I0831135

SYNC CHROME CITY

Sync Chrome City

SHEL GRAVES

CONTENTS

Sync Chrome City

First Printing, 2025

ISBN: 979-8-9985486-0-4

For permission requests, contact Shel Graves,
info@shelgravesanimal.com, www.shelgravesanimal.com.

Cover Artwork and Design by Shel Graves

I was inspired to write this novel after Alaska Airlines Flight 261 crashed into the Pacific Ocean, January 31, 2000. Eighty-eight people were killed on their way back from Puerto Vallarta, Mexico, including a group of friends I had celebrated that momentous Y2K New Year with and felt I was just getting to know well. Sending love to all mourning losses from this plane crash. May their memories be a blessing.

This book is dedicated to the Underdark Calligraphy Club — and to my beloved Sam.

PROLOGUE

In the distance, on the horizon, the corrosion of the Rust Sea rises slowly submerging the islands of Pacifica. While many of the smaller fish have died, some in the sea like the sensitive sharks have silently developed resistance and embraced the deadly rust while Varuna the Whale sings and dives deeper to escape it. Yet, we begin in the remains of the most beautiful places in the world; the Cascadian Wilderness, where blackberry vines cling to slopes and towering evergreen trees often burn, and the northern islands of Pacifica, where madrona trees hang over the rising waters, the color of their peeled skins perfectly matching the color of the red seas.

Off continent, many wondrous islands with white, black, pink, and beige sands await. Occasionally, we see glimpses of the once sparkling blue and green waters surrounding them. More often, the grey-green plastified waters slosh and churn. Nonetheless, surfers travel from beach-to-beach and wave-to-wave carefree, communing with each other and enjoying the freedom to see the world while they may, as absentminded men fretfully try to restrain and employ them. The surfers do their best to stay far ashore of the United Government and its industries and travel any other way than in the lurching containers of AeroFlux planes.

Pay attention and the variety of birds and fish on Earth still astound, while populations of mammals surge and wane around fluctuations of human tragedies. When humans retreat and die off from manmade disasters, other animals may return to prowl.

On the edge of Cascadia, in the basement labs of New West University, researchers attempt to combine mammals, fish, reptiles, amphibians, and birds quickly into new shapes to withstand the environmental damage men have wrought.

The 'Way, the great grey stretch of asphalt that divides Cascadia's competing political utopias, New West and C-Town, contains unwelcome refugees with their multifaceted minds harboring so many unwelcome thoughts. Out here, men use genetic manipulation to give themselves new features: fur, feathers, scales, and tails. Generations despondently yearn to be more animal, but most do not know how to access their animalness other than in this superficial and manipulated way. Some howl and gyrate as they listen to Giovanni Hastings Musica, a mix of old and new instrumental sounds. Songs contain hope and inspire listeners. Animalness lies within in every cell and soon in every grain of sand.

In other parts of the United Government, animals are largely tortured and eaten though some crawl underground and some escape notice. The landscapes remain vast, after all.

On distant planets, men work in the Spire Mines to provide resources for other richer, absent men and they dream of home and imagine the beauty of the Earth. Further away lies a planet made of tiny organisms living lives like sand for now untouched by human thought.

Eventually, human thought expands for good or ill.

Wisely, look to the animals. Ask: What are the animals thinking? How do the animals feel? Yes, you can tell by the way they hold their bodies and the choices they make with them. Yes, we too, are embodied. Look to animals, as small as they may seem, for clues to our destination. Find yourself: suddenly prescient and amazed. Animalness remains.

A parrot squawks revived by aliens. Taste the slippery orange fruit. Be transported to sacredness, power, and an earthly unearthly island.

Isn't it strange how some humans have ignored even the largest animals like Varuna the Whale? Her vast intelligences know many secrets. She communes with beings underwater. She understands better than most the fate of the oceans within which everyone's fates flow. She sings.

On the edge of Cascadia, great transformations rise above the horizon.

In the heart of Cascadia, evolution continues to unfold on Earth and in the universe.

Beneath the drowning islands of Pacifica, a compassionate civilization awaits.

As you envision the future, hold your loved ones close. Let them burrow near your neck and feel their sharp claws, scaly fins, and slick fur.

May you feel loved.

We begin our approach to this future, heads held high, with the story of a heedless young woman raised by utopians, a college student at New West University, Geneva Teresa Weltraum.

But first, there is an angry man.

~ 1 ~

THE FREEWAY

"Some mistakenly believe Geneva Teresa Weltraum to be the originator of society's psychic transformation but, in fact, before The Awakening many youth displayed heightened awareness, although their abilities were repudiated and ridiculed. C.G. Burrows, arguably among the first Dawning Psychics, was one of these pariahs. His own abilities were limited and came at a cost. He could hear others' thoughts clearly, but only those directed at him. This limited telepathy caused him great pain. Thoughts entered his mind "like needles," he said. He considered his ability a great curse. He was an outcast and a misanthropist. " — *Becoming Psychic 101, A History and a Primer*

On the other side of someone else's vision of utopia, the manicured territory of New West, those people deemed unworthy of paradise camped on the Freeway. Tents littered the top of the mud-streaked asphalt. They blended together makeshift, weathered and covered in soot, as did the men who ambled between them bearded, hooded, and hunched. C.G. Burrows kept apart from this human refuse as long as he could stand to, living in the forest they feared, until his loneliness grew unbearable, and he ventured close to make another attempt to join them. Despite the pain people caused him, Burrows craved their company like a drug. Thus, forced from hiding, he approached the masses on the Freeway. Low hanging branches clipped him as he paced the tree line. Black smoke from the kerosene campfires stung his eyes as he scanned the pavement looking for a tent with red and beige flaps. That tent was not much different from the others, except that it had the person he needed inside, his only friend on the 'Way, his dealer, Mace.

Burrows hadn't seen Mace since his last failed fix: a dose of old therapeutic that hadn't helped his condition or got him high. He'd retreated to the forest and stayed there, alone, for weeks. Now he couldn't be sure something hadn't changed on the 'Way. Maybe Mace had moved on, decided to make the trek south for warmth. Although, he would have had reason to stay. This part of the Freeway was prime real estate, just out of sight of the white arching entrance to New West on the hillock of clipped lawn, but close enough to draw the occasional guilty emissary out. A few of the rich bastards would occasionally bring fuel, food, and apologies to assuage their guilt. Tents further down the corridor got none of this false regret. Charity made this part of the 'Way crowded and aggressive, a belt of opportunistic and ever hopeful beggars. No, Mace wouldn't have left. He had to be here, somewhere.

Finally, Burrows glimpsed a spot of red in the canvas sea. He shifted the weight of his knapsack and warmth trickled between his shoulder blades. He hung his head and stepped onto the asphalt. He began weaving though the squatters: head down, eyes up. Almost immediately some guy was on him, staring at him with narrowed eyes. Burrows braced for the impact.

The guy pounded him: *What you got in there? Looking to deal?*

Every word struck and stung.

"Leave me the fuck alone," Burrows said.

The guy sized him up. Burrows got: *Fine, big man*. The pain eased as the guy turned his attention elsewhere. Burrows hunched and hurried on, but now he'd attracted attention and more desperate thoughts: *Looking to deal? Looking to deal? Deal. Deal.* He looked back at the forest with longing, but he was already a few hundred tent-covered yards away from refuge with at least 50 people between him and the quiet. It was just what he'd been afraid of, a mind field, and he was trapped in the middle. They needled him all around and he couldn't yell because it would bring more of them on him. Anonymity was key. He struggled in silence. And suffered, yes, always suffered.

Shut up. Ignore me, he thought, but he knew they wouldn't hear. His was a one-way curse.

"Back off," he grunted, pulling his jacket around him. He wished, just once, he could fire back at the crowd, press his own thoughts directly into the heads around him, let them feel the hard jab, the echoing sting, the after burn and see how they liked it. "Back off!"

No one ever got him. He was a receiver, a one-way street leading out of New West. There was no way in for him. He hurried on, but the tent he'd started toward turned out to be the wrong one. Still, no Mace. If Mace had moved on, could he find a new dealer, pick another quiet mind out of the hustle? He wasn't sure he was up to it, and the time he'd spent isolated in the forest wouldn't make it easier. He felt monstrous and, by now, had to look the part.

He stopped and turned to a dirty young woman beside him, brown-scraggly hair and a musky urine-tinged stench. She opened the flap to her tent and held it wide. If only it could be that easy, just go inside and see what she had. He made eye contact and stepped toward her: a mistake. She blasted him: *What's he got in that sack? Not a bad looking guy. How much will he want? Could be a protector, scare off the others.* All her scheming speculation pierced him. As the pain intensified, from everywhere he got: *violence, a show, should we stop him, he's hurting Allison.* He looked up into the woman's bulging blue eyes. His hands were high on her shoulders inching up her collarbone to her throat. He was strangling her. He wanted to silence her thoughts, to end his own pain. But if he gave in to it, then the rest of them would be on him pinning him with all their incriminations. They would never leave him alone. Instead, Burrows inched his hands back down the woman's shoulders and shoved her into the tent, "Shhh." She stumbled back onto a pile of tattered clothing.

Burrows' restraint had the desired effect turning a murderous impulse into the kind of fleeting violence common to life on the 'Way. He felt the minds around turn away, bored. He hurried on. So, that was it. There was no way he could handle meeting a new source. He looked toward the forest ready to bolt. Then, at last, he spotted it, Mace's tent, in exactly the same place it had been for the past two years. Going for it, Burrows made himself slow. The minds pulled away from him as the squatters forgot him and returned to their preoccupations. He swung the sack off his back and held it up. Dark stains crossed the canvas. The patch of dried blood tightened across his back as he braced for the initial jolt.

"Mace," he said.

Mace stuck his head out of the tent. The thoughts he directed at Burrows struck in two dull thuds: *Burrows. Meat.* It hurt, but it didn't floor him. Mace was one chill dude. Burrows shook the bag and went fishing for information, "You got something good for me?"

Mace took the bait. He shrugged, but he couldn't help thinking: *SLO-42. Da Lime. Really good score.*

"You look like you got your hands on something," Burrows said, rubbing the side of his face along his rough bearded jaw. Mace had to be about his age, in his 20s, but all the refuse on the 'Way looked weathered.

"Yeah, it's new. You take it and you get to experience what it's like to be someone else. It's made out of someone else's neuro...something, whatever, brain juice," Mace said.

After a bout of zipping and shifting nylon, he stepped out. He flashed the inside pocket of his tattered United Government issue jacket and Burrows caught a glimpse of neon green, possibly the cure he was looking for, or at least a reprieve from his continual misery. "So, it's good?"

"Depends. Mine is," Mace said. Burrows followed his gaze to the lone truck coming at them, making its way along the shoulder of the Freeway past the tents. It glistened white, free of the pale gray soot that covered him, Mace, everything else. The forest-green New West logo shone inside a yellow circle.

"Mace, trade?" Burrows said.

"Hang on," Mace waved the back of his hand. "I want to see what this one is."

The absence of pain Burrows felt as Mace's attention completely left him provided only bitter relief. It quickly turned to annoyance.

"Mace, trade." Burrows said, wanting to get this over with and get off the 'Way. But Mace was focused on the truck like a well-trained dog.

The truck rolled to a stop beside a group of tents and a man and woman got out, a matched set. They were dressed in identical boots and jackets, but there were no logos on their clothes, or when they lifted the back door of the truck, on the pile of burlap sacks inside. They were do-gooder missionaries acting on their own outside of New West's authority.

"Flour," the man said into a small, white handheld megaphone. His voice carried over the crowd amplified by a tinny echo. "We want you to know the revolution hasn't ended. There's still a place for you in New West. We've brought flour and stoves. Anyone can ask us what it's like inside."

As the man spoke, people began to crowd the truck and the woman started handing down sacks. Burrows hefted his bag of meat up over his shoulder again and adjusted the weight across his back watching the weak people clamoring. Handouts. He didn't need handouts. The New West bastards had taken everything but his freedom, and now they were offering flour in exchange as if it were a fair trade. Fuck that.

Burrows dangled the sack in front of Mace again. "Rather have meat?"

"I'd rather have both," said Mace with his ever-practical, adaptable chill. "Gotta go. You want to trade or not?"

Burrows couldn't stand Mace's good nature. From what he knew of Mace's history, the guy had reason, even more than himself, to be pissed off at anything that came out of New West. Instead, he let himself be reduced to a pathetic beggar. It made him want to club some sense into Mace with the bag of dead rabbits, but he couldn't let himself get testy, not with the one guy out here whose company he could briefly tolerate. "I'm not sure. Let me try some, see if it's as good as you say. Use your tent?"

Hands in the pockets of his grey camouflage jacket, Mace shrugged: *Sure, I ain't got nothin' in there you can steal.* "Sure," he said and handed over a rig half-full of green liquid: *Da Lime.* "It goes in your eyes. They connect to your brain, man."

"Yeah, I get that," Burrows said, rolling his eyes. He was not some ignorant junkie. "Who did you say this comes from?"

He ignored Mace's rambling explanation because he got his answer clearly: *Kendra LeMay.* He knew the name. He took the rig, stepped into Mace's tent and zipped it up behind him. The inside smelled like a dank concentration of the rest of camp: feces, musk, urine, sweat, black smoke. Burrows rummaged around. Mace wasn't wrong. There was nothing of value here. He found a bottle of rubbing alcohol, matches, and some cotton.

He settled on top of Mace's tattered sleeping bag and heated and swabbed the syringe. The green drops in the rig looked dirty in the yellow cast of light filtered through the tent. What made Mace think he'd actually scored some of Kendra LeMay, the Friend-Me inventor? It seemed unlikely, although he'd heard rumors around the camp about plans for a new Friend-Me factory. It could be built just outside of New West on the land along the Freeway so the company could make use of the cheap labor. The 'Way had been abuzz with the news, with the hope of work, but so far, nothing had come of the rumor. LeMay had chosen to stay in New West under its restrictions. It wasn't a smart choice for an entrepreneur. New West's brand of perfection was the death of invention. In fact, LeMay's Friend-Me journal was the only thing new to come out of New West since the revolution, and only little girls got excited about diaries, no matter how techie Friend-Me made the journals.

Burrows leaned back and positioned the tip of the needle in the corner of his eye ready to inject the green fluid into his optic nerve. He doubted he'd get a glimpse into the mind of Kendra LeMay, but he wasn't really concerned with the experience itself. He was after a side effect: anything to keep other people's thoughts out of his head. He depressed the syringe and the liquid surged around his eye. He blinked twice, as his vision turned puce. He sat back and waited for the kick. It worked fast gliding over the blood-brain barrier like caffeine. The stench in the tent became unbearable. He smiled even as he stumbled out of the tent and caught his breath. The drug had definitely come from a female anyway. She couldn't stand the reek of sour male sweat and now it repulsed Burrow's drugged senses, too.

Outside the tent, the New West logo on the truck caught his gaze. At first, he wasn't sure whether his reaction to it was drug induced at all. As usual, the truck represented rules and he wanted to avoid it. But in the SLO-42 haze, with somebody else's perceptions riding over his and guiding his emotions, there was also curiosity. *Could this really be Kendra LeMay?*, he wondered.

As he stared at the truck, a drug-induced memory played over the top of his natural vision. He saw a little girl on an empty playground with her arms wrapped around a willow tree. The school grounds and everything from the tetherball pole to the sidewalk graffiti glimmered. Energy flowed into the little girl as she plucked a frond from the tree. She waved the leaves back and forth and spun round. Then, a nimbus of golden light surrounded her. A word came at him as if spoken by a crowd: *destiny*. It rang his mind like a bell. Its chime came at him from all sides and Burrows reeled. He tripped on a tent stake and dropped to one knee. Underneath the excitement of the drug, the word surged into his mind and expanded fast, filling his head. Pressure pounded at his temples. He exhaled, shallow panting breaths. Then, the memory stopped. He looked up at the truck again, deflated. He quickly found Mace and traded his two rabbits for another dose.

That night, he and Mace shared a campfire with the New West emissaries, Vic and Perla Freeman. Burrows was used to inhaling lung-scarring fumes from a kerosene flame or, by himself, burning wood, which smelled better, especially with meat cooking over it, but the smoke still stung the back of his throat and left his voice dry and husky. The Freeman's, however, lit one of their clean electric blue stoves. Vic set the swirls of yellow and purple light high so they could almost see the faces of the nearest squatters. The glimpses Burrows caught of the shadowed squinty visages surrounding them made him cringe, but his recent dose of SLO-42 dulled the thoughts the campers shot his way. They came through in manageable thumps: *Lucky. Bastard.* Vic adjusted the scent of the stove through lavender and sea spray to settle on clean pine. It was just another example of how everything had to be better in New West, Burrows thought. Even a campfire wasn't good enough for those...the drug smoothed away his habitual *bastards.* It dulled his cynicism. Instead, the thought felt true. Everything was better inside New West. It surely was.

The Freeman's shared food with them: savory mashed hazelnut and shiitake cakes and stone-ground wheat crackers washed down with sparkling blueberry cider. Perla served them cinnamon Pink Lady apple tarts on clean tin plates. The drug enhanced the flavors too, Burrows thought. It allowed him to enjoy the tastes without judgment. The buttery graham crust seemed a good enough reason alone to embrace New West.

"Pretty fancy-pants for the 'Way. But I can't complain," Burrows said. He really found he could not. Because that almost, but not quite, bothered him, he laughed. His mind really was not his own. Maybe next time he could get away with just half a rig of Kendra LeMay (if that's who this was).

"What do you normally eat out here?" Perla asked.

"Whatever you send out. And there's some trade." Mace said.

Burrows didn't mention the woods, his hunting. It wasn't good nighttime conversation.

"That can't be enough to feed everyone," Vic said.

Mace took another bite of tart. "A lot of people headed south."

"People camping on the Freeway outside our gates without food. That's not what we had in mind," Vic said.

Even through the SLO-42, Burrows got twinges from the Freeman's guilt: *Terrible. What we've done to you.*

Even through the drug, their guilt disgusted him, but the person whose perceptions he was riding didn't share his anger. She was a problem-solver.

"So, what's the political situation?" he asked, to get the Freeman's out of his head and talking.

Perla leaned toward the flame. She wanted to explain. Burrows heard her soft beat: *Don't blame me.*

"A lot of people feel we made some mistakes," she said. "We knew we couldn't convert everyone to our way of thinking, and we couldn't create the society we wanted to without a unified effort. So, we asked those who disagreed to leave. A lot went to C-town. Most were happy to go, I think."

Burrows nodded. "My parents were."

Before the economic collapse, they had been some of the wealthiest, most influential people in the Northwest. Then, in the depression, they'd lost everything: money and power. The New Westians had foreseen the financial chaos. They'd swooped in with their savings and encircled their bastions, the seat of government and the university, along with some neighboring farmlands and a few small towns. They'd created New West on the high ground no one else wanted. His parents had left voluntarily taking Burrows with them to C-town. Not everyone was so lucky. New West forcibly removed a lot of undesirables: the uneducated, homeless, drug addicts, dissidents. When he couldn't handle C-town — the incessant mental anguish of being a refugee in a city where everyone felt bad for him — a brain hammering chorus of *Sorry. Sorry. Sorry.* — Burrows ended up here with all the other castoffs outside New West on the Freeway. And then, entered the forest.

"I was never political. Just poor," Mace said, digging his hands deep into the pockets of his U.G. jacket.

"New West didn't have much choice. The old system left behind so many problems. We wanted to make a fresh start," Vic put his arm around Perla. "But our new government is stable. We've got our infrastructure in place. Things are good now, very good in New West. We're working on an alliance with C-town and granting amnesty to those who agree to try the new society."

"You're opening the gates?" Mace asked.

"We hope, eventually," Vic said. "Friend-Me Co. is also looking at building a factory outside New West and I think, this time, the government will allow it."

That rumor again. Maybe, just maybe, things were looking up, Burrows thought.

The next day, Burrows brought his own tent out of the woods and pitched it next to Mace's. Mace handed over two more vials of green, "I think things are going to change for us, bro. Pay me back later." They helped the Freeman's distribute the remaining bags of flour. On full rigs of SLO-42, Burrows head throbbed tolerably even in the August heat with all the squatters gathered around: *Me. Me.*

Give it to me. Even with the headache, he felt better than he ever had. In the forest, he'd been physically pain-free, but alone. He'd forgotten how much he actually liked people, when they weren't hurting him.

"Are you going to try to go to work for Friend-Me?" he asked Mace.

"Nah, I'm gonna get in to New West if I can. I've had enough of this here. I want to be clean and well fed. Something I can get used to long-term."

Vic wiped his brow. "We have a couple passes. We can bring you back in with us if you want. You'll have to complete studies at New West University to make your residency permanent, like any other citizen."

"Maybe," Mace said. "I can see myself settled in to one of those nice little towns."

"Deming or Linden are real nice," Perla said.

Burrows thought about it. He could not picture himself in one of those hick towns, but he could see himself at the capitol, New West, at the university. College was what he'd always wanted until his dream had been derailed by the revolution. He'd been 16, about to enter university and more than ready. He'd barely survived high school and all the stabs of *loner, creep* he'd endured. His junior year, he got taller and broader than the rest of the guys and let a slutty girl hang around him to deflect attention. The clangs of *nice tits* were annoying, but not directed toward him, not blows. Still, he'd clung to the idea of escape. One more year, and he'd go relatively unnoticed at the large university. He'd study to be a surgeon, maybe even a neurosurgeon. He liked the idea of being able to mess around inside someone else's head for a change and when they were too doped up to think about him at all. Anesthesia would mean silence. That could be perfect. His parents would buy him a condo off campus. He was finally going to get away. And then everything had gone to hell. Political machinations he had nothing to do with and couldn't control.

Now, with the Freemans, Burrows saw a way back in, a way to reverse time. Maybe everything would be better in New West. That night around the campfire he asked Mace for more SLO-42 and got the last rig. "Sorry dude, it's a limited run. So, what do you think? Was it LeMay?"

Burrows nodded. "Could be. Positive, a real go-getter anyway."

That night he left the campfire early. The SLO-42 was wearing off and his head was starting to throb. The next morning, he caught Mace making last minute trades and packing up his gear.

"You going to New West?" Burrows asked.

Mace didn't look up. He was squatting in the dust, hunched over a collection of white packets and pills laid across a strip of canvas sorting them into piles and counting. "Yeah, why? You were."

"You can't seriously think that's a good idea. That they are going to let you in. No." Burrows stepped over the canvas casting the goods in shadow. "Dumbest idea, ever. It was just the drug talking."

Mace squinted up at him: *Comedown's a bitch.*

The words fell on Burrows like fucking hammers.

"It clouded my perceptions like New West wasn't so bad. But you can't forget what the revolution did to us." Burrows ground a boot into the ashy pavement. "Not here. They're using that drug to control us. You think it's a coincidence SLO-42 from LeMay shows up and she's planning to open a factory out here? She's looking for friendly slave labor. That's what it was. It's another huge scam aimed at us losers."

"That was all you. I was never on Da Lime. My mind was my own. I've been thinking pretty clearly for myself. Just back off, OK?" Mace pulled a corner of the canvas out from under Burrows' boot. "You changed your mind. Fine. I got things to do, a place to go."

"It's not like you can take any of that with you. You'll be nothing, have nothing in there. Think about it. They want us to fall in line under their rules." Burrows knelt. "I'm never going to do that. I'm never giving up my freedom. Think about it. That's what you're doing."

The thought of Mace leaving, his one contact out here, made him so angry.

Mace didn't blink. "No, I'm taking opportunities. I can set myself up there." He began rolling the goods up. "Tea, bandages, aspirin: it's all legal. The Freeman's are leaving tomorrow and I'm going with them. Don't worry. I'll still be able to work trades out here. I'll come back with something for you." Mace shoved the roll into a knapsack and shot off: *Junkie.*

Burrows grabbed Mace's shoulder and held him low. "No, you gave me that woman's Lime. You owe me."

Mace froze. Like a rabbit. *Man, dude's whack. He's going off again.*

The drug was gone now, completely, and the thoughts thrust into Burrows head stinging and burning like nettles. Burrows' hand dropped from Mace's shoulder. He was staggering to his feet when Mace launched his next round: *You want to live like an animal out here, fine. You probably couldn't handle the city. I'm going in.* "I don't own you nothin'," was all Mace said.

Burrows stumbled towards the forest. Jumbled thoughts chased him as he ran through the tents, checking people as he went. *Hey. Where's he... Why's he... running to? Who's that? Look at that. Some crazy motherfucker.*

Out of the heat, in the forest, Burrows pressed his head against an evergreen. He ground his face into the bark and then began to pound his head against it until it felt better, the physical pain superseding the mental. He slid down and huddled at the base of the tree. As the voices ebbed, he drew his legs up under him and rolled, fetal, in the evergreen needles, pulling at the roots of his limp damp hair. The pain didn't stop. No words came at him, but pressure crowded his skull. He looked up into the trees and — *destiny*— that golden word, sprang at him from the branches. It clawed at his skull and sunk its teeth into his brain. He didn't know what the drug-induced memory of a little golden girl meant to its owner, Kendra LeMay. For it had been Kendra. To him, the borrowed memory showed that the pain in his head could get a lot worse. It would come out of New West. It would find him in the forest. It would be more than he could stand.

When night came, Burrows crept back into camp. He snuck into Mace's tent, placed a knee on his chest and wrapped his hands around his throat. It felt good to be doing something, on the offensive. He wouldn't wait around to be a victim. When the body stilled, he claimed the rubbing alcohol and the matches and headed for the New West truck where Vic and Perla Freeman slept. He didn't even know they'd had a little girl with them until he saw her run from the back of the smoking truck into the tents. She looked like a miniature of her parents, no hint of gold nimbus as in his dream, so he ignored her. He drove the truck with its flaming corpses into the woods to burn. The traces of lavender, sea salt, and pine that had lifted in the propane explosion faded into the toxic smoke of burning vehicle, bodies and old growth wood. Burrows had always thought the other transients weak, too afraid of the rumored voices in the trees to live on the soft forest floor where the hunting was good. Now he'd felt the evil screaming from the trees: *destiny*. The rumors had proved true and he wanted to engulf the whole forest in fire.

It didn't matter who favored heading to New West University, the capitol, or settling in a little town like Linden. No one was going back into New West with the Freemans. But Burrows could not return to the forest, either. He pulled his new U.G. issue camo jacket around him and, in the pocket, flipped the Freeman's pass card. He had his ticket into New West. He would wait near the border until the threat came — the stab of *destiny* — and then he would hunt it down.

~ 2 ~

BLACKBERRY CORDIALS

"The economic collapse of the United Government led the way for social transformation. It was a time of great change. The educated elite of society had predicted and prepared for the downfall. They led the revolution and founded their utopia: New West. These visionaries created a stable social structure that allowed for the next, unforeseen, stage of evolution, an internal transformation we refer to as the Psychic Reformation. Key founding figures of the New Westian Revolution included the Weltraum and Freeman families. This alliance brought Dawning Psychics, Geneva Weltraum, First Psychic Sender, and Valerie Freeman, First Psychic Receiver, together. At the time, no one knew how the girls' powers, once awakened, would clash."

— *Becoming Psychic 101, A History and a Primer*

Many people, the majority, thought they had succeeded in creating a utopian society in New West carved out of the remnants of the United States in the Pacific Northwest. They had chartered an ordered government, which created a secure environment for its citizens to pursue their own interests and intellectual growth. Yet, they had attained peace with unforeseen and uncontrollable consequences. Perfection came at a price, and so, with some sense of loss. In much the same way, as soon as her new sister appeared, Geneva Weltraum came to regret ever wishing to improve her family. Why had she ever longed for and begged for a sister?

When Geneva was six, Valerie Freeman came to live with the Weltraums. At the time, Geneva's family was the only world she knew. Valerie's arrival was her first experience with sudden change: a negative one. She lost her status as an only child in one nightmarish evening. One night, soon after she'd been put to bed, Geneva's mother had woken her, "We're going to help a friend." She'd led Geneva, bleary-eyed in her nightgown, to the car. Because her family rarely drove anywhere, this woke her fully. She watched as they sped out of Linden past the neat neighborhood houses, down the main street where blue solar lights lit the high school and through the forested outskirts of town. Shortly after the black expanse of low-growing soy fields began, the warmth of the car and the whir of its electric engine lulled her to sleep again. Her parents' voices soothed her into sleep as she curled in the back seat wrapped around the fluff of her blanket. She woke up when her mother sobbed, "But why? It was over."

When the green security lights flashed over them, she sat up as the car crossed the border and the high, white, illuminated arch passed over them. On the other side lay darkness. It was the first time Geneva had ever experienced the boundary of her world, Linden in New West on one side, everything else unknown on the other. She huddled in the backseat. She felt her world's smallness and her own. The car slowed as they left New West driving along the shoulder of the Freeway under the line of evergreens. "Hurry," her mother said. But her father said no, they might hit one of the people living on the road. Geneva had never been to the Freeway, only heard adults arguing about it. Bad people lived there. One day, they might get into New West. She hoped not.

When she heard shouting in the distance, her father stopped the car. She could see shapes moving nearby. Behind them, reddish light shone around billows of black smoke. “Stay here,” her father commanded. “Don’t move.” A burnt smell entered the car as her parents left it. Alone, Geneva huddled with the blanket over her head inhaling its lavender scent. Even without her father’s admonishment it wouldn’t have occurred to her to set foot outside the car here. She wasn’t a curious child. She was lawful. Footsteps, then the brush of someone passing along the side of the car, brought her out from underneath the blanket. A figure loomed outside the window. Scratch, thunk — the door handle lifted. She shot across the seat, reaching for the opposite door, but stopped when she saw her father's hands. He lifted a girl onto the seat beside her. The girl smelled of smoke. Her hair and pajamas were smeared with soot and stuck with pine needles. As her little shoulders shook, she made sounds like rubbing tree limbs. Geneva wrapped her blanket around the shivering girl, then drew away. She rubbed the silky corner of her blanket between her fingers. She wanted her blanket back and the girl away. The girl didn't feel safe. Nothing about this night did.

When they got home, her mother tucked Geneva back into bed and petted her hair. "Val lost her parents last night, Gen, she's our responsibility now. You have a sister." Geneva barely slept. She’d always wanted a sister, but her parents had said one child was enough. Now Val was here. Geneva wondered if it was too late to change her mind. She hadn’t known she’d be this scared of the sister.

In the morning, the girl sat at the breakfast table with them, terribly silent. Geneva had never known anyone whose parents had died. The way the girl looked — frozen — it was more awful than she could imagine. It was as if Val had stepped out of a nightmare and stayed. Geneva shied from the strange girl as if she might lure monsters out, at any moment, into the sunny kitchen. The girl had streaks on her face where tears had dried, but she didn't make a sound now, not even when she cried. In a way, that was good. It would be more frightening if the girl spoke, if Geneva had to talk to her, because she wouldn't know what to say. Instead, she stared at the bony, dark, pale girl. No one would believe they were sisters.

After breakfast, her mother sent them out to pick blackberries. During the revolution no one had had time to fight the encroaching Himalayan blackberries, and now they grew ripe and wild behind the house. Her father had talked about taking shears to them, but he hadn't gotten around to it. Geneva hurried to grab her silver pail. She could already taste the sweet tart juice and the buttery crust of her mother's pie. She was excited to get started, but she had to take Val, too.

Val walked too far into the bramble in her short sundress unwary of danger. Thorns hovered just over her pale skin. She faced straight ahead and plucked at the branches. Her long dark hair hung past her shoulders and into her face. Geneva wondered if Val could even see. Sometimes her fingers caught a berry and sometimes not. She dropped leaves and clusters of green and white nubs into the silver pail.

"You're supposed to only pick the ripe ones," Geneva said.

The girl flinched and red lines rose on her arms and legs as the bushes around her shook. There were pricks of blood on her fingertips.

Geneva filled her pail quickly. "Come on. It's enough."

When Val didn't say anything and didn't move, Geneva grabbed her arm and pulled her away from the bushes. Val’s dress snagged and Geneva unhooked each of the thorns while she stood there. When Geneva had freed her, Val ran ahead of her into the house. Geneva spit on her hands and rubbed the blood off the long scratches on her calves before following her in.

It had been like that ever since. Geneva, although she was actually a year younger, took care of careless Val. They'd become roommates at New West University against father's advice. "It would probably be better for both of you to be apart," he warned. In a show of newfound independence, Geneva disregarded him. It was only the second time she'd ever done so. The first time was when she'd bought the new Friend-Me Journal.

As it turned out, Geneva's father was right. The girls rooming together had been a terrible idea. In the spring of their junior year, Geneva and Valerie were studying for their finals at New West University when Val began to scream. The shriek brought the university security guards, two of them, both with blond hair nearly the same color as their jackets. They stormed into the dorm room in a rush of reflective yellow and tackled Val where she writhed on the ground her keyboard still clattering. As one of the guards hit the floor, he thrust an elbow into Geneva's open Privacy Law book and crumpled its pages. Geneva heard the tear, a low rip through Val's cry. Then the guard reached across Val's heaving chest and pinned her with his thick forearm. The other guard held her down, his hands on the short bare expanse below Val's skirt. Val's skin reddened around his fingers. Geneva had no idea what was wrong with Val, what had started the screaming or the spasms. The eerily quiet Val she'd grown up with seemed to have departed this loud, violent, irrational body.

"Don't hurt her!" Geneva yelled, but in her typical passive take-what-comes fashion, she didn't try to stop them. Her side ached where Val had thrust a thick-heeled black boot into her ribs. Geneva clutched the side of the armchair where she had scuttled out of the way of Val's flailing limbs.

The guard near Val's head wrenched the virtual reality glasses from her face. Val turned her head to the side, heaved and puked. The room filled with a stench of chocolate and vomit layered over a thick masque of cinnamon oil: Val burned drops in the tiny brass lamp beside her computer. She said cinnamon enhanced her mental abilities. Val would do any little thing to get an edge, to race faster through the virtual world. Maybe the cinnamon was to blame. Maybe she had gotten too fast. Maybe, underneath the wires where Val spent most of her time, something had gone wrong. Definitely, definitely something had gone wrong.

Val stared up unblinking, but her eyes still scanned side to side, up and down. Her fingers still twitched rapidly over the air. She gaped and stopped screaming. Geneva could still hear the piercing echo of her screams. She hadn't imagined Val could even be that loud. If she hadn't seen her mouth stretched wide, she wouldn't have believed that Val was making the sound. She still didn't connect the noise to Val, not really, it seemed to emanate from everywhere. Now Val sucked in air, her entire body arcing as the men held her.

"Looks like we've got another case of EHBF," said the guard at her feet.

Sirens blared outside the window. A medic in a white lab coat wheeled a stretcher into the room, he mumbled into a snail shell phone as he did so and waved the guards over. They manhandled Val ignoring Geneva until a guard turned to her, "What happened?"

Geneva looked at the frothy almond milk and brown chunks on the crème carpet and started to gag. Her mouth still held the taste of chocolate, now bitter, in the back of her throat. She wished she'd spent the day studying with Val instead of taking the extra shift at Ruby's. She'd tried to make up for her absence with chocolates. She remembered the chocolatier placing four blackberry cordials into a silky pouch.

It had started out as such a bright, beautiful spring perfect New West day. Geneva had left Val in the dark cave of their dorm room, put on her somewhat faded but still bright ruby-colored uniform, and headed across campus. She'd stopped at the landing by the student union building which overlooked the bay. There was a sculpture of jagged white arches framing the view: the bright blue bay and the deep green brambles of blackberry on the steep slope below. There were whale spouts in the harbor. There were eagles perched in the evergreen trees. A squirrel chittered in a nearby madrona. It was gorgeous and full of life. But if anyone else had been standing beside Geneva they might have pointed out the warning signs to her. There was a red tinge along the edge of the horizon where the sea was turning to rust the same color as the red-tipped thorns among the blackberry brambles. The whales, along with other ocean refugees, were coming closer to shore to escape the poisoned seas. But Geneva saw only what she wished to, and had been taught to observe, a bright peaceful serene place, the alluring utopian vision of New West.

From there, she hurried on to Ruby's not because she needed to work, but because she enjoyed the community and serving the diners there. She also liked the baker, Nate, who made Ruby's blackberry scones, muffins, and pies. Nate had lived before the revolution and outside of New West. He was her parents' age but well-traveled and more forthcoming. He occasionally shared stories and sometimes leftover goodies, contraband, and forbidden flavors. But today she'd worked a standard shift, the only surprise was the unusual tip a customer had left for her after devouring a slice of blackberry pie. Geneva stopped by Tim's Chocolate Shoppe with the gold coin on her way back up the hill to campus.

Tim, the chocolatier, had flipped the pure gold coin between his fingers, "Are you sure you want to spend this?"

Geneva wasn't. It was the first time she'd had one of the commemorative coins in her possession. Her first thought had been to take it back to the dorm and give it to Val directly. In between ferrying plates of food, she'd rubbed her fingers over the evergreens imprinted on the coin in her pocket. She liked that New West had minted the coins out of real gold so that they had actual value. She appreciated the heft of it in her hand and in her pocket. But the more she thought about it, the more she realized Val would not like this reminder of the founding of New West 25 years ago. Val's parents had not, technically, died in the struggle. They'd been killed six years afterwards when the revolution was over. However, Val didn't see the distinction. She still blamed New West for her parents' death. Besides, she would point out, New West's supplies of solar and wind power were worth more than its cache of gold.

So instead, Geneva had detoured over to the chocolate shop. She nodded at Tim and took the bag of chocolates. Tim's Chocolate Shoppe, and its blackberry cordials, had been one of the first discoveries she and Val had made together at New West University. Freshman year they'd trekked down the hill for them before every tough exam. This year, as juniors, they hadn't come to the shop at all. She and Val were still roommates, but they didn't hang out anymore. Val was becoming a regular Plug-In. Even when she was in the dorm, her mind was virtually elsewhere. Geneva had been spending most of her time at the greenhouse in Varian Hall, the environmental psychology building. Geneva wasn't sure what had changed, but they just weren't as close, and she missed the connection with her older adopted sister. Blackberry cordials might not be the solution, but they weren't a bad start. Besides, they were a delicious indulgence, perfect for finals week.

Leaving the shop, Geneva stuffed the pouch into the front pocket of her Ruby's uniform. Now she had two reasons to hurry. She needed to get back and start studying for her final and it was a rare spring day actually warm enough to melt chocolate. Heading up the hill towards campus, she could see the water shimmering in the bay to her left. Ahead, the evergreens encircling campus stood in stark relief against the perfect blue sky, but mid-air the sea-pine scents mingled. A sheen of sweat broke out on her forehead as she strode up the hill along the brick path beside Old Main. In a hurry, she'd forgotten to take the long way around to her dorm. Sure enough, the three gray-haired protesters were there with their faded yellow signs. They were standing on the stairs to the administration building as if they had nothing better to do. Their signs read: "Get R.A.P.T.! ," "We want PSI!," and "Problems, Solutions, Innovations." As she passed, they cocked their heads and gazed at her. Geneva hugged her arms to her chest and hurried away from the weirdos. These women could have told Geneva about the dangers of the encroaching rust red sea.

The protesters were fixtures on campus, as much a part of it as the evergreens and the madrona trees, the red bricks and the ivy covering Old Main. They'd positioned themselves in front of the administration building and had been there every day for years. The first day Geneva had visited New West she'd hardly noticed them. She'd been with her parents and Val checking out the school.

Her father had pointed at the three women huddled on the steps of the building and elbowed her mother. "Does that remind you of something?"

Her mother shrugged.

"Wasn't that us, in the early days, getting together, ready to raise hell?" he said.

Geneva looked at the people sitting and humming with their hands on their knees. They didn't look especially rebellious.

Her mother laughed. "Ha, they remind me more of homeless people. Remember them?"

"In New West? Never." Her father laughed, then said, "I don't know, those psychics look pretty serious."

Her mother snorted. "Well, they can relax. The Revolution's over. They ought to just leave well enough alone." Her mother put an arm around Val and drew her in. "Just concentrate on getting your education."

Geneva and Val both rolled their eyes. Their parents were reminiscing again about the old days, "When times were hard and people had had to fight..." Blah, blah, blah.

"Back to the future, OK. Let's be present. Be here, now," Val had said using their parents' usual admonishments against them, and they'd continued their tour.

Since then, except for the times when the protesters got new yellow signs or were written about in the student newspaper, *The New West U Review*, Geneva hadn't paid much attention to them, mostly.

One day, this past winter, one of them had startled her. She'd just looked at Geneva strangely. The woman's head had jerked around when she walked by as if she had called out. The woman's eyes went wide. Her look was expectant. It made Geneva feel exposed and the feeling clung.

Then, it happened again. Another day, another intense look. A different protester, but that same jerky movement, those same wide eyes. The next time all three of the women had started to turn toward her as she walked by. Geneva attracted the protesters' attention, as if she'd suddenly appeared in front of them. They weren't just looking either. She felt them reaching out to her as she turned away. To avoid their creepy stares, she usually took a longer route across campus, veering through the madronas and crossing in front of the student union building.

She'd forgotten in her hurry and there they were at it again. They stared at her open-mouthed as she walked by. She looked behind her to see if there was anyone else the women could be staring at. Nope. The path was empty. She had one more year left at New West University. She wouldn't miss those three strange women.

Geneva walked faster tugging down the hem of her short Ruby's uniform dress and reached the lawn in front of her dorm, dotted with students. Textbooks were splayed in front of them, but no one was reading. The students lay on their backs, eyes closed, lips slack. She wanted to shrug off her flour-dusted Ruby's uniform, flop down on the grass and bask with them.

But it was finals week. She had to study. Until Nathaniel had called and begged her to fill an afternoon shift, she'd meant to spend the day reading. She wanted to nail her test. Then she'd be home free until graduation. She also wanted to encourage Val. At the beginning of spring quarter, Val had received a warning notice from the university. She had been spending a lot of time in virtual reality and that winter all the online slacking had finally skewered her grades. Graduating from New West University was a requirement for permanent citizenship. If someone got booted from the university, they could be thrown out of New West onto the Freeway. It was a serious consequence. Still, even after the warning, Geneva didn't think Val had attended many classes this spring, either. Fortunately, most of Val's classes were in her major, quantum information theory, which were easy for Val. She needed to ace the finals but could do so with just a little study. Geneva was frustrated. Val wasn't putting in the little bit of effort it would take to prevent a crisis, while she had to bust her ass just to maintain decent grades. Geneva had always been annoyed by Val's tendency to float by obstacles in the past, but now she was worried.

Geneva couldn't quite give in to the indolent spring day, but she settled for taking off her shoes as she crossed the lawn. She wiggled her toes in the grass and admired the way her Toad Vapor polish sparkled. As she walked across the lawn, Ruby's wingtips in hand, a flock of AeroFlux Butterflies flew by and a bare-chested boy in board shorts lunged past her twirling to grab a handful of the disks. Geneva noticed his long lithe torso, warm skin, and slim muscled calves. She watched him leap over one of the girls lying on her belly on the grass and snag the edge of his target. He spun in the air with the Butterflies in hand so that he landed on his ass facing the girl. He winked at her and then grinned. The girl laughed shaking the blond ponytail that hung down her back, apparently not minding the intrusion.

"Hey, Ruby!" A voice called. It took Geneva a second to realize the guy was talking to her. It was her uniform, the monochromatic ruby-colored dress. She turned and the guy was there. She was looking at the wishbone arch where his chest ended and his abs began.

"Wanna play?" he asked.

She caught her breath. He had full lips and gleaming teeth and his hair fell in natural brown curls to his sun-kissed shoulders. He grinned and bounced on the balls of his feet like he was flush with energy but had all the time in the world to spend it.

Geneva shook her head.

"Got to study huh, Ruby?" he said and bounded away, over the path and across the grass, flinging Butterflies to another boy. She tried to imagine standing in her stiff, stick-straight Ruby's smock pointing her arms up into the air and stumbling after a Butterfly. Just then the blond ponytail girl stepped by her. The girl looked nude at first in her bronze bikini until Geneva saw the thin line of a strap under her blond hair. The ponytail swung back and forth across her back like a metronome keeping time with her hips. She leapt like a dancer and caught eight Butterflies flung her way. Geneva noticed she wasn't the only one watching ponytail move.

Just as well, Geneva thought, let the other girl distract the beautiful Butterfly throwing boy. She had an upcoming exam, the last significant one of her college career. After three years of effort, this test was worth the sacrifice of one more spring day. Next year, she could take electives, do an internship, and figure out what to do with the rest of her life. She quickened her pace.

At Inu Wood Dormitory, Geneva pushed open the door to her dorm room. The air inside was hazy with cinnamon-scented smoke: Val's incense. Val was there, in total Plug-In mode, just as she'd been when Geneva left. She wore slim, black, virtual reality glasses, a purple snail-shaped cell receiver in one ear and a silver one in the other. Insulated as she was, Val could probably ride out an earthquake, even Cascadia's long awaited Big One, without looking up. Geneva winced at the way Val was sitting. She was perched on the narrow chair. Her long legs, encased in her favorite kick-ass, thigh-high boots, were slung sideways and tucked under her butt. It was an ergonomic nightmare, but somehow, Val managed to hold that twisted position for hours.

Geneva went to the kitchenette, poured a glass of almond milk and set it down beside the computer. Val snaked a hand out, wrapped it around the glass and brought it to her lips. Her other hand maintained its flight path over the keyboard whirring as her fingertips depressed keys. On the monitor, information spiraled around the screen and then came to a stop as Val pulled off her headset.

"Hey, Gen. You're back." Val wrinkled her nose. "And so smellin' like fried soy."

Geneva shrugged. "I tried to smell like chocolate." She reached into her apron pocket, pulled out the Tim's bag and handed it to Val. "To help you study."

"Cordials?" Val reached into the bag and then held up one blue and brown smeared finger. "Yep. Ah, thanks." She put the bag aside.

"Sorry. It was warm and I dawdled. You get some studying in?"

"Ah sure, Mom. I think I got it under control," Val said. "Don't worry. They try to kick me out and I'll just remind them my parents died for the cause."

Geneva turned, stung. "OK. I guess."

"Hey," Val called as Geneva headed down the short hallway. "I still think you should dye your hair. Everyone already calls you Ruby. So why not go with it?"

Geneva slipped out of her uniform and took a quick shower. A package of Wicked Sprites hair dye in Gator Tongue red was displayed on the bathroom counter. She smiled as she secured the wet sable strands of her hair into two ponytails and put on a white

T-shirt and khakis. Val didn't seem to get that she already attracted more attention than she wanted. In the living room, she took one last look out the window. Through the dark slats of the blinds, the long lines of sky and lawn were now cast in an orange glow, the first hint of sunset. She closed the blinds and wrested the oversized armchair around to face into the room.

"Val, is it OK with these closed?" she asked turning on the floor lamp.

There was no reply. Val had left real-reality. Geneva wondered when talking to Val had become mostly habit, like talking to a pet. She didn't expect a response. Still, in front of her, Val filled the room with companionable silence. Val rustled the air and sucked it in. She swung side to side on her chair. Her fingers on the keyboard produced soothing insectoid sounds. Val muttered to herself in breathy half syllables as she did — whatever it was she did — online. She provided just enough noise and movement to make the room feel occupied, exactly the right amount of company. Val's reaction to the cordials had been disappointing, but what did Geneva expect? A few chocolates weren't going to make them kids again. Growing up meant growing apart, and maybe their more distant relationship wasn't bad, just different. Geneva sunk into the armchair and hefted the Privacy Law book onto her lap. She turned to the section on Neo-Privacy and started reading.

Snap! Geneva looked up as Val undid one of her many pockets, extracted a vial of gloss and whisked the brush over her lips. Geneva smiled. Val had been wearing that same vampy shade of plum since junior high. It matched her Wicked Sprites Nightshade colored hair. She noticed how the ends of Val's hair fell forward in a sharp angle under the headset and smiled again. On the other hand, Val had a new haircut almost every week.

Geneva returned to her text. It was time to get serious. She needed to think of a mnemonic device to remember the names of the plaintiff and the dissenting judge in the landmark neo-privacy case. She sounded out a sentence slowly, driving each word into her head, "The Supreme Court upheld the *Hales v Friend-Me Co.* ruling in an 8-1 decision with the dissenting opinion coming from..."

Then Val started screaming. Her high-pitched wail shook the room streaming from everywhere at once. Geneva had to identify the source of the sound visually — Val's plum-smeared mouth stretched wide. Val jerked backwards in her chair and then fell from it onto the floor. She writhed. Her limbs struck the metal chair as she continued to scream.

The law book crashed to the floor as Geneva jumped to Val's side. She fell back striking her tailbone as Val kicked her in the side.

"She...she just started screaming," Geneva said to the medic. "I was studying here and she was online and then..."

"How long?" the medic said.

"Hours."

"No, how long was she screaming?"

Geneva shook her head. It felt like hours. She began to tremble. The numbness that had reined in her panic at the bizarre situation left her suddenly, releasing her to a cold quake.

The medic extracted a finger-length wand from his front pocket and waved a point of light in Val's eyes. They were laced with red, sunk deep into the sockets. The flesh around them puckered.

"Optic neuritis," he said. He filled an eyedropper with liquid from a vial in his coat pocket. From it, he squeezed green drops into Val's eyes. Then he placed a black patch on her forehead. A wave pattern appeared after a few seconds. He spoke into his snail shell as he worked. "There it is, the spike and wave. And there's the ELF. Definitely an EHBF. What's your name?" he asked.

Val stared up vacantly. The drops made her irises swell. "Val Freeman," she whispered.

"Where are you?" he asked.

"New West University," Val said her voice steadier. Then she jerked and grunted, "Get...off...me."

The guards started to back off.

"Keep holding her." The medic told them. "I'm going to give her something to relax."

He pulled a syringe out of his coat, peeled down the top of Val's boot and lowered the plunger into her thigh.

Geneva edged off the armchair, “Wait.”

But Val was already sinking into stillness. The guards released her and the medic hoisted her up. She hung limp as he belted her onto the stretcher. Under the thick straps, in her black T-shirt and short-pleated skirt, Val looked delicate. She would hate that. Bruises were already beginning to form in a row down her thin arms where they had struck the chair. Her head lolled. Geneva reached over and tucked a strand of hair behind Val's ear. Her hair and forehead were damp.

The medic began to move the stretcher forward. Geneva started to follow, but he stopped, grabbed her arm and pulled her aside.

"Here, take this." He handed her a business card. "Call her family and tell them to call this number."

She started forward again as Val was wheeled from the room. "I'm family.”

"No," he said, his voice low, his fingers tight around her arm. "You should stay here. You're shaking. You want something to calm you?"

She shook her head. It was true that she could not stop shivering, but she felt too calm as it was. She should be doing something. She wanted to run after Val, but she didn't trust her legs. The medic had stepped around in front of her, blocking her.

"Well, here, take this, if you want, for later," he said. He handed her an eyedropper filled with green liquid. Her fist closed around it. When she looked up again, she was alone with the two campus guards.

"Jeez," one of them said as they left. "What were you girls doing inside today anyway? Inside on a beautiful spring day, it'd make anyone crazy." He pulled the door shut behind them.

Geneva looked down at the card in her hand. The card's embossed green pyramid logo glittered. She went to the lamp and read: New West Mental Health. Details of Val's seizure began to shine out to her like the words on the business card and she connected them with bits she'd learned in psychology and science classes. The diagnosis the med-tech had given Valerie, ELF, these were low frequency electromagnetic waves, brain waves. She'd seen the label on the drug he had given Val, Thorazine. That was an old anti-psychotic, but with a new modern use the professor had glossed over, that she could not recall. She saw the words Sync Chrome City stretched across Valerie's chest on her t-shirt and thought she'd seen them somewhere else before. She began to remember the crazy rumors, of something like this happening to other students at New West. She may have even seen flyers on campus about it — a place the government had taken students, usually Plug-Ins, referred to as The Camp.

Just when everything seemed out of her control, at the same time, everything felt connected. Geneva had the feeling that if only she'd been paying attention, she could have anticipated this and spared herself and Valerie a painful shock. She could have done something to prevent this. She promised herself that now, now that her roommate, her sister, her best friend had been taken, she would be more aware, she would notice. Things had been happening in the world around her and they mattered.

~ 3 ~

QUILLS

"Most are in agreement that the Psychic Reformation likely would not have occurred without the establishment of a peaceful enclave that allowed Generation Utopia to focus on a high level of self-actualization. However, many (notably: S. Sherring in *Save Giovanni: The Lost Men of the Psychic Wars*) have speculated about the role of C.G. Burrows and whether the trauma of those first Awakenings could have been avoided. In hindsight, we can argue that the New Westian Revolutionaries should have tried to repair the immense social damage created under the United Government, rather than attempt a pristine utopia. In addition, many have criticized New West for its failure to enact a psychic education program sooner. Had it done so, undeniably, suffering could have been avoided." — *Becoming Psychic 101, A History and a Primer*

Just outside of New West on the 'Way, C.G. Burrows was taking his time plugging black ink into his thigh bead by bead. After each prick came the ooze of entering ink. He finished the tail of the "e" on his left thigh and started in on the "d" on the right. The design was nothing fancy, just black block letters he'd been working on a little each day, ever since he'd moved his parents' R.V. up from C-town and opened his Vary shop inside. For six months he'd been clean. An assortment of drugs had failed to keep the needling voices out of his head, even here, closer to New West, where there were fewer people. Of course, he'd never been in a hurry to finish the tattoo. That was kind of the point of the long Latin phrase he was embedding into his skin — *Omnis festinatio ex parte diaboli est* — all haste is the work of the devil. He was taking it nice and slow. The needle pain was his new remedy for his psychic distress.

This morning, he'd heard about another way of keeping the voices out of his head. He'd found a link to the Noetic Sciences Institute — the headquarters located far down the 'Way — and the Society for Psychical Research, located far off-continent — on the Psi-Aware website. Noetic meant intellect, and he didn't think the Psi-Aware group had any. The idiots were interested in enhancing and developing psychic skills and spurring change in a rapid fashion as ignorant as New Westian rebels. Their naïve expectations regarding the ecstasy of psychic experience ran counter to Burrows own experience with telepathy. It just caused pain. The desires of these factions were the stuff of Burrows' recurring nightmares: the one where he stood in a crowd of silent people stabbed by the thoughts of a similar crowd over the next hill, or even worse, the one where he stood alone in a clearing with no one and nothing in sight but trees, still pinned by a crowd of pricking thoughts as if he were trapped in an ancient torture device, a psychic iron man. So far, these psychic wannabe groups had not found support for their plan to develop psychic abilities in the general population. So, his nightmares were still only nightmares. The only thing he agreed with them about: It was possible.

Unlike the Psi-Aware activist naïfs, however, the Noetic Institute had done actual research into psychic abilities and their research had application for his own interest: controlling his psychic piercings, reducing his pain. The institute wrote academic scientific papers filled with multi-syllabic garble that concluded: psychic powers can be controlled by meditation. It was a slow and time-consuming solution he hadn't tried and wasn't going to. He'd stick to the ink. When he focused on the pain, he could keep the intrusive thoughts out of his head. He practiced slow tattooing as pain management.

Burrows looked at the clock and laid aside Faust, his favorite needle, a nine-incher. It was time to open his shop. Not that anyone was likely to come in before it got dark, but he had to keep to a schedule, or he'd lose his mind out here. He made a quick post on *KillGiovanni* to keep the content fresh. Then he turned on the vid screens displaying his handiwork in the showroom, lit up the neon pink "V" over his R.V. and put on his lab coat.

He was sterilizing his needles one by one over the stainless-steel table when the kids intruded: two minds pierced his. A girl, impatient: *Where's the owner?* And a boy, bored*: There's no one here.* He clenched his jaw and tapped his temples with two fingers, twice, hard, mimicking the pain in order to dull it. He liked to be sitting out front when the customers arrived so he wouldn't be surprised. He could handle the pain better if he was prepared for it.

Let them wait. He didn't need psychic ability to know they were college students, coming into the Freeway so early, on a lark. He finished sterilizing the set of two-inchers and walked out into the waiting area when he felt the boy about to leave: *There's no one. Let's go*. He stroked Faust's steel in folded gauze as he approached them.

Sure enough, college students, too clean to be anything else. They were a little sweaty and scraggly from the walk past the gate, but they were obviously from New West although they'd put some effort into appearing otherwise. The boy had matted hair and the girl dark gunk around her eyes. Both were in clothes that hung off their scrawny limbs. They looked like rag dolls, but he could see their stuffing and it was clean. What would their parents think? The revolutionary generation had worked so hard to keep the rabble out of New West, only to have their children idolize the castoffs and scheme their way out of utopia.

The boy was nervous, spooked probably, by the dirt and disorder of the ‘Way and maybe a little turned on by it too. Everything that was so carefully maintained in New West came undone on the Freeway. It was New West with its corset unstrung, exuding carnal entropy. He remembered what that felt like the first time, being cut loose onto the ‘Way. Frightening, but invigorating, before it wore you down.

The boy's eyes flickered around the shop unable to settle on any of the screens flashing images of blood and body parts from finished and in progress Varies. The guy finally saw him and nudged the girl who was also staring at the screens. He nodded and Burrows just stared back until the girl — *Over here!* — talked. "I'm here for quills."

The girl’s voice in his head was needy and insistent, particularly biting, and it was Burrow’s pleasure to ignore her. He turned to the guy and testily countered with a string of his own verbiage, "You from New West? You sneak over the border and walk into the first Vary shop you see on the road, that it? So what do you think? What can I do for you? Give you a special on detachable tails? I got some real pretty custom exotics."

Burrows had learned to be a fast talker. It was the only way for him to fire back at the unsolicited thoughts he got from others, since no one ever "got" him.

It was insulting to suggest they wanted something so tame as tails and Burrows knew it. The kid, on the defensive where Burrows wanted him, puffed up at first, then he decided to play cool and sunk into a chunk of the mustard-colored foam in the waiting room.

"No detachables. Quills," the girl said.

"Yeah, she hardcore?" Burrows asked the boy. Then, still focused on him dismissed the idea. "Nah, those are real uncomfortable."

The guy pointed at the girl and shrugged. She looked into a glass case at back of the R.V. "Serious, I know what I want."

"OK, sure. I'll take your money, if you've got it," Burrows continued to address his comments to the boy while the girl's indignation grew—*Hey. Prick. Over here. I'm the customer.* It amused him to annoy her, but he was going to have to deal with the headache sooner or later. "I'm not one of these Vary guys that tries to mess you up and laughs at you later. What you want is what you want, but I know my business." He jerked a thumb at the girl. "I don't think you want quills."

"You can't look at me and think you know what I can handle," the girl said.

He snorted. "Handle, sure. In case you haven't noticed, I haven't even looked at you." She'd left greasy handprints all over his showcase. He finally gave her a long look. "Like I figured, you look more like tail."

Asshole. Her retort slammed him, reminding him that he was having too much fun. Pissing people off was the one thing he enjoyed about his "gift." He could push people to the brink of anger and still end up with their money. Time to get charming. "But who cares, I won't see you in here again anyway. She wants quills, she can have quills."

The boy took the cue. He reached into one of his many pocket and flashed his circle of New West green and yellow. These college kids always had lots of credit. "I think that'll cover it," the boy said. He crossed one baggy-pant clad leg over the other, sprawling, taking up space, relaxing into the insulation like it was home.

"Now we can talk," Burrows said to the girl in a low voice, the one women especially liked. "I'm Burrows." He extended his hand. "And you are?"

Eve. She thought it. He knew it. Her name penetrated his mind and then she said, "Eve." It was like living in a damn canyon. He liked it better when people lied. It was less repetitive.

Eve pointed to one of the long black quills in the case and he opened it up and handed it to her. She ran a finger along it as the boy came up beside her. He reached a fingertip out and jabbed it on the point drawing blood, "Yaaah!" Burrows swiped the quill from Eve and swabbed it with the gauze.

The boy jammed his fingertip into his mouth and sucked. "Damn, those could do some serious damage. Where you going to put them?"

Eve pulled her shirt up and placed her hands around her hips just under her belly roll. "Long ones from my back to just about here that stick out." She slid her thumbs down from her hipbones till they met in a point just under the waistband of her black pants. "And then a triangle of shorter flat ones in between where the points meet."

"Oh great," the boy whined. "You want to kill me?"

Eve curled her lip at him. “You wish.”

Burrows unlocked a smaller case and extracted one of the gold quills. He held it up to the light so she could see its glowing core.

"See, that's pretty," he said. "The inside captures the light and it has a russet tone." He touched the transparent tip. "And it's longer than it looks too, surprising. Now, these are what you want. Not those black ones, too obvious, garish."

Eve, mesmerized, nodded. "Yeah."

He knew she'd like those. They were a total mismatch with the persona she was trying to pull off: black clothes, dyed black hair, kind of witchy. But they reminded her of someone: *Coco.* Some other girl, he figured. A pretty girl. No, his type. Better than pretty, he imagined — fine.

Burrows began to gather an assortment of the five, three, and two-inch gold quills. When he had a fistful, he jerked his head at the door to the surgery and said, "Come on behind the curtain. I'll let you watch me alter your girl's abdomen."

He pulled the curtain aside to reveal the most sterile place outside New West — his operating room, one stainless steel table and a collection of needles. It wasn't what he'd envisioned when he'd dreamed of becoming a neurosurgeon. It was what he had, the meatloaf he'd made out of the scraps of life he'd been left. He waved Eve toward a stainless-steel table. "Climb up there."

She hesitated at the door. "Do I have to put something on? Like a gown or something?'"

"No, just pull up your shirt and take off your pants."

He looked at the boy. The two kids had exchanged moods. The boy was the cool one now and the girl was nervous and struggling not to show it.

"So, serious, you do know what you're doing, right?" she said. “I mean, you must've been doing this awhile."

Accusations were flashing through her head — *Hack. Waster. Perv.* — He felt each one: prick, prick, prick.

"Yeah. Good question," Burrows said. "Why don't we talk about this while I'm working? This could take time."

She pointed at his lab coat. "Are you wearing something under that?"

The boy snickered and that made her shut up and drop her pants. She sat up on the table. "Fine."

She had flat white thighs and black cotton underwear. He wheeled his chair and tools over and swabbed her abdomen with alcohol. She didn't squirm much. That, and the way she hadn't complained about the cold table, told him she'd probably be good with the quills. He started to look forward to this.

"You know, actually, I haven't been doing this long," he said, when he had the first quill poised over her side.

She shot him a look. He hadn't left himself much room. She was one comment away from slamming her hands down on the table and jumping off. He looked up at the boy who was already starting to lose interest, pacing around the backroom.

"But she's in good hands," Burrows said. "Before I did this, I was gonna be a surgeon. You know, back when people wanted to be beautiful. But don't worry, I didn't get shut out of New West for malpractice or crime."

"What happened then?" Eve asked. "How did you get here?"

Burrows inserted the first quill in her side. "Steady now. Let's just say some people didn't like my opinions. They had their revolution. I was on the wrong side."

"You could come back. There'll be amnesty," the boy said. "Especially for a doctor."

"Interesting riff. Heard that before. You don't listen," He began to stick in the second quill. "I'm not a doctor. I was going to be."

The boy: *Whatever.*

He stuck the girl harder than he needed to with the third quill. She bit her lip, real quiet now. She was concentrating on her own pain, not thinking about him at all anymore. She was staying in her own head, good girl. That was the best part of the Vary work, making people quiet. The boy stood by watching the infusion of quills into his friend's side. It shut him up for a while too, but not for long. He was a twitchy little guy.

"So when did you get all that work done?" he asked.

Burrows paused and ran his hands over the "work," the kid was referring to, the long hard spikes around his neck and the rubbery black nubs over his jaw and cheeks.

"I didn't, 'get-it-done'," Burrows said inserting another quill in Eve's side. "I did it. You have to trust a guy who does his own face, right?"

"Yeah," the boy said.

"I wanted to make sure I would never be tempted into going back into New West again, since they wouldn't take me like this, it all works out."

The kid stopped asking questions. The girl was flat on her back now. Her chest heaved like she might hyperventilate. Her eyes, glazed and unfocused, were muddy brown like the edge of the 'Way along the forest. She was beginning to feel high from the pain. Burrows zoned in on his work. He poked the thick end of each quill under the white flesh, watching the blood rise to the surface and seep out around the end in small circles. Eve's sides were starting to swell and purple where he'd stuck the first quills. He finished on her sides and began to set the shorter, softer quills into her lower abdomen.

He was getting into a rhythm, laying them down fast and smooth, when a spasm of thought knocked him off beat. He jerked back, jabbing his finger with one of the quills as the kid stabbed him: *It's him. It's the killgiovanni guy!* He whipped around and saw the boy hovering over his computer.

Then the kid was at his side in full twitch mode. "Is *Kill Giovanni* your site?! No way, everybody loves it! Do you run it? Did I introduce myself? You said you're Burrows, right? I'm Grugel."

Grugel was not this kid's name, which explained why the kid hadn't given it to him sooner. A name was usually the first get people would hand him. Everybody wanted to be known. This kid, some kind of schemer, stayed inside, a proper liar, but he was telegraphing now as he rambled on. Grugel was spinning ideas about whether he could get Burrows to come into New West with him, if there was a way to make some money.

"I have a cult site too. It's called *Sync Chrome City*. Giovanni is one of the security codes."

The kid sent tornados of geek enthusiasm migraining into Burrows. It was a pain, but also flattering. Apparently, Burrow's site, his little counter revolutionary hobby, *Kill Giovanni Hastings*, a stab at the popular children's book, had gained some kind of following. After a few beat downs in elementary school, Burrows had learned to disguise his weak-looking reflexive wincing with a pissed off mocking sneer. He used it now, turning this face to the source of the migraine. "I thought all you kids liked Giovanni Hastings — the voice of Generation Utopia?"

At this, Eve hoisted herself up on her elbows. Her stomach rolled out, now nearly coated in gold quills: like a bloody, prickly, teddy bear tummy. Her lip curled.

"That was our parents' idea. We can't stand that sunny-day story. Giovanni Hastings ends up king of the world. But what really happened? Nothing. Our parents got to have a revolution. We got nothing: static. What am I supposed to do when I finish college? More of the same. Some lame job in New West. Giovanni's just a fairy tale."

"Well, yeah." Burrows rolled his eyes. "More like propaganda. So, you're running to the 'Way? Taking up residence? Finding work, maybe, at the Friend-Me factory?"

"No way," she looked around. "Just visiting, maybe hitting one of the bonfires. We don't want to make slaves of ourselves and live in the dirt out here. I'm just saying it's not perfect in New West. Not so perfect as they like to make it out."

"Hey, I like to make out," said Grugel, and was ignored.

"Just better than here," Burrows said. "Because you're bored?"

"Yeah. Basically. Perma-bored. Stuck."

Grugel hopped around. More astute than the girl, or maybe just less self-absorbed, he actually noticed how the comments burned Burrows. "Eve, piss him off when he's done sticking you," he warned.

"Yeah, I'm about done," Burrows gave Eve's forearm a little shove. His antagonism toward the kids had become more serious, less entertaining. He hated that they had what he'd once wanted: comfy, little college lives. "Lay back down and let me finish this."

He flicked in the last quills.

"That you too, Grugel? Going nowhere, bored? Way's too poor for you?"

Grugel: *Is he crazy? No one lives on the Freeway unless they have to.* "Not me," he said. "I mean I'm not going to have some lame job. College is just like, my cover; I have my own business."

"What kind of business?"

The kid shrugged. "I do some tech." But Burrows got another much more interesting answer: *SLO-42.*

The kid was dealing. No surprise there, what other kind of business could a college kid have? But SLO-42. That was rare. Burrows kept his expression neutral, but he had to work at it. SLO-42 was complicated to manufacture, and you had to have a source, someone who people wanted to experience. Did this kid know Kendra LeMay? Burrows hadn't got his hands on that supply for years. He'd given up on the drug altogether after a few bad trips sampled from dull minds. He didn't need to experience the perspective of some guy on the 'Way. He already got that.

He hadn't had a good trip since the dose Mace had given him. He was sure now it had really been off the famous entrepreneur, LeMay. He grimaced remembering how he'd last seen Mace. The worst part had been the expression on his face, not even surprised, like he expected Burrows to kill, just like he'd expected him to steal. The next worst part was the intensity of his thought, completely focused on his murderer as he struggled. It had come at Burrows like a spray of buckshot; the pain delivered on a mundane last thought —just a denial — *No!* Then the pain ebbed. The thoughts had faded. Mace had gone inside, silent, his life flashing before his eyes, Burrows supposed. And Burrows had rushed out of the tent and continued to live up to low expectations. He'd given up on drugs, for the most part though, and settled for solitude to avoid the pain of people.

He pushed back his stool and, even distracted by his memories, he couldn't help but admire his work. The girl's pierced belly was almost pretty now with its prickly golden sheen. Eve sat up and carefully ran her hands down the quills.

"It'll look better without the blood and bruises. You're done," he said.

Grugel handed over payment, a circle of green and yellow. "Hey, don't forget we want one of those tails too," Eve said. She pointed at a Golden Tamarin — a long fluffy noncommittal variant that, in truth, had no genetic relation to any kind of off-continent creature. It got its lush fringe from Golden Retriever and its long curling tail courtesy of an inventive rat-cat hybrid. Not that these kids knew the difference between their animal parts.

"That doesn't look like it'd fit either of you," Burrows said.

"No, it's for a friend. She was too scared to come," Grugel said.

"Then she doesn't deserve this," Burrows said stroking the tail, which was still one of his favorites despite its inauspicious origins. The geneticist had made the best of the inferior raw materials available. "Why give her an edge she hasn't earned?"

"Oh, as if," Eve said. "She wasn't scared. She wasn't allowed. Her father's got her in chains."

"Father?" he asked, to see if he could get it. He already knew they were talking about the fine girl, *Coco*, who Eve idolized and was so overshadowed by that she'd gotten quilled to try to stand out. Too bad for her, he doubted it would work out. Classic beauty always trumped trying too hard.

Eve: *President Sherman.*

Another surprise. These kids! They knew the daughter of the head of the university, the de facto leader of New West, and they had access to some kind of SLO-42. He couldn't help but hope it was the Kendra LeMay variety. Now they were getting interesting.

Burrows shrugged turning the New West electronic coin over in his hand. It was just a credit card, but everything had to be tweaked in New West, made better. It had the heft and glint of coin, embossed with the New West emblem, a circle of yellow bisected by a line of trees. He scanned it, took his due, and as he handed it back to the kid asked, "So what if I decided to come visit? Would you have a place for me to stay?"

"Yaaah! People would want to meet you," Grugel said, failing an attempt to suppress a geek spasm of excitement. The kid was like a series of electroshocks. "Check out my site, some time. Here." He handed over another coin, this one glossy black. A line of skyscrapers cut through the circle in place of the trees on the New West coin. The cityscape pictured on the coin was anti-New West in every way but reminded Burrows of the black windowed Mirror building at the center of C-town where his parents lived. C-town was another enclave that had formed in the economic collapse, but the people there had taken the opposite approach: preservation. They had liked things the way they were and tried to keep them that way. It was a dull, predictable scene.

"Those are the access codes. Tell me what you think," Grugel said.

At that, both the kids' minds flashed, pinning Burrows brain from either side: *Check out Sync Chrome City.* And from the boy: *Yaaaah!*

After the kids left, dragging their Tamarin tail behind them on their way to a Friend-Me bonfire like it was freaking spring break, Burrows flipped Grugel's Sync Chrome City link into his machine. Twenty minutes later he was reeling, gasping for breath. Ten minutes later he had a blade on his face digging into his flesh to remove the nubs. He had to push the scalpel in deep to get them out. Removing the quills from his neck was even more painful. The delicate skin tore loose. The flexible quills didn't help and after he pricked his fingers a few times he broke off the sharp ends to get them out of the way while he worked. When he finished at about 2 a.m., his head, ear to jaw, was a bloody mess. Blood streamed through the stubble down his neck and pooled in his collarbone. He sponged the worst of it off and applied some anti-microbial jelly. He'd wear a collar. He'd grow a beard. It'd be fine. But he was going back into New West and he couldn't have people looking at him and sending hard thoughts his way.

He'd put in the quills and nubs to fit in and establish his business out on the 'Way. Now, he'd ripped them out so that he could pass back into New West. He told himself that it was not about scoring SLO-42. It was what he'd experienced on Sync Chrome City that drove him, but in truth he couldn't get Kendra LeMay out of his mind. She'd opened the Friend-Me factory just down the 'Way from New West like she'd planned, giving the ruffians work and holding the monthly bonfires to keep them happy. The hedonistic celebrations drew the college kids down like flies. They didn't want to work as "slaves," but they were more than happy to party like them. So, Kendra was close, but still too far away to please him. He'd seen the potential of Sync Chrome City, so it was time to go into New West. If he managed to score some SLO-42 made from Kendra LeMay, so much the better.

~ 4 ~

FINAL EXAM

"Perhaps undue attention has been given to the fact that Geneva Weltraum, Mother Connectress of Minds, was so solitary in her younger years. Many have countered that her studies of psychology, even though her focus was primarily plants, not people, indicate her empathic leanings. However, the portrayal of Geneva as a loner is, for the most part, accurate. It must be remembered that she manifested first as a Sender: a telepath, not an empath. The repellant nature of Sender and Receiver, referred to today as "annihilation," caused trauma that could have been avoided if the government had embraced psychic abilities rather than treating those first manifestations of the transformation as mental illness." — *Becoming Psychic 101, A History and a Primer*

Rumor had it that a few New West students each year suffered psychic seizures, and that the university had been removing them to a remote facility. Whether the purpose was to help them, study them, or just isolate them; no one knew. They called the mysterious off-campus location, The Camp. Now Geneva knew another alias: New West Mental Health. That was where the medics had taken Valerie after giving her thorazine. Geneva had remembered its other use: a psychic suppressant. Groups like Psi-Aware, advocates for supposed psychic evolution, wanted the drug banned.

Did the university think quiet Val was psychic? How could they know? Was she sick? Could it possibly be contagious? In tears, Geneva called home. She was relieved to hear her father's voice. Usually, she disliked talking to him on the phone and immediately asked for her mother. Ever the scientist, her father didn't converse: He relayed information in terse, tense phrases. Now she was grateful for his laconic style. She didn't want to talk or to try to explain what had happened. She just wanted help. Unsure where to begin to sort through her fear, sadness, and the first seeds of anger, Geneva began in a manner like her father, concise and factual. "They've taken Valerie."

Her father listened to her blunt story and then his voice lifted as he zeroed in on key information. When he spoke, it was in the slow, moderated tone he used when he did research, talking to himself as if reading his thoughts aloud as they scrolled by. "OK, the business card. Just read me what's on it."

She did, and her father responded with silence, the way he so often did. He'd stop in the middle of a conversation to ponder a subject unrelated to what you wanted to talk to him about, possibly a new species of rodent he was studying. There was nothing to do but wait him out. If interrupted, he'd forget what he'd been about to say. Geneva grew impatient, she wanted reassurance that Val would be OK.

"Can I talk to Mom?" she asked.

There was another pause, and she strained to hear him catching only, "Sorry." before he hit full volume. "Your mother's on assignment in C-town."

Of course, she was. Her mother had been "on assignment" since Geneva had hit puberty. She glanced at the door, still seeing, in her mind's eye, the dark top of Val's head disappearing as the medic wheeled her out on the stretcher. "I shouldn't have let them take her without me. I should go after her."

"No," her father said, in the firm tone he used to announce new research. "I was thinking I know where they are taking her. That place. It's nearby. When did they leave?"

"Minutes ago. They'd take her all the way back to Linden?"

"Yes. You've seen it. That clinic. The building was by your high school," he said. "You remember, in the forest."

Geneva didn't.

"I'll meet her there. Sit tight. I'll call you when I have news," he said.

"Wait, what about this green drug?" she asked.

But he was already gone. Her father didn't say goodbye. He never did. He had no sense of phone etiquette, as though he didn't really believe the device was connecting him with another human being just the information that person contained. Geneva detached the phone from the curve of her ear and stared at the purple snail shell in her palm. The display read 11 p.m.

Her father had sounded so sure about his strange conclusion. If they'd taken Val to Linden, that was at least a 30-minute drive away. Val wouldn't even be there yet. Her father wouldn't call until he had concrete information. It'd be an hour at least, after midnight, a new day.

If The Camp was real, why had the medics taken Valerie there? As far as she knew, Valerie wasn't any kind of psychic. And they'd both been healthy. Her mind raced, and the dorm room felt constricting. She replaced the phone on her ear, grabbed her key card from the pocket of her Ruby's uniform, and headed out the door down the empty hallway.

She wanted to bang on one of the doors, find someone, and tell them everything to dilute the contents of her spinning mind, but she didn't know anyone who would unquestioningly invite her in at this hour. Val was the one person in her life she could talk to about anything, anytime. As she left Inu Wood, she caught a glimpse of a couple cuddled in the lounge in the glow of a screen. She'd met them but couldn't remember their names.

Maybe her father had been right when he'd said she and Val shouldn't room together. Val had been her built-in best friend ever since she'd come to live with the Weltraum family. When the economy collapsed, the government and all the schools had shut down. Restoring the educational system had been New West's priority after the chaos of the revolution, but it had happened slowly. Her parents had taught them at home until high school. If not for Val, she would have been alone. When the high school opened, Val had welcomed it. She'd made new friends. Geneva could just as easily have stayed at home helping her father identify new species of rodents.

"You're more like our mother," she'd said to Val once in high school meaning it as a compliment.

"Your mother," Val had said. "And I'm not."

Her parents were not technically Val's, but they'd always said "our mother" before. Val's rejection hurt, but Geneva excused the slight. Maybe Val was upset because their mom had been away on diplomatic missions so much. She felt abandoned sometimes, too. It had to be worse for Val, but they'd never talked about it.

When they'd moved in together, Geneva had been happy. She thought it would bring them back together and heal the places where they'd grown apart. You couldn't get closer than roommates; problem solved. Maybe rooming with Val had kept her from making an effort to meet any other people on campus, so what? She didn't need a lot of attachments. She was focused on her studies, and, after all, one close friend was better than a bunch of acquaintances.

Geneva headed across campus without any particular destination in mind just seeking more space for her thoughts. Lamps along the brick paths cast an orange glow. She soon reached the west edge of campus overlooking the dark bay. She leaned against the railing looking back. A sliver of moon hung over the evergreen covered hill behind the cluster of brick halls. Through the madrona trees at the university's heart, the administration building was as still as the rest. The stairs leading up to the giant double doors were empty. The protesters had gone home for the night. Geneva wrapped her arms across her chest and rubbed the goosebumps on her arms. The campus was still tonight, its students tucked away cramming for finals.

The snail shell balanced lightly on Geneva's ear. She wished it would vibrate and she would hear her mother's voice. She missed the mother she remembered from childhood: a more serene version, she thought, before Val had come to them and before she had taken the government job. The breeze off the Salish Sea cooled the tears in the corners of her eyes. The moon appeared to waver as she blinked them away. Val had changed their lives. Sometimes Geneva wished she hadn't.

It's happening again, Geneva thought, nothing will be the same tomorrow.

She bit her lip and veered over to the Student Union Building. The Big Top Valerie had called it in an editorial she'd written for *The New West Review* and the name stuck. She'd opined that the building's design reflected the architect's disdain for students. It looked like a circus tent. Disdain was a frequent theme of the paper especially on the topic of "their generation," Gen Utopia. They would be the first to live out their lives in New West and benefit from the social order and the soundness established by their parents, The Revolutionaries. They would all be educated and economically upper class and would not have to worry about political upheaval, an economic crisis, or environmental chaos: the three plagues that had occupied their parents. They were free to spend their lives at the pinnacle of Maslow's hierarchy of needs and devote themselves entirely to self-actualization. The newspaper editor railed against the labeling of their generation and liked to point out this left Gen Utopia in "no place" with nothing to do. Although she'd never shown much interest in writing before, Val had picked up the paper's note of disdain perfectly in her commentary. She'd always been persuasive in a quiet way.

"The Big Top exemplifies how they see our role in this society. They expect us to live delighted within their arena, like children at a circus. We are their perfect denouncement. At the same time, our entire generation could slide into the sea, and it would not spoil the show. Perhaps the best we, Gen Utopia, can hope for is some looming natural disaster to give us purpose. That's why everyone talks about The Big One, the earthquake we hope will shake us out of our ennui, and why the psychology, geology, and environmental studies classes here at New West are so full. When were not self-absorbed in actualizing, we're hoping Nature will give us something more worthwhile to do."

Looking at The Big Top it was easy to understand how it got Val thinking about natural disaster. Nearly half of the hulking octagon hung out over the bay supported by steel beams. Geneva identified with a lot of the sentiment in Val's article especially the feeling of ennui, she didn't know what she wanted to do after university either. But she disagreed with the scathing tone. It was disrespectful. Their parents had devoted their lives to that transformation of society and had solved a lot of pressing problems. It seemed ungrateful to be bored. Geneva resented Val's slam on "self-actualizing students" and attack on psychology and environmental fields, her own double major. If Val thought her studies were self-absorbed, she could have said so to her face instead of writing about it in *The Review*. Val's editorial had widened the rift between them.

Papers flapped on a nearby board. Geneva looked to see if, among the flyers for bands, shows, and clubs on campus, any warned of psychic seizures and The Camp. A fluorescent pink paper caught her eye. Smoothing it down to get a look at the message, she shivered. That stripped feeling came over her like when the psychic advocates stared. She repressed an instinct to look around. No need to be paranoid. Then she remembered the self-defense training she'd learned in the dorms: It's safer to meet a stranger's eyes.

As she turned, a hand dropped onto her shoulder. "Yaaah!" a voice behind her shouted. "End of the Year romp!"

She spun around snaking her arm out, her fingers cupped to strike the attacker's neck. Her fingers twitched when she saw the guy behind her. He was about her height with a wild mat of towering hair. Emblazoned across the front of his T-shirt in fire engine red was the word, "Dickwad." It was just another student. At first, she was proud, then scared, to note that her fingertips were poised just like she'd learned in the class at Inu Wood, poking towards his windpipe. Another few inches, a clean strike, and she could have collapsed his throat, maybe even killed him. But he'd caught her wrist. The grip of his hand made her give him a second look. His forearms were sinewy. Muscle packed his frame. He was small, but tougher than his goofy expression and the paunch of belly hanging over his belt suggested.

He released her wrist and winked. He was somewhat bug-eyed and his open eye bulged at her so she could see his sea green iris clearly even in the faint light. He held his arms out on either side of her and pointed with both hands wagging. "This ain't no average, ordinary hallucination. New West, Dark Wave with the electric light stylings of DJ Leo Love brought to you by..." He moved his hands in an arch over her head and wagged them to the left. "The Mansion Expansion."

He pointed at Keller Hall. The dorm was a windowed wedge. A cliquish group of plug-ins and ravers called it home. This guy, a hybrid, had the pockets of a plug-in, but his bright orange half-shirt screamed raver. Val had been spending some time over there lately. Did he know her?

He reached into one of the many pockets on his green cargo pants and handed her a flyer identical to the one she'd just been looking at. "Yaaah. Supa Stella!" He arched his arms over to the Mansion again. "So, you must be one of Leo's girls. Want to party?"

When she didn't answer, he cocked his head at her shaking his plume of hair. He narrowed one eye. The other widened. He pointed at her pocket. "Party?"

Geneva looked down. In her Face in the Crowd T-shirt and khakis it had to be obvious she was not his scene. Then she registered the green glow spreading through the pocket of her pants. She reached in and brought out the dropper half full of shiny green liquid that the med tech had left her. “You want something to calm you?” he'd asked.

The spaz boy snatched it and raised the dropper. When he looked at her again, green liquid streaked down his face. The whites of his eyes glowed and his irises had turned from light green to emerald. "Yaaaah, that's it." The look he gave her made her feel unwrapped. "Sure, you don't want to party?"

He held out the dropper. But she shook her head. "Um, no I have to study. That's OK."

He pocketed the dropper with one hand and grabbed her hand and gave it a violent shake with the other. Then he shook pointed fingers at her pistolero style. "Bummer. Right on."

Her phone began to vibrate. She lurched and it fell off her ear onto the brick. The guy squatted and grabbed it. His toenails were the same orange-red as his shirt. She snatched it out of his open hand and placed it on her ear. "Dad? Dad, are you there?" she asked. She turned her back on Dickwad.

"Geneva, I'm at the clinic. They're evaluating her for treatment," he said. He sounded stilted as if he were reading lines. “An apparent psychotic break. That's what they said.”

It was as if Geneva was standing in the dark on the middle of campus alone again. She didn't know what to say after that, and if her father did, he was taking a long time thinking it over. Psychotic: Geneva struggled to remember the clinical definition. It wasn't something that came up often in environmental psychology. It meant Valerie had lost contact with reality. For a plant, losing contact with reality wasn't a condition, it was a death sentence. Plants needed their roots in soil or water to grow, but people could become detached and still survive. Behind her, Geneva heard a patter on the bricks and knew the weird boy was loitering behind her continuing his restless dance.

"I don't understand. She's been fine," she said into the phone.

"No," her father said, and for the second time she heard his harshest voice directed at her. "She's not fine and she hasn't been fine. She's had some kind of breakdown. Whatever you've been doing up there, I don't know, but we're going to keep her close."

The silence was so long she was sure he'd disconnected. When she turned around Dickwad was still there, hopping. Whatever drug the medic had given her wasn't calming on this guy. When she started to walk away, he darted in front of her and gave her his pistolero fingers again. "See you tomorrow night."

She crumpled the flyer and shoved it in her pocket.

Suddenly, her father was back, "They say they'll be keeping her over the summer."

"Summer? But she can't miss." Geneva looked up and saw she'd instinctively headed to her safe place, Varian Hall, which housed the greenhouse and most of her classes. "It's finals week."

"Finals?" Her father asked. Of course, he didn't know about Val's slumping grades or the warning letter.

Geneva sat on the steps. "We both have big tests tomorrow."

The chill marble seeped through her pants.

"So, she was studying when this happened?" her father finally asked.

"Not exactly." Off to her right, a movement caught her eye. She turned and saw only moonlight reflected in the waxy azalea leaves.

"But you were, right? You weren't on the computer?" he asked.

"No." She wished again for her mother. Her father, the scientist, liked to analyze, pick things apart one at a time and classify them. Her mother, the diplomat, was great at listening, multi-tasking and making connections. She could have dealt with Val's emergency and been there for Geneva, too. Her mother would at least ask how she was feeling. Her father continued to use the harsh tone with her, and now she was confused by his barrage of questions and sudden interest in studying. She tried to reach him and let him know what she needed some fatherly reassurance. She said quietly, "Dad, I'm scared. I feel like, somehow, this is my fault."

In response, she heard only muffled voices in the background. She rose half off the stairs. The azaleas shook. Her father returned. "Geneva, there are some papers I have to sign. Don't worry about your test. You'll do fine."

The test? Wasn't that the least of her worries? "Dad? Goodbye? Goodbye?" But this time, he was really gone.

The azaleas rustled again, and a low growl rose out of them. She walked toward it crouching to peer into the shadows beneath.

Through the leaves, she saw hands running down a bare back and fingers plucking at the strings of a bikini strap. "Animal," she heard a girl's voice and giggling. Blond hair swished across the back. The girl she had seen chasing Butterflies was in the bushes with some guy. He made the sound again, a mock growl like a human purr.

Geneva stepped back. She wasn't the only one who'd caught the couple. She saw a flash of orange around the corner of the building: Dickwad. She hadn't meant to see either the couple's naked lust or his naked jealousy. Suddenly, it felt like there was too much company on the college campus, and too much emotion. Geneva was exhausted. She turned and headed back to the dorm. She collapsed on her bed and stared at Val's empty one. Her mind cycled between worry, confusion, and fear until she fell asleep.

The alarm clock went off at 6 a.m. Geneva let it blare. She lay in bed surrounded by pillows in the windowless dorm room. Her head ached with the retort of Val's scream, fired off like a concealed weapon carried within her usual quiet. Geneva kept hearing her father's accusation, "Whatever you've been doing up there...we're going to keep her close." What did he think they had been doing? She tried to reassure herself that Val's sickness, whatever it was, was not her responsibility. That's what her mother would have said if it had been her on the phone last night. She often chided Geneva for taking "too much on her shoulders." Her father, on the other hand, reinforced her own tendency to be analytical and try to solve every problem she encountered. "Sometimes all you can do is cry, and that's enough," her mother liked to say. Maybe it had been true when she and Valerie were in high school and their problems were mostly silly and social. They were struggling to fit in and beginning to grow apart and make different friends. Was it true now? Shouldn't she be more responsible? She was on her way to becoming a citizen, after all. Her father had questioned her and sounded critical as if Val's breakdown was something she could have prevented.

As she got up and began to get ready for class—because what else was she supposed to do—the situation made her angry. This was Val's fault. It was a stupid time for her to go crazy. Graduating from New West was the first thing they had to do on their own, their first chance to screw up. If Val was going to freak out, any other time would have been better. Now, although there was no way she could possibly concentrate on it, Geneva had no choice but to take her Privacy Law final. It was what she had planned.

As she crossed campus, other sleepy, scruffy students stared at her. They paid sudden attention to her as if they were all Psi-Aware protesters. A shivering girl in a tank top shot her a sympathetic glance. A huddle of guys in ball caps parted to let her through. It was as if everyone could see the misery inside her. Geneva hurried head down along the brick walkway until she reached the steps of Varian Hall. She already felt bad for blaming Valerie. Thanks to her stupid psychology classes, Geneva knew she was only angry because she felt powerless. She didn't know what to do to help and she felt so lost she couldn't even cry. She was studying psychology not because she understood people, but because she knew she didn't. She felt more comfortable around plants: They were simpler. But of all people, she'd thought she could always count on Val. Now she couldn't. She'd thought they'd understood each other. Clearly, they hadn't. Worst of all, she'd thought they'd always be there for each other, and now she'd failed that too. She'd left her friend alone thrashing on the dorm room floor. She hadn't been able to help. If Geneva didn't understand and couldn't help Val, then she wasn't of use to anyone.

Up the steps and into her seat in class, Geneva tried to switch tracks and think about passing her exam. It was useless. She couldn't recall anything she'd studied, not a single fact. Val screaming. Val flailing. Val lying on the stretcher. That was all she had in her head.

When she looked up, the professor was done giving instructions, the same ones she'd heard a million times, for taking the test. She didn't say, "My friend went insane last night. Can I take this test later?" because it wouldn't matter. It wasn't as if she would feel any better about taking this test in a couple of days. If Val was an unknown variable, then everything in the future was uncertain.

The class clown, sitting beside her, shot her a pained look. She looked down and pulled up the exam on her desktop. Essay questions appeared on the screen. "When the Supreme Court upheld the *Hales v Friend-Me Co.* ruling in an 8-1 decision with the dissenting opinion coming from..."

She froze. It was the exact same sentence she'd been reading just before Val's seizure. She heard a cough behind her. The professor leaned over her shoulder. "You don't have to do this."

She turned in her seat. "But I..."

"Nonsense." He ran a hand through his thin hair as if brushing something aside. "Look, I know this is not a good time for you. Shhh. Listen. Rules make humanity, but they don't trump it. Quietly take your things and go. No, no. We'll talk about the make-up some other time, Geneva."

She grabbed her knapsack and staggered out of the room keeping her head down to avoid the gaze of the staring students all the way across campus. Back in the dorm, she dry-heaved over the toilet. Before today, she hadn't even thought that professor knew her name. She was a diligent, anonymous student. Her adviser Robin Roundtree was the only one who'd ever paid her any attention in class. Now, she still wasn't speaking, but it felt like everyone on campus was listening, when she wanted to be inconspicuous. Geneva had never felt so afraid, and she was trying to tamp it down, bury it inside of herself. If she gave in to her fear, if she let herself, she'd be on the floor screaming and they would take her away, too.

~ 5 ~

MANSION EXPANSION

"In addition to the serene social conditions within the New West enclave three factors fostered the environment that allowed the rapid emergence of psychic abilities:

The Friend-Me Journal — created the precedent for information sharing among large populations and the predictive empathic element of the Friend-Me Couriers.

Sync Chrome City — although the computer program induced mental trauma in unprepared young minds, this artificial Psychic Space model introduced and adapted the Dawning Psychics to the speed, heightened awareness and collective thought they would later share without the aid of devices or drugs.

SLO-42 — this chemical replica of a neurotransmitter conveyed empathy and stimulated neural pathways in the Dawning Psychics.

A fourth factor may also be considered, although its impact is still being analyzed by botanists (including R. Roundtree) and geologists, the natural event of the earthquake along the Cascadian fault line some call the Psychic Quake." —*Becoming Psychic 101, A History and a Primer*

Geneva held her head under the faucet in the bathtub and watched Gator Tongue dye stream out of her hair, coloring gallons a rusty red. Whenever it seemed about to run clear, she'd tousle her hair and more red would gush forth. With her head doused in cold water, the answer to the test question — "What was the reasoning behind Justice Grace Vinton's dissenting opinion in the *Hales v Friend-Me Co.* 8-1 ruling?" — came easily.

The neo-privacy lawsuit was about Friend-Me Journals. The journals were new and all the rage when she and Valerie were preteens. The controversy was with the sophisticated database, which tracked and fed the girls' journal entries to the corporation. Justice Vinton had argued that because the consumers were minors when they began to give Friend-Me Co. access to their personal information they could not legally give consent. Geneva's father had had the same opinion. "You're too young. You don't even have control of yourself yet, you're too young to give it away." He'd wanted to forbid the girls from getting Friend-Me Journals, sure the corporation would abuse its link to the subconscious of a generation of teenage girls.

Her mother, however, had insisted the girls be allowed to decide for themselves. Valerie, in a rare display of conformity, quickly got a Friend-Me. Geneva, going against her father's wishes for the first time, did too.

Geneva massaged her hair again and the water turned rosy. She turned off the faucet. Pink droplets spattered the white tile as she reached for a towel and wrapped it around her head. Of course, her father had been right. Friend-Me Co. had come up with a way to profit from all the information they were getting from the girls. After five years, the company launched its courier service. Using its enormous database filled with teen girls' wants and desires, the company developed an intricate caching and retrieval system. Zeroing in on product names and cross-referencing them with key words indicating levels of interest, analysts at Friend-Me developed a program that could extrapolate a user's future desires based upon their journal entries.

Prescient deliverymen, the Friend-Me Couriers brought you exactly what you wanted even before you knew you wanted it. Most devoted Friend-Me users raved about the new service. The deliveries cut through uncertainty by providing an instant, tangible answer to everything. Even if you didn't know exactly what you wanted, Friend-Me knew. It reviewed your recorded emotions, ran a comparison to a database of other users, and linked them to a corresponding product. The Friend-Me goods had an 89 percent acceptance rate. The couriers were as difficult to deny as a craving. That was the crux of the *Hales v. Friend-Me* litigation.

Too young, Geneva hadn't paid much attention to the death of Sherri Hales until it was required reading for her Privacy Law class. But her parents had often talked about the case and the woman's Friend-Me assisted suicide. The Friend-Me courier had brought her a bouquet of Lilies of the Valley. Hales ate the datura leaves and collapsed. Neo-Privacy advocates brought a wrongful death lawsuit against Friend-Me Co. on behalf of the woman's daughter, Eve. The suit accused the company of bringing the means of death to a depressed woman's doorstep and the privacy advocates argued furiously against Friend-Me's use of Sherri Hales' teenage diaries filled with vampire fantasies: death and resurrection.

The justices, with the exception of Vinton, disagreed. The court said that the women had established a precedent by confiding in the journals and accepting Friend-Me deliveries on numerous occasions. Users' consent for the couriers was implied when they logged in to their journals.

As Geneva dried her hair and secured it into ponytails in front of the mirror she was startled by the effect of her garish red hair. It made her green eyes pop, looking large and alien. The rest of her slim pale features — nose, cheeks, and lips — appeared to retreat behind them. She swabbed some of Val's Plum Ice gloss over her lips. The clash of red, green, and purple turned her triangular face into an exclamation point.

Now she was ready. She was done with feeling powerless. She'd decided to follow her instincts and problem-solve. First, she had to find out what Val had been looking at when she'd lost it. In the living room, she put on Val's glasses and scrolled through the history. There were two sites: NWU-Physics and *Sync Chrome City*. Geneva went to the physics site and it took her into Val's e-academics folder. Val's final was there in her quantum information theory class. Geneva scrolled through and was surprised to see Val had filled in most of the questions. There was still time. She guessed on the final few questions for Val and submitted the test. While waiting for the confirmation, she scrolled over the *Sync Chrome City* link.

She felt bad about checking up on Val, but when the reply came, "You have completed your QIT final." she clicked on *Sync Chrome City.* The words flew into the corner of her vision. Skinny right leaning letters in script the mirror image of Val's glowed cerulean. They read: *I am not an average ordinary hallucination. I am going to mess you up, bad. Welcome to Sync Chrome City.* "Ooh, la, la," a voice trilled. "Gunk-Secured content."

A series of crisp video images —roaches, bombings, and mutilations — flashed in front of her. Geneva couldn't handle even the first round of hard-core content. She lifted the glasses and tossed them aside. "Ugh, that's what I get for spying. Damn, Val what were you into?"

Geneva, rocking back in the chair, almost tipped to the ground when she heard a courier call "Friend-Me" outside her door. She went to answer it, determined to auto-reject the delivery. Today, her life was too complicated to want anything that came in a box. When she opened the door, the courier knelt before her on one knee in a spotless forest green cloak.

"You want this," he said packing persuasion and subservience into the few syllables. The green box he lifted out from under a fold of his cloak glittered. He held it up to her in the palm of his hand.

She knew it was just packaging, but she could already feel her resolve caving to curiosity. According to Friend-Me's database, her history indicated a desire for whatever was in that box, right now. It was a message from her childhood self.

Probably sweets again, she thought, reaching for the box. "I'm not hungry." But she stroked the velvet lid and opened it. With a knowing smile, the courier transferred the box to her hand and bowed sweeping the cloak across his body. "On your account, of course."

Geneva nodded and pushed the door closed. She sunk to the floor with the box in hand. On the satin lining, the cluster of tiny leaves looked especially dry and brittle. But her memory was fresh. She had plucked the leaves from the towering willow tree on the edge of the school grounds on her last day of first grade. In that moment, her emotions surged. She'd stared up into the branches spinning around with the feeling that she was about to be caught up in something enormous and wonderful. She'd heard a voice, the word — *destiny* — and reached up to the tree and shook a branch as if she were sealing a pact with it. Then the feeling faded. She'd put the leaves in a scrapbook that she hadn't touched since buying the Friend-Me journal.

For the first time, Friend-Me was wrong. This wasn't what she wanted. That feeling of destiny, purpose and wonder was exactly the opposite of the one she had now and the memory of it made her despair. She didn't think she'd ever feel like that again. Geneva lifted the leaves out of the box, and they flaked onto the carpet. Underneath the leaves was a slender black stylus just like the ones that came with all the Friend-Me journals. She picked it up and realized why everything about this delivery felt wrong. The courier's knock had startled her. She'd been at Val's computer, not connected to her Friend-Me journal at all. So where had this "gift" really come from? She spun the smooth stylus and ran her fingers over the engraving. The silver read, "Sync Chrome City."

Geneva stumbled as she entered The Big Top teetering on Val's boots with their 9-inch heels. As she stood in the doorway, looking into the room filled with dark spaces and flashing lights, she felt relieved. No one turned to look at her. The stretchy black fabric of her short, pleated skirt was almost obscured by masses of shiny silver snaps. Light reflected off them and colored spots darted around on the floor in front of her. Although she couldn't have felt more conspicuous, she blended in. Everyone here wore plug-in clothes, practical black adorned with buckles and snaps to secure all the pockets that held their electronic gear. Thumping beats allayed her fear that the thoughts pounding inside her head were audible outside it, too. Instead of turning to her, everyone at the Mansion Expansion dance seemed immersed in their own worlds, their bodies spinning solo in restless intensity.

It wouldn't be hard to get caught up in it. Geneva stepped onto the dance floor and swayed. She needed a break. She didn't know how to have an insane friend. She couldn’t wait for the quarter to end, for campus to empty out and everyone to leave. She was tired of telling people that Val had gotten ill and gone home for the summer. It was the truth, and it wasn't. She wanted to bring Val back in time to continue fall quarter and ignore the weirdness. She knew she couldn't do both. She had to find out what had really happened. *Sync Chrome City* was key, but she was too afraid to enter the site. It wasn't just the disturbing Gunk gross-out images; she was scared to let her mind run wherever Val's had gone. The lurid pink flier, pimping the Mansion Expansion dance, had given her another idea, brought her here. Just like *Sync Chrome City*, it claimed to be "not just another average, ordinary hallucination.” Maybe she’d find a clue here.

Geneva maneuvered through the dancers around the edges of the octagon looking for Dickwad. At first, she couldn't find him, then she spotted his frizz of hair bobbing through the lights. He had on another orange T-shirt. This one said, "Kill Giovanni." He was smash dancing into a guy twice his height with sleek dark hair that shone blue in the lights. The tall guy danced head down, jerking on the hinges of his elbows and knees, gliding in circles around Dickwad. Silver flashed across his black T-shirt and after a few rotations she made out the words: *Sync Chrome City*. What was this, suddenly everywhere, city?

Geneva made her way towards the men dancing pressing through the crowd. Even on heels, she lost sight of Dickwad but she tracked his tall-dark companion. She was greenhouse hot and misted, moving through the dancers, by the time she got near him. She reached for his shoulder just as Dickwad slammed into him. Tall-Dark's elbow struck her chin and she went down, landing on one knee. It was Val's damn towering boots. The guy turned to see what he'd hit, but the crowd closed around him blocking his view.

The music changed. A discordant cello and electronic mandolin duet replaced the pumping sets. The crowd on the dance floor thinned. A circle of seven guys in black joined Dickwad and Tall-Dark. Geneva crouched just at the edge of a pink spot of light that opened up in the center of the dance floor. Two girls gyrated up to them. She recognized the blonde by her metronome hips as Ponytail from the Butterflies and the bushes, although she wore her hair loose and wavy tonight. A black stretch dress rode her curves made out of a chameleon fabric that matched colors with the lights playing over it. Ponytail wrapped the end of her detachable Vary, a golden-fringed Tamarin tail, around the back of Dickwad's neck flirtatiously, but they seemed an unlikely couple.

Geneva hadn't seen the other girl, squat and witchy looking with curly dark hair, before. And she'd never seen a Vary like that. The V of red-gold quills that lined her stomach below her triangular half-shirt was clearly from The Freeway, not something you could get in New West. Geneva didn't know why anyone would risk going out there, but the Vary definitely made the girl look exotic. Without it, she might not have gotten a second look. Whereas the tail on the blonde was a redundant accessory. The golden girl didn't need any help to attract attention.

With the rest of the crowd hanging back, the small group's dance became a performance. The song had unintelligible lyrics that resonated from a low male voice as if he were singing from inside a hollow tree. A celestial chorus of women trilled behind it. The dancers mouthed all the words, but the chorus rung in a crescendo of voices as they sang along and now, she could make out some words, "Harvest Sin and Chrome and Sea. Come and intertwine with me." The DJ melded the music and the lights with his Sound-wield set. Even with her limited knowledge of the equipment, Geneva appreciated the DJ's prowess, the way he spun, weaving the lights through the crowd. Val, who could have appreciated the tech too, would have been in awe.

Geneva watched the DJ hanging in the darkness near the roof of The Big Top on a three-legged silver stool. When the new student union building was erected, the architects had insisted the design was an homage to higher thought. It was meant to look inspiring. But with the DJ spinning in the center of the sloping ceiling it looked even more like a circus tent. He leaned back arching over the dancers. The curled ends of his hair dangled as he swung from side to side waving the Sound-Wield wand to adjust the lights. She watched until her neck ached and then looked back to at dancers to see what effect he was having.

Now thick pink ropes swooped through the dancers linking each of them with light. The girls' sinuous movements went staccato. The whites of their eyes shone. The dancers leaned to the right, twitched, and shook. Their limbs flailed as the music rose to a pitch. Writhing, they collapsed on the floor as the music stopped. Geneva's knees buckled as everyone else began to applaud. Only she seemed disturbed by what she had recognized in the grotesque movements. They were stylized, and somewhat slower, but they were dancing psychic seizures: flailing, writhing, and twitching just like Val had while screaming on the dorm room floor. But it was all a performance.

Geneva stood, both repulsed and fascinated, by what she'd seen. She was curious, but afraid. She wanted to ask them what they were doing and find out what they knew, but the encounter with strangers seemed more than she could handle tonight. She wished she were back in the dorm room in her Face-in the-Crowd clothes with her long brown hair down over her eyes and a book in front of her like a shield. A chain rattled just behind her ear. She lurched back and found herself staring into the upside-down eyes of the DJ lowering his stool down beside her. When his sparkling black eyes were level with hers, he flipped and landed upright beside her. "Intense. Very intense."

Those were her thoughts exactly. He stood so close it felt like they were touching. She swayed back and forth in her boots. He put a hand on her back, to steady her and it felt hot.

"What band was that last song by? It's amazing," she said.

He nodded. "Giovanni Hastings Musica from down the 'Way. No one's sure if it's really a band or all synth and marketing though."

"What's your name?" she blurted.

"Leo." The DJ pressed her hands lightly between his. "Love."

She flushed. He tapped his chest twice with his forefinger. "Leo Love." He winked. "I know you. Ruby, everybody. Everybody, Ruby." He gestured in a circle at the ring of dancers surrounding them, many of them had glowing green eyes. They looked like Dickwad after he'd used the drops the medic had given her. Leo made a quick round of introductions, while Geneva paid just enough attention to get that Dickwad went by Grugel, Eve was the witchy girl with the killer Vary, and Tall-Dark Streker wore the Sync Chrome City T.

Every one of the DJ's friends oozed charisma, and she felt dweebish in comparison. Meanwhile, she was sure her fascination with Leo had to be apparent. Eve, with her hands on her hips just above the quills, looked like she wanted to stick Geneva with them. They could probably all tell she was a poseur. She had to look ridiculous in Val's clothes. Worse, now that the music was off, she had that stripped feeling again like everyone could hear her thoughts. She'd never been in love before. She imagined it would be a heavy-handed mystical experience and that was exactly what this felt like—love, falling, at first sight. She tried to think about anything but love, Leo, or otherwise. She was here to ask about *Sync Chrome City*, the psychic seizure, the green drug, and The Camp where they had taken Valerie.

While she tried to screw up the courage to ask at least one of her questions, Ponytail sauntered in and draped her arms around Leo's shoulders. She wrapped her fluffy golden tail around him and kissed his cheek. Leo purred and nuzzled her neck. "And this is Coco," he said. The heat drained from Geneva's face as she recognized the animal noise Leo had made. He was the guy she'd seen playing with Butterflies and heard in the bushes with Ponytail girl. He looked so different as a DJ in the dark with his lithe body encased in black clothes. Of course, Ponytail— Coco—was his love interest. She stepped back, letting Leo's friends edge her out of their circle.

"Nice to see you again," she whispered as she headed for the exit. It was too much. She'd had enough. She needed the night air to cope with what had happened to Valerie, not a bunch of new people. As she strode across campus, through the courtyard, she broke into a teetering lope. The chill air wicked sweat from her skin. Then she jerked forward as the heel of one boot caught in a gap in the bricks. She broke her fall with her forearms and sprawled. Pain keened as she examined the red raw scrapes. She sat up, unzipped the boots, and pulled her striped stocking feet free. As she did so, she saw why the boots had been so uncomfortable and unwieldy all night. It wasn't just the high heels. She'd been wearing them on the wrong feet. No doubt then she'd looked dumb in front of Leo and his friends. She was such a clumsy dweeb.

Thankfully, it would be summer soon. Everyone would leave campus and the only person she'd have to deal with would be her manager at Ruby's. Geneva yanked the boot heel free and began to laugh. There was nothing else for it. It was all she could possibly do.

~ 6 ~

MISTRESS M.D.

"We considered those men collateral damage. We made the decision to look to the future. The past was too desecrated to repair. Forced to make the decision again, knowing the costs and the consequences, I would do the same, abandon those men, C.G. Burrows among them. I cannot regret how we created New West. But many of our decisions were wrong, including how we handled the emerging empaths. The psychic internment camp at New West Mental Health was a gross mistake. We acted out of fear both for our youth and of them. I feared for my daughter. Constance Monica was always foremost in my mind." — *Save Giovanni: The Lost Men of the Psychic Wars*, S. Sherring

Under a black light in his surgery, Burrows gripped a white marker and sketched routes into New West across his thigh. He thought up lies as the glowing lines appeared until his bowels grew painfully heavy again. In the outhouse for the third time that night, his gut twisted. His nerves were acid. He felt sick planning to sneak into a place where he rightfully belonged. Burrows wiped his ass with a page out of a pre-revolutionary copy of *InkSkins* and let it fall. The door to the outhouse banged shut behind him. He would do what he had to. If there was psychic spread coming at him out of New West, he'd find the source and stop it. He had to take it one move at a time. First, get into New West. Then, find the kids. Follow his instincts. Act.

Burrows stripped off his lab coat and took a deep breath. The night air billowed over his bare chest. He palmed the warm tin of Black Gold wax in his pants pocket. He popped the top and smeared a corner of his lab coat with the grease. Evergreen needles skittered as he pulled the tarp off Mistress M.D., his Mercedes. It was time to take her for a ride. He stroked the car in circles with the polish until her surface gleamed. The shadows of his broad torso in her black depths as he leaned over the hood gave him smooth certainty. The wax had the same leather and oil scent as the inside of his car, but with a soapy undercurrent. It was the scent Burrows found most comforting, although not his favorite. His favorite scents were girls and warm snickerdoodles like his nanny used to make and, in the best of all possible worlds, girls who smelled like cookies: sugared cinnamon and vanilla. In his worn button-up shirt and Mace's old U.G. Jacket, Burrows slipped into the driver's seat as if it were a silk suit. He drove the Mercedes, a vestige of his parent's wealth, to the border. Razor-edged coils of concertina wire glinted along the top of the fence while lamps and moonlight lit the arch over the entryway to New West. It glittered silver and white shining unmercifully through the dark like the gateway to a prison or a paradise. The false lure of the place was what he hated. He wouldn't want to be trapped inside, but he couldn't stand being excluded either. He brought Mistress M.D. to a stop beneath the arch.

Behind a plate glass window, the border guard raised his eyebrows and shrugged. "Where'd you get a car like that?"

Burrows got a better look at the guard's scrawny shoulders and the green and gold New West badge on the breast of his jacket. "My parents, Marlee and Arlan Burrows." he said. "They live in C-town now."

From the agent he got: *Those rich bastards?*

"C-town, eh?" the guard said, still elevated, probably standing on tiptoe in a pair of heavy black boots.

"It didn't agree with me. I grew up in New West. I guess you could say I'm looking to come home," Burrows said, although he hadn't talked to his parents in years.

The guard lowered a few inches, giving Burrows a better view of the stubble on the roll of flesh under his neck. "Hmm, my mama always said home was wherever she was." His eyes flicked to the side and then back: *Am I going to have to shoot you?*

The green tint of the glass the guard stood behind gave him a reanimated look. Burrows held out the Freemans' pass he'd swiped off of Mace along with the jacket years ago. He hoped it was still good, but there was always Plan B.

The guard studied the pass like he was going to be tested on it later. Possibly he would be, that fit New West's over-educated style. While the guard looked vacuous, he undoubtedly had some degree that qualified him to do this job: probably political science or psychology, in the old days it would have been criminology, but who needed that now? New Westians disbelieved in crime. They'd excluded that element from their social planning, too. Education didn't make the guard smart though. Burrows prepared to floor the gas–Plan B drive real fast. He'd found it didn't pay to over think and if the guard was even allowed a car to chase him down with, it'd be one of those low-powered jobbies unable to keep up with his Mistress. As he pressed down on the gas, a bank of green security lights shot down from the arch and scanned over the car. A glowing tag now marred the pristine black of the Mistress M.D.'s hood. They'd given him a driving pass. He would be privileged not to have to ride the New Westian buses. What those freaks had against cars; he did not know.

"That's good for six-months. Then you have to renew," the guard said. "I guess New West and C-town are becoming best buds. Enjoy your stay."

As he passed through the gate, he switched Mistress' control panels over to electric and solar. There'd be no place to fill up the car with gasoline in New West. "Sorry to tame you girl," he said. "It's just while we're in enemy territory." Like that, Burrows was on the other side of the border. He drove past miles of soy and pea fields and small towns lit by pale blue solar lights straight to the university. He remembered the way, although he'd visited it last in high school. There were buildings and green open spaces now where there'd been parking lots, but it was easy enough to find a place to put his car on the street. In the darkness, Burrows could see only the edges of the long dark lawns and the clustered stalwart buildings in the distance. His chest expanded as he inhaled the warm pine and sea scented air. It sunk to the bottom of his lungs. So fresh. A white monument sign with New West University etched into the marble sparkled at the entrance to campus under a bright lamp. Burrows ran his hand over the letters—New West. The edges were sharp, although the institution was more than 200 years old. Burrows put his hand to his face. The sides of it were pitted from where he'd pulled out the nubs and his fingertips came away wet. The skin was rough on his cheeks and around his eyes. He felt like an old man sneaking onto campus on a summer night. It was the opposite of what he had wanted.

He strode past the shadowed buildings, heard a cry and stepped around the corner into a brick courtyard shadowy with amber solar lights. A girl sat in the middle of it, her arms hooked over her knees. Stiff curly ponytails stuck out from each side of her head. She was staring between her legs as if he'd caught her in the middle of midnight sit-ups. As Burrows watched her, she started to shake and then he heard laughter, high-pitched and somewhat hysterical. She took off her boots, padding towards him in striped stockings. She swung the long boots beside her, so they almost kicked the ground. Her red ponytails danced. Burrows staggered back as her thought stabbed him: *Sometimes, you just have to laugh.*

The thought nicked him, knife to stone. The suddenness of it caught his breath like a sucker punch. He didn't think she could even see him from where she'd been sitting in the dim light. This was not the way it worked. They weren't supposed to be able to get him randomly. He couldn't have dealt with every stray barb. It would've killed him. He froze in place, panicked, and then filled with a cool rage. This effect was confirmation of exactly what he had come to New West to stop. Let these people keep their thoughts to themselves. He didn't want them out infecting the 'Way with their thoughts. As she got closer, she started. Her red ponytails jerked back before the rest of her, and the coils sprung as she came to a stop: *I didn't see...Big scary guy. Danger.*

She looked light. If she dropped the boots now and started running, he didn't think he could catch her. Instead, though, she'd stupidly come to a halt. He could reach out and take her shoulders in his hands. She was not his type, dressed like a distressed doll, but she was just what he'd been looking for. She would know the way.

"Where've you been?" he asked.

She rushed him: *At the dance. All the plug-ins. Sync Chrome City. Valerie. Leo. What can I do?*

A barrage of thought came at him, a battering, far more than he was used to at once, and he couldn't make sense of it. The thoughts weren't all directed to him or even remotely about him. She must be drunk, he decided, caught up in her own world, projecting at everyone. He wanted to get away from her, but it was like he was in the middle of a storm being struck repeatedly by lightening. He couldn't move until it had passed. He hunkered down. Over and over, he got: *There's nothing I can do to help her. I can't even walk in her boots. I'm ridiculous. Stupid.*

Well, he agreed with her there. Shut up and vomit, he thought, as he weathered her silent barrage of words and finally picked out what he needed from her mess of a mind: *Mansion Expansion. The dance. The Big Top.*

"Yeah, so that way?" he pointed across the courtyard. Got: *Yes.*

Then, as a bonus, he got a last thought from her: *Just let this be OK, and I'll never walk alone on campus at night again.*

It almost made it up to him, for all the painful thoughts, that she was scared of him. She should be.

"You know," he said. "You really shouldn't walk alone at night. Perhaps you would like me to walk you home?"

She thrust back: *No.*

Instead of wincing, he took the pain and leered. "My placc, perhaps?"

Then she ran. He watched the pleats of her skirt flap over her taut haunch, as her thoughts grew faint. A smoky cinnamon scent lingered in the air where she'd been standing.

"Mmm, hmm," he said, enjoying the low vibration of the sound in the back of his throat relieved that she was gone, and he was alone in his head again, but regretful, too. It was always pain or nothing, and just when he was having fun. "I'll just carry on without you then."

He headed across the courtyard until he came to a new dome-shaped building that had to be The Big Top. Students dressed in black and shiny clothes milled around the entrance. One of them would know the kids he'd met in his shop. The helpful, painful girl had pointed him in the right direction.

As Burrows approached, the students averted their eyes. They raised their voices appearing immersed in their own conversations. From them he got quick appraisals: *Who's that? Not a student. Looks tough.*

Then the thoughts snapped studiously off. If he left them alone, they would leave him alone their thoughts said. Burrows could almost like these kids, his kind of people, even if he had some 15 years on them. He was clearly not a student, but the been-through-it look of his face and his natty camo jacket bought him some cred. Or maybe it was his size—the one lasting advantage he'd gotten from his father. Either way, these kids respected his solitude. They had a code of privacy that he could exploit. Any adult would have questioned him, knowing he didn't have a good reason for being here, and therefore bad intentions. They would have been right.

Instead, some lanky kid nearly his height approached and offered him a hit. The kid drummed his fingertips with their matte white nails against his shirt pocket and lifted and lowered a dropper: green glowing inside. It took Burrows a couple of ticks to realize what he'd seen. Da Lime. SLO-42. He hesitated and the kid moved on. Burrows hadn't had another opportunity to get the drug, since he'd ditched Mace and sworn it off. He shoved his hands deeper into the pockets of his coat. He was tempted, but no. No drugs, especially not SLO. If he ever killed again, he wanted to be certain it was solely his decision. He had a goal to achieve and couldn't let himself get distracted under somebody else's influence.

He watched the pusher kid move through the crowd and stop to talk to another kid coming out of the building. There was no mistaking that head of rag hair. It was Grugel the *KillGiovanni* fan boy with his hair dyed the same orange as his shirt. Burrows took a few steps out of the crowd and into Grugel's line of sight. In a moment Grugel came at him buoyant and grinning like a clown. It was perfect. He was even wearing his KillGiovanni shirt. "Burrows, my man!"

"Fanboy!" Burrows said.

Grugel bounced at him, shaking little droplets of sweat on Burrows' jacket. When he got close enough Burrows got: *Freak, man!*

Grugel was staring at his face, noticing his new scars.

But he also got: *Sweet! This is gonna be sweeeeet.*

The kid was cool. He turned and waved the drug pusher over.

"Streker. Streak, man. This is the guy I was telling you about. The one Eve and I met out on the 'Way. C. G. Burrows, the host of KillGiovanni."

The kid was practically panting with enthusiasm. The pusher looked at Burrows. His girlishly big eyes widened: *Whoa!*

He was not a deep well. Grugel put an arm around the pusher's neck, reaching to make up for the height difference, but making it look easy, and drew him in. "Streak works with me on *Sync Chrome City*," he said, pointing to the kid's black and silver t-shirt as if it weren't obvious.

Burrows nodded. "I came to see your set up."

"Yeah, you know it. Matter fact, we were just heading back to The Mansion," Grugel said. He pointed across a lawn at a long windowed one-story building.

"You're running it out of a dorm," Burrows said. "You live, there?"

"Yeah," Grugel bounded ahead and Streker followed. The pusher carried a constant shrug, his shoulders high around his neck.

Grugel opened a door to one of the rooms from the outside. It had a huge blind-covered window like a cheap old motel.

"Welcome to Sync Chrome City," Grugel said, as he held open the door. Burrows ducked under the threshold. The squarc room smelled rank and stale as a tent on the 'Way.

Grugel turned on a black light. A jolly roger glowed on a flag hung over the far wall. There were two narrow beds shoved to opposite sides of the room. Burrows wondered how these kids got laid. He looked at them and smirked: yeah, probably not a big concern.

"Give me a hand, Streak," Grugel said, as he stood on the end of his bed and reached up to unhook a corner of the pirate flag. The cloth dropped to the floor revealing a panel of electronics. Micro-sized versions of microphones, speakers, lights, recording devices, hard drives and consoles were packed together around three huge monitors.

"Yaaah! That's what I'm talking about," Grugel said grinning maniacally. He reached down behind his bed and the room started to hum. The words "Welcome of Sync Chrome City—population 1,274" popped up on the monitors. Grugel began blinking rapidly, his eyes darting from screen to screen.

"Yaaah, lots of people on board," Grugel said. He turned and bumped up against Burrows' chest. He leaned back, looked up and drew circles in front of his eyes with his pointer fingers. His eyes glowed gray. "I got the contacts. Do you want one of the headsets?" Grugel: *This will blow your mind.*

The kid's thoughts hit him like a hangover. The sensation was not entirely unpleasant. He was enjoying Grugel's enthusiasm. Being around the kid was like doing shots and immediately paying the price in rapid succession. "Brilliant, fanboy. Nah, I already perused your city from the 'Way. Lots of options. So, how much are you charging?" Burrows asked.

Grugel shrugged.

"Would that even be legal?" Streker asked.

"If people want it, it's legal." Grugel said.

"Right, very admirable. Listen," Burrows said. "I'd like to stay around awhile, really get to know your system. We can talk business."

Grugel: *Oh, yeah? Moneymakers? You don't look money, but I'll show you off. The KillGiovanni guy.*

Burrows was still getting his head around that latest round when he got pressed again, this time, by a new voice: *He's here!*

Eve walked in. She was wearing a short black skirt that made her legs look thick, but he had to admit that the Vary he'd put in was doing her favors. The v-shape elongated her short waist. She looked better.

"It's OK. She's cool." Streker piped up from where he was sitting on the bed. He patted the spot next to him, but Eve stayed standing.

She didn't look happy to see him, but he got: *He's here! You came!*

"You guys going to be ready?" Eve said, with the practiced nonchalance of an ill-favored woman.

"We're showing Burrows *Sync Chrome City*," Grugel said. "He's got some ideas."

Eve bent down and reached under one of the beds. The hum stopped. The room went still. She pulled a large black case out from underneath the bed. "You guys haven't even started to pack," she said. "Do I have to do everything?" Eve detached a speaker from the wall and placed it in the case. "What ideas? There's no time to mess around. We're out of here tomorrow."

"Yaargh! Don't mind her," Grugel said. "Going home makes her bitchy."

"Just put the monitors in the case and don't touch the screens," Eve said.

"Yeah, gimme a hand," he said to Burrows.

Burrows liked the bickering. It kept the kids' thoughts off him. But he didn't like watching them disassemble Sync Chrome City. "I thought we were doing business."

"It's summer," Grugel said.

Burrows stared at him. "So? Am I interrupting something?"

"Dude, nobody stays around in the summer," Grugel said. "But, hey, you could come with us. We can work on it at home."

"Right. Where's he going to stay?" Eve said. She had her hands on her hips just above the Vary. "Your father won't be cool."

Grugel shook his head and pointed at Eve.

"No way," she said. "It's just bad timing, you know."

"No, it's fine," Grugel said. "He can stay with Strek."

They all looked over at Streker, who was sacked out against the wall chewing his white-coated fingernails. He looked up when he heard his name. "Dude, I think I'm eating paint. Think it's toxic?"

"Streker," Grugel said. "Lydia will be cool, right?" He pointed at Burrows. "He needs a place to stay for summer so we can do stuff. Why not Deming?"

Grugel: *That crazy bitch won't even notice you, Frankenstein.*

Streker looked at Burrows: *Stray cat.* "Sure," he said. Shrugged. "Shouldn't be a problem."

"Don't think so," Burrows said. "I'm the kind you don't take home to mother."

Streker stopped gnawing his nails. "We'll almost have the place to ourselves. She's all the time at Psi-Aware meetings or meditating."

Psi-Aware. Well, that might make a detour to Deming worthwhile. Burrows could feel everything lining up. New West was sprawling for him.

"OK, I'm for bed. You guys finish packing," Eve said. "The Shadow Bus leaves at 8 a.m."

"No," Burrows said. "Take your time. No bus. I have this invention. Called a car. You'll like it."

Streker was a blank, keeping his thoughts, if he had any completely to himself. Eve scowled at him wordless, but he could feel the ache of her wanting. Grugel's grin went maniacally wide again. From him Burrows got: *Man! Dude! Yaaah!* The kids' enthusiasm gave him a migraine. But it was almost worth it. *KillGiovanni*, a car — Burrows felt like a real celebrity here and he couldn't wait to surprise them.

~ 7 ~

NEW WEST MENTAL

"What was once considered an illness, a defect or a harmful mutation affecting Generation Utopia is now seen as society's greatest gift. It is ironic that the First Psychics were deemed unfit when they developed the same neural networks that children now achieve in elementary school. The lesson is powerful: the permutations of what is possible, what is normal, what is gifted, and what is ill are ever-changing. It was once common belief that people used only 10 percent of the brain, that they could not learn past a certain age, and that psi-abilities were extremely rare or quackery. Today, these notions seem ridiculous. As you meditate and develop your awareness and connections, remember that the brain is indeed 'wider than the sky.' There is no ceiling to our thoughts." — *Becoming Psychic 101, A History and a Primer*

In the outdoor dining area of Café Ruby's, the sun shadowed the customer's face so that he looked up at Geneva with dark eye sockets, "That's not what I ordered." She swept the offending Ruby's Special away promising to bring the soy "salmon" burger instead. Inside, she apologized to the chef pushing the plate back under the heating lamp. He shrugged. "It all starts to sound the same after a while, doesn't it? You're still one of the best. Try to fit in a break soon."

She was at Ruby's full-time during the day for the summer. The money was good, but the work was draining; filled with forced music, loud conversations, and the pervasive scent of grilled soy. It didn't help that everything in the restaurant was red. On her first full day, by the end, in a fit of sensory overload she'd wanted to rip all the menus and napkins to shreds. Now, after an hour on the job, her senses shut down and everything looked like Gary the manager's stash of pre-revolutionary memorabilia—plastic. She couldn't wait to go back to the night shift when summer was over. It was soothing by comparison. The lights were dim, the red looked ruby, the customers were fellow students, and the orders were simple: shakes and fries or pancakes and coffee.

After the irritated customer ate his salmon and left a meager tip with his bill, Geneva caught a break. She leaned against the brick wall in the alley behind Ruby's, feeling the hard warmth between her shoulders. She closed her eyes and imagined the sun burning through the stale soy particles embedded in the fabric of her uniform. She thought about the DJ, Leo Love. It was becoming a habit, an embarrassing one, even in the privacy of her own head. She could see him dancing over her. His locks fell forward to touch her shoulders. His lips were on top of hers, kissing. The fantasy was becoming more intense but less satisfying each time, as she let herself drop irresistibly into the pleasure pangs of hope.

When the door beside her creaked, she opened her eyes and jumped to see Gary glowering. She shoved her hands into the pocket of her apron. She wasn't sure what, if anything, she'd been doing with them, but she felt guilty about it. Gary had that look: stonewall with a glaze of pity. It was the look he used when he was trying to explain to some curious customer what was in a Ruby's Special.

"You've got a call from your father. He says it's urgent."

It had to be about Val. She swallowed hard. "My dad, calling here?"

She followed Gary and took the call standing beside his desk in his tiny office. It was filled with a stash of pre-revolution era culinary supplies. There were clunky, colorful plastic appliances and cans and boxes and bottles labeled in unintelligible, off-continent writing. Glossy photos of cakes and salads topped with strange pink, orange, and green sliced fruits plastered the walls. Gary said he liked everything about the revolution except the food. He'd had a fancy restaurant before and constantly reminisced about the menu when there had been key-lime pies, Cajun-seasoned swordfish, and Sloe Gin slushes. Now, he said, Ruby's serves a Pacific Northwest-Cascadian-American Indian-West Pac Rim fusion. "Get it, fusion?" he'd say and howl. But except for a couple of the older chefs, who sighed sympathetically, none of the waiters got the joke. She could tell Nate, the baker, got it, but he always rolled his eyes.

In a Social Justice class at the university, Geneva had learned how New West had moved to self-sufficient production of its own food supplies. It was both socially responsible and an economic necessity as the United Government could no longer be relied upon to provide enough goods to support the population. Besides, importing had been a heinous abuse of resources, which had caused a host of environmental and human rights abuses. It was far more efficient to live off the land. As well, the foods naturally produced each season were the healthiest to eat. New West had ceased importing and exporting operations. It became completely autonomous, producing everything it needed locally. It received nothing from the United Government and nothing from off-continent.

Occasionally, some of the older generation grumbled. They missed this or that product that they had enjoyed in the past, especially on holidays. Many of them kept caches of canned goods stashed like buried treasure in the backs of storerooms. Most people Geneva's age thought this behavior silly. Geneva was sure, no matter what they'd imported in the old days, it couldn't have been worth it to forfeit their self-sufficiency, not when what was locally available was plentiful and delicious. She was even wary of the mission her mother was on now to open limited trade between C-Town and New West. She wasn't sure it was such a good idea. Although they were in the same eco-system, it still seemed a bad precedent to allow New Westians to come to depend on goods that they couldn't produce themselves. And from what she'd heard C-Town ate a big diet of lab-grown meats, which sounded disgusting. But it was impossible to argue with Gary and the chefs at Ruby's when they began to reminisce about food. They would say, "Well, you never tasted them. You wouldn't know." True enough, and that was fine with her. She couldn't be missing much. If Gary and the chefs really thought so, they would have left New West. They looked horrified at the suggestion, "There's always C-town."

"No, no, out of the frying pan," Gary scoffed and then he'd turn back to reminiscing about a certain fruit or vegetable with a private wistfulness. He talked about shipped and imported foods the way she fantasized about Leo, milking each little memory for maximum pleasure again and again.

Still, Geneva would rather listen to Gary babble about the past than hear her father's shaky voice on the phone now, "They were supposed to release your sister today. But there's...a problem."

Geneva tensed. Gary was shuffling just outside the open office door. She didn't want to have this conversation here at work. She leaned against a stack of boxes wishing she could shrink into them.

"You need to come home now," her father said.

"And leave work?" she asked for Gary's benefit.

"You need to come home now," he said. "She tried to commit suicide." He said more after that, something else incomprehensible. She heard the words but wasn't ready to deal with them yet. She tucked them away for later.

"But she's OK, right?" Geneva asked.

"Just come home," her father said.

Gary was beside her nodding as soon as she hung up, "Family emergency. You do what you have to do."

"She's OK, right?" Geneva asked still trying to make sense of her father's words. She stared at Gary blankly. He looked miserable. She tried to imagine him lumbering from table to table trying to do her job. Could she really just leave in the middle of her shift? If she left, there wouldn't be anyone else to help him. She should probably stay. It wasn't like she could just blow off her job. She was supposed to help. Besides, how fast could she get home, anyway? It wasn't like there were bullet trains to Linden. And when she got there? What could she possibly do? How could she help?

The truth was, she didn't want to go. Knowing Val was at New West Mental Health was one thing but seeing her there would be another. Gary looked at his watch and his face flushed. "Unless you can finish your shift. It's just an hour, and we're swamped. I won't be able to get anyone to fill in."

An hour wouldn't make much difference. She nodded, relieved to have the decision made for her. She went back out on the floor and took a family's order. She had their pile of burgers and fries hefted above her shoulder when her hands began to shake. Her chest tightened. Ruby's melted into a neon-red blur. Her conscience caught up to her. She thought, Val could be bleeding to death right now. The tray fell from her hands. Plates slid across the concrete floor and shattered. The sound cut through the blaring music. Conversations stopped. The family stared at her and two out of three children in the restaurant began to cry. The smashed burgers and ketchup splattered fries squished underfoot. Gary appeared at her shoulder. "I've got it. Just go."

Dazed, Geneva walked out of Ruby's into the heat and headed up the hill to the university. It had been a long time since she'd spoken to Val. After Val had been admitted to New West Mental, Geneva had called often. Each time the conversation began all right, but by the end Val was babbling. She kept muttering something about getting reconnected. She kept saying Sync Chrome City and asking for a Friend-Me stylus. The conversations were exhausting. They went nowhere. Val seemed trapped in a cyclic delusion impervious to logic. She was unreachable. Eventually, Geneva had stopped calling. It hadn't exactly been weeks since she'd last thought of Val, but it had been weeks since they'd spoken. Meanwhile, she thought about Leo, a guy she didn't even know, every day.

Recently, Geneva had been having nightmares and it didn't take a psychology major to know why. She felt guilty. In the nightmares, she was in a classroom, alone, taking a test, nervously running her hands through her long reddish-brown hair. Then, in a dream shift, her hair was cropped and black and the classroom was filled with old women staring. They surrounded her and her hair began to drop onto her desk in chunks. The dreams were so filled with the classic symbols of a troubled psyche that it made her laugh recalling them. But knowing that worry and guilt were fueling her nightmares didn't make her feel any better about them or herself. She felt powerless to help Val, but that seemed a poor excuse not to even try.

Geneva broke into a run, anxious now to make up time. She shouldn't have tried to finish her shift at Ruby's. Any compassionate person would have headed home right away. She took the fastest route across campus, past Old Main. As she passed the building, the protestors turned to her, startled. There were more of them this summer. Geneva counted seven men and women. Deep creases lined their eyes. Their probing looks added to her rising panic. She shouldn't have stayed at the university this summer. She should have quit work—but she liked helping there—and spent the time in Linden near Val—but what would she have done there?

Her uniform trapped the heat around her and it grew heavy with sweat as she ran across campus. It stuck to her legs as she sprinted across the field to Inu Wood. When she reached her dorm room, she shucked off the sticky dress. She changed into a pile of clothes on the floor and grabbed a few things for Val—clothes and a vial of plum lip-gloss—and stuffed them into a knapsack. She rushed down the hill to the bus station. At least she was finally doing something, even if she wasn't sure what.

Then she fidgeted, at an enforced standstill again, waiting for a Shadow Bus. The buses, painted black with surplus paint, were hard to see and would have caused accidents but for the lack of traffic. They also had high beam lights and were wrapped in iridescent yellow wire lights meant to look like a security system, but everyone knew they didn't work. The government wouldn't allow them to be equipped with actual electrodes. A public entity didn't have as much leeway to accidentally zap a civilian and there were too many children and elders at the bus stations, not to mention punks who were most likely to trip the security by goofing around the station. The buses would have been tasering everyone, all the time, if they were really armed. The lights had been installed back when it was trendy to put pretend deterrents on everything as advocated by Mindfare, the now defunct philosophical/marketing movement. Mindfare had moved to C-Town after the revolution, but there were remnants of its advertising campaigns in New West.

Geneva sat on a concrete bench and remembered what her father had said just before he'd hung up. Fear sharpened his final words to her, "She tried to commit suicide. The doctors are afraid she might be susceptible to some new virus. Before they release her, they want to talk to you."

Geneva didn't know why she was important, but she knew there would be questions and answers: right and wrong, like a test. All she wanted was to pass so that she could get Val out of there and back to New West in time for fall quarter. Then everything would be all right again.

When the bus pulled into Linden station, Geneva shielded her eyes from the sun and looked for her father. She stifled a gasp when she spotted him in the shadows. His face was gray and blotchy and his eyes sunken. Possibly he hadn't slept a full night since Val's collapse. She went to him and he held her, squeezing her shoulders tight, so long that she began to squirm trying to create room between them for cooling air to flow. "Dad?"

He released her, his jaw trembling. His vacant eyes shifted. He avoided holding her gaze.

"What happened? What is it? Is Val OK?" she asked.

He sighed. "Geneva, you're here." He inclined his head toward the street and the family's compact green Enviro-Car. He didn't speak again until they were both wedged in. He pulled out into the narrow empty streets rubbing one hand nervously along his thigh as he drove. In profile, the edge of his brow and the corner of his lip twitched. "They said she tried to commit suicide. But she didn't. She didn't succeed. I don't understand. She was fine at home. They say there had to be something up at the college."

Geneva pressed back against the vinyl seat and looked down at her sneakers. "She seemed OK." All summer she'd been trying to avoid this conversation and the accusation that she should have noticed something unusual about Val long ago, some observation that could have prevented this. But she hadn't noticed anything. The truth was Val had been keeping to herself a lot lately, zoning out under her glasses and leaving Geneva virtually alone in the stark dorm room. Between Ruby's and the hours she spent in the greenhouse, Geneva had barely registered how often Val was plugged-in and unavailable.

As the car passed the high school, her father stopped to let a pack of teenagers cross in front of them. He focused his gray eyes on her. "But she wasn't OK. And you were with her. You must've seen signs of something."

Geneva lowered the window. She needed fresh air. The teenagers laughed as they headed over to Rome Subs, a favorite hangout. She was too nervous to eat, but the smell of fried comfort foods, potatoes, and breaded onions, made her stomach rumble. "I'm sorry. I wouldn't have let anything happen to her. I don't know what went wrong."

After they passed the high school, the town gave way to forest and the air in the car cooled. Geneva grasped the side of her seat as her father turned sharply onto a gravel road just wide enough for the car. "You're studying people," he said.

Geneva looked back at a sign angled away from the road. Underneath a film of brown-green moss, she read the words, New West Mental Health. "Environmental psychology," she corrected. "It's mostly plants."

Her father stopped the car in front of the building. Evergreen branches brushed its roof. "Just talk to the doctors. Maybe there's something you saw but didn't notice. Talk to them, please. That's all I'm asking."

Geneva frowned as she got out of the car. The building looked more like one of the high school's portable classrooms than a medical clinic. Her father followed behind her as she climbed the rickety steps. There was no reception, just a claustrophobic entryway and two steel chairs. Her father shuffled from side to side, his shoulders stooped before collapsing into one of the chairs.

"Shouldn't we tell them we're here?" she asked.

He pointed up at a translucent camera mounted in the corner. She settled into the other chair and studied her sneakers until she felt a hand on her shoulder. She sprang to her feet and looked up into a woman's face. She had sharp features. Her eyes were even wider and darker than Val's. She wore a lab coat and a cold air of authority. "Geneva, I'm Dr. Montgrave, Valerie's doctor, please follow me."

Geneva looked back at her father. His head rested on the wall and his long legs stretched out in front of him. His eyes were closed, but his face was ashen and contorted. Low rhythmic grunts escaped through his nose.

She left her sleeping father and followed the doctor behind a door down a hallway rank with mold. They took a couple of turns and passed through a few doors until Geneva was sure she could no longer find her way out on her own. They entered a white windowless conference room just big enough for one folding table and an old vending machine. Geneva shivered and understood why the doctor was wearing a high-collared sweater under her lab coat in the middle of August.

"Valerie?" Geneva asked, ignoring the audible rumble of her stomach. "I came to see her. Is she OK?"

"I have a few questions first." The doctor gave her a crimp-lipped smirk— the kind of cold smile professors used before tough exams. "We're trying to help your friend..."

“My sister,” Geneva corrected.

“Yes, well, I'm hoping you can help us figure out what happened. We've ruled out any neurological disorders or genetic predisposition. But you were with her most recently. If you'll give us some time, maybe we can find out what triggered the seizure.”

Geneva sat in one of the cold folding chairs. She looked at the dingy carpet and the flecks of black mold where the walls joined the ceiling. She listened to distant footsteps, a creaking door and then silence.

“Would you like coffee? Something to eat?” the doctor offered.

"No," she said. She couldn't eat here; it would feel too much like acquiescence. It reminded her of mythology class: like Persephone eating pomegranate seeds in Hades. If she ate food here, it would give them power over her and she might not be able to leave. It was unreasonable, but she preferred her gradually growing hunger to the quick pain of forcing down fear. She knew it was a bad sign, psychologically, that she was letting superstition drive her actions. It meant she felt out of control. She wondered what pomegranate tasted like and if it were one of the foods Gary missed. She'd have to ask him. Why had Persephone eaten only the seeds?

Across the table, the doctor's persistent silence was oppressive, and it made Geneva want to fill it, which she suspected was the point, a trap. At last, she rushed into it, "I'm sorry. I feel horrible. I mean I didn't notice anything symptomatic in Val's behavior. I can't believe she's here. The guards said she had EHBF, I remember."

She didn't expect the doctor to be forthcoming, but Montgrave said, "Extraordinary Human Biological Function. Uncontrollable psychic reception."

"Psychic reception," Geneva echoed, and this time she waited out the trailing quiet until the doctor spoke first.

"Well," Dr. Montgrave said, after an interminable pause. "In an untrained brain, EHBF causes imbalanced electrical activity in the two halves of the brain, EEG asynchronicities — seizures. The more the seizures are allowed to happen the more likely they are to reoccur. The brain learns to activate that firing of synapses: a kindling effect. The repeated use causes psychic disorder."

"They gave her Thorazine, an old anti-psychotic," Geneva said. "And a psychic suppressant."

Dr. Montgrave took out a small notepad and a stylus from her lab coat pocket. She rolled the green stylus across the table. "Don't worry. No one's blaming you. Have you seen one of these before?"

Geneva rolled it under her fingers. "Uh, yeah. It's a pen."

The doctor lowered her voice. "A Friend-Me stylus. It's also what your sister used to try to kill herself."

The pen clattered as Geneva let it fall. She stared at it on the table and imagined Val thrusting it into her throat in a deadly tracheotomy. It was a horrifying idea, but she didn't buy it. "How?"

"It's been modified to emit ELF, that's extreme low frequency electromagnetic waves," the doctor unscrewed the stylus and showed the stretch of clear fibrous wires between the pieces. The wires were notched and lined with spirals of metal. "This modification could be used to jury-rig a kind of external neural net, an almost direct connection between people. There have been reports of people doing this, taking their conversations offline, turning their biological brain networks into a kind of server. It's the kind of thing advocated by Neo-Privates. I don't know how much your father told you, but we've heard reports that this kind of thing is spreading, as if it were a game at the university. But it's dangerous. The brain is not a toy. We're concerned. These technological extensions hardwire harmful connections and are basically creating a new viral form of mental illness. It spreads from brain to brain like a cancer. Normally, electricity is biologically propelled through a nerve, but this modification bypasses normal chemical inhibitors. It sends out constant stimulation. The neurons literally fire themselves to death."

"We're trying to find the students who are doing this. Valerie won't tell us anything. She's too caught up in it to see the harm." The doctor let Geneva digest this information and then pressed her, "Did you notice anything unusual about Valerie's behavior before you witnessed her seize?"

The doctor leaned forward. Geneva wanted to push her chair back but at the same time she could not look away from the woman's face. Her engaged, yet calm, expression reminded Geneva of photos of her mother taken in the days before the revolution. Afterwards, her parents had tried to cultivate in their children this same intense awareness. But Geneva did not feel focused on her parent's world. She felt worried, guilty and something worse. There was a needling feeling her under her skin she couldn't identify, and she hoped it would go away before she did.

"Well, Val's definitely a plug-in. It started in college. She's been plugged-in a lot recently. We haven't talked much lately." She shrugged. "I don't know. It didn't seem odd to me. It's what people my age do." Geneva didn't feel like volunteering specifics, but she was starting to guess that the source of Val's illness, if that's what it was, probably had to do with the Sync Chrome City site.

"Well, I'll tell you what I noticed," Dr. Montgrave said, and her voice became soft and low. "Almost immediately." She leaned forward and looked over Geneva's shoulder with an intense gaze that was even more uncomfortable than when the doctor eyed her directly. The roped copper chain of her necklace bounced along the high-rolled neck of her sweater. The 8-shaped pendant swung round. "I tell you this outside of my official capacity here: There is a quality of amorous sadness about your friend, an intoxicating ennui. Such a thing is often a harbinger of change. It requires our full attention, if you understand me."

Geneva didn't, and her confusion showed. The doctor promptly leaned back and resumed a business-like demeanor. She wore the expression of a student in the front row of a lecture. She reattached the pen and poised it over her notepad screen. "Now, my questions, which you will do your best to answer before you may see her. She's been asking for you, you know."

Dr. Montgrave's stylus glided across the pad as Geneva reluctantly answered questions about Val. At first, the information seemed trivial: Val loved orange juice and chocolate, slept five or six hours a night (unless she was pulling plugged-in all-nighters, Geneva omitted) and listened to trance music or soulful folk. Then the questions got harder: Yes, Val spent at least four hours daily in virtual reality. No, Geneva didn't know what she did there. She didn't know why. She didn't know when she had started doing it. She didn't know who Val hung out with in person or plugged-in.

She really didn't! Being asked the questions made Geneva feel like she should know the answers. She nervously twisted her ponytails around her fingers. There wasn't a clock in the room. The only decoration, aside from the vending machine, was a tattered poster of a girl spinning with her arms outstretched under a tree and a clear blue sky. It looked like the cover of an environmental psychology textbook. At the bottom it said, "The brain is wider than the sky. — Emily Dickinson." She put her head in her hands and spoke to the tabletop through clenched teeth. "No. I don't know. I really don't know. I don't know. I really don't."

Finally, stonewalled, Montgrave ceased her barrage. She paused, "OK, fine. Just one more thing. What about partners? Is Valerie seeing anyone? A boy or a girl?"

Geneva looked up. That was it. She wasn't going to talk about this. Val had no trouble attracting a certain type, brooding plug-ins, and she had been spending lot of time at the Mansion. But if love was the reason, Val kept it to herself as was her right. Val's sex life or romantic status, if she had one, was no one's business. The table bucked as Geneva slammed her hands on it and stood up. "Forget it. I'm done. She's not a freakin' Neo-Private. Listen. Please. I'm starving. I'm tired. Just let me see her. I need to see that she's OK."

Dr. Montgrave sighed. "We're trying to help your friend. Are you sure there isn't anything else?"

Geneva pressed her lips together. There was one secret of Val's she was privy to that maybe did matter, and she hadn't mentioned—the warning notice about Val's expulsion from the university. But this clinic couldn't give a damn about that, or they wouldn't have yanked Val out of school. Besides, she definitely wasn't spilling a true secret. That would be a real breach of trust. Already, she regretted blabbing as much about Val's personal life as she had. Val had always been loyal. If the situation were reversed, she thought, ashamed, Val wouldn't have given the doctor any information at all. "How exactly is this helping Val?"

The doctor's serene expression wavered which Geneva took to mean it wasn't or at least Montgrave had her doubts. "All right. I'll take you to her now. I should tell you though; it's a bad day. She's rather upset that we took the stylus. She wants to use VR, but I'm sure that would do more harm than good."

As she rose, Dr. Montgrave adjusted her swinging necklace. Her voice dropped and she trained her distant gaze past Geneva again. "It's an infinity symbol. Not a figure eight or a woman meditating, no. Yes, you see, depending on where we are sitting, our perspective changes."

At last, the doctor led her to Val. For a moment, Geneva watched her friend through the tiny pane in the thick door. She had hoped Val wouldn't be strapped to a bed or anything macabre the way she'd imagined. She wasn't. Val sat beneath a barred window surrounded by white pillows looking thin, pale, and startlingly familiar. Instead of a gown she had on pajamas. They made her look more like a philosopher than a patient. Dr. Montgrave placed a hand on Geneva's shoulder and pushed the door open, "Go on in. It's safe."

The room, small and austere, reminded her of their dorm room, but it smelled of mold not cinnamon. A low moan of wind rattled the roof of the clinic. Pinecones clattered. Tree branches brushed the window, casting shadows on the opaque glass behind the bars. Val sat with her legs folded up to her chest and her head flopped over her knees. Her dark hair fell forward along the line of her chin and covered her eyes. The posture exuded sadness. Geneva wanted to go to her friend and comfort her, but she found herself at a loss, afraid to step into the room. What good could she possibly do?

Geneva stood by the door willing herself forward until, at last, Val looked up. "Nice Gator-girl hair. So, I leave and you finally listen. Figures. C'mere."

Geneva twirled her fingers through her Gator Tongue ponytails as she entered the room. She perched on the end of the windowsill seat across from Val and watched the door swing shut.

Val rolled her eyes. There were dark bags under them, and her lips were pale. She spoke with her head down between the shanks of hair that fell across her face. "I so did not try to commit suicide. They tell you that? So not my style you know. If I did that, how would I know how everything turns out?" Val slapped a hand down on Geneva's bobbing knee. "Stop. Nervy-girl. Did you bring it?"

Geneva unsnapped a pocket on the side of her pants, extracted a vial and handed it over.

Val shrugged and smeared some of the lip-gloss over her pout. "Thanks, but I meant the stylus. I need the one you got from Friend-Me."

Geneva's shoulders tightened as she hugged her knees to her chest. "How did you know?" It was disturbing that Val knew about the unexpected Friend-Me delivery, but worse that she'd asked for the stylus, the same kind Dr. Montgrave said she'd used to try to kill herself. She watched Val's keen dark eyes. She didn't think Val would harm herself, but Geneva didn't trust her own judgment. She'd been missing so much of her best friend's life, lately. She shook her head and held up empty hands.

Val sighed. "I love you, but clueless-girl, I wasn't trying to die. I was trying to get connected. Listen, you and me have nothing to fear from wideware. The adults are just jealous that their stale old brains can't take the tech. Yeah, I want to do something radical, but death, so not what I'm going for. Not in the middle of a revolution. There's a lot more to do. A lot more. We have to keep at it for all those other people on the outside, on the 'Way."

Geneva tucked her chin to her knees. For the first time she thought Val really might belong in a mental ward. "Not over? What? Those people on the Freeway want to be left alone. It is, definitely, over."

"No," Val said. "Things are changing."

"Things changed," Geneva lowered her voice. "Val, I'm sorry. But the revolution? It ended the day those people killed your parents. All we have to do now is graduate New West. Keep the peace. You know it's OK for us to do that. It's OK."

Val raised a hand and leaned toward her. Every line in her face was tight and turned down. "It's so not OK to just sit on our asses while this goes down. Look where I am. But yeah, sure, you be peace-girl. That's so like you. I wouldn't want to spoil it."

Geneva knew Val would never hit her, but it looked like she wanted to. On the pretext of grabbing a pillow, Geneva shielded her face as she set it in her lap.

"Ugh." Val spun off the bench and folded her arms across her chest. "If you're so afraid of me, why are you here? To tell me to calm down? Like that's going to help in any way?"

"I've been worried," Geneva said, kneading a corner of the pillow. "I want you to be able to come back to New West, to finish your degree. I want to help."

"Really? You've been all worry-girl, helpful for me?" Val said. "Or do you want what you've always wanted, what your parents told us to want: a quiet place in a perfect little world? Here's the problem: There's no such thing as a bloodless revolution. Why don't you tell me what you have been doing all summer? Because you haven't been here."

Geneva rocked with the pillow.

Val leaned forward again, fists on her hips. "No? Nothing? Fine. I'll tell you what you've been doing," her voice got louder. "You've been worried about serving people burgers. You've been thinking about some guy. You so haven't been thinking about me. You could have come anytime. You're here now because they said I tried to kill myself. Why not care about my everyday life as much as my possible death? Make me be drama-girl because that's what it takes to move you. You so haven't been paying attention. And I can't believe you're scared. Of *me.* Coward. You're afraid and you don't even know what you're afraid of."

Geneva felt Val's breath on her cheeks. She stood up and stepped to the side to get some distance. She had to look down to see into Val's glossy eyes. She realized Val was barefoot and without her boots several inches shorter than usual. Even so, it was true. She was afraid of tiny, quietly forceful Val, who'd she'd known all her life, as if she'd been transformed into some strange creature. It was fear of the unknown. She didn't know what to expect from her friend anymore. They used to know each other. Now she didn't know what had broken them apart, so how could she manage to mend the gap? It shamed her to realize, that for her part, Val had resorted to brinkmanship. She had pretended to commit suicide to get Geneva to the clinic. Was that really the extreme it took to make Geneva break her routine — a near death experience? It probably was. Even now, if she could, she'd rather be at Ruby's doing predictable work than having this nebulous argument with Val. How could she repair the damage between them? "Val, I...sent your final in for you. So, you're on track to graduate," she said, lamely.

"You touched my computer?" Val followed Geneva's gaze to her feet and sighed. "No. That's fine. That's great. You want to help me. But the New West way so doesn't work, withdrawing or erecting walls. Isolation invites evil. To create utopia, everyone has to participate. Everyone has to connect. You want to understand just give me that stylus. I want to get out of here, too. I so do."

Geneva fingered the stylus in her pocket wondering how the tiny every day object could possibly be as dangerous as Dr. Montgrave had implied. She hated the fact that she didn't trust Val with such a small thing. "I can't."

Val put a hand out palm up. "Yeah, I know. You think that. But we're family. You can't be too afraid this time. You know I know what I'm doing, or I wouldn't ask. Do you want to help me or not? We're together in this."

Geneva scanned the room and slowly pulled the pen from her pocket. "There's no port here. What are you even going to do with it?"

Val slipped her hand around the instrument. "I don't need a port."

In seconds, violet light flashed in the air around them. Outside, branches splintered.

"Sync Chrome City Psi-Girl," Val sighed sounding like a computer shutting down and her arms dropped to her sides. Her body began to convulse in rubbery waves. She collapsed toward the window seat.

"Val!" Geneva grabbed at her friend's waist, caught her shirt and fell forward with her onto the cushion. Val's forehead knocked against the bars over the window. Geneva groaned. She lifted herself off Val's side and turned her over. Val's back arched. Her head dropped exposing the long taut line of her throat.

Geneva slapped the side of Val's face. "Don't do this. Don't make this my fault. Don't."

Val's head jerked up, a red patch forming on her forehead where her skull had struck the bars and another along the side of her jaw where Geneva had hit. Her eyes rolled into place. "I'm fine. Tell the doctor it's OK."

The door creaked and Dr. Montgrave pushed Geneva aside placing two fingers on the side of Val's neck. "What did you do? What did you give her?"

Val's eyes flicked to the side in the direction of the stylus lying just at the doctor's feet. Geneva pocketed it, but not before the doctor noticed.

"Hand it over," Montgrave said.

Geneva extracted a slim black tube from her pocket and gave it up. Val sat; her face flushed. "I'm fine." She took the vial from the doctor's hand, opened the tube and ran the wand across her bottom lip. She smirked at the doctor with her Plum Ice smile. "Lip gloss, just what I needed."

A lab tech entered the room, and while the doctor talked to him Geneva whispered, "Sync Chrome City?"

Valerie pulled her in close. "Listen, you don't want to deal. Fine. I'll respect that. You're off the hook. Thanks. It was enough. I'll be home soon."

"Run some more tests," Dr. Montgrave said, as she grabbed Geneva's elbow and steered her to the door.

Geneva turned her head as she left the room and saw Val peering around the lab tech at her. The look in Val's eyes—What was it Dr. Montgrave had said? "Amorous sadness." — made her want to stay. She wanted to finish the argument, figure out when Val had become so angry and why she felt so responsible.

"Is she going to be, OK?" Geneva asked as she tried to keep pace with Dr. Montgrave's stride down the hall.

"We don't know. Every time she seizes, it reinforces patterns. It's more likely to happen again. She needs to stay out of VR, before the pattern becomes permanent. But there's nothing more you can do," she said.

In the waiting room, her father was awake now, staring vacantly. There were shadows embedded in his brow and worry lines slicing from his nose to his lips. Her father, a biologist who was most content researching rodents, had joined the revolution. He'd dedicated his youth to establishing utopia. Then he'd taken in Val, his best friend's daughter, and instead of following his own passion had devoted his life to making sure his children could enjoy the prosperity of New West. Now, what he had worked for was unraveling. He looked drained. His eyes were watery. His lips quivered. He looked pleadingly at Geneva.

Nothing more she could do? If that were true, then Geneva had absolutely no control over a situation affecting the people she loved. She cared deeply and could not accept it. She twisted her ponytails around her fingers and pinned down the needling feeling she'd had: hope. It was a small, despairing, persistent feeling that she knew, uncomfortably, she would have to pursue. Now that everyone was telling her to never mind, she would do the opposite. Her stubborn streak, as her mother called it, had kicked in. She would make a difference. She would find Sync Chrome City. That she could do.

~ 8 ~

DUMPED

"Prior to the Psychic Awakening, those who considered psychic abilities possible were marginalized. One of the main effects of the Awakening was the institutionalization of empathy and the introduction of psychic curriculum into the public school system. Early fringe factions included:

Noetic Sciences Institute — a reputable, scientific organization of people sharing psychic research and practicing collective consciousness using modern methods although, pre-Awakening, with far less dramatic results.

Psi-Aware — a radical group of former revolutionaries, protesting for psychic awareness, rights and the introduction of psychic curriculum into the schools. Few members were able to demonstrate psychic proclivities.

The United Government — highly-classified groups within the government or operating under government grants secretly testing psychic abilities such as remote viewing, primarily for military objectives, with 50 percent success rates.

For further study: What other factions now marginalized might be advancing tomorrow's thought forms? Recall that before the printing press was invented even silent reading, the idea of hearing words in your head, was regarded as an impossible mental skill. Consider the psychic botanists and geologists whose teleological theories and attempts to tap into the *unus mundus*, or world mind, many consider to be extreme, impossible, or ridiculous." — *Becoming Psychic 101, A History and a Primer*

Living with Lydia Streker in Deming over the summer had been a surprising boon. The dowdy, frizz-haired hippy wasn't his type, but Burrows liked the sugary lard she served up in her bakery, and in her bed. It had been a while since he'd used his telepathy to work a woman and he'd forgotten what could be accomplished when you knew ahead what they were thinking. Usually masochistic pleasure, the pain of other's thoughts, was the best he could hope for when he manipulated people. Lydia had unwittingly taught him some tricks, however. In her quest to become psychic, she was big into meditation. Playing along to ingratiate himself, he'd found that the techniques helped him control his migraines. Although it took a lot of concentration, he could dull the pain.

Fortunately, before he got too comfortable mooching on the couch of New West, Lydia invited him to come to one of her Psi-Aware meetings, as he'd hoped she would. He needed to find the threat, the person who would bust minds wide-open, make privacy a thing of the past, and cause himself intense, inescapable pain even out on the 'Way. He needed to find the threat he'd glimpsed in Sync Chrome City and eliminate it.

Unfortunately, in this regard, Psi-Aware was a huge disappointment. No one in the group had any ability. In fact, he'd never met a group of less intuitive people. They were all a bunch of middle-aged wannabes like Lydia, true believers, but not in the least psychic. He couldn't resist showing off a little and they began to look to him for advice. When he meditated with Lydia, their adoration was even bearable.

He'd started to have a bit of fun with his ipso facto leadership role, seeing how far off-kilter this group could get. They were rabidly loopy, and he was good at inspirational speeches. "Now, I think we all know that if anything's going to get done, it's going to get done at a grass roots level. Even the national chapter of Psi-Aware has gotten far too conservative and cautious. And I'm tired of waiting. If the Deming chapter has to make it happen, then so be it. We just can't have people being kept down like they are now, struggling for no good reason."

After that, they'd given him a standing ovation and it got him thinking. He seemed to have tapped a vein with his oratory persuasion. They gushed enthusiasm. These Sync Chrome City kids were working out better than expected, giving him all the right connections. He was beginning to feel very hopeful about his prospects in New West. Forget about simply stopping the psychic threat. There was a chance he'd even been wrong about that. Nothing he'd seen so far indicated that anyone had that kind of potential. Maybe his ability was an anomaly. Now that he was here, he could turn his own pain to his advantage, extract his revenge. New West had shut him out, now he would shut it down. He could feel the "utopia" on the brink of crisis pressed on one side by the psychic wannabes and on the other by the privacy advocates. It had been too calm too long. Entropy and chaos were the natural order, the place where Burrows fit in.

Another entertaining side effect of bedding Lydia was the reaction of her son. Streker had figured out that Burrows wasn't in line to be "daddy" and was probably up to no good with mom. While Lydia herself had low expectations, older women tended to be realistic about their self-indulgences, it made her kid peevish. As fun as annoying Streker was, Burrows was due for a break. He would have accepted the kids' party invitation just to get out of the house. For variety alone, he'd trade the suspicious pains of Streker to endure the jabs of fawning Eve. It was a significant sweetener though when he found out he was to be a guest at President Sherring's home to celebrate the twentieth birthday of his daughter Coco. Yes, New West was just a land of opportunities. For a malicious outcast who'd scored an invite, Burrows was starting to see a lot of them.

Eve had mentioned Coco's birthday party casually, but he'd gotten: *Save me!* and knew she wanted him to provide her a bit of distraction from The Coco Show. Burrows was only glad to be used. If Eve got sick of glow-glow Coco, she was welcome to hang out in Burrows' shade. Meanwhile, he'd get a handle on the psychic landscape—find out what the politicos were planning—and where they were weak. To ensure your own security, you had to think big, long-term, get involved. You couldn't let people make world-changing decisions with life-threatening implications like—hey, I know, let's change the entire structure of people's brains so we can all have nifty psychic powers—without your involvement.

The only downside to the party was being foisted off on Leo. Eve had spent the night with Coco as a guest. To get in, Burrows would arrive at the party as a friend of Leo's, Coco's boyfriend. He'd gotten to know the guy pretty well—and didn't like him. It was two long hours on the back of Leo's scooter to get to the president's mansion. No cars were allowed on Route 9 around New West so they couldn't take his Mistress. Leo was a quiet guy inside. In that respect, he reminded Burrows of Mace. He gave Burrows little, but still managed to grate on his nerves. On the surface he was energetic, always moving. The guy was so juked up to see his girlfriend at her little birthday party he was practically cartwheeling. Being around Leo made Burrows feel every day of the nine years he had on the kid.

Leo parked the scooter at the gate and vaulted off it. On the banks of Silver Lake, the New West President's palatial estate rose before them. Burrows imagined the white columns of the house on fire like in an old movie. He unbuttoned his collar, wicking his shirt away from his chest and rolled up his sleeves. It had been years since he had been anywhere so clean—the place reminded him of a fresh wound. He squinted as he strode along the sparkling sidewalk, past an expanse of lawn and grazing goddamn horses. The New West he remembered was a soggy haze filled with chill tension that made your bones feel brittle. This was something else.

"Oh yes, electric! And we call the dorm a Mansion!" Leo exclaimed. “This is the real deal.”

As they walked up the steps and stood at the president's door, Burrows looked over at Leo with his curls and his scooter helmet tucked under his arm. Leo was wearing a pair of tailored pants and a lime-striped shirt both a bit tight and short like he'd bought them long ago and hadn't worn them enough to notice he'd outgrown them. He stood with lazy knees and elbows, showing a lot of teeth. The guy had no clue. Leo's role as campus DJ and Coco's erstwhile sidekick had given him delusions. The kid thought he was carrying cool currency, but he'd enter this house with an empty plastic card.

"Hey, wait," Leo said, grabbing Burrow's wrist as he reached for the brass knocker. "Before we go in, look."

He reached in his pocket and pulled out a velvet jewelry box.

"For Coco," Leo said. "Do you think I should...?"

Burrows got: *Love her forever.* And cut the kid short. He didn’t have time for schmaltzy kid crap. "How should I know? I haven't seen her. Put that away. Let's go in."

Burrows lifted his hand, but Eve opened the door before his knuckles struck wood. Her expression was sullen. Burrows marveled at how she could mold her face into such disdain. She looked tired from the effort. He leered at her and she lost it, the corners of her mouth turned up. She was wearing a sleeveless black dress that made her shoulders look beached. It reminded him of doing her Vary, her black underwear and flat white thighs. The lacy leftover prom dress bunched around her widening hips and chest.

"Hey, good to see a familiar face," Leo said.

Eve shrugged. "Coco's still getting ready."

"You look good," Leo said.

"You too," Eve replied.

One advantage to being psychic, no one lied to you about how you looked.

Eve looked at Burrows with no concerns for his appearance at all. She thought at him: *Please, make this less lame.*

"Wow. Check this place out," Leo said, ogling the closest crystal chandelier.

Burrows peered into a ballroom. Behind French doors, arrangements of flowers, Hollyhock, Columbine, Fireweed, and Bleeding Heart, and platters of food, deep leafy greens and red and blue berries, splayed down elongated tables.

"Check out the spread!" Leo said.

"Fit for a princess," Burrows said.

Coco made her entrance descending a winding staircase. She wore a red dress with a plunging v-neck. The sateen fabric clung to her hips and flowed around her legs. Her hair was pulled back in a low ponytail. Gold hoops dangled from her ears. Beside her Eve looked short, dirty, and adolescent.

Burrows looked at Eve and let pity show in his eyes. Her reply snapped: *Ugh.* He extended a hand to Coco and she enclosed it in soft fingers. "I'm Burrows—a friend of Leo's. Happy birthday."

"Happy birthday!" Leo said, stepping between them.

Coco embraced Leo, "Thanks Leo Love."

He went wet sugar limp in her arms.

Burrows hung out with the students until the guests arrived. Then, Eve helped Coco greet them at the door, Leo accosted the buffet table, and Burrows mingled listening. Most of the guests were well-dressed, middle-aged politicos. Few people spared Burrows a thought other than: *Ah, security.* It helped to be a big guy.

Most of the conversations were local politics: debates about New West's new trade negotiations with C-town, flame vs. electric shock alarms, and neo-private legislation. Boring. It wasn't like anyone here was going to say, 'psychic'. If anyone needed a map to where that would put you on the political landscape all they had to do was look at Psi-Aware, an organization so far out in the boonies of influence it could have been off-continent. Burrows started to think the party was a waste of time, but the food was good, if strictly vegan, and he enjoyed watching the women shimmer in soft gowns. It seemed like years, not months, since he'd been surrounded by the filth of the Freeway. He grabbed a pine nut tart off the buffet table, which, of course, brought him dangerously close to Leo, the feeder, again. He overheard the kid talking to Coco.

"When are you going to introduce me to your father?" Leo asked. "I thought he wanted to meet me."

"Trust me, he's been checking you out all night," she said, touching her lips to his cheek. "But he's busy. Schmoozing."

"Well, now he's schmoozing with my mom," Leo pulled Coco toward a tall woman with black braids talking to an even taller white-haired man. "Time to introduce myself."

Burrows recognized President Sherring and Kendra LeMay, the owner of Friend-Me Co. He stared at Leo's back in his too tight pressed shirt and tried to process. The goof Leo was related to the Friend-Me founder—she was his mother. He followed the kids into the two leaders' conversation and found the two people in New West who weren't afraid to say psychic—the president and the entrepreneur.

"Psychic education. Completely open our minds?" Sherring said, opening his hands at the same time, hands even larger than Burrows' own hands, with long fingers and pink palms. "That's an extreme point of view even for a neo-private."

LeMay shook her head, hands on her hips. "I'm not advocating any agenda, but I'm a futurist. I don't think the issue is going away. Remember, before the advent of the printing press something as benign as silent reading was considered practically paranormal. The fact is there are 100 billion nerve cells in our brains all with the potential to connect and interact. If we're not using them all, then we don't really know what we are capable of. We haven't even touched the surface of possibility, yet. In the long run, Psi-Aware is right. The future will be about going into our own heads, expanding and exploring our own capacity. That's the next space we have to conquer."

Her hands, at the end of her long bare arms looked disproportionately thick, hammers stuck to wire, and her knuckles were worn, dry and cracked. LeMay paused to encircle Leo with her arm. The kid didn't flinch. He stood there like it was the most natural thing for a guy his age to remain under his mother's wing. Burrows felt a twinge of jealousy. Possibly the best time in his life, the most certain anyway, had been that week on the 'Way drugged on LeMay, under her influence.

The president nodded at Coco. His face froze into an attentive expression as LeMay continued her argument. "You know, I had my doubts about doing business in New West. When I started Friend-Me, I had lost my tech job in the depression. I staked everything on my silly invention—that's what every investor said about a diary for girls. I worked harder for myself than I ever had for an employer, in part, because I was terrified. I was pregnant with Leo at the time."

Leo grimaced as his mom drew him tighter. "I was on my own. My idea had to succeed so we could support ourselves. I had such high hopes. I think hope is the female equivalent of men's lust—an intense and painful obsession."

At "lust," Leo detached himself from his mom's embrace. "Coco, let's dance. This sounds serious."

Coco took his hand. "It's supposed to be my party, but with my father it's always politics."

LeMay and Sherring smiled distractedly at their children. Neither noticed Burrows standing next to them. In this ballroom, with these important people, his head was silent and numb. No one spared a thought for him. LeMay turned to Sherring. Her black eyes shone. "I almost left when you were creating New West. I loved the idealism of it, but I hated the rules. Utopia is not an innovative environment. I stayed because I felt so strongly about New West, both ways. When emotions pull at you like that—love-hate, hope-fear—you have pay attention. As it turned out, New West was the right place for Friend-Me. New West and Friend-Me both work because they fill the same need—connectivity. People want to be in a system that's small enough to interact with them, where they matter as individuals. I wasn't the only little girl sitting alone, writing in her diary, wishing for a response and someone to talk to."

Behind LeMay and Sherring, Leo pretended to waltz Coco around the dance floor. Her dress hung low in the back, and he had his hand on the girl's bare skin. Many of the guests had turned to watch them. The girl beamed. LeMay and Sherring continued to stare each other down. Burrows, beside them, still got nothing. Sherring's long hands hung at his sides.

LeMay talked with her hammers. "I've learned that having my own business, makes me more dependent on other people. What happens in New West affects Friend-Me and being stagnant isn't good. The depression and malaise that plagued the United Government remain. New West hasn't cured us. To maintain this utopia, we have to move forward, we have to train people to use all of their minds. It's coming whether we like it or not. What I'm saying is, ignoring the problem could undo all you've achieved here. We have to think of our children. That's why it's so important that New West fund our research."

At this, president Sherring held up his hand, long fingers pointed to the domed stained-glass ceiling. "We'll talk real business tomorrow."

LeMay dipped her head as Sherring turned and, finally, Burrows got something. Sherring noticed him: *Who? So close. That's not one of my men.*

Burrows scars stretched beneath his beard as he smiled. "I'd be careful, president. What Ms. LeMay says sounds like a threat: either you help the psychics gain access to your heads or you face the possibility of civil war. Meanwhile, your kids aren't fighting."

Burrows got a quick slice of animosity from the president before his attention turned to his daughter. LeMay and Sherring looked to the dance floor to see what had been entertaining the rest of the party. Leo dipped Coco and swung her back arched, blond hair skimming over the polished ballroom floor. They all looked down the smooth line of her chest. Her hair shook as he righted her, face flushed. Then Leo got down on one knee and opened a tiny box to her.

The president stepped quickly forward, raised his hands high and clapped twice. "Attention," he said. His voice boomed. All eyes turned to him. "As you know, it's my daughter's 20th birthday. Please stand and sing with me."

Leo, interrupted, stood up, flustered. Coco beamed, unaware, easily exchanging one form of attention for another. The guests started in on the song. Waiters in white coats flowed through the ballroom with plates raised over their heads. They distributed pink-frosted cakes decorated with glazed berries and one lit candle each to the guests. The room filled with glow and sugar-scent.

"Let's make a wish," Sherring said.

Leo stood just behind Coco, stunned and forgotten. The president and LeMay shared a distressed glance. He looked angry. Burrows was sure if he'd been LeMay he would have gotten: *Keep your son away from my daughter.*

LeMay lifted her cake, pursed her lips as she blew out the candle and winked at Sherring. "Well, you know what I wished for."

She dipped the tines of her fork into the frosting and tasted it. "Mmm, strawberry."

Burrows stared at the dainty cakes, the shiny curtains, and crystal chandeliers. He recalled spring on the 'Way when he'd found a cluster of strawberries growing wild on the forest floor. There were only three worth eating, the size of your fingertips. He'd wanted to show them to somebody, share them, but most of the outcasts on the 'Way were afraid to come into the forest. None of them were friends. He'd put the berries in his pack and found them at the bottom of it weeks later: three moldy lumps soaked in rabbit's blood. The wax from the candle dripped onto his cake and hardened in the frosting furrows. He set it down, still lit, on the buffet table.

LeMay was right: hope hurt. Wishing was a painful, useless, obsession. There was no reason to endure the anguish. If you wanted something, you took steps to make it happen. Burrows looked around the room again and saw all the instruments of New West's demise laid out in front of him, shiny and sharp as a row of surgical steel. The waiters flowed through the ballroom again distributing champagne flutes filled with light liquid and popping peach-tinted bubbles. He grabbed the president's arm.

"I'd like a meeting with you too, Sherring. I have some information for you," Burrows said, and he braced for the pain that came when the president turned his full attention to him, angry, irritated thoughts falling on Burrows in heavy blows.

After the party, Eve paddled over to the stairs of the pool and hung on the top step with her legs behind her and her chest floating forward in the hammock of her bikini top. "I bet I could get any one of those suits to sleep with me."

"Yeah," Burrows said kneeling by the edge of the pool. "So, why are you wasting your tits on me?"

Eve: *Asshole.*

Ignoring Eve's splashes and her opinions, he looked up to the house where politicos lingered with the president. Satisfied with the proceeds from his own schmoozing, he'd followed Coco's friends to the pool. He returned his attention to Eve.

"Sure, those guys would gladly drain you of your youth," Burrows said. "But why would you want them to? Oh, wait. Don't tell me." He leaned forward and dipped his hand into the pool in front of Eve. "You'd like the attention."

He had to steady himself on the pool's edge as he got: *Look at my chest.* As if it were possible not to. He could also see the backs of her dimpled legs magnified in the water. Fat hadn't disqualified Lydia, but he would never sleep with young Eve. Her wasp's nest of thoughts tormented him enough. He wouldn't want her thinking of him more, although he couldn't seem to resist baiting her.

“You know what kid, fact is, sooner or later, everybody's mother dies. It's no excuse: Eve Hales versus Friend-Me. Yeah, I've been paying attention. New West’s a small town. Your parents all know each other.”

He looked up at the balcony, where Leo leaned on the railing staring into a room with movement behind him. "That Leo's one lucky guy, isn't he? Coco is one fine bit of birthday cake."

This time Eve didn't bite though. Her thoughts drifted elsewhere. She was used to her place in Coco's shadow. "She's a daddy's girl. Sherring throws this party every summer. Next year will be big, Coco's turning 21. They’ve probably already started planning,” Eve said, sounding blasé, but not sarcastic. Coco did seem to be at the center of the kids' world: Eve’s and Leo’s anyway. For Streker and Grugel, it was Sync Chrome City. “I don't think Leo's lucky tonight though."

"So, you guys are going back to school soon?" Burrows asked.

"In a few weeks.” Eve said.

"Well, you shouldn't have to live in that fishbowl dorm again, kitten. I've got another option," Burrows said. He watched Eve's eyes narrow: *Kitten?* She was wise enough to tell he was pandering but didn't quite have the willpower to resist it. "For you, Grugel, Streker."

Burrows got a strong spike of interest from her like the pull of a fish on a line and then Eve's thoughts flicked away. She looked past him at Leo, who was stalking towards the pool, walking heavy like he'd stored the buffet in his legs. "Hey, Burrows. Party's over. Let's motor."

"Oooh, with a rebel yell," Burrows said to Eve. “Boy’s gone fierce. What's gotten into him?"

"Coco dumped him." Eve said. "Again."

Burrows started to take off his shoes. "I was just starting to enjoy myself."

Leo looked to Eve and back and spiked a thought at Burrows: *Letch.*

"Sure got the impression the President didn't like you." Burrows said.

"Yeah," Leo said. "He told Coco to stay away from me."

Burrows dipped his feet into the pool. "Can't blame him for trying to protect his daughter from the taint of mediocrity."

"The taint?" Leo said. He glared but gave Burrows nothing. The ends of his thoughts all pointed in. "Man, what's your problem?"

"Same as yours." Burrows said. "And my mother's not even the head of a Big-Time company." To his mind, the party had been worth it just for that bit of knowledge. DJ Leo Love was aka Leo LeMay, the son of Kendra LeMay, owner of Friend-Me Co., New West's biggest, most innovative and, therefore, controversial company which also had a huge factory out on the ‘Way. It made everything just a bit more interesting. Even more delightful was the fact that Ms. LeMay, who almost hadn't made the cut to stay in New West herself, and President Sherring didn't exactly agree on the definition of utopia and Sherring abhorred her son dating his precious daughter. Then there was Coco’s best friend and jealous rival, Eve, the daughter of the woman who'd been killed by a Friend-Me flower delivery. There were so many cracks in the walls, Burrows wasn't sure where to strike first to bring them down.

"Right. I don't think Friend-Me helps my case. My mother tends to piss people off. She's always pushing," Leo said. His gaze drifted up to the balcony. "I just don't understand why Coco listens to him. Her father said he was worried about her 'associations.' He wanted her options to be 'limitless' so that she could make choices without any 'hindrance.' Whatever. What's that about?"

"Um, hindrance, that would be you. Kid, you just don't fit into their plan. Don't they teach you history? That's New West's M.O., get rid of what you don't like, move on. Keep only perfection."

Leo stared down into the pool. "You can read it like that. But I'm thinking, it's simple: Coco's afraid to stand up to her dad. She just needs some time."

"Hey, feel free to draw out the pain," Burrows said, rubbing his thigh. "Always a good distraction. I ought to know."

"It worked last time," Eve said. She was sitting on the stairs now. Her arms wrapped around her knees. "She got back together with him in the fall."

"Oh, evil," Burrows said. "You let her play with you? You her cat toy?"

Eve and Leo went quiet, and Burrows followed their eyes and watched Coco stroll out of the house. Her rolling walk made a very fine silhouette.

"Hey guys," she said, as she unwrapped her towel and laid it across a chaise lounge. In the shadows, as she walked around the pool, the bikini ties that dangled down her thighs and swung at the back of her neck hinted at clothes. When she perched on the end of the diving board, the clinging bits of her swimsuit shimmered in the soft surrounding light. She stood with her heels raised, her calves long, a glimmer between her thighs. Light rippled over her torso. She unloosed her hair and the waves fell past her shoulders. She dove.

"I can see why you'd be tempted to be her whipping boy," Burrows said, while they watched Coco glide under the water towards them. "But you have to figure a girl like that will get what she deserves. Better."

Leo didn't respond. Not even with a thought. So, he agrees, Burrows thought.

Coco surfaced near them with Eve paddling in the water beside her. "Come on. Swim with us."

"No," Leo said.

"Don't be like that on my birthday," Coco said folding her arms over the ledge of the pool. "Swim. Daddy won't mind. You can even spend the night."

Leo turned away. "Yeah, thanks. I don't think so. It's past two and we've stayed plenty late. Burrows, let's get."

"You go," Burrows said, unbuttoning his shirt and dropping his pants to reveal black briefs. "I feel like plunging in. Now, I'm sure I can figure out some way to get home."

Burrows enjoyed the jolt of the girls' appreciation, his lean years looked good on him, as he jumped into the pool. He surfaced next to Coco. In the water, she glowed, just like the little girl from his drug-induced premonition. Was that about 15 years ago? Then, today, Constance Monica Sherring could be the one about to make minds explode.

He answered her unasked question. "The ink says, 'All haste is the work of the devil.' It means, wait for the right moment."

This could be it, he thought. Now that he knew what mattered most to the President of New West and most to Kendra LeMay, the owner of Friend-Me Co., he'd found what mattered most to him. There was no need to wait any longer. He dove underwater hiding his grin, watching the girl's legs churning the water. Here he was, a shark among seals.

Burrows took a trip with the kids: Grugel, Streker and Eve to the 'Way. There'd be no more dorm life for them. They brought back his Vary shop, a silver bullet of an RV, and he had them set it up with all their electronics: Sync Chrome City on wheels. Come fall, he'd split his time between them at New West University and Lydia Streker in Deming, between Sync Chrome City and Psi-Aware, plotting the end of New West. It was cocky to think he could wage a one-man coup, but with time and technology on his side, he was pretty sure he could.

~ 9 ~

FRIEND-ME COURIER

"As misguided as the early attempts to access psychic potential through wideware, technological extensions to the brain, may have been it is true that an external focus or vision can help people tap their potential. Each person is unique however, and technology is just one of method of accessing our higher, connected selves. Just as individuals may more easily learn conventional, teleological information by visual, auditory, or kinesthetic means, each person must identify their own best avenue into Psychic Space." — *Becoming Psychic 101, A History and a Primer*

Inside Varian Hall, the environmental psychology building, philodendrons with face-sized leaves climbed the walls of Dr. Robin Roundtree's office. The vines ran over the small skylight in the ceiling, their unfurled leaves casting faint green into the room. It accentuated the chlorophyll tinge of Professor Roundtree's hands and face that students said was due to the pitchers of Herbbank Farm alguice he drank during lectures. He stroked one of the waxy leaf tips that hovered along the trim line of his beard across his plump cheek. "It's a good plan. I have some projects in the greenhouse you can work on for elective credit this winter and in spring you should look into an internship."

Geneva nodded, peering down at the schedule she'd scrawled into her notebook. Despite her academic adviser's assurances, she wondered if she'd outsmarted herself packing all the rigorous classes for her last year at New West into fall quarter. Environmental Science, Natural Psychology and Chemicals and Physiology were all in her major, so she'd do well. But she wasn't Valerie; she'd have to work at it. If everything went as planned, she'd graduate at the end of this year. Still, she had no idea what came next. Between these classes and her shifts at Café Ruby's, she'd have no time to think about the future.

“You look pensive. Let us see," Roundtree turned and for a moment his head and shoulders submerged into the dark mass of leaves behind him. He returned balancing three books in the crook of his arm. "It seems I have extra copies of the required texts." He pushed them across the mahogany desktop. "You may borrow them."

On the cover of the thickest book, *Natural Psychology*, a smiling man and a woman read together beneath a cherry tree. It looked like most of the books in her major, but this one was by Professor Roundtree himself. Geneva placed a hand on top of the books and calculated that by giving her the books he'd just saved her a few months' work at the café. "Thank you, really, this helps so much!" She lifted them into her knapsack.

Roundtree's voice dropped into a Hort-Audible coo, a tone usually reserved for talking to plants. "You're a rare student, Geneva. I must nurture you with the richest soil just as I would any exotic orchidaceae. Ah, like our Nootka Rose-Orchis. Have you seen her in blossom? Extraordinary." Roundtree grabbed the edge of his desk and pushed his chair back into the vine-covered bookshelf. Leaves flopped over his pate, hiding the bald patch in the middle of his ring of red hair. "We're finished here, aren't we? Come with me to the greenhouse on your way out. I think I have something else to help you. I don't like to see you feeling the loss of *unus mundus* too deeply. You remember, *unus mundus*, from class?"

Geneva hefted her pack onto her shoulder and followed him. "The world?"

"The world mind: our connection to it and to nature," he said.

The loamy scent of Roundtree's office wafted behind him, replaced by traces of strawberry and hyacinth as they passed through the arching double-doors into the greenhouse. Geneva tied her jacket around her waist as he led her back to Special Projects.

"You've finally blossomed for us." Roundtree cooed over his pet orchid. The scent of wild roses flowed around the camouflage of his corduroy jacket. She peered around him at the Nootka Rose-Ladyslipper hybrid in full bloom. The center lips of its three-petal blossoms protruded. They were bright pink with deep red striations. "Oh, it's..." She reached for it and Roundtree stepped aside so she could cup one pink bud in her hand. "Lovely." It looked delicate as folded wet moth wings, but the petals were orchid thick.

She tried sub-vocalizing, "You're a beauty."

Roundtree cocked his head at her. "Yes, but it's a little further back. Hort-Audible should sound like two teak branches rubbing together." He placed two greenish fingertips along her throat and wiggled them up and down her windpipe. Her voice dropped an octave. "There, that's right. Perfect. Would you like to take her home with you?"

Geneva shook her head. "What? To the dorm? Oh, no. Not a special project."

Roundtree lifted the plant and placed its ceramic container in Geneva's arms. He continued to talk in coaxing Hort-Audible. "Oh, I think she's ready. Not all learning takes place in class, you know. There isn't a class for everything. Nootka can help you regain *unus mundus*. She will ease your sorrow. They say a feeling of oneness with the universe is the highest experience the brain has to offer. If this were any sort of real university, I would offer you that at least. But Nootka will have to do her best." The rose scent enveloped Geneva as the two-foot-tall plant trembled. Bits of blossom fell onto her head. She followed Roundtree out of the greenhouse as he cooed instructions. "Practically speaking, I want to see if she's ready for cooler temperatures and drier climes. I'd love to plant some of our starts outside in spring. Keep her in the bathroom at first and then gradually move her out. Keep a record and let me know how she does. Consider it an internship."

Outside the greenhouse, he resumed his normal human-audible tone. "So, you are on track to graduate." He pinched the bridge of his nose, the way he did in class to right himself when he realized he'd digressed. "Almost."

The rose-ladyslipper's thin thorns pricked Geneva's face as she jostled it.

"I was surprised to see you had an incomplete last quarter," he said. "So I wanted to make sure to mention it. You missed a final, was it? Just be sure to take care of that. I know you are still undecided about your future. Don't worry, you've time. I offer this advice: In looking for self, pay close attention to that which both attracts and repels. That's good. That's all," he concluded abruptly, muttering to himself as if he were checking boxes off of some internal list. "Now, do you need some help with that? Nootka is heavier than she looks and awkward to carry."

Outside Varian Hall at the top of the steps, Geneva glanced between the rose-ladyslipper stems in the direction of the bookstore. If it weren't for the rose, she'd probably go there to browse anyway even though she didn't need to buy books anymore. Everyone would be there. She'd thumb through some of the texts outside her major while the freshmen darted around. She maneuvered down the stairs, shifting the rose in her arms so she could catch glimpses of her tan sneakers landing on each step. Would she have seen Leo Love? Did the DJ dance in the music or art history aisles?

She rolled her eyes and blew a strand of hair aside. She could not believe she was still so pointlessly obsessed, even after her talk with Valerie. Before the dance she'd never seen DJ Love, not once in three years, not in class, in the crowded bookstore, or in passing on campus. Their paths didn't cross.

At the bottom of the steps, she turned toward her dorm, Inu Wood. Students' sandals slapped against the bricks as they passed in a blur of brown, green, and black backpacks. Crossing the open field, she remembered the one other time she had run into Leo and glanced to the side looking for him and his AeroFlux Butterflies. Then—squish—she stumbled forward as the ground went soft beneath her, burying her shoes in mud. She mucked back to the brick path. Of course, the soggy field was empty. No one was playing on the lawn today. As her toes turned icy inside her sneakers, she shivered and looked down at her jacket still tied around her waist. She shifted the weight of the smooth ceramic pot, pressing it into her side so that she held it as much with her torso as with her numb arm wrapped around it. The rose thorns poked her chest and shoulder through her thin T-shirt. The plant's leaves drooped. She hurried on, her shoes squeaking along the alameda of Japanese Fire Maples on the path to Inu Wood. These solitary trees had turned to pinkish orange spires. Others, on the hillside behind campus sharing oxygen with the evergreens, remained pale green or yellow.

At the dorm, she fumbled with the door, watching the plant's reflection in the glass window. In three years, she'd never thought to bring a plant back to her room. Valerie would have hated a pure pink rose, but she'd like the professor's vermilion orchid hybrid. The pot slipped under Geneva's arm. She clenched it to her chest with her limp arm but recoiled when the thorns stabbed at her throat. She spun on the slimy soles of her shoes and the pot slid away from her, crashing onto the brick. Its blossoms landed up against the door. Slim white roots showed through the soil surrounded by ceramic shards. "Oh no, the *unus mundus,*" she moaned pushing soil over the roots. "Not air." She ran to her room. "Val, quick, I need a..." She grabbed a container from the kitchen.

Outside, she replanted the rose in a popcorn bowl. She carried it straight back to her bathroom. A few buds and leaves fell onto the bare countertop as she set it down and filled the sink with hot water. Steam rose along with the scent of crushed wild rose. The Nootka's branches were intact. Her choked voice fell naturally into Hort-Audible. "I'm not trying to kill you, special project. You're the world mind. Be strong."

The Nootka lifted the faces of its rare blossoms, but its leaves wilted and clung. Finally, she left it alone in the bathroom shutting the door behind her. "Val, did you see that? I almost killed my professor's plant."

Geneva dropped her pack on the bed, went to the closet to retrieve a sweater and stopped cold. Usually there was a sharp divide, where the light matte palette of her Face-in-the-Crowd outfits ended, and Val's shiny dark Plug-In gear began. Now the light blue wall continued past her clothes. The closet was half-empty. Val's clothes were gone.

Geneva darted to the bathroom and pushed open the door confirming what she'd observed, but hadn't registered, when she'd placed the plant down on the bare countertop. The bottles and vials that made up Valerie's collection of cosmetics and hair goo and dyes were also gone. She opened the cabinet. There was only her own wood-handled hairbrush, a jar of apricot kernel skin softener, some tubes of plant wax lip balm. All the glossy, slick products were gone except a short row of Wicked Woodsprite nail polishes and the container of Gator Tongue hair dye both gifts to her from Val.

Her breathing slowed when she saw the computer still hooked up in the living room because she could not think that Val would have left it behind. Beside it was an envelope propped against a glass of orange juice. Her full name was written across the front of it, tilted sharply left in Valerie's skinny script. The letter began without endearments:

Geneva,

I'm still on campus. But I've decided to live with some new friends at the Mansion. We came and got my stuff while you were out. I left the compu because your parents bought it and you might need it for class. The guys are a bunch of plug-ins and they have a good lab set up at the Mansion. We share interests. There's more to life than graduation, you know! But, yeah, don't worry, I will still try to get out of here, but, it's a big world out there. Anyway, I hope you get a cool new roommate, someone you have a lot in common with, and I'm sure I'll see you around. I know this may sound cruel, but I've thought about it a lot, actually, and I think living with you made me a little crazy-girl. You don't seem to want to deal, so...I'm just getting out of your hair.

Still love your new red 'tails by the way, go gator-girl,

Val

Geneva clutched the letter and circled the dorm. "Your parents? A new roommate? See you around? This MAY sound cruel. MAY?"

She ended up in the bathroom, the letter clenched in one fist, yelling, "A letter? She leaves a fucking letter!" at the Nootka Rose, until she collapsed to her knees beside it overwhelmed by loss, *unus mundus*, and deep, insatiable sadness.

That afternoon, Geneva commandeered the computer. She'd stopped crying but she was still angered by Val's abrupt departure. Her legs splayed across the chair as she leaned into the screen. She stretched Valerie's custom virtual reality glasses apart to fit around her wider face and lowered them, wrapping herself in darkness. The silver letters Sync Chrome City flew into the left corner of her vision. This was where Valerie had been when she started screaming. "Since when is hanging out with Mansion Expansion freaks more important than graduation?" Geneva queried the dark.

A pixilated flashing skull appeared. Blue flames shot out of its eye-sockets. After the trill, "Ooh, la, la. Gunk-Secured content." the skull dissipated, and a series of crisp video images flashed. Geneva rolled her eyes and sat tight. Shaded gray tubes writhed on top of still gray, black, and white shreds. She tried to decipher the image and pinched her eyes shut as soon as it crystallized — maggots crawling on a chunk of rotting torso. The image repeated until she forced her eyes open and watched.

Then in a flash of blue, more words appeared silver and wavy as mirages: *I am not a rub on Aladdin's lamp.* More video followed. She identified it faster this time. The corpse of a young man shed strips of skin as he spun around his limbs lined with fishhooks. An electric crackle accompanied the words: *I do not exist for your entertainment.* Shades of pink filtered onto black-and-white, video-colored flesh still attached to the joints of protruding bones in a pile of bodies. Geneva's temples and fingertips tingled as an electronic buzz, feedback, amplified into a thumping pulse: *Prism people, fractured all.*

The music trailed away. Everything went white. Light glowed through the white letters: *Sync Chrome City, mind-expanding speakeasy. Operate EveryMan?*

"Wow, paranoid, much?" Geneva responded. Gunk was one thing, a half-assed security system that tested a user's will to sit through horrors in order to get to the main attraction. EveryMan, on the other hand, was serious neo-private security. It open sourced a user's data logs baring a computer's soul. In theory, it created a screen of privacy behind a thick fog of information. Valerie wasn't a neo-private, but she'd installed EveryMan and had it set on Deviant. While she was on Sync Chrome City, her computer would browse porn sites while broadcasting her files. Geneva twirled her fingers through her ponytails and set Every-Man to Numbingly Normal so it'd hit only a random-selection of top-rated sites.

Submit to screening process?

She hesitated then clicked *Sync///chrome///city.* She had to find out what Val was into. Aluminum bubbled before her, words wavered across reflective surfaces: *Welcome to Sync Chrome City. Four questions secure your admission.*

Are you big?

Do you use it all?

Anything unusual today?

Giovanni Hastings?

Geneva typed yes four times smiling for the first time since she'd turned on the computer. Giovanni Hastings (it was also a book, a movie, and a short story) was her favorite game to play as a kid. It was about a nerdy child who grew up to rule the world, if you played it right.

Choose your method of locomotion: movement, people, computers, nature.

She hit nature in spite of her accident with the Nootka, the plant looked as though it had a fair shot at recovery, and a little clock appeared, and the machine began to whir. The time warp installation was the most devious security measure of all since most plug-ins abhorred wasting seconds. To sit still for it, Val must have been motivated. The delayed install took forever. While she waited, Geneva painted her toes Smashed Violets and fell into a reverie. She imagined DJ Leo Love's hands wrapped around her feet. He massaged her soles. Just as his fantasy lips touched the tip of her toes, a rap on the door made her kick back rocking the chair and nearly toppling.

"Friend-Me," the courier called. "You want this."

As she leapt to the door, she noticed she'd tracked mud all over the crème carpet. "Damn!"

The courier held a hand out from underneath a flap of the usual forest green cloak. A purple velvet box rested in the palm of his hand.

"You want this," he repeated, and she reached for it.

"Yeah, sure." She stroked the velvet box, listening to the whir of the computer as it loaded Sync Chrome City. The courier already had his back to her. She grabbed the felt of his cloak. "Hey, I wasn't actually using Friend-Me so you shouldn't be here. How do you know what I want if I'm not journalizing?"

He turned around and her eyes scanned over the Friend-Me badge on his breast, an official silver, equilateral triangle with thin green letters, or a perfect replica. She looked up at the courier's face and DJ Leo Love stared down at her just as he had from the ceiling of the Big Top at the Mansion Expansion dance.

He swept the formal Friend-Me bow, turned again, and walked away.

~ 10 ~

IN IVY LEAGUE

"As disturbed as I was by Burrows' threat to my daughter, it was this conversation that led me to act. He accused us of simply shutting out what we did not like—accurately—I thought. I then had to admit to myself that I was acting out of fear. Our minds could not and, in fact, would not, stay closed. I did not want to be held hostage by man or fear. And I wanted to prove him wrong."

— *Save Giovanni: The Lost Men of the Psychic Wars*, S. Sherring

As C.G. Burrows stepped onto the New West University campus, he resolved to begin his conversation with President Sherring amiably. The irony of pretending to talk to the president on behalf of Psi-Aware was too rich. He could see the ivy-covered administration building, Old Main, across campus and guessed that the jade green climbing it was not alive. It looked natural from a distance, but as he approached he could see the ivy leaves were too regularly spaced. Unless trimming them was someone's full-time occupation, the placement of the vines was unnaturally perfect leaving an eight-inch margin around each window.

Real ivy, he assumed, would not be allowed in New West. It would grow in and force the bricks apart. The live stuff would have been poisoned and replaced. A tamed synthetic would impart the institutional aesthetic: We've been here forever (a lie) and there's no going back (a fantasy he'd dispel). Old Main itself, undoubtedly, was centuries old. Built long ago on the slope of an evergreen-covered hill, the building had probably withstood several earthquakes and might even remain standing after the fault line below split into the latest and greatest, overly anticipated, Northwest natural disaster. It was the recent incarnation of the college that needed the façade of ivy. New West University had been here less than a lifetime.

The steps of the building were close together and many. Four tiers of stairs and landings led up to the doors. Burrows stretched his steps over four or five stairs at a time. When he reached the top, he adjusted the collar of his jacket. Across campus, the emerald tip of a pyramid pierced the gray sky. The construction of Friend-Me Corporation's headquarters on the southeast corner of New West University was nearly complete. Nearby, lines of students filed out of the bookstore by the bay. He wondered if any of them knew the university was building a psychic research center for Friend-Me Corporation with their student fees. Probably not. They couldn't see more than the next red brick in front of them on their way to class. They couldn't think past their next big test. The greater consequences of the society they lived in eluded them. Only he was aware. He had to put a stop to it, turn the president against Friend-Me.

Burrows ground his knuckles into the scarred craters knotting at the base of his neck. His skin was still numb from when he'd yanked out the Vary implants. He entered Old Main. The administration building was filled with stale citrus-scented heat wafting off the polished pine banisters. He walked three more flights of stairs to the President's Office where a blue uniformed New West officer, an older, stouter version of the campus security guards, stared sullenly. Burrows got no twinges from the guard and figured he looked passably benign. The officer, probably thinking only of his next pay raise, hadn't spared him a thought.

Similarly, the receptionist waved Burrows painlessly into the president's office. Inside Sherring stood, arms crossed, at his third-floor window in a parody of idle time. But Burrows could feel him busy, thinking, thinking migraines at him about their upcoming meeting. The information came at Burrows in onslaughts, streams of consciousness followed by sharp conclusions.

From Sherring he got*: Why is C.G. Burrows interested in Friend-Me Corporation's funding? What is his connection? What does he know? He's trouble.*

Burrows wanted to retreat from the pain, turn and slam the door behind him, but he'd lost the option to go back when he'd left his Vary Shop in the 'Way. Maybe other people didn't understand, but that's how it worked. When you decided to do something, it was done. You got one chance to choose and then it was over. There was no longer any choice involved. Teeth clenched; Burrows stepped further into the room. He held very still while he waited for the shards of information about himself to pass through. It was like running through a window in stop motion.

Sherring continued to project*: Burrows is: a counter-evolutionary who has been living on the Freeway running a Vary shop, an aspiring surgeon who lost his chance to go to New West University during the revolution, the son of wealthy socialites now living in C-Town.*

The president's objective focused analysis dealt Burrows near crippling mind cramps. Sherring knew a lot, but he was still seeking answers, asking questions, trying to gain an advantage. Burrows could see why the people in power were so stalwartly opposed to psychics. They didn't want to lose their edge. They were practiced at extrapolating from every bit of surface knowledge they could glean about a person: his personnel file, his history, his non-verbal cues. They used this expertise in human behavior to see inside other people's heads from the outside. They didn't want psychics to one-up their advantage. Later, when he was in less pain, Burrows would appreciate what he and Sherring had in common: They saw other people first as foes.

At last, Sherring turned and acknowledged Burrows.

"Mr. Burrows come on in, welcome, please have a seat," Sherring said, leaving the window and settling into his faux leather chair. "So, are you here to see me in my capacity as the President of New West or as the President of New West University?"

Meanwhile, he was assessing Burrows: *A nice suit. Conservative cut, not too stylish. He could still be his father's son. But don't jump to conclusions. The revolution created a rift. The beard is troubling. He's hiding something. Vary scars? Likely Vary scars.*

Burrows struggled to keep his forehead smooth, his reactions hidden, while the president's sharp interest cut across his brow. It was hard to be charismatic with a migraine. This guy was a real thinker. Burrows was glad he'd worn the suit. A nice suit went a long way with a guy like this. If there was one thing his telepathy had taught him, it was that appearances mattered. "I'm here to see the President of New West," he said.

Outwardly calm, the president showed stress in his stream of analysis: *No, this is not routine. He doesn't just have a complaint. He has an agenda. He already looks uncomfortable. He's not intimidated by me, and he's intense. The way he's standing, he looks like an enforcer. He looks like he's going to tell me what to do, not ask. At least he'll be direct. McDougall's on security duty today. He's reliable if this gets out of hand.*

Burrows lost his line on Sherring's thoughts for a moment, as he did when a person reached back into their own minds, remembering. If Sherring was already thinking about security, he realized he didn't have much time. The president returned abruptly from his inner voyage to pound Burrows with: *This is about the war.*

Burrows stumbled forward and slid into the chair in front of the president's desk. Even on the 'Way few had the courage to call what had happened war. People had to bleed in war. They had to die. The deaths of the revolution had been indirect. Among those hardest hit, it was called an opportunistic seizure, a grab. Everything had gone to hell and a few people had made good.

New Westians stuck to an official line. During the Greatest Depression, a group of people had banded together. They had foreseen the collapse of the markets. They had pooled their considerable funds, drawn a net around the institutions they cared about and protected them from ruin. Amid chaos, they had created New West. Everyone had had a choice to abide by the new government or to seek a way outside of it. The intellectuals had kept the transition orderly.

Burrows sat back in his chair. He uncrossed his legs and let his arms hang loose at his sides, giving the president cues that he was at ease. He had to strike a pleasant tone, establish some trust. He began by telling the man what he already knew. "After the revolution I never thought I'd come back. I opened a Vary shop on the Freeway." He stroked the side of his face. "I gave myself some pretty nasty looking implants. I was angry, I admit. I was a young man at the time. I didn't understand all the politics, didn't want to. I just wanted to go to my father's alma mater and study medicine to help people. But then a group of people, brilliant people by all accounts, for reasons I didn't understand, forced some changes. I didn't have a choice about that, but in doing so they denied me my opportunity, my education."

From the president, Burrow got an answering jab*: Yes.*

He had struck a nerve: New Westian guilt. He'd known it was there from his time around the electric blue pine-scented fire with the Freeman's, but he had not been sure it reached all the way to the top, to the instigators of oppression. They had made some coldhearted calculations to attain a fresh start for their new utopia, but they had been aware of the costs. They had sacrificed a generation of others' children, banishing them to the old 'Way, in order to make a new way for their own progeny. Burrows understood that he was here taking action just in time. The original founders, with their historical memories, still had regrets. Saul Tillitat, for example, had taken his riches and retired to the island of La Merde in Pacifica so he would not have to see the refugees. Generation Utopia, when it took power, would not regret. Those kids: Leo, Eve, Coco, Grugel, and Streker. They would owe Burrows nothing. Now was the time to use this remorse to his advantage. "I never even had a chance to understand what their issues were," Burrows said. "Because I wasn't allowed access to the information and the knowledge they had. To them, it was a necessary sacrifice, but I saw myself as a casualty—of war."

Burrows paused. His use of the word, stolen from the president's own internal narrative, had the desired result. It got Sherring's attention and his empathy. He leaned forward, his arms folded over the papers on his desk.

Yes.

"Those combatants chased out people they didn't agree with. They chased my parents out because they didn't fit into their new perfect society. They chased me out onto the Freeway; a place they said wasn't fit for anyone. They condemned class warfare, but they reinforced that divide, that chaos. The way I saw it, at least the 'Way had freedom, autonomy, independence, privacy — a few of my values were intact out there. So, I left. But then, what? After all the grief they caused, then what did the New Westians do after their so-called revolution?"

Burrows let the question sit. He watched Sherring's eyes. His head stopped aching as the president's thoughts wandered away from him again. Then Sherring returned and gave him: *I'm sorry.* He'd struck the guilt. Those two sharp veins striating his brain: I'm sorry. Now he'd mine it.

"Nothing. They rebuilt society exactly the way it was." Burrows took a deep breath. "Except with me and my family shut out of it. They ruined my life."

As he said that last though, Burrows instantly heard himself as a teenager, whiny and adolescent, and wished he could take it back. He guessed he'd overplayed his hand and was correct. The president watched Burrows steadily, his blue eyes barely blinking, but he'd become defensive and then bored: *Right, sir, this is the part where I let you talk. You talk, I listen. You go away happy, heard. You burn away your energy in words. You forget what you wanted. I'm a sounding board. I'm an apologist.*

Hearing the president had no patience for self-pity, Burrows switched tactics. "But I've forgiven them," he said, evenly, moving on, leaving all of the wrongs done to his family on the cutting room floor. "I'm thinking about the future. I've met some students, some very bright young minds, and I've found this Utopian generation to be appreciative and understanding. We have some things in common. I know that you played a key role in keeping things the way they are, from getting out of control. I'm worried about those young people. You share my concern, I know. That's why I'm here."

With that, he had Sherring's attention again, he got: *OK, now we get to it. Get to it.* He pressed his hands together fingertips intertwining. "Mr. Burrows, what can I do for you?"

Burrows glanced at the collection of photos of Coco in an assortment of silver frames on the president's desk. He saw Coco as a girl, her fine pale hair in faintly curling ponytails, sitting on the steps of Old Main; Coco, with curls cascading from underneath a red mortar board; and Coco lying on a beach, somewhere off-continent, surely, with pink sand and turquoise water behind her, her hair pulled back, resting her head in her hands and smiling. It looked like where she belonged. Did the president regret that he had stranded his daughter in the enclave of New West, that he had denied her the world he had always known and she only briefly? Or was he grateful that global events had intervened in her transition to adulthood (probably she would have chosen to study abroad) trapping her close where he could hold on to her childhood a little longer?

"You are a hypocrite," Burrows said. "And you are setting yourself up for a civil war. The Neo-Privates won't like to hear that the New West government is funding Friend-Me Corporation's psychic research. LeMay misrepresented herself. She's very anti-privacy. Her company is all about evolution. Its experiments are dangerous."

"There's nothing wrong with research," the president said.

"You know it's gone way beyond that. You have to end it."

"Mr. Burrows, let me speak candidly, since I see there is no point in trying to disguise what you already know. You are right, we have made discoveries. But," the president shook his head. "It would be wrong to end the experiments. I think this change in our society, in ourselves, is inevitable. I don't think we can stuff it back in the box, at this point, just because it makes us uncomfortable."

However, the president was not thinking what he was saying. Burrows could tell by the complete absence of pain, a total misdirection. He was lying. Burrows took a guess about what and went fishing. "But that's exactly what you are doing."

The sink line paid off, he got: *New West Mental Health.*

"Oh, that's rich," Burrows said, quickly making the connection. "The kids are manifesting psychic powers; you don't know why and you've created some kind of place to shut them away. That's New West's answer to everything, isn't it? Shut out what you don't like. Do you know what's causing the powers?"

He got nothing. The president didn't know. But Burrows had a good idea: Sync Chrome City. That was a bit of information he could use, later.

Burrows picked up the photo of Coco lying on the beach. "You're willing to sacrifice Generation Utopia? Her? Listen, Friend-Me is not the answer. You can't let these abilities develop.

It's not an option. Do you want your daughter to grow up in a world where anyone can get into her head? It's mind-rape."

From the president, he got: *Leave Constance out of this.*

Sherring's expression didn't change, but Burrows knew he'd struck a nerve.

"You'd better try. Friend-Me Corporation has been producing drugs. SLO-42 made with the son's oxytocin. Ever wonder, how your daughter became so interested in a loser like Leo LeMay? Drugs, maybe? Makes a lot more sense, doesn't it? If you let Friend-Me carry on with this 'research,' you'll give other people the power to control how your daughter thinks."

Burrows gripped the arms of his chair, half raising out of it, not caring anymore that he was beginning to make a bad impression: *An enemy we created in my office. Stop talking about Constance.*

The president stood up. "Put that down. His tall body shook as if the window had opened to let in the fall chill. "McDougall," he shouted, his voice hoarse. For a moment, Burrows' mind filled with flashes of red and a roaring crescendo. He rarely got emotions from people, just words and pain, but when he did, they came in a rush. Then the president switched off his anger and regained his logical pace of analytic thought: *Wait, Constance's 20th birthday. You were there. Why? How long have you known my daughter?*

Burrows took blows from Sherring's mental jabs. He dropped the photo of Coco. The metal frame clattered as it hit the floor, glass shattered, and shards slid over the polished marble. Burrows lowered back into the chair. It was all he could do not to clutch the sides of his head an instinctive reaction to the pain that he'd fought to suppress since childhood. It gave him away. It made him different. He sprang from his seat and lunged at the desk, placing his hands in the center of the president's desk to steady himself, knocking over Coco's graduation picture and the one of her as a toddler. The president didn't move. His eyes locked on Burrows. He landed a thought. It sunk in like a long, slow injection: *Stay away from her.*

It sent Burrows reeling. The chair's legs screeched against the floor as he stumbled over it. He staggered back and hit a wall of uniformed flesh. The New West officer clenched Burrows' shoulder. Burrows time was up, but he wasn't sure he'd gotten what he wanted. The president squared his shoulders and righted the picture of Constance.

"What about Friend-Me? Are you going to let them?" Burrows shouted as the officer jammed two sharp prongs into the small of his back.

"You're going to leave now," the guard said.

"Your daughter. I'll drug her myself," Burrows said calling the president's attention to him. "What are you going to do about LeMay?"

The president took the bait and Burrows got: *Friend-Me will have to go.*

It was the response he had wanted. He sank into the officer's grip.

"Did you hear that threat, McDougall? Mr. Burrows will be ending his visit now. Please provide him an escort."

The officer piloted Burrows into the elevator, kept the taser on him all the way down and then shoved him out the front door of the building. As Burrows stumbled down the steps propelled by the officer's grip, he kept his eyes trained on the tip of the Friend-Me pyramid. The sides of his face pulled taut. The scars beneath his beard stretched tight. They burned with the sensation of a numb limb waking when he smiled.

The guard released him at the bottom of the steps, where 30 members of the Deming Psi-Aware chapter hoisted yellow and red signs: Psi-Now. Burrows raised his voice to address them. "No progress. We're at an impasse. The protest continues. The president refuses to see reason. If non-psychics don't take us more seriously there will be civil war."

Behind him Burrows heard a soft but steady snikt, snikt. As he watched the protesters mount the steps, he saw a slim figure dangling beside one of Old Main's windows. A man in brown overalls and a green painter's cap was holding a shiny pair of shears. He was trimming the live ivy. It occurred to Burrows, for an instant, that he didn't know New West as well as he thought.

Burrows was relieved fall classes were starting. The Utopian kids had almost unlimited reserves of adulation.

Streker: *Whoa, man, I'll just get out of your way.*

Grugel: *Dude, you can really work it.*

Eve: *So interesting.*

There was only so much of that he could take within the confines of mobile Sync Chrome City, the cramped RV outfitted with the kids' tech. With summer over, the students fell back into their routines and self-absorption and gave him more mental space. He had them pegged now. They manufactured drama-laced lives fueled by simple motivations.

Streker: Love

Grugel: Money.

Eve: Love *and* money.

Security. That was the prize they were after, at the root of all their angst, but it was impossible to get at by thinking small. So, he'd get them thinking big. Get them ready to take it up a notch. Grugel said he could have the tech ready in time for New Years. He'd blow the lid off Sync Chrome City.

~ 11 ~

SYNC CHROME CITY

"The physical and chemical effects of the psychic state are well documented. Meditation stimulates the alpha waves in the brain and the release of the amine, serotonin, and peptide, oxytocin. Psychically active minds achieve a state of internal synchrony. All nerve cells fire simultaneously. However, the psychotropic nature of the experience remains unexplained. The feeling of interconnectedness with the universe is similar to the effects of psilocybin. Our empathic connection to all surrounding minds, our creation of an external neural net, our Infinite Lattice, our Connected Ego, remains a mystery." — *Becoming Psychic 101, A History and a Primer*

Geneva shoved the purple box into her pocket and followed the green cloak of the Friend-Me courier. All summer DJ Leo Love had been in her mind manipulating lights and sound behind her eyes and delivering kisses in dreams and daydreams. She'd wondered if she'd ever see him again. Then he was at her door, a Friend-Me Courier. How many times had he delivered to her? How many times had she passed him on campus and not even noticed? Maybe Valerie was right. She wasn't paying attention. What else was she missing? She'd only noticed the DJ when it had been impossible not to, when he'd been swinging over her like a star. There was no guarantee she'd see him again. She wanted to know who he was, where he lived, and how she could find him again, so she followed. It was a drunken impulse; hope drowned her inhibition but without the heady time warp. She didn't have seconds to reconsider. She just went, trailing behind him so that she wouldn't be seen, tracking him in his green cloak across campus.

There was an oceanic roar of chanting as Leo headed towards Old Main. On the lawn in front of the administration building she could see the crowd of protesters had grown. They were 30 or more strong waving signs and yelling "Psi-Now!" in unison and there was a smaller group holding up pictures of sad-looking lab rats. Geneva shied away from them afraid that they would turn to her en masse. But Leo stopped in front of them. If he turned now, he'd see her standing behind him, obviously going nowhere, following him. She glanced up at the ivy-covered building and veered up the steps ducking into the mob for cover.

Leo stripped off his cloak revealing a white T-shirt and long forest-green pants. He sprinted at a group of students jousting with live steel on the lawn. He finished his dash with a forward handspring, and he landed in front of them.

"Leo!" the fencers bellowed. One tossed a flail. Leo caught the hilt, yawped, and parried. The others grabbed their swords and engaged. From the steps, Geneva gawked. With some quick thrusts and a deft lunge, Leo disarmed his opponent and held the tip of his sword to their chest. His opponent dropped to a knee. Brandishing the sword, Leo pivoted towards the steps, nodded his head and yelled, "Geneva."

She shrunk into the crowd, but it was no use trying to hide now.

"Geneva," he yelled again looking right at her. "It's you right? From the dance."

She waved a hand in Leo's direction. She hoped his next question wouldn't be, "Why are you following me?"

He introduced her around again to Grugel, Streker, and seven others who looked vaguely familiar from the Mansion Expansion dance. This time she got all their names: Chris, Michael, Don, Eli, Tod, Roger, and Andrew. "We all live in The Mansion. We were just about to go get some food. Do you want to come?"

They went down the hill to Ruby's, of course. They crowded into to the biggest round booth in the back, the one the waiters called The King's Table when the tips were good or the 'Way Back Booth when they weren't. Geneva ended up in the middle of the ring of loud college friends across from Leo. They were a classic case of big eaters, bad tippers. She wondered who would be serving them.

She was surprised when Gary the owner came over to take their orders and felt a flash of guilt that Ruby's was so short-staffed. "What will you have?" he asked.

She shrank in her seat. His eyebrows arched when he saw her. "Hey..." he was about to say something embarrassing, then caught himself. He took down the orders for burgers and fries. "Just tea for me," she said. He winked at her.

"So, I'm thinking it's time we break out, do something big," Grugel said. "I'm working on some code to spark the process. We haven't even touched capacity. It'd be like adding fuel to the fire."

"We'll have a party for the roll out," Streker said.

"Are you talking about Sync Chrome City?" Geneva asked.

"You a citizen?" one of them asked.

"No, I was trying to enter. I got interrupted."

"This'll be beyond you then," Grugel said. "We're talking about an amped up version."

The food arrived. The friends dove in. Geneva sipped her tea and tried not to get caught staring at Leo. Then Gary returned and set a head high sundae down in front of her. They all looked up as he pushed it across to her and handed her a silver spoon with a curled handle. It looked long enough to dip down through all the layers of creamy whip to the ice cream below.

"I didn't order this," Geneva said.

Gary smiled and leaned against the table. "This contraband isn't on the menu—yet." He winked. "I'm not leaving until I see the look on your face when you taste it."

Drizzled over the top of the sundae were sunshine swirls of orange and yellow sauces. A sweet citrus scent rose off the sundae. The others stared at her as she lifted a spoonful. It tasted like not-quite orange and lemon, the flavors were infused with some far away tang. The nuts sprinkled on top were unusual too. They were crisp instead of crunchy, and lightly oiled. The best part was the ice cream itself. It was a smooth confection of an unfamiliar flavor, fresh, new, exotic—not butter cream or maple or strawberry—that reminded her of longing.

She took another bite and then passed it down the table. "Everyone's got to try this."

Gary leaned across the table and whispered. "That's toasted coconut ice cream topped with mango and passion fruit syrups and crushed macadamias. You couldn't get further off-continent. That's what you've been missing. That's what all us old chefs have been talking about, the paradise outside New West. I figured I'd give Geneva here a taste since her mother's helping to negotiate the trade with C-town. Who knows how they are getting these tropical goods, but that's what we used to call utopia, the places where you could get fruits like these."

By the time the sundae returned to Geneva only two melted lumps of white ice cream remained. Now that, with Gary's help, she had the friends' attention, she asked, "After this, show me Sync Chrome City?"

Back at the Mansion, they took her into the City. They brought her to one of the fishbowl dorm rooms outfitted with a panel of screens and closed the blinds. Geneva sat on the end of a bed next to Streker with a row of his friends alongside and another across from her on the other bed all wearing black razor glasses. Leo perched on a swivel chair next to her and handed her a pair. She pulled her ponytails out from under the sides of the glasses as she put them on.

At the front of the room, Grugel knelt beneath a screen and tapped electronics. The silvery equipment glowed. The onyx screens glimmered. The words Sync Chrome City ran across the largest screen in tall, stretched type. She gripped the edge of the bed.

"Let's have some music," one of them said, and from under the bed the drum-bound strings of Giovanni Hastings Musica began to flow.

The tat-tat-tat of Grugel's rapid typing continued. "I'll get us in quick, go around all the security straight to the source," he said.

When the first security flash appeared—swollen red and purple-banded worms writhing through torn gray flesh and bandages—Geneva squeezed her eyes shut. The tapping quickened. She peeked between her fingers, and they were blowing by slick, heavily-coded decoy sites: the towering black spires of Sin Rom City and the deep silver pools of Synchronicity. She opened her eyes wide when they landed on the doorstep of the real Sync Chrome City—a flat screen with the four questions: Are you big? Do you use it all? Anything unusual today? Giovanni Hastings? They ran across the screen in a textbook font on matte black with a flashing green prompt. But there was more. Geneva felt she could scoop her mind out and squeeze it in looping spirals onto that black space communicating with the masses like icing on cake. She felt that she could go into to the netscape of Sync Chrome City but didn't understand what it meant.

"OK, I see it. But what is it, exactly?" she asked.

"Yaaaah, it's the same as utopia. Nothing really," Grugel said. “No place. Like where we’re going Gen Utopia. The big zero.”

"It’s true," Streker said leaning in, breathing against her shoulder. "That’s what utopia really means. The guy who came up with it was being sarcastic."

Geneva lowered her glasses.

"What? Don't look at me like that," Streker said. "I'm a philosophy major. It was Sir Thomas More. 16th Century."

She rolled her eyes. "Jeez, at least with environmental psychology I can work in a greenhouse. What are you going to do with that?"

Streker shrugged. "I'm doing this. It started as a social network, some Psi-stuff I bought into as a kid, some games, just playing at trying to expand each other's minds—but it was all kind of flat. Then I met Grugel here and he advanced the tech. He hit on some juice. A formula that, like, sparks the mind, taps the wires. It's a trip. You'll see."

He watched her as he spoke, his eyes staring into hers. His hair gleamed blue in the low light reflected off the screens like dark wavy leaves. She raised her glasses again. "So, you're kidding me, Grugel's probably the only one of us here with a viable major..."

"Computer science," Grugel said. "But I haven't been sweating it. This makes bank. Don't worry, first ride's free."

Beside her Leo swiveled in his chair, his vinyl pants making swish-stick sounds. "And I have a decent shot with my music. Not that some people think so. Just take her in. Get her past the bouncer."

Streker turned to her. "The questions are just a screening system. We didn't want to let in people who couldn't get it. If they can't experience that space out there, this looks lame. They'd talk smack about Chrome City, say it sucked."

Leo: Swish. Stick. Swivel. "The questions don't really matter. You get in, if you're ready. It's a trigger."

Under the glasses, Sync Chrome City expanded like an oil slick, colors swirling. Geneva forced her eyes from the screen and lowered the glasses again. The room was still there. Its black walls a fuzz-edged enclosure.

"Kind of like hypnosis." Geneva raised the glasses. "Ready."

Streker talked as he tapped through the answers. "The questions refer to your mind and your self-perception. Are you large? Do you contain multitudes? Or are you a lone ranger? Most people, if they are paying any attention to what's going on outside themselves, have unusual experiences that they can't explain."

"The brain is wider than the sky," Geneva said.

"A nice way to put it," Streker said.

“Dickinson,” Geneva said, feeling a bit silly she’d got the quote off a poster, but Leo’s friends seemed very intellectual, and she wanted to keep up. When he got to the last one, Geneva put a hand on his shoulder. "Giovanni Hastings? What’s that mean?"

"Yaaah, goody-goody," Grugel said.

Streker shrugged. "Oh, nothing. Really. Nothing. I just like him."

"No. It's cool, really." Leo said, swiveling in time to the music. "It fits with what people can experience here. Being greater than they are, unexpected world rulers in a way like Giovanni. Maybe that's what our generation is all about really. Forget Gen Utopia. We should call ourselves Gen-Giovanni."

"Yeah. My kind of my hero." Streker said. He tapped again and they arrived at the last screen. It looked like the others but read, "Choose your method of locomotion. Movement. People. Nature."

"This is the key. It tells us the best way to tap a person in. What did you choose? No, I know..."

"Nature," he and Leo said together.

“The environmental psychology major,” Streker said.

The final keystroke clicked, and Sync Chrome City went live. "I'm a big kid," Streker said, as the blackness morphed to jungle night green.

Vines looped out of the darkness and unfurled body-sized leaves. Juices coursed, slurping through thick translucent veins. Geneva tried to lower her glasses with her palms, but she lost track of her hands. The plants pressed against her intertwining with the purple cords in her head.

"Rocket, we're in." Streker said.

Inside Sync Chrome City, on the periphery of her own perception, Geneva could see the vines pulsating as multicolored laser beams or surging with corpuscles as interwoven red veins. Those were Leo's and Streker's interpretations of the experience: movement and people. She tried again to move her hands and this time her fingers fluttered like the tips of fur-lined leaves. Streker leaned against her, his shoulder tree trunk firm against her knee. He whispered, his voice rustling through the vines, shaking the leaves. "Feel them," she heard him say and then felt the echoing press of his thoughts: *Feel them.*

She sighed and her hands dropped into her lap as she became aware of the other minds. There were less than a hundred of them connected to Sync Chrome City. They dangled together like ripe fruit in the space. She pressed a thought out to them— *Hello.*—and the vines rose and fell, rippling from 'h' to 'o'. The minds bounced as she ran her thoughts along them, down the vines, touching the tops of each one. One by one, she met the people connected to Sync Chrome City. The seven in the room and other students at New West, the same faces she saw in passing each day lugging packs on campus. But they came at her in three-dimensional layers. Instead of eyes and ears and mouths, she identified them in a glance by experience, personality, and injury. He played the oboe, had grown up on the 'Way, rose to meet her, mind open wide, with high levels of serotonin afraid of very little since his father had abused him. She studied biochemistry, had been off-continent and spoke Chinese, and stayed deep inside herself with low levels of serotonin used to being sheltered. They danced up to her freed in this space to be themselves. Geneva knew these students. There was more to know. And she knew as much as she needed: *It's an external neural net.*

Streker: *One big party. And everyone knows everyone. Really knows them.*

Leo: *A group of people with something in common who'd go to great lengths for each other, a reunion.* His laughter thumped giddy through the greenery and Geneva heard it pounding as though it came from within her own heart.

The circling vines swelled looping over each other. Geneva mingled. It was like being at the Mansion Expansion dance where she'd been fascinated by the people around her, except that she was one of them now. She could stay here, forever, in their company.

Hours later, Leo lifted her glasses and helped her off the bed. She staggered lightheaded; her legs numb. The others were still, motionless under their black razor glasses. They looked strangely unlike themselves now placid and uniform in plug-in clothes, now that she'd seen them vibrant inside Sync Chrome City and gotten to know them. She was glad she'd been able to meet them in person, before getting to know them in Sync Chrome City and that she'd had her first experience in the city in the Mansion with people nearby rather than all by herself in her dorm room at Inu Wood. It dulled the shock of leaving the City and finding herself suddenly alone, to see them there and have Leo nearby.

"I think that's enough," Leo said. "You get the picture. It's pretty addictive."

"Yeah," she nodded. "Is it dangerous?"

"Anything is—in excess. I mean, for one, you have to remember to eat and stuff."

He walked her back to her dorm. She felt like she knew him very well now and it was comfortable to be beside him and natural to slip her hand into his. But at Inu Wood, she realized she'd forgotten her passkey, locked herself out of her room when she'd chased after him, Leo Love the Friend-Me Courier.

"Come on back to the Mansion, sleep at my place," he said.

She twirled her hands through her ponytails, uncertain what he was asking.

“Just sleep," he said.

And she did lie beside him that night, but she didn't sleep much. The dorm bed was narrow and covered with worn flannel sheets. She drew next to his warm curled body and after inhaling his scent, sugar-dipped pine, began thinking about how he had swayed over her at the dance. She memorized the sound of his steady whistling breaths and marveled at his stillness. Her lips brushed once against his back covered by a thick cotton T-shirt. She awoke from a dream remembering a pattern of green and blue-green and purple-green shades laced through the treetops below. She'd been sitting cross-legged beneath an evergreen tree. Then needles clattered down beside her, and she rose into the air, arms outstretched. The sun on her back made her afraid to fall like Icarus, so she skimmed low like a hawk over the forest listening to whispered voices below saying unfamiliar, but potent, words. She felt tangy, light and delicious as an off-continent sundae.

Like that, she became a regular at the Mansion. She didn't spend much time on Sync Chrome City, instead hanging out with Leo in real life listening to him play music and watching him work his Sound-Wield set. Coco and Eve avoided her making it awkward. Leo caught her watching Coco once. "Yeah. She's cool. She's very confident. Sometimes I think you can keep more hidden if you make people think you're giving everything away."

Now that she was part of the Mansion crew, Geneva could keep tabs on Valerie, who spent most of her time in the Sync Chrome City room. But mostly she was absorbed with Leo. He seemed to live a whimsical, spontaneous life the opposite of her habits. Although she'd freely shared her mental space in her Friend-Me journal, she'd never made a physical connection until the night Leo embraced her. It felt good, but it couldn't last.

She hadn't known for sure until she'd had sex with Leo, and then, lying in his arms, afterward, it had been obvious.

"You still love her," she'd said.

"Coco." Leo nodded. He'd placed his hands on her shoulders. "Honestly? Yeah. Even though she just gave me up like that, without a fight because of her father. I think if I had the chance..."

Geneva had known what he said was just true, he wasn't trying to hurt her. She wished that she were a different person. Val often said "all's fair in love and war," but Geneva didn't believe it. There were too many excuses in the world to pretend like other people didn't exist. Love couldn't be one of them. When Coco wanted Leo back, she wouldn't stand in her way. Coco and Leo looked like they belonged together and all the Mansionites had enjoyed the couple's radiance. But it was worth it to hang around in the meantime and be near Leo while she could. She just tried to remind herself, it wouldn't last. She thought if she was logical about her decision, it would hurt less when it ended. When it did, she told herself that was true.

It happened as fall quarter came to an end. Coco made up with Leo and Geneva just stopped going to the Mansion. She spent a lot of time in the greenhouse, avoiding going back to her empty dorm room. She hadn't gotten a new roommate. Screw that, it was her senior year, she wasn't taking the time to get to know some stranger's quirks. She put in extra time at Ruby's to pay for a single room. Valerie had been a total plug-in last year, so she'd figured living alone wouldn't be that much different. It was.

She couldn't keep up with all that had been happening. She felt like a leaky vessel. She couldn't seem to get to class on time. No matter how hard she tried, she got to class later and later. She'd begun to make ridiculous excuses, which her professors believed. Then she felt guilty. Her mind couldn't keep up with the world and she began to lose her physical grip on it too. She kept losing things just when she needed them: a stylus, a disk, her passkey. She'd never realized how many separate, small objects she had to keep track of in order to live, until she began to fail at the task. She'd taken to wearing pocketful plug-in clothes, which helped, until she put on a clean outfit and left everything she needed behind her in a dirty wad on the floor in Inu Wood.

Once in early winter, she stopped by the Mansion. She wanted to check in on Val, see the guys, and maybe Leo, too, but she didn't have a passkey to the fishbowl dorm because she wasn't a resident. She spotted Eve going in and called after her, but Eve never looked around and pulled the door tight behind her. Geneva realized she'd lost not only Leo, but her access to the Mansionites and Sync Chrome City, too.

~ 12 ~

DA LIME

"It had become shamefully common to experiment with the brain chemistry of our children. We medicated them for perceived mental defects. We did so out of guilt. We were so sure the rigors of our modern society had left them diseased and corrupted. We mistook their terror and unrest for teenage spiking hormones aggravated by drug use, lack of sleep, and poor diet and exercise. It never occurred to us that while we were in shock, they were evolving." — *Save Giovanni: The Lost Men of the Psychic Wars*, S. Sherring

On New Year's Eve, Geneva went to the Mansion again. Tense, lonely, she wanted to catch Valerie before she went out, if she was going out. She peered into the fishbowl and knocked when she saw Eve. This time Eve opened the door, but she didn't step aside. She was dressed for a plug-in party. She had on the same outfit she'd worn at the Mansion Expansion dance, a short black top that showed off her red-gold Vary quills with a flowing black skirt, and she'd taken some time to pin back her masses of wiry curls.

"I just stopped by to say hi," Geneva said. It was stupid to explain. She had every right to visit the Mansion. She hadn't seen Val for months, but Val was still her sister, still her best friend.

Eve glared. "Well, no one's here."

She could tell from her tone that Eve probably thought she'd come here looking for Leo. It wasn't a bad idea. He was usually in the center of everything anyway. "What about Leo?"

"Probably with Coco," Eve said and started to close the door. She was still playing watchdog.

"Great, I'm just looking for Val," she said.

She was ready to give up, when she saw Leo coming down the hall. He saw her right away, waved and Eve stepped aside as if she'd just opened the door.

"Hey Leo," Geneva said trying to sound nonchalant but working to get out the words. Leo wore black, too, loose pants and a flowing shirt that made his upper body look broad. She'd forgotten how nervous he made her. She couldn't help thinking of him as DJ Leo Love. Val would have mocked her with, "fan-girl," if she'd known, and Geneva would have deserved it. Looking into Leo's thickly lashed dark eyes made her feel pathetic. She wanted to curl up and cling to him like frazzled lint. She shook her head and looked around. "Where's everybody?"

"Mostly in VR," he said.

He meant the guys she hoped, not Val. Months later, she still had a fear of virtual reality headsets. "On New Year's Eve?"

"Yeah, yeah. It's some kind of online party. Some kind of launch. That's why everyone stuck around campus. They could have done it from home, but they wanted to experience it together," Leo shrugged. "Everyone's all geeked out about the Bonfire."

"I thought I'd noticed a lot the Mansionites around for winter break," Geneva said. "Val isn't with them, is she?" She winced at the way the words came out, brusque and high. She sounded like her mother checking up on Val.

Leo shook his head and Geneva relaxed.

"What about you? The Bonfire?" she asked.

"No, I plan to check out a live action party," he said. "There's a place, Sync Chrome City on wheels. Do you want to go?"

He sounded so casual. But it wasn't. She wanted to check up on Val, but she didn't want to crowd her. She wanted the chance to be near Leo, but she didn't feel like competing for his attention. He seemed to want her to go. But Eve, sullenly standing by, obviously didn't. And where the hell was Coco?

She spun her fingers through her hair, twisting her ponytails into curls. She really had come straight from the greenhouse. She was in her old Face in the Crowd clothes and probably smelled like soil. "Um, I'm not really party ready."

"Val and Coco are already there," Eve now volunteered. "A nice ride came and picked them up an hour ago."

Eve had meant that to be discouraging, but that settled it. Geneva wanted to see Val. It had been so long. Still her voice wavered, "But yeah, OK."

They piled into Eve's Cadillac, sitting up in front, because the back was cluttered, filled with big piles of dark stuff. They squeezed in together, thighs pressed, Geneva in the middle and too aware of their legs touching on both sides. Eve reached over her, pushing Geneva's knee aside to crank up the heat and fiddle with the defroster. Leo began to riff in his smooth voice, dropping in some eerie minor chords. As they headed out on the highway, encircling New West, it started to snow.

They drove a long way out of town and eventually pulled into a trailer park landscaped with weeds that were gathering snow. Geneva sat forward. The worry she had pushed aside earlier had crept back into place on the drive over and she was anxious to see Val. They drove to the back of the park and pulled into a lot that had a bit higher gravel-to-weed ratio in front of a crooked trailer. There were few lights. The nearest trailers to the side were a ways off, and beyond the tilting trailer there was nothing but black. The trailer was on the edge of a marsh, or most likely, from the smell creeping into the Cadillac's vents, a landfill. As Geneva scooted out of the Cadillac, one whiff of the air, heavy with decomposition, resolved any doubt.

The trailer looked all the more shoddy next to the swank black Mercedes parked in front of it. Walking by, Geneva jumped back as she spotted red and orange flame emblems on the car's bumper, warning of a fire alarm system. She didn't want to get charred.

Leo put a hand on her back, "Don't worry, it's not that sensitive."

Geneva leaned into the tingling sensation of his palm wanting the touch to be more than it was, coincidental. "Are those even legal, the flame ones?"

"I think so," Leo said striding ahead.

As she approached the trailer, Geneva recognized Giovanni Hastings Musica, drumbeats electronically fused with shrieking strings. Inside, it was pitch black, but as her eyes adjusted, she saw glints of silver. Expecting a dive, Geneva thought the walls were covered in aluminum cans until she could see well enough to discern the high-end electronics. They were wall to wall, top to bottom. Layers of slim Plug-In gadgets were packed next to lab equipment and Vary Home Surgical Kits. One of the newer Sound-Wield Sets took up a lot of space in the back. A monitor lined one side of the trailer with one big velvet armchair at a console in front of it. It was a small but spendy space. There had to be a good air-filter system among the tech, because the air wasn't tainted like the outside. It smelled of cinnamon.

She spotted Val in a corner talking to a tall man who looked vaguely familiar. Val looked comfortable enough, leaning against a paneled side of the trailer, nearly invisible in all black, except for the luminescent blue drink in her hand. Geneva waved but got no response. The man's huge shoulders probably took up most of Val's view. She twirled her ponytails as she took a better look at him. His age set him apart from the crowd. He had a beard, a bald head; a heavy jacket pulled up around hunched shoulders, and a rough look. In that respect, he fit in better here than she did. She looked down and noticed that her chest was glowing, her unobtrusive white T, gone disco in the black light. She pulled her brown jacket around her and held it in place with crossed arms.

Most of the party people, in black Plug-In clothes, sat on cushions strewn across the floor. Coco was in the middle of them dancing in a short gold dress to the Giovanni Hastings hit. The lead singer had an androgynous voice that dipped drum deep and then rose stringed up. Geneva listened carefully trying to discern if the music had real voices and instruments or if it was completely melded synth. As the final chorus of the song played, everyone mouthed the lyrics, while reaching for Coco's swaying Tamarind tail, "Intertwining fingers on your soul, invade your heart and make it whole, harvest Sin and Chrome and Sea. Come and intertwine with me." Along with everyone else, Geneva watched Coco twirl to the last notes of the song, spot Leo, and grab his arm. Her tail swatted Geneva's nose as she spun round. Leo sat in the center of Coco's circle. As she finished her dance, she sunk to the floor beside him. Her tail curled around his leg, her bare knees touched his, as she threw her arms around his neck.

Geneva decided to take off her wet, muddy boots before she destroyed all the silk pillows. She knelt to unlace them, wondering what she was doing here. Nothing had changed. Leo and Coco were still together, and she was out of place as usual. Val seemed to be getting along fine without her, too. She was listening with an animated expression to the tall man. Geneva had the impression—the cinnamon scent, Val's relaxed demeanor—that she'd been here a few times before. Worrying about Val was just paranoid. She shook her head and stumbled as she yanked off her boots. A hand reached down and righted her.

"Welcome, my lady." Her rescuer — a gangly Plug-In — bowed sweeping the long jacket he wore behind him. He took her hand, held it to his lips and kissed it. His thin lips warmed the back of her hand. "Always nice to meet a new lady. I'm Streker."

She blushed; glad it would be hidden in the reflected glow of her shirt. "We've met before."

Streker cocked his head at her and blinked both eyes, one blue, one brown. His face had slightly distorted features, like he'd been punched a lot. His look told her he didn't remember. She took a step back to make room, but his coat still brushed against her. He reached into it and held up a test tube filled with glowing liquid. "Some Lime for the lady?" His half smile revealed crooked eye-teeth. He tipped a silver syringe into the tube filled it and then, "Last chance before we start the festivities."

She shook her head.

He placed the tip of the needle in the corner of his eye. "Suit yourself. I'm your host, not your feeder."

She turned away to miss the injection and when she turned back, he was staring at her with glowing green eyes and grinning.

"Do you know why they call me Streker?" he said. "Because I let it all hang out. No secrets. I expose all my data to everyone. Of course, I've got nothing to lose. But it's what I do, shock people out of their little worlds within. Ask me anything. Ask me."

"So, you're a true neo-private. Well, what's your take on Giovanni Hastings?"

"My favorite story."

"No, Musica. Are they really a band?"

"No, just some local synth pretending to be imported from down the 'Way. You?"

"I think it's a band. I want it to be anyway. There's too many different sounds and it has a raw feel. Those haunting voices, I want them to belong to people. Someone I could meet."

"I know what you mean, but there's really good synth out there."

She nodded toward the older guy. "What about him? Who's he?

Streker looked sad. "Our star power, Burrows, the host of *Kill-Giovanni.*"

"Kill who?"

"Kill Giovanni Hastings. It's kind of a cult site. A parody, you know, of the book. Grugel and Eve met him on the 'Way last summer, when Eve got her quills."

Geneva clutched the ends of her coat over her glowing midriff and shivered. She loved the Giovanni Hastings story and its odd little hero, a kid with supernatural powers who conquers the world. Kill Giovanni Hastings? Who would want to do that?

C.G. Burrows watched the college kids lounging around the trailer injecting drugs into their eyes. Grugel waved a fluorescent green syringe in front of him, "Hey, why don't you give this a try. It's a party. It's New Year's Eve."

Burrows rolled his eyes. The kid was trying to pressure him, unbelievable.

"I know you're more into the meditation thing like Strek's mom. But it just gives you a different perspective. It really works." Grugel nudged him, made twin pistols with his hands and shot an arc of imaginary bullets around the room. "Don't you wonder which one of them is the source?"

Burrows didn't. Grugel gave him the name: *Leo.* But he didn't get why Leo's head was in demand. If he was going to shoot up with one of these kid's personalities, he'd pick one of the girls, Coco probably. She looked like something he'd like to get inside: shapely curves that moved well, undulating, with warm skin and hair that glowed. Her dress was simple, well-cut. Even flirtatiously short, it was classy. He'd watched her dancing earlier, they all had, a potent promise of warmth and softness. She gathered their attention and radiated it back like a power source. Sex. He got that from her. Instead of a sharp pain in his head, it came like a low throb in his loins. OK, not really. Wishful thinking. He got: *Checking me out?* He got: *Who are you?* Anyway. That chemistry, that perspective, might be fun. But, Leo, hell, he looked like one of the dimmest bulbs here. The way Leo kept smiling at him, at everyone, maybe he had no thoughts at all. He certainly wasn't giving Burrows anything. The guy hadn't given him a second thought or a first for that matter. Nothing. He'd never run across anyone who didn't strike him at all.

Meanwhile, Coco was hanging all over Leo. Another girl, who didn't have a chance, was looking at him longingly and kids were shooting him up left and right. Burrows was annoyed. He'd been hanging around these kids too long. They were starting to get to him. Their heads were textbook-laden, introspective. This party was bringing back distasteful memories. He'd been denied a chance at college by these kids' parents. Damn revolutionaries. He didn't need to fit in. He needed to relax. He had a plan, and it was coming together. He could probably relax a little, "OK, yeah. Give it to me."

Grugel waved the syringe again, "Want me to do it...?"

Burrows lifted the flap of his brown jacket to the side to reveal a holster of needles he used to perform his Vary work, including the monster, Faustus, he'd used on his own tattoo. He rolled his fingers over the cold cylinders, which responded by casting glinting light around the room, as if, in the dark glow of the R.V., they were one with the electronics. Burrows took the syringe from Grugel and squeezed the liquid into the corner of his eye before the kid could finish his sentence. "You forget, fanboy, I'm familiar with needles."

In the wake of the SLO-42, Burrows' animosity faded fast. He blinked. The green cortisol-based fluid washed over and behind his eyes. Grugel smirked knowingly and slid into the chair at the console beside Eve. Burrows wiped away a tear and stared at it on the tip of his finger. It appeared to him as three distinct aspects. There was the lime color, the rolling shape, and the dancing viscosity. Glancing up, the disorienting view rocked him. The trailer was a black and silver block. It had flashing lights and slow jerking bodies inside. His eyes couldn't settle, and he lost his balance and fell back on the floor cushions. He closed his eyes and when he looked at his fingertip again the triad of images coalesced. The tear was easily identifiable again as the sum of its three parts: green, round and fluid.

He knew roughly how the injection of Leo's neuropeptides was supposed to work as it shot back behind his eyes and coated his neocortex. But the experience was nothing like his telepathy, the cutting thoughts that came at him. Instead, the SLO-42 created a haze over his own perceptions so that everything he experienced was filtered through a foreign point of view—Leo's. Burrows sank back into the cushions. He could feel the corners of his mouth curling up into a goofy grin.

In Leo's world, the trailer was bigger. The tech was brighter. The party was stimulating, and he was at ease. He liked the people around him and they, certainly, liked him. Coco was still gorgeous, but glossier, slippery looking. The other girl he'd seen watching Leo, *Geneva, Gen, Genie,* now he got her name loud and clear—was prominent in Leo's periphery. And wasn't she cute: lithe and flexible, with glowing hair and skin. *Willowy. Earthy.* She fit into an overall feeling he had: that the world flowing around him was about to pop like a canister of confetti and fall into his hands. Burrows, affected by Leo, couldn't take his eyes off Geneva. Everything was going to be great.

"Now it begins," Grugel said. The huge monitor lit up displaying an image of a stack of logs piled high, leaning away from a video moon. It bathed the room, and the side of Grugel's angular face, from the point of his chin to the spiked peaks of his hair, in amber light. His mouth stretched wide, "Bonfire!"

Geneva did not like the way that man who'd been talking to Val earlier was looking at her now, with an unnatural smile, like she was his New Year's resolution. It figured, the creepy older guy giving her attention. She checked her watch, nearly midnight. She hoped Leo and Eve wouldn't want to stay long after.

The light flickered and the countdown started. Everyone in the room chanted, "10, 9, 8, 7, 6..."

Grugel, Eve and Streker hunched over the console. Just before midnight, the video logs burst into flame. "It's time to jump," Grugel said. Everyone screamed, "Midnight!"

But Val didn't stop. Her voice carried on. Her wail rose to a pitch. It sounded as though it was on top of them, but Val herself was far away inside the fire. Geneva stared at Val's open mouth; her lips smeared with plum gloss. That frozen feeling spread down her limbs. She couldn't believe it was happening again. It seemed that if she concentrated, she could make Val stop just by becoming more aware of her, like a lucid dream. Instead, she lunged.

Val began to twitch in a parody of the Mansion Expansion dancing, her limbs crooked her body jolting, her head down eyes up. The only difference was that it came with a tight sporadic flailing that could not be consciously imitated. Her ankles twisted out from under her. She began to fold and fall. Streker caught her waist in the crook of his arm and lowered her. Geneva was at Val's side, cradling her head before it touched the floor. Val wasn't breathing.

She pointed at the nearest spectator, Grugel, "You get help. Call an ambulance."

She tilted Val's head back, opened her jaw and swept a finger along the back of her throat. She breathed into Val's mouth and watched her chest lift. Ripping open the front of Val's shirt, exposing her white chest and black bra, she placed her hands atop each other in the hollow between Val's ribs. With her elbows locked, she pressed hard and fast. Val's chest flexed under her hands: thunk, thunk, thunk. She breathed for Val again. When she looked up, Coco knelt beside her ready to help.

Geneva let her take over the compressions. Sweat beaded on her forehead as they worked on Val in rhythm. Finally, Val's chest shook and rose on its own. Geneva turned Val's head to the side. Coco rolled her over. Val spluttered, coughed, and vomited onto a silk cushion. Caught between the sweetness of Coco's floral perfume and the stench of Val's upturned stomach, Geneva gagged.

"Where are the medics? Where's the ambulance? Shouldn't it be here?" She pointed at Grugel again. He was still standing in the same place. "You called them, right?"

He shrugged. "We can't have any greenies out here."

"But we need to get her to a hospital."

Around the room, people were either staring at Val or at the floor nearby. Leo was beside her, eyes downcast. Only the older guy looked directly at her, smirking like he was watching a show. "Fine." she reached down and pulled Val up by her armpits. Coco helped her hold Val there. No one else moved.

"We need to get her to a hospital," she said looking at Eve. Eve shrugged. Streker came forward and placed his long jacket around Val's shoulders but stepped back at a grunt from Grugel. Grugel, Streker and Eve began to argue as she and Coco carried Val out of the trailer. Through the dim blue lights and the falling snow, she could see the black car in front of her, the keys in the ignition. If no one would help her, she'd help herself. Passing Val to Coco, she waved Coco away from the Mercedes' flame bumper emblems. She didn't know how far out the flames would shoot or for how long. She took off her brown jacket, wrapped it around her arm, turned her head aside and reached for the door.

Leo gripped her forearm just before she touched the handle. "No. It's OK. Eve will drive."

"It's not OK!" Geneva yelled. She didn't turn until she heard the Cadillac start and saw Eve at the wheel.

Leo, Coco, Geneva, and Eve squeezed into the front seat laying Val across their laps. Geneva held her friend's head in her hands and stroked her soft dark hair. "What happened to her?"

"It might have been the Lime." Eve said.

"The drug. What is it?"

"You've heard of SLO-42, right? That's Lime." Leo said. He was looking away out the window, watching the snowfall, avoiding her gaze.

She frowned. She had learned about SLO-42 in class. Psychotherapists had developed the drug before the revolution in response to growing public apathy. The chemical was manufactured from a person's neurotransmitters. It gave the user a peek inside someone else's head, a truly different perspective. It was hard to make and had little street value, unless it came from someone people really wanted to experience. Its popularity had peaked when the mind of a serial killer had made the rounds. Then it had been outlawed. A bad reaction to the drug meant a bad source, like that creepy guy Val had been talking to. "That guy."

"No, me." Leo said.

"You?" Was he some kind of monster? She leaned into Coco and stared at the falling snow. The Cadillac headed uphill towards the university. "Why aren't we going to Bayside?"

"She won't want to go there," Eve said. "We'll just get her back to the Mansion."

Geneva lunged across Leo and grabbed at the steering wheel. "What's wrong with you? Take her to the hospital."

Val's eyes opened wide. Her lips parted. "No."

Eve sneered and pushed Geneva's arm away. "See."

"But she needs help." Val's eyes, were wide, scared.

The Cadillac stayed on course. As they approached campus, lights flashed through dark plumes of smoke obscuring the snowfall. Fire trucks blocked their view of the Mansion. Eve lowered the window as a police officer approached with his hand out. "Stop here."

Cold smoke stung Geneva's eyes.

"What happened?" Leo asked.

The officer made a quick backhanded gesture, "An incident. Fire. Some students at a party. We haven't really had time to investigate." He placed a hand on the window, leaned into the car. "What's wrong with the girl?" he turned over his shoulder, shouted, "Medic."

Leo, Coco, and Eve turned away from the Mansion. In the flashing lights surrounding it were fire trucks and ambulances. Medics eased Val out of the car. Coco, Leo and Eve stumbled out together and held each other in a tight knot. Geneva stood outside beside Val as the medics loaded her onto a stretcher. But the New West officer in his green uniform held her back, his fingers digging into her arms, as they closed her into an ambulance. "You can't go with her."

As the ambulances sped down the hill, he released her behind the plastic tape barrier. She stood beside Coco, Leo and Eve and watched the dorm burn as the snow fell. With the added height of the columns of flames, the one-story building looked like a true mansion. The heat radiated over her face and torso. It was a while before she felt the pain in her feet. Her toes were white on white, as she stood barefoot in the snow. In her hurry to help Val, she'd forgotten her boots.

~ 13 ~

NEW YEAR'S DAY

"I disagree with those who see C.G. Burrows as a sociopath with unfathomable motives. In fact, I count him among the Dawning Psychics. It is easy to understand his animosity, his hatred, for our children. He had been like them, with all their potential. Yet, they had everything he had wanted, while he had been cast aside. To him, it was justice, seeing them grow up and also become worthless." — *Save Giovanni: The Lost Men of the Psychic Wars*, S. Sherring

Burrows woke up on New Year's Day in a companionable drug-happy haze. Streker drooled and Grugel twitched, sprawled on the floor nearby. As the SLO-42 wore off, the trailer darkened. Burrows' hangover started as soon as he moved. Grimacing, he struggled to lift himself out of the sunken chair. He felt pieced together, slow. When he was high last night, that girl, Gen, had glowed. She'd leapt with feral speed to the thrashing girl's side. She'd pounded on the girl's chest like she was fighting for her own survival. Soon, he vowed, she would be.

That slight girl was a powder keg. He'd seen through the bramble grown wild over her explosive potential. He rubbed the side of his aching jaw. He'd been stupid, thinking Coco was the one about to pop, thinking she was the golden girl of his dreams. Blame it on having lived too long away from women on the 'Way. Being lead around by your dick felt nice until you saw where you were headed. He'd forgotten.

Streker interrupted. Shot at him: *You don't even care about her.*

The kid meant his mother. He'd become obsessive on the topic. Burrows stared at him until the kid blinked and looked away. It took a fraction longer than he liked. Last night, in the chaos, he'd gotten a similar bit off Leo. While Coco and Gen were on their knees lifesaving, Leo had thought: *Mom.* That was the guy everyone lusted after, just another mother obsessed man-child. New West: creating a nation of pansies. "Who was she?"

Streker: *Val.* He groaned. "Oh god, what happened? That was so wrong. What did we do?"

Burrows looked around at the glinting electronics. This set up had served its purpose. "I think you overloaded her, kid. Maybe we should find out if she's a total vegetable. Where do you think she'd be?"

"The hospital, Bayside," Streker said.

Grugel sat up, combed his fingers through his hair so it spiked again. "Nah, Eve said she'd make sure they didn't take her there," he said. "We're cool. They'll be on campus."

"Nice job, Greg Lionel. We still need to get this out of here. Drive this bucket back out on the Way. Streker, come. We'll go find the rest of them, don't want them saying the wrong thing."

Grugel: *Man, you're tweaking.* "Relax, they're cool. Even Coco. It's her rebellious phase."

"Yeah?" Burrows asked. "Even ponytails? She looked a little upset."

Grugel: *Ugh, just chill.* He shrugged. "She's Val's friend."

"No worries, Val and Gen go way back," Streker said.

"Really? That's not selling me. I think you've got a problem." Burrows said.

Streker: *You got us into this.* "They're like sisters. Seriously, Val came to live with Gen after her parents were killed, in a fire or something."

On dawning New Year's Day, that was all Burrows needed to make the connection that had been just out of his grasp. He grabbed his jacket and stumbled out of the trailer towards his car. He wrapped his arms over his throbbing head shielding his eyes from the light. In the new day's light, he remembered his history: Gen was the golden destiny girl he'd seen in the forest wearing Kendra LeMay's perceptions. Val was the waif he hadn't bothered to chase down after he'd killed her parents Vic and Perla Freeman. He still knew their names. They haunted him. That he'd seen the girls together last night, just as they were expanding the limits of Sync Chrome City, smacked of synchronicity, an incident that screamed, "Pay attention!"

He'd talked to the girl, Val, last night for a while and her brooding had seemed more genuine than these other kids' angst. He'd gotten pangs of skepticism: *So, what are you doing here, old man? Slathering after Coco? What's the point of KillGiovanni?* He could see it now for what it was: the inheritance of a childhood in mourning. She wanted a revolution. She wasn't just a Sync Chrome groupie. She was a believer.

The trailer door banged as Streker emerged. He was, as usual, wearing a too tight sweater, that made him look even reedier with his trademark black pants and trench. Burrows started Mistress M.D. and sat inside as the kid scraped frost off the windshield. He didn't like his connection to the girls, the feeling of unfinished business. But it was the perfect start to the New Year. No one in New West needed horn-blowing festivities. They needed to smack up against the terror that came when your mind expanded. They needed to cower under the weight of their own capacity. If they manifested psychic abilities, it would mean a complete loss of autonomy and privacy. It would be a pandemic of mental anguish and pain, which maybe New Westians deserved, but the people on the Freeway did not. SLO-42 had given him a taste in Leo of New West's perky hope. The morning after the inside of his mouth tasted of rotten orange. Hope was a downer, a hangover. Disgusting.

He lowered the window, "Get in. Good enough."

Mistress M.D. slid across the slick of frost-covered mud as they left the trailer park. Burrows gripped the wheel. "Hey, you got any more Lime on you?" he asked.

Streker shook his head: *I'm not your dealer. It's Leo's Lime.*

When they reached the road, Burrows pressed his foot to the floor.

They smelled the smoke long before they saw the black clouds over New West University, which dissipated to a gray haze across the bay.

"Not the Mansion," Streker pleaded, as if he couldn't see the sodden ashes in front of them and the green fire trucks spouting arcs of water on the ruins.

If he'd been alone, Burrows would have skipped up the walkway. It had worked. Crashing Sync Chrome City had caused this damage, no doubt. He could see the kid wasn't making the connection. His eyes were unfocused underneath welling tears. If the kid knew he'd caused this, it would crush him.

“Not the Mansion,” Streker sobbed.

Ah, innocence. You learned that it didn't matter if the people around you were ready or not. If you saw danger you acted, even alone. You moved with a single mind until disrupting lives, counting casualties, and killing dangerous people became incidental.

A man yelled, "Psi!" Burrows looked his way and saw the crowd of protesters. Flakes of ash floated through the air above them. The scene was pleasantly apocalyptic. Burrows rocked on his heels and a chill crossed his gums, as his lips parted wide.

"Is that Psi-Aware?" Streker said. "Mom?"

The kid took off running past the Mansion to people. He darted around them like a dog after gulls. Burrows followed, his hands in front of him pointing the way. The kid finished a lap around the crowd and came to a standstill beside Burrows winded and dazed.

"Lydia ain't here, kid. Too embarrassed, probably. It looks like the group is finally taking their crusade to the next level."

"Yeah," Streker sighed: *Now will you leave mom alone?*

Burrows reached forward, palmed the kid's head in one hand and squeezed. These kids kept thinking harder. He tousled Streker's hair to disguise his anger as he pulled away. Sure, kid, sure.

Desperate as Streker was for a father, he'd strained things with the kid when he'd moved into Lydia's bedroom. Fine, he was about done with her. He'd gotten what he'd wanted. The loonies were hell-bent on pushing their "teach us to be psychic" agenda and looking damn silly doing it. They couldn't see the real deal, psychic potential crackling around them well-disguised as it was, hidden in unlikely vessels. Speaking of loopy kids, "Is that Leo?"

"Hey, have you guys seen Gen?" Leo asked looking around. "She was right behind us and then she was gone." He touched his forehead, stared down at the bricks. "She probably went to Val. I think they took her to Linden."

Leo looked up, gestured toward the Mansion. "Ah, Streker, man," Leo put his arm, encased in puffy parka, around the kid's shoulders. "I have to tell you..."

"Wait. She'll be at the bus station then. Streker, go after her."

"Me?" Streker asked, rocking on his heels pivoting towards Leo. "Shouldn't you?"

Leo shrugged. "Nah, she's got to be sour on me, Da Lime, me."

"It wasn't your..."

"Guys," Burrows said. "We're in a hurry here."

He had just one last task for the boy. He pulled Streker aside. "Go, now. That girl shouldn't be alone. Follow her. Stop her in Deming."

Streker stared at him with those long dopey eyes.

"Just take her to see your mom."

The kid started down the hill glanced back and then broke into a run. His feet were practically spinning at the bottom of his black trench coat. His long legs must really be churning. Good boy. Go fetch.

"Good," he said. "So everyone here all right?"

Leo shook his head, no. He got: *Seven guys.*

Burrows reeled from the hit. He fired back, "Where's your stash?"

Leo: *Friend-Me.*

"You got any on you?"

Leo: *Damn.* "Just the last of the latest batch." He opened up his jacket and there were four syringes. He handed three of them over. *You take the fall.*

Instead of backhanding Leo, Burrows took the syringe and shot it into the corner of his eye. He barely felt it when Leo punched him with: *What are you doing shooting up in front of all these people?*

He was starting to feel good and happy. Now all he needed was a nice pair of dead girls. In the distance, Burrows saw the top of the Friend-Me corporation pyramid, a green triangle, rising out of the haze. In Leo's perception, it beaconed to him like a Shangri-la invoking feelings of loyalty and responsibility. He looked at it and saw his destiny, but it also provoked rebellion. He heard music in the background of Leo's thoughts. He wanted to pursue his own course. So, this was what it was like if you were supposed to take over your family business.

He could not stop thinking about Geneva. Last night seemed to have capped it, turning his attention from Coco to Geneva. Burrows wasn't sure how much of this was Leo's perception and how much of it was his own, the feeling he'd woken up with this morning that she was the key, the place to focus his energy. He understood the different psychic potentials. Geneva and Leo were senders, broadcasting their thoughts: the girl powerfully, constantly, unfocused and Leo only as a DJ unconsciously but controlled. The other girl, Val, was a receiver, taking it all in. She got everything. More than her mind could handle.

Burrows got the location of New West Mental Health by asking probing questions at Bayside Hospital. On his way to Linden, driving Mistress M.D., and riding Leo's happy thoughts, he obsessed about Geneva as he watched the New West landscape, the brown, soaked, snow-spotted fallow fields of winter, pass. He imagined the red-ponytailed girl in the middle of the empty fields and along the roadside and was content. He was headed in the right direction here in New West seeking out the girl. But underneath all the good feeling, his latent cynicism nagged. The drug wouldn't last, and he feared the betrayal of this hope would cause a return of his murderous rage. The towns seemed barren and lonely, and he sped through them to the clinic wanting to be with people on New Year's Day.

Inside New West Mental Health, a shoddy, ill-equipped building that looked no more like a hospital than his Vary shop on the 'Way had looked like a doctor's office, Burrows heard screaming. There was no one at the front desk and no one prevented him from going back. He could distinguish voices in the screams: men shouting and groaning and one distinct female yell. He passed the lab filled with stretchers and movement and went back to a smaller room where there were bars over the windows. The screaming began to oscillate. They were moving the girl about, perhaps putting their hands to her mouth. He looked in the room and saw the dark-haired waif. They had the girl bound hands and feet and were stuffing a cloth over and into her mouth. Two scrubs were doing the dirty work while a distraught woman in a longer lab coat stood nearby.

"Excuse me," Burrows said. "I think I can help."

He felt how the doctor was relieved at the interruption and knew he had an in, this would be easier than he'd thought, maybe even less violent. Interning a few random students who'd been spending too much time online hadn't bothered her, but the implications of the sudden collapse of so many young minds on New Year's had frightened her. What they were doing now—from her he got: *imprisoning* and *suppressing a generation*—crossed some line she'd set for herself. Well, he could use that.

The SLO-42 helped him make a nice impression, the way it had made Valerie's parents, The Freemans, like him. He was relaxed and easy going, with an air of natural authority.

He was Leo when he asked for the girl. "The danger has passed. She's OK. Let her go. C'mon, let me take her home."

The medics relaxed their grip on the girl. Valerie stopped struggling. Everyone saw the value of diplomacy. If nothing else, it was a chance to catch their breath. They turned to the doctor, awaiting her response.

"She's a danger to herself."

"Danger? Or something you don't understand? Maybe she's handling this just fine. Why don't you ask her what she wants?"

The girl was not stupid. He saw shrewdness in her eyes. She clearly understood the trap. He'd now opened up an option to her, but she was still limited to two: stay here at the clinic or go with him. He felt the doctor and Valerie sussing him out and it was a pretty good try from both of them. The doctor even knew what she was doing. He felt a searing press of hot needles, but he met her with a blank wall. The girl's attempt was ineffectual. His mind was closed to her. He was a receiver like her, a one-way street. He gave them nothing.

"I want out of here. I want to go with him," Val said. "There's nothing wrong with the way I think."

Burrows got a more conceited version: *Can't hold me here. I'm the future.*

The doctor looked down. She pressed her hands together. Then she took off her lab coat, and he saw her breasts in a soft-looking warm-colored sweater, her hips rounded and wide even in black pants and a copper necklace, an infinity symbol, drawing his attention back to her breasts. She folded the lab coat and draped it over her arm. She looked apologetically at the medics.

"I can't do this anymore. I can't be a part of this approach," she said, and then turned to Valerie. "As far as I'm concerned, you may go."

Burrows caught a last stab of fear from the woman: *Careful.* The SLO-42 was fading and the thought stung. He pulled the girl to her feet and shoved her ahead of him down the hall.

As they left, he heard the doctor tell the medics, "There has to be a better way. We need a decision."

As he touched Valerie's shoulders, Burrows was aware how close he was to his own conclusion. He held half of the psychic threat in his hands.

"You are the future," he said, and he felt the words relax her. She thought he understood. She didn't know it was the future he feared.

Outside, Mistress M.D. was waiting for them, and Burrows was sad to see the car looked like it had seen better days. The gleam had worn off her. Bits of evergreen littered her hood. She could use another coat of polish.

"Where's Sync Chrome City?" the girl asked, as if the transportation he'd brought her wasn't good enough.

"I put it in the trunk," he said, not a bad idea, actually. It'd be a great place to hide the tech.

He disarmed the car and popped the trunk and the girl went there and stood beside it as though she was really expecting to plug back in right now outside the clinic. *Junkie*, he thought, and wished just once someone would get him.

"I've gotta get back in. What was happening was incredible. What we're going to be capable of, they don't even know," she said.

"I know," Burrows said, and he shot her a look. He saw her and her friends their minds unleashed streaming everywhere like an EMP.

From her, he got a sudden awareness: *You don't want.* She was a sharp kid.

"Pain," he said. "Like razors. I feel it coming and I just want to be alone."

As he said it, he felt the SLO slipping away making it true. How alone he wanted to be: alone. He'd get the other girl, finish this business off, get out of New West and then maybe go south down the 'Way. He turned to the girl and saw the fear in her eyes, and the fight, but he wasn't afraid of her anymore. He had come so far, and he was so close to the end.

~ 14 ~

STREKER

"It is important to place these historic events in a cultural context. Understand that people at that time had rudimentary ideas of what it meant to be psychic and they were each bound to a Single Ego. They had no knowledge of connectivity. The idea was foreign and terrifying. They valued independence and autonomy. They feared the loss of privacy. Some called telepathy invasive others went so far as to use the loaded term "mind rape." The older generation didn't want the youth to gain abilities they could not. People thought the older brain was brittle and weak. It was a radically different time." — *Becoming Psychic 101, A History and a Primer*

Rumor had it that seven of the guys had been critically injured in the fire. No one mentioned Valerie. Leo, Coco, and Eve spent the night huddled in Geneva's room at Inu Wood. Coco could have gone to her father, but she said, no, he was busy and she would stay with her friends. They felt safer in each other's company. In the morning, a resident adviser knocked on the door. He was going around to all the rooms. He told them winter quarter classes would start the next day as usual. The university was holding a meeting to discuss the tragedy and would provide temporary housing for residents of the Mansion. They began walking up the hill to the Big Top.

Eve and Leo flanked Coco. Eve held her hand. Leo sheltered her, his arm around her shoulders, "It'll be OK. It'll be OK." Geneva trailed them. Acrid smoke hung low in the heart of campus. Some students were standing, watching the fire trucks stream water onto the hull of the dorm. Leo, Coco, and Eve squeezed together and entered the Big Top murmuring, heads down. They didn't look back when Geneva stopped at the door. She stiffened. Other students corralled into the Big Top after them, quiet and still. She glared, feeling like she could pierce them. It sickened her to see them simply doing what was expected when their friends needed them. She was jealous, too. They fawned over Coco while she was so alone without Val.

She turned her back on them. There was movement beyond the Madrona grove. She cut through the trees toward a distant hissing. She heard someone yell, "Psi!" as she walked in front of the New Year's Day protest. There were so many Psi-Aware protesters, she couldn't see the steps of the administration building or the bricks of the walkway leading up to it. The hiss-yelling grew louder as the people chanted, "Psi, psi, psi!" Clouds of white breath puffed into the sepia haze. They were bundled in coats and hats and scarves and coated in a fine layer of gray ash from the Mansion. Only a band of their faces showed: red cheeks and dark eyes. They stopped speaking. As one, they stared at her.

She stared back, stood her ground for a moment, her eyes darting from face to face to face before she turned and ran. Water rushed over the charred remains of the Mansion. Pain pricked across her cheeks, the sudden return of sensation after a chill. It wasn't fair to be angry: with Leo, Coco, Eve. The university would tell them to go to class. If they didn't know what else to do, they would go. It was just that she couldn't, this time, continue to do as she was told. The medics had taken Val to New West Mental again. Probably the guys were there, too. She went to the Shadow Bus station and bought a ticket for the next departure. Outside the terminal, she pulled her scarf tight around her neck as she shivered beside the black buses, black screens over the windows for privacy, looking for the one that would take her to Linden.

The bus was half full. Riders cloaked in privacy webs sat in back. She took a seat, reached up, and pulled the black fabric down in front of her face and all around her. Inside the enveloping darkness, she couldn't get a full breath. Her chest heaved halfway up and stuck. She cycled through her fears: that Val and the guys would die, that her new friends were also in danger, that she would never be safe again. Shut away behind the web, she saw the protesters' eyes. She felt them on her skin. She yanked the web up and released it so that it shot back into place on the roof. Inhaling deep breaths, she moved to the front of the bus. She had to get to Linden.

Finally, a woman in uniform approached. Geneva gawked as the bus driver boarded. The woman looked like an over-sized character in a children's book: glossy and bright. Her hips spanned the seat as she settled into it and hunched over the huge wheel. As the bus lurched forward, Geneva glanced out the window. A lanky figure loped after the bus. "Hey wait. That guy."

She caught her seat as the bus jerked to a halt and Streker stepped on.

The driver looked back at her and winked one huge blue eye. Lashes like shredded black butterfly wing dropped over it. "Ha! No problem. I don't suppose anyone here is in too much of a hurking rush to get to Linden." The driver winked again. Her yellow ringlets bounced.

Geneva raised her hand as Streker went by. He reached out, caught it and kissed the top of it, swaying deftly as the bus pulled away from the station. "A pleasant surprise, the lovely lady. May I?" He sat down beside her, his legs splayed, his knee touching hers.

"I never wear a web," he said, looking around at the shrouded shapes at the back of the bus. "But it's nice that there's someone here I actually want to talk to."

"Are you going all the way to Linden?" she asked.

He grimaced and shook his head. "No. Home. Deming. Just out-side."

"Deming's home? You seem more city."

He shrugged. "Nope, home is where my mom is, that's Deming. I thought I'd better get away for a while."

"Last night wasn't your fault," she said. "And I'm not angry at you guys. I know I was just projecting. A similar thing happened to Val last spring, and I just stood there. I didn't do anything. I felt so stupid. Not that you guys were stupid. I just remember what that's like. You are so shocked you can't move. Totally understandable. I just couldn't do that again. I had to act."

He looked away. "Yeah, well, the people at your party are your responsibility. But it's not only that, I'm worried about mom."

"Why? No. That's OK. I respect your privacy. Hey, wait though, Neo-Private. Isn't spilling your thing? You put it all out there."

He held up his hands with his wrists clenched together and shook them at her. "You caught me. Cuff me."

She crossed her arms. "So, what's with your mom?"

"Well, she's been having migraines and she's a member of this group, Psi-Aware. You heard of it?" His eyes flicked back and forth between her face and his knee.

"Yeah, they're always on campus. Today, there were many," she shrugged. "I don't really get them. They think they have ESP or something. Not sure what's to argue about. Does your mom? Have ESP, I mean"

He looked away again. "Uh, no. Not a bit actually. There's no way. There's so many things I've hid from her. But that's the point. That's what the Psi-Aware people are pissed about. My mom and her geek friends don't think they are psychic. They think that they *could* be. Should be, but the government's keeping it from them. Nobody teaches psi. If we started at a young age, we'd all know how to read each other's minds as easy as English."

He fixed his gaze on her. His blue eye was very light, the brown eye almost hazel. "Yeah, they're convinced that it'd be really easy. We all just need to learn how."

"What? You mean like a class at New West? Becoming Psychic 101?" She started to laugh, but stopped short when Streker said, "Exactly. But the government won't do it. So, it's a conspiracy."

She held a hand over her mouth to hide her residual smile. It took her a while to sound serious. "Oh, but what do you think? I'm sorry. Do you think we could be? Psychic?"

He shrugged. "Could be, but, honestly, it's not my thing. I don't care. I don't want to look into other people's heads and nobody has to look into mine. As a neo-private, I run around naked. So, what's the point? I'll tell anyone whatever it is they want to know. What you give away can't be taken."

She tugged her jacket around her and turned away to look out the window. "Sounds scary." She could still see the red tops of some of the New West buildings surrounded by evergreens and the triangular green tip of the new Friend-Me building. It was the beginning of the quarter, and she was leaving campus. She still hadn't scheduled a retake of her test from last year because she still hadn't had a chance to study. It was twisted logic, but she couldn't help think how in some ways Val was the lucky one, again. She didn't have to worry about tests, homework, a job, or grades. She didn't have a choice, so she didn't have to choose. Her problems took that away, reducing her options to one clear path—clear to Geneva anyway. Val had to get help. Geneva still had to make decisions though, and maybe she was making the wrong one right now, leaving campus. What she was going to do when she got to Linden, anyway? She wanted to be there, but what good was that? She pushed the doubt aside, having made the decision. She had to be there, had to. Maybe it wouldn't make a difference, she didn't know, but this time she had to be by her friend's side.

"Hey, wait." She turned to Streker. "Are you sidetracking me? Conspiracy theories, psychics, it's interesting, but what's it got to do with your mom?"

He cringed, his shoulders hunched, and he made the "cuff me" gesture again. "That guy from the party last night. He didn't have a place to stay when he got here this summer, so he stayed at my house."

"The creepy guy?" she asked.

"You think so?"

"Well, yeah. He's mammoth and older and he's not a student, right? So, why's he here? And last night, he was giving me weird looks." She crossed her arms over her chest again. "Maybe it was just the Lime. Was it really Leo's?"

"Yeah. But Leo's a good guy. I don't think that caused Val to flip." Streker looked at his hands and seemed to fold around himself. His gangly body took up even less room. "I don't know. I didn't really have a problem with the guy until he started sleeping with my mom. Not Leo. The creep guy, Burrows. I didn't mind so much at first. She seemed happy. But he was using her, trying to get close to her Psi-Aware friends, I guess. Except now he doesn't seem into them, either. My mom's headaches are getting worse. And it's bad timing. She and her Psi-Aware friends think something is going down."

Streker's shoulder brushed hers. "But you said they aren't psychic."

"No, but they are so well-connected and whack. It's almost the same thing." He leaned on her shoulder and sighed. "You know, I'm comforted with you here after last night. You seem solid. I just don't know many good people like that."

Solid. She wanted to believe him, but she felt so unsteady. She was on a bus instead of in class. She'd altered course and inside she felt like she was down on the floor with Val in spasms, screaming. At least it didn't show.

"Yeah, I'm glad you're here, too. I've just felt so alone. Since, last year."

"You should come meet my mom," he said.

It sounded so sweet. She thought about her mom taking care of everything when Val first came to live with them. Baking pies. Outside, the land had flattened, and patches of farmland began to appear between clusters of evergreens. The bus rumbled by. Streker took her hand from her lap and stroked it. When she didn't pull away, he put his head on her shoulder and lay there with easy affection like an animal. She smoothed his dark hair across his forehead and stroked his chest through his green sweater, fuzzy and coarse, like moss.

"I like this." she said, plucking at it.

"If you stopped by my place, you'd get to Linden even faster. I could drive you. I have a permit."

"Yeah, so why aren't you driving now?"

"A friend asked if he could borrow my wheels last night and I said sure. He'll have it at my house soon."

"You gave him your permit?" This was the most unbelievable thing Streker had said, and she was sure it was a lie. It was hard enough to believe he had a permit. Cars weren't allowed to travel outside city limits without one and the government didn't issue many because people were supposed to use the buses and trains. That's why the buses were mostly painted surplus black. No one would pay to put advertisements on them anymore because few people saw them pass by, no traffic. If Streker actually had a permit—doubtful—it wasn't the kind of thing you let someone borrow. It'd be foolish to trust anyone that much. The price of a permit would pay her student loans. But maybe he was a better person than she was, less cynical. "And you're sure, he'll have the car back? No, I don't think I can stop."

"Too bad. I'd like to find out how you do it."

"Do what?"

"Be you. Be so together."

Suddenly, she was tired of holding it together while the people around her freaked. If college had made one thing obvious, it was that her dad had been right. The world was in stasis. She looked out the window and the view confirmed it. The scene was the same as ever: a long gray road banked by fallow farmland, with a gas station and the pointed tops of houses appearing as they approached the town. All the significant events and inventions had gone before. Gen Utopia had only toys: AeroFlux Butterflies, Sound-Wield Sets, Friend-Me Journals, nothing that would make a difference. Maybe that's why people didn't like the Giovanni Hastings story—jealousy. None of them would experience a transformation like that. It was a lie, a tease. Nothing would change for herself and her friends. Where she was resolutely headed, out of college and into the working world of New West, they would all wind up. It had been handed to them. Geneva had been planning her life carefully day by day, but just to fill it. The foundation of her life was as arbitrary as her economic theory classes as made up as mathematics and flowing along in history like everyone else's. This point in time ebbed.

As thc bus drove through Deming past a coffee shop, bakery, diner and bar, Geneva felt anything but together. As long as she was being pushed apart, would it hurt to take the next step voluntarily? She was a child of her generation. There was no use resisting. When the bus stopped in sunny Deming, Geneva placed her hand in Streker's and stepped off. She didn't like those Psi-Aware eyes on her, accusing her. Of what? Maybe Streker's mom could tell her.

~ 15 ~

CRÉME-FILLED

"In elementary school, you learned the tenets of extrasensory perception. You were trained primarily as a Sender, to push your thoughts out to others, or as a Receiver, to catch those thoughts. You identified your psychic learning style, learned meditative techniques and sent your first tendrils, wires or waves (however it fit you best to visualize it) out to touch the Lattice. Now that you are sure in your individual identity and have learned emotional control, you will attain the next level of psychic skill. You will enter the external net and join us on the Lattice. Let your teachers guide you." — *Becoming Psychic 101, A History and a Primer*

Stepping off the bus in Deming with Streker felt like skipping class. Geneva was happy, excited, and instantly guilty.

"Not in such a hurkin' rush to get to Linden at all. No one ever is," the wonderland driver said as the doors wheezed shut.

"Cool." Streker said, releasing Geneva's hand as she stepped to the ground. "You really will like my Mom."

He bobbed as they strode through the town's main strip. He stopped in front of the bakery, Lydia's, and pointed at a tray of doughnuts puffed so full of cashew cream it spilled out and pooled on the waxed paper sheets. A bell rang as he pulled her inside the shop and inclined his head at a pink-aproned, pink-cheeked shop clerk who emerged from the backroom. He extracted a doughnut from the case and presented it to Geneva on a square of waxy paper. Even so, the doughnut's sticky sides slipped around and smeared her fingers as soon as she took hold.

"I can't eat this. It's like the size of my head," Geneva said. "And shouldn't you pay for it?"

"Nah," Streker shook his head, taking a bite. Globs of cream slopped onto the linoleum. She went for napkins to sop it up as Streker stood rocking back and forth on his heels, his face stretched blissfully smooth. "Yeah, that's the stuff." He turned to the clerk in between bites. "Is Mom here?"

"Upstairs," the clerk said, swiping her hands back and forth over her apron and releasing clouds of flour. "She started the cinnamon rolls this morning and went up for a bit. Headaches again. Go ahead, step through the back."

At the mention of headaches, Streker stilled. Then he resumed his languid swaying. Geneva inhaled the shop's yeast and maple sugar scent. She wouldn't have imagined Streker could look so content outside of the electronic lined RV. "This where your mom lives?"

Streker nodded and gestured back at the writing in reverse across the shop window, "Lydia's." Then he pointed up. He took Geneva's doughnut-free hand and pulled her back behind the counter. Enormous steel ovens warmed the bakery. Mounds of dough rose in belly-sized bowls under towels. Frosting udders lay supine on silver countertops.

"This way," he said pointing to a door at the end of a hallway lined with bags of flour. He paused and turned to a shelf filled with bottles of colored sugar crystals. He plucked one, opened the top and grabbed Geneva's wrist. He tilted her hand back, so the doughnut lay flat and shook the bottle over it. Pink sprinkles scattered over its wet sugar surface and began to melt. "There, that's better. Come on, you gotta try it."

“Yeah, that’s what it needed, more sugar,” Geneva said.

He pulled her down the hall and up a narrow staircase while she buried her face in the sugar dough. Cream squeezed away from her mouth. Blobs of it fell onto the stairs and rolled in the dust. She started bouncing up the stairs after Streker in a shared sugar high. It reminded her of how she and Valerie used to act coming up the hill to campus from Tim’s chocolate shop. The memory scalded her with guilt. Val had probably woken up this morning scared and alone at the clinic. Geneva should be with her now. Across the door at the top of the stairs, gold letters spelled Streker. Before she could help Val, she needed to know if there were answers behind it. Did the Psi-Aware advocates know what was happening to the New West students, and why?

Layers of cinnamon smoke swirled as Streker pushed the door open. Geneva blinked while her eyes adjusted to the bluish light. Stacks of books filled the room piled on end tables, climbing up corners. Titles like *The Lusty Rogue* and *The Courtesan and the Pirates* ran across the paperbacks in metallic scripts. Block letters covered hardbacks with combinations of the words: universe, quantum, hologram, and consciousness. A few trails of shaggy brown carpet wound around the books. Geneva looked for cats but didn't see any and the cinnamon smell inside reminded her of Val. Sugar fueled a rush of anxiety. The woman, she was about to meet — no mere crazy cat lady — was a Psi-Aware member. Geneva noticed her hands were suddenly empty. She'd inhaled the rest of the doughnut and dropped the square of paper on the stairs.

"She's probably in her meditation room," Streker said.

"Val?" said Geneva, distracted.

Streker shook his hair back from his face and behind his shoulders. It was almost as long as her own. "No. My mom. That's what she does when she has migraines, meditates."

He led her down a carpeted furrow to a small room in the back of the apartment. In the middle of a worn tatami mat, a flour-dusted woman lay on the floor with her legs and arms spread wide as if she were in the middle of making snow angels. Her eyes were closed and, asleep, she buzzed and whistled exhaled breaths.

Streker sighed kneeling. He patted her shoulder. "Jeez, Mom."

The woman opened pale green eyes. "You're not the Buddha," she said staring up at Streker. "I fell asleep again, didn't I? I'm terrible at this." She winced and closed her eyes again. “My head still hurts."

Streker put his hands to her temples and began making small circles there with his fingertips. "You really should just take some aspirin."

The woman grunted. "Don’t you start. I've told you drugs cloud the mind."

"Aspirin? Besides, it's not working. You aren't getting psychic."

"Uh, uh. Don't waste your time scolding today. This is no time to doubt."

As mother and son fired sentences at each other, Geneva looked around. The room was mostly bare except for a low table with four cones of incense smoking on a saucer and a satisfied jade Buddha settled in one corner. Above the Buddha were five framed certificates. They said; Lydia Streker, visionary leader, Noetic Sciences Institute; Lydia Streker, president Psi-Aware, Deming chapter; Lydia Streker, baking certificate, Lakeview Community College; and Lydia Streker, doctorate in physics, Massachusetts Institute for Technology. The final certificate was a cross-stitch sampler. It read, "There is only one time to awaken. That time is now. — Buddha."

"So, how's your sex life?" Lydia asked.

Geneva snapped around. She flushed before realizing the question hadn't been directed at her.

Streker's face and neck reddened.

The woman was still lying down feet pointed away from the door. "I'm your mother. I have to ask."

Geneva wondered if Streker had to answer. He'd seemed adamant about his Neo-Private philosophy. Maybe this is where he drew the line.

"It's, um, different and, um, kind of on hold," Streker reached down and tapped his mother's shoulder. "Can I introduce you to my friend now?"

The woman opened her eyes. They rolled back in her head as she looked at Geneva. She flopped over on her mat. "Oh, Streker, is this...? " The woman pressed herself up, her ash-colored hair a nimbus of frizz. Across her bosom and pouched belly, her T-shirt read "Deming Fest: Dem Right!" She certainly didn't look psychic. Although, sitting cross-legged on the floor she had a distinctly eight-shaped figure that reminded Geneva of Dr. Montgrave's infinity symbol necklace. Lydia stood, lifting from buoyant hips. "Oh, Push-Me! I mean, Geneva. What a nice surprise!" Upright, she grew animated. She pressed her hands together and dipped her head. "Namaste! How nice! How nice!"

She reached out, brushed the side of Geneva's face and held out sugary fingertips. "I see you've been to my bakery. I'm Streker's Mom. You can call me Lydia. Right then. We'll go back down and finish the rolls up quick, quick, quick. My Psi-Aware chapter will be here any minute. This is so exciting."

She bustled out of the room singing, "You want to know what I know."

Streker smiled and shrugged. "That's my mom. Just go with it."

They followed Lydia out of the room. "About Psi-Aware?" Geneva asked.

"Just let me grab a snack," Lydia called out as she went down a hall.

Geneva followed feeling disappointed. The woman had not fixed her with a strange glare. Aside from her meditation and cluttered house, she seemed friendly and normal, not at all what she'd expected from a Psi-Aware member. It had been a mistake to stop here. She should have gone directly to Val.

In the kitchen, the light in the apartment turned from hazy blue to puce as, instead of filtering through smoky incense, it passed through chlorophyll. Plants filled the space instead of books. Most of the vegetation appeared connected to one matriarch philodendron winding its way along the window intermittently unfolding shiny green leaves. In off continent tropical jungles, the leaves of the philodendron could grow to the size of a small child. Some of them were approaching those dimensions in Lydia's kitchen. The plant appeared to originate from a huge yellow pot in the corner while rooting along the windowsill in a collection of white, blue, red, and green hand thrown and painted pottery. Lydia grabbed a handful of raw almonds from a bowl on the table and chewed. Geneva crawled across the breakfast nook and peered through the blinds. There were no cars on the street. "The car?"

Streker looked around, his eyes scanning as though he expected the car to unfurl in the kitchen, "Don't worry. It'll be here soon."

She wasn't so sure. Streker's friends weren't the kind you could trust with a fancy vehicle and an expensive rare road permit. She could be stuck waiting for the next bus. She shouldn't have stopped here. Sitting in the corridor of plants, she wasn't even sure which way to go to get out of the apartment. Another sampler hung on the wall by the stove beside Lydia's head. The words, speckled with orange grease, read, "All we are is the result of what we have thought." — Dhammapada.

"When you feel uncertain about something, it's a good idea to ask yourself how you got where you are." Lydia Streker said. "What brought you here today?"

"Streker," Geneva said.

"But how did you decide? Was it a gut choice or a decision?"

"Gut," Geneva said, as the half-chewed gobs of dough wobbled in hers. She imagined curdling cream-filling. "I wasn't thinking. That's my problem. I just go along."

"It was probably the right choice, then. You see, that's the way our brains work, the processing happens behind the scenes. It's almost impossible to think about the future We have to rely on our intuition," Lydia said.

She held up an almond to the light peering at it as if it were translucent. "This is the same shape as the amygdala, the most primitive part of our brain. It's the seat of our emotions, the source of our sadness and confusion."

"I've heard sadness is a loss of connection to the world mind," Geneva said.

"Hmm, the *unus mundus*," Lydia chewed a few more almonds and swallowed. "That's a way to look at it. All these ideas are connected. This way," she said and led Geneva through the book maze back to the bakery.

Downstairs, Lydia took a pound of plant butter from a refrigerator and dropped it into a white ceramic saucepan decorated with tiny red flowers. She dusted one of the countertops with flour, overturned a bowl of dough and divided it into three sections. She threw one to Streker. He peeled off his sweater. Underneath he wore a thin long-sleeved Sync Chrome City T-shirt. He pushed up the black sleeves and tied back his hair.

Lydia placed a lump of dough in front of Geneva and demonstrated the kneading motions. "Up to speed. Down to business, dear."

Geneva looked over her shoulder. A row of shiny buttered, brown-topped wheat loaves lined the narrow opening from the bakery to the shop. Past the bread and through the pink swirl—s'aidyL— across the front window the street looked empty. "The car could be here soon. I don't really think we have time."

"Don't worry. I'm an expert. We can finish these fast. Or Cinda will." Lydia nodded behind her at the opening and the back of the shop clerk's pink-kerchiefed head. "Besides I think better when my hands are moving. You're studying psychology?"

Geneva nodded.

"That makes it easier. You know a little about the brain. You understand how it works? Electricity leaps from synapse to synapse and, voilà! we are alive, Frankenstein style. Brain cells store and access information like a computer." Lydia dipped her head from side to side. "Left brain logical, over here. Right brain creative, over there."

Geneva pressed the dough under the pads of her hands. "No. Not quite, it's way more complex than a computer. It's really a combination of chemicals and electricity. And that whole right brain, left brain thing is really outdated. There is no right-side, left side; it functions together."

"Mmm, hmm, that's right. Now fold the dough together and squoosh it again. Squoosh, that's a technical term. Good. Good, they are teaching you something in that university. Neither one nor the other, neither right nor left. Both. Much more intricate. Organic. Adaptable. Interwoven. We call it the community of the mind. The brain has far more possibilities for connections than stars in the universe." Lydia inclined her head at Streker. "He hasn't helped me in the bakery for a very long time. But see?"

Streker kneaded the dough moving it through his long hands like liquid.

"Plasticity. Even now his synapses are reestablishing old connections." Lydia said. "And strengthening new ones. Our brains have the ability to change rapidly with experience and the more experiences we have the more we are capable of. We create our own possibilities. Start at any idea, anywhere and you have immediate access to the entire potential content of your consciousness.

All the options, unlike any device. The brain is totipotent —capable of all possible futures."

Steker snorted. "My mom's really into wetware."

"Shush, skeptic. Don't roll your eyes at me. I know what I'm talking about. Even if you think it's foolish. I don't know why you are so interested in computers when I've always told you, you have the untapped potential right here." She thumped him on the side of the head with a floury hand.

"I'm studying philosophy. I don't think you're foolish, I just..." Streker said.

"Yes, you do." Lydia reached across him for a tube of frosting. She squeezed a drop of icing onto her fingertip and smacked her lips around it. "Mmm, taste," she said dotting the tip of Geneva's own fingertip with icing. It tasted faintly of orange.

"Matter used to be the gold standard, then it was energy," Lydia said. "We found smaller and smaller particles capable of testing the limits of what we thought was possible. We found particles that responded differently in controlled tests depending on the expectations of the researchers. The particles moved as the researchers thought they would." She flicked some flour from her fingers at Streker. "Now tell me that I am making some fantastic leap. I am not. It is the teeniest, tiniest step through time and space, from where quantum physicists have explored to what the ancient shamans believed. Sentient awareness is the basic substance of the universe. It's the material that connects us all." Lydia raised her arms up over her head and brought her hands together: clap, clap and a shower of flour. "Thought."

"Mom, I know you're not stupid." Streker said. "You just get so drama, and I really don't think..."

"Give me," Lydia held out her hands and took the satiny lumps of dough from Geneva and Streker in each hand mashing them together. She unhooked a silver rolling pin from a collection of utensils clanging overhead. She rolled the dough into a thick sheet.

"It isn't such a stretch to believe that everyone has a great deal of unused potential." She sighed. "Here we are having this conversation instead of simply understanding each other. But at least we're going to get some sweets out of it."

Geneva looked over her shoulder again. There was still no sign of the purported car. "So you earned your doctorate in quantum physics?"

"Yes, yes and then you want to know why I have a bakery in Deming? The answer is because I've always wanted to have a bakery in Deming. Because they shut down the space program when the economy collapsed, and this was my opportunity. But the real reason is that our minds are the next frontier, the greatest exploration we will ever undertake." She pressed her hands to the sides of her head pressing down her frizzy puff of hair. "This is the space I'm interested in now. If we apply what we know and observe about the universe to ourselves, if we take our intuition seriously, then we, we scientists and bakers, become telepathic. We've always had the innate abilities. We just need to learn and connect those neural pathways like anything else."

Lydia grabbed the saucepan of melted butter and poured it over the dough. She made butter waves spreading it around with her fingers. She shook a jar of cinnamon sugar over it. The lighter particles of cinnamon wafted up. The heavy bits fell. Streker sneezed. Lydia laughed and poked him in the side.

"Meanwhile, even skinny, skinny skeptics have to eat. And it might as well be cinnamon rolls." Lydia rolled the dough over the layer of butter-soaked cinnamon sugar turned rich earth black. "You know, they say cinnamon enhances psychic abilities. I am constantly testing that theory." She winked. "So that's the answer to your question. People are gathering in New West because New West was supposed to be moving forward with our exploration of minds. It was part of the promise of our utopian vision."

"Now that's what's stupid," Streker said. "People don't want to be psychic. That's never what New West planned. That's all you."

"Well, you could be right. People are afraid. But I don't think we have a choice. They triggered it, so now our chapter of Psi-Aware is asking the government to take action, to take responsibility for what they began."

"Mom, don't. You shouldn't put yourself out for those wackos. They laugh at you. They don't care about you. You are not psychic. You're not gonna be. Not even a little."

Lydia took down a large clean-edged knife and began to slice off ends of the roll. "We have cut the brain into the thinnest slices and inspected it, but one aspect remains a mystery: consciousness. The mind-brain dilemma. How do all the chemicals, sections, synapses, and cells that we do understand account for and create an individual's sense of self, which we don't? This is the question that we will answer in your lifetime. That's your question too, Geneva. Your burning question: What does all of this have to do with me?"

Lydia looked at her out of the corner of her eye as she sliced the dough. Geneva leaned forward. *Yes. This is it. Tell me why I'm here*, she thought.

"The answer is: nothing," Streker said. "Mom, that's enough. Leave Gen alone. This is your thing. She doesn't care about any of this." Streker grabbed her arm. "Come on. Let's wait outside."

Geneva pulled her arm free and pushed Streker aside. "No. I need to hear this." She thought she heard a car approach now, a crunch of gravel, but she didn't look back.

"The car," Streker said.

She ignored him. She stepped toward Lydia. "Why are they are always staring at me?"

"Because we can feel your thoughts dear. You're projecting outside yourself, outside your head. We call you Push-Me," Lydia shook her head. She brandished the knife in between cuts. "No, not pusher. Push-Me. Like Push-Me-Pull-You. That's what it feels like when you think: a push. Anyone paying the least bit of attention around you gets it."

"But I'm not doing anything," Geneva said.

"Oh, but you are. Trust me." Lydia said. "Were you always this way?"

No.

"Leave her alone," Streker said.

"Any idea how this happened? What does your intuition tell you?" Lydia asked. "If it's about your friend, why are you here?"

"Mom, let it go."

Val. Val. I just want to help Val.

Lydia turned to her and fixed her with that Psi-Aware gaze, the one that made her feel as though she were thrust on stage in front of a large crowd. A connection sprang to the front of her mind. *Val! Sync Chrome City.* It landed. Snap. *We're in danger.*

Lydia Streker reeled. She clutched her head, nicking her forehead with the knife, and teetering back. She elbowed the pot of butter on her way down. The delicate red flowers spun around the rim. Streker lunged to catch his mother as the ceramic pan lurched off the counter hitting his arm. Hot butter slopped onto Geneva's thigh. It slid down Streker's arm. The knife clattered. The pan shattered on the floor.

Lydia sat among buttery shards. Blood trickled down the side of her face and flecked her forearms. She began to cry. "That was my mother's pot."

Streker threw off his shirt. Geneva stared at the sudden exposure of skin. His pale flesh hung close to his bones. His shoulder and upper arm were shiny, bright red. He bent his shoulder into the sink and turned on the tap. "Burned?"

Geneva's thigh pulsed heat when she looked at it. A grease stain spread across her khakis. "I'll be OK."

"No, take off your pants." he said. He shrugged his shoulder at the running faucet. "Put it under cold water."

He turned away and offered a hand to his mom. Geneva stepped out of her sneakers and pulled down her pants. She jumped up on the counter and wedged her leg under the water. The cold felt good until she looked down and saw how her thigh was a bright match with her silk scarlet panties. She wished she'd changed out of her party underwear and vowed never to have such a stupid thing again. It served her right for thinking her underwear could be seen in a desirable situation to be caught out now, ridiculous. She heard a car door slam just before the bell rang.

She pulled her shirt down between her legs and looked up to see the creepy older guy from last night's party standing in the doorway with a half-eaten Bismarck and a creamy smile. "Well, what have you been up to? Ready to go?"

Streker knelt at his mother's side. He helped her to her feet, his head bent low to her ear whispering, "Please don't go with him. He doesn't care about you."

Geneva sat in the sink still holding the ends of her shirt down, knees pressed together. Lydia followed Burrows upstairs to get her things. She took Geneva's pants to the clothes washer and promised she'd bring something else down for her to wear.

"Are you OK?" Streker asked. He gently placed his hands on either side of the reddening blotch on her thigh. The soft flour dusting his palms tickled. Sparse, black hair trailed across his chest and in a line down to the top of his jeans.

She touched his shoulder above the burn. "Yeah, you?"

He flexed a freckled arm. "It's OK. I don't think it will blister."

"It's not true, is it?" she whispered. "I'm not a whatever, a Push-Me. I mean, you can't feel me?"

Streker's eyes flicked from her thigh to her neck. "Now?"

She flushed. "I mean, thinking."

He knelt to press his forehead to hers and pulled back.

"You have to tell me," she said. "You won't keep secrets."

"Not if you ask. Then, the answer is: yes." The word pressed out of his thin, thin lips. "At first, I thought you were just very intense. Then I realized I could actually hear you, words. It's OK. You're very, very nice. Don't be afraid. Not of me. It doesn't feel bad to me, your thoughts. It's just different, lady."

As he placed his lips on hers, they felt full and warm. His kisses were soft and kittenish, harmless. She tensed as the faucet pressed into her back and glanced at the stairway.

"It's OK. It doesn't have to be such a big deal. You can relax. They'll be awhile," he said. She caught the bitterness in his voice and felt sorry for him. She wanted to comfort him, soothe herself.

Streker put his fingers to her mouth and traced them lightly across her lips. "I want to think about something nice."

He put his arm around her and drew her in. It was a turn on to let him touch her, she felt generous as though she were bestowing an ill-deserved gift. She felt pleasantly free of herself. He moved his hand and kissed her again until she wrapped her arms around the back of his neck. His tongue licked the traces of grease and sugar from the corners of her mouth. She stopped thinking, on purpose.

Her burn brushed his jeans. It stung. She was still very conscious that she wasn't wearing pants but becoming less and less embarrassed by it.

Then a pair of large hands gripped Streker's shoulders and yanked him from her arms. The creepy older guy said, "It's time to go."

Lydia stood behind him, her eyes red and swollen. She tossed a pair of white drawstring pants to Geneva who jumped down from the sink and pulled them on. The guy grabbed her arm as soon as she was standing upright before she had time to put on her shoes. He steered her to the door. "Enough fooling around."

Streker stood at his mother's side. He put his arm around her shoulder and drew her in. "What's wrong?"

"You were right." Lydia said. "Happy? He doesn't care about me."

Compared to the guy who held her, they looked so small: Streker a mere slice, Lydia dwarfish. "Yeah, you'd think, Lydia, if you were psychic, you would have seen this coming," Burrows said as Geneva pulled away. When he didn't let her go, she kicked. "I'm not going anywhere with you."

He absorbed the blows and held her fast. "Yeah, 'fraid so. Didn't kissy-face here tell you that was the plan?"

"Let her go." Streker said. "I said I'd bring her. I never said I'd let you take her. Not if she doesn't want to go."

Geneva went limp. "*This* is your friend?"

Streker shrugged scrawny shoulders. He seemed sad, but he always looked sorrowful. "You didn't ask."

Creepy older guy gave her a yank. "You think we're having a conversation, people?"

Her feet flew out from under her. She managed to get a foot on the ground and catch her balance. She twisted around and planted a foot in the guy's groin— heel first, Tae-Kwon-Do style, just like in the self-defense class at Inu Wood. It worked. She felt the give in his jeans under her bare foot. He folded at the waist and released her. "Ungh."

She turned and ran for the stairs. She made it more than halfway down the hall when he caught the tail end of her shirt and swung her sideways. Her foot twisted into one of the bags of flour. She spun into the pantry shelf and scrabbled at jars of cake decorations. Colored bottles flew off the shelves shaking sugar-crystals. One of the containers popped open. In a shower of pink sprinkles, the guy got a grip on her shoulders. "Fun," he said. "But not very friendly."

Slip, she thought. And he shook her so hard her neck torqued. It stunned her. She couldn't think.

He walked her to the door, smashing scattered sprinkles underfoot. The bell rang again as Burrows directed her out of the shop, with a firm hand. Geneva turned her head. "Why? What about Val?"

Streker, shirtless, cringed into his collarbones. He didn't make a move.

Creepy older guy manhandled her into his car. "All that tussle and you never asked where we were going. I'm taking you right to your best friend forever." He nodded at Streker. "Just like he promised."

Finally, in the creep's black Mercedes, Geneva was headed at top speed toward Linden, exactly what she had wanted. Except now, she knew she was a freak. The Psi-Aware protesters, who wanted everyone to be psychic, were listening to her thoughts and somehow this whole idea was putting all her friends in danger, if they were her friends: tough to say, since her judgment was clearly impaired. The second boy she'd ever kissed had already betrayed her. Follow your intuition because your brain is a step ahead of you, Lydia had advised. But if that was true, then Geneva's subconscious was seriously defective. Maybe her gray matter wasn't working right. Or maybe she was thinking too much.

Her twisted ankle throbbed and her neck ached. At least she didn't have to ponder the source of her sadness. Her trouble wasn't Val, the loss of connection to the *unus mundus* world mind or the firing of the primitive, emotional center of her brain the almond-shaped, amygdala. She looked at her kidnapper. Her problem was him. *Who the hell are you, creepy older guy? What do you want with me? I hate this.* The car swerved and Geneva clutched her burning thigh.

"My name is Burrows," he said through clenched teeth. "And 35 is not that fucking old.

~ 16 ~

BREAK OUT

"Be prepared for your first entrance into the external neural net to be disorienting and quite unlike your earlier psychic experiences. The main difference is that instead of your mind being used as an extension of your body, you will experience your body as an extension of mind. Instead of your one separate ego connecting to a few minds as you may have experienced in small group work, your ego will be subsumed by the larger Connected Ego. A common experience is to perceive the Connected Ego as a very literal interpretation of the inside of the mind as moist, dark, warm, electrical coils often accompanied by blue or violet flashes of light. Later experiences may be quite different. The Connected Ego has been perceived as nature (clouds, forests, mountains, or seas), patterns (tapestry, wires, or cells), or as mundane places mimicking virtual realities in libraries, schools, or city streets. Sexually active students familiar with entering a state of communion with another person will more easily access the Connected Ego. It has been said that the experience is similar to orgasm. Certainly, it produces similar patterns of activity in the brain." — *Becoming Psychic 101, A History and a Primer*

Burrows pulled over on the highway just outside of Deming. Even though he had practice, it was harder than you'd think to fit an unwilling 19-year-old girl into the trunk of a car. He didn't bother being gentle. He could still feel the ache in his groin where she'd landed him one. It was all about control. He held her as if she were a snake, squeezing the back of her neck. Still, she could kick and she had a lot of leg for a short girl. She'd actually been more trouble after he'd blindfolded her and tied her hands behind her back. Once he put his hands on her, lifting her up, she'd lashed out with those legs. Up until then, he supposed, as long as he was going her way, she'd been willing to give him the benefit of the doubt.

He skewered a knee up into the small of the girl's back. She arched instinctively and he used her momentum to force her into a forward fold. He hadn't meant for it to go down like this. After six months of careful planning to remove the psychic threat and bring down New West, he'd ended up with victims in the trunk of his car like some cheap serial killer. It bruised his ego. This wasn't the way he'd meant to operate. It wasn't who he was. He'd been all finesse turning Sync Chrome City and Psi-Aware in his direction. Now this was a come down. He couldn't chance the border with her in the trunk. But in the car, beside him, she'd been thinking migraines at him. Unbearable.

At the same time, even through the headache, he'd liked her there on the seat beside him twirling her ponytails around her fingers and biting her lower lip so hard her hair and lips were the same shade of red. Cute. He knew he hadn't thought she was adorable before and suspected the SLO-42 had worked him over. He hadn't meant to scare the girl. But he'd seen that joker Streker kissing her in her underwear, and he'd reacted. Then, he'd had to fight to get her out to the car. It had to be residual SLO-42 fuzzing his thinking. Yeah, maybe, literally, fuzzy. Like small, brown and fuzzy. Like voles. He remembered reading something about SLO-42 in the C-Town *Mirror* when he'd lived with his parents. The headline had said blah, blah, blah FEMALE ORGASMS. That caught his attention. It was probably the reason that rag, *The Mirror*, had done the story in the first place, anything to put the word orgasm out front. SLO-42 was made of two neurotransmitters. One of them, oxytocin, had been linked to lovely female orgasms and, far less sexy, maternal instincts. In male rodents — voles — they'd found it triggered bonding, monogamous relationships. Bottom line: men didn't have a biological excuse to screw around because voles were committed. Yeah, someone had really reached for that one. Who woke up in the morning to study vole sex? What loser got stuck with the job?

Anyway, when he'd seen Streker with Geneva, he'd lunged like some kind of sightless tunnel beast thinking, "Mine." So, there was a good chance that goof Leo wasn't interested in Coco anymore. The kid might not even know it himself, but his fresh batch of SLO-42 held a bit of bonding to this girl, Geneva. He eyed the band of red underwear across her buttocks showing through the sheer white pants, as he tucked her head under the metal lip of the trunk. Too bad she was such a pain, maybe he would have worked on changing her impression of him.

"You know most women find me really attractive," he said.

In return he got: *Creep.* Again, with the creep. He should have been mad, but it was kind of endearing. Damn drugs, he'd never had any fun with them.

She caught him a good one above his knee and he dropped her into the trunk.

"Sorry, sweets, what we have just ain't real. It’s all in his head."

The nice thing about there not being a lot of traffic in New West was that he didn't have to worry about being seen along the highway. He just kept a look out for Shadow Buses. But these unpaved roads were hell on Mistress MDs wheels. The potholes!

Geneva landed in the trunk of Burrows’ Mercedes. The lid slammed over the top of her, rocking her back and forth so that she got a feel for the space: tight. She gummed the wad of gauze stuffed into her mouth trying to find a comfortable place for her tongue to rest behind it. Her eyes were bound under another cloth and her wrists wrenched behind her. It all seemed a bit much. She got the feeling she had really bothered creepy older guy, personally. Why? What was she to him? Better question, why was she worried about the kidnapper's feelings?

She should have jumped out of the car when she'd had the chance. But he'd said he'd take her where she wanted to go, to Val. Until he'd freaked out, trussed her up, and stuffed her in the trunk, being in his car hadn't seemed so bad. Now it was bad. She strained her fingers behind her to see if she could reach her bonds. Instead, she touched smooth cold skin. She pulled her hands back. Was that really skin? Cold, dead skin? She wasn't sure. How cold was dead? She hadn't taken anatomy yet. And it was winter. It was cold in the trunk anyway. Her own hands were probably cold, not dead cold though.

If there was another body, no, another person, in here with her, it would have to be small, no he/she would have to be small. Maybe that's why it had been so hard for the kidnapper to get her into the trunk. Or it could be a big person, a big body, in pieces.

She reached out again tentatively. This time she ran her fingers over thick satiny fabric. She touched something cool and smooth, a button, no, a snap. She poked her hand down behind the button into a pocket of the slippery fabric — snaps, pockets — plug-in clothes. The body — *no, don't think that* — the person, behind her jerked. She reached back again and felt the cool skin — hands. The fingers wiggled in hers. Thank goodness. Live hands, her size hands, maybe a little smaller with slimmer, longer fingers. A live person. Then underneath the medicinal smell of gauze, she caught a whiff of cinnamon.

Valerie? It had to be Val. She felt relieved and terrified. If that was Val, they were together again, but in the same predicament. Worse, but better. She tried to take a deep breath through her nose, but there was barely room for her chest to lift. She squirmed trying to create give. She needed to breathe, think how to get out of this. The top of her head struck metal. She went still.

Then it felt like someone pulled her hair: *Gen.* She was lying on top of one of her ponytails. She wiggled and got her hair out from under her, but her hair still pulled at her neckline. Her fingers fluttered behind her.

Yank: *Gen.* The hands grasped hers.

Yank: *Gen. It's me. Relax.*

She thought she heard a voice, but the voice didn't sound like Val. It sounded too close and metallic. It reminded her of a sleepless night when she was very ill as a small child with a high fever. The voice had said: *Geneva.* It had called out to her from a nightmare: A dream about a blaze in the middle of the 'Way. Her mind re-envisioning the night they had rescued Val maybe. The voice had called *Geneva* from the middle of the fire insistent, urgent. The voice had licked her like flames.

This voice was similar. She listened to the muffled hum of the car tires on pavement and felt the vibration beneath her and realized the voice wasn't a sound at all. It was a physical sensation. She felt it inside her head, behind her eyes, inside where she herself was, within her own thoughts. The pressure was like thinking very hard, like learning a difficult subject for the first time, or studying for a final exam in a foreign language.

Gen. It's OK. You can hear me?

It tapped at the back of her head. It gnawed. It burrowed in bringing bad news. *He wants to kill us. We need a plan.*

Kill us. It really hadn't occurred to her. It seemed so out of the realm of possibility of what someone would actually do. She retreated from the thought.

The trunk had the ambience of a cold womb. She curled there. As a child, when she'd dreamt about the fire, she'd woken up and pulled the covers around her head leaving only a breathing hole.

It wouldn't keep the monsters out, but it'd be better to go with her eyes closed. She'd lose in a struggle, but the fear would be the worst. The monsters could eat her, so long as she didn't have to watch. She'd slept that way ever since, hiding.

Tap: *Gen.* Tap: *You idiot.* Tap, tap: *Don't shut me out. Hello, stop being so morbid.*

Geneva bounced as the car went over a bump. Slam: *I've had it with you.* She pulled her hands out of the ones behind her and tried to press them down against her back. That voice wasn't Val. Val wouldn't say that. All she'd been doing was worrying about Val, trying to help her. If she hadn't been, she wouldn't even be here. She'd be finishing school. Since last spring, she'd been worrying about Val and maybe even always, since Val came to live with them.

The voice: *Spare me, Gen. Spare me your denial and guilt. You haven't been thinking about me. You haven't even been paying attention.*

Geneva moaned under the gauze and squirmed trying to stretch her cramped limbs. That had been Val. The sentences vibrated with a tinny twang like someone talking through the end of an aluminum tube, but the tone was definitely Val's. It was her scathing voice—the one she used when she thought she knew more than a professor, "He keeps making these analogies to string theory but he never shows us any equations." or when they were both mad at their mother, "I think if we want to see mom again, we're going to have to move to C-town." or when they made fun of their father, "OK, here comes Vole-Man to the rescue — for all your obscure rodent knowledge needs." It was not funny being the recipient of the sarcasm. *I was worried*, she thought, and I *saved your life*. Just *last night*.

From the voice—Val—came: *Did you? Or did you just turn me in so they could lock me up again at that clinic. Turn me in so Burrows could find me. You don't know what's going on. You don't know what's happening to me — everyone. You're just worried it will mess up your plans.*

Now she was sure she was in the trunk with Val, hearing Val's thoughts. But she couldn't believe what Val was saying. How could she be critical at a time like this? Sometimes it was too hard to be her friend. She just didn't get where Val's head was, anymore, if she ever had. Now that they were going to die at the hands of some psycho, she just wanted Val to know that she loved her, cared about her. At a time like this, that was all that mattered.

Val: *That is so lame ass. 1. I'm not going to die like this. 2. You have to figure this out.*

Val grabbed her fingers and squeezed them hard. She twisted them wringing them around. Stinging shocks replaced the numbness in Geneva's hands. At the same time, she felt a thrust: *Here!*

What she got was a chunk of thought, Val's thought. A memory that shoved her own reality—panting for breath behind a cloth—aside. She recognized it immediately. It was a moment from her childhood. Val had had severe asthma as a child, but she hated her inhaler and often forgot to carry it. Geneva had been with some new friends across the playground when Val had collapsed.

This time, in the memory, she was Val sprawled on the fresh mown lawn. Geneva stared at the pink daisy sandals that had been Val's favorites at age 7. She wheezed. Her ribs felt like armor over her tight, flat lungs. She took deep pulls through her nose trying to lift them, let in some air. Her chest constricted. There was barely room for her pounding heart. Breathless moments passed. She tried to focus on the pink daisies. They spun round and turned purple. She was drowning without water. Everything was tinted blue: the grass, the schoolyard, Gen running toward her. She couldn't breathe. She could not breathe. Gen pressed the inhaler into her hand, held it to her mouth helped her pump the fumes into her lungs. She relaxed, waited. They expanded, opening wide. She lay back on the grass, arms wide looking up into the sky, air everywhere, drawing breath. Euphoria. Breath. Breathing.

Geneva shook her head from side to side, the cloth between her teeth, herself again. It had been like being in a demo of a virtual reality game, where you are someone else, but not in control.

She was still trying to reorient when Val slammed in another chunk of memory, this one unfamiliar, at first. It placed her in the middle of a blaring black swarm. It snapped into focus when she looked down and saw the thigh high boots. Val was in college at a concert surrounded by Plug-Ins, dancing up on the speakers, and loving it loud. Her skull vibrated. Her body rocked. The walls were coated in electronic finery. She felt hands on her hips and turned to see a bare undulating torso. The stomach in front of her was nearly convex with sparse black hair. She grew warm feeling Val's lust. Then she looked up the trail of curly black hair up into the face and the eyes: one blue, one brown. Possibility. Maybe even love. She saw Streker. Streker and Val, together.

The memory released her. Streker: Val's boyfriend. Oh, shit. Shit. Geneva went cold, trunk in winter cold — not dead cold, she was pretty sure. She'd been kissing Val's boyfriend. She should have known. How long had they been dating? She was surprised at how easily she knew the answer once she thought about it: Since this time last year when Val had started spending more and more time plugged-in and at the Mansion. Val and Streker had been together a year. And she'd kissed him, today, for no reason at all, just a distraction.

Val was right. She hadn't been paying attention, didn't want to. Maybe worrying about Val wasn't the same as caring about her at all. Maybe it was just avoidance. No, wrong. In the stillness of the trunk, Geneva realized Val could be reading her thoughts — right now. She didn't want Val to know about this kiss, didn't want to damage her friendship any more than she already had. Instead, she thought about the one thing that made it impossible to think of anything else — Val's parents, how they had died.

Val: *Fuck you. Everybody dies. It's no excuse, bitch.*

The car lurched and swerved. It sped up and then it went quiet. The vibration of the engine stilled. The car had stopped somewhere. There were footsteps, then a screech of metal on metal like a key being scraped along the outside of trunk. There was a dull thud and a steady—thunk, thunk—across the top that grew faster and faster. Geneva flattened trying to get away from the roof.

Val: *Relax. He's just whacking off.*

The sound stopped. She heard footsteps and the hum returned. The car lurched. Geneva braced and spared herself another lump on the head. The hum came high and long. They were moving fast.

Val: *Forget, apologies. I've had it. If I'm stuck here with you, I can't wait for you to come around. I can't let you ignore me. If you care, you'll get this.*

The thrust thought came again. She couldn't tell at first if she was Val or not. She was disoriented, unsure. That didn't feel Val-ish. The new place was black, filled with dark tangled shapes. It could have been the trunk they were in or maybe the backseat of Eve's car. Her limbs were cramped and bound, and she was still stuffed into the space, but it was hot and moist. She looked down to see what kind of shoes she had on. There was only blackness below. She struggled against the thick cords binding her. They released her and she plunged forward into black space. Then the cords yanked her back and sent her ricocheting. They began to glow. Neon purple coils lined the walls of an open chamber and sizzled with current. She flew past them and landed, free, on top of a pile of greasy ropes.

What was this? A virtual reality? A techno sauna? A plug-in theme park? It wasn't a memory. Maybe it was a dream. *No*, she thought, *this is Val's mind, I'm in.*

Geneva searched through the piles of cords, holding each one to her ear until she located the source of the echoing whine. When she found the one humming, it slipped from her hand again and again until she wrapped it around her wrist, a purple, fluorescent bracelet. She followed it stepping over and under the other cords. A goo like melted blackberry cordial coated her arms. As she walked, the whine got louder and shriller and the cord began to pull. She stumbled forward trying to keep her balance on the slick surfaces. She ran, then tripped, dragged forward through the ropes. They lashed her face and smeared it with warm mush. She started to scream.

Then she arrived at the memory. She knew it, instantly. She looked down and saw the thigh high boots tucked beneath her. She was Val studying in the dorm room last spring screaming loud and shrill. She was on Sync Chrome City opening to the minds around her and then she was off in space. Off the net, detached, but still linked to a sea of minds. She was scared, but not terrified—thrilled. Every few seconds, Val took a breath and could have stopped screaming. But she elected to howl: a joyful catharsis, epiphany, power.

In a flash, from outside the memory, Geneva saw the purple cords, strung tight, vibrating. The neon flickered. The cords sizzled and went black. A burst of burnt sugar steam rose from the cords. It smelled of charred blackberry pie. It stung the back of her throat.

Inside the memory, Val's scream changed to that wrenching, throat about to be torn out, shriek. She fell off the chair and started to convulse. She looked at Gen watching her, wide-eyed and frozen. Help me, she thought. She couldn't breathe.

The car lurched. Geneva was jolted back to her own senses. The memory released her. She thought hard trying to make sense of what she had experienced.

Val: *I need you. Do you get it? Did you see? This is it. Final exam.*

Sync Chrome City had awakened something in Val's mind. It wasn't bad. For a moment, it had been amazing. It wasn't an illness like they said. It was a new ability. A sense. Something changed.

Val: *Forget it. I don't need you. I'm on my own. Again. I'll fight this guy, get out of here myself.*

Wait! *Wait!* Geneva thought, but this time she imagined gripping at the purple cords. The thoughts pressed out of her. *I don't understand. Is this some kind of evolution?*

There was a long silence. Stillness. The car had stopped again.

Val: *Yeah, maybe exactly.* Geneva also felt Val's emotions: Relief. Excitement. Val had been so scared, alone. They had both felt so alone.

Geneva thought out*: I think I got what was going on with Sync Chrome City. But what about that other part: the coils and the neon. What's all that?*

There was silence—then footsteps.

Val*: I don't know. You're the psychology major. Listen, about Streker. I know. It's not your fault. He's like a big dog, needy. And he took some of that Da Lime. It's OK.*

Geneva sighed. She was trapped in a trunk and suddenly unafraid. Possibly the least afraid she'd ever been in her life. *Euphoria. Possibility. Power.*

Burrows opened the lid of the trunk. He looked down at the two trussed girls, one in white, one in black, lying yin-yang curled like seeds inside fruit holding hands behind their backs. He stepped back, his head pounding. His instinct said, *close the trunk, get away.* He almost listened.

~ 17 ~

FAUSTUS

"It is possible to use psychometric tools to store aspects of one's thoughts or to help gain access to the Connected Ego. However, use of Faustus Implements by students (popularized by sympathetic retellings of C. G. Burrows' role in the Psychic Dawning) is generally discouraged. They are unnecessary to psychic development and there is no reason a student should feel compelled to expend undue effort to the task of creating one. Because Burrows used his Faustus as a murder weapon, some schools strongly oppose the creation of any such mind-imbued matter. Despite its nefarious origins, however, there is no reason to believe psychometry is anything other than a harmless diversion." — *Becoming Psychic 101, A History and a Primer*

Burrows reached under his brown jacket to the side holster hanging beneath his arm. He unclasped the leather pouch, rolled his fingers over the smooth, cold cylinders, and withdrew Faustus, his favorite nine incher. With his thumb over the blunt end of the needle, he reached into the trunk. One of the girls was kicking now, jamming her heel against the inside of the taillight to no effect. The other girl lay still, facing up, her head swaying from side to side, blind, but aware of him, listening. He reached for her, plunged Faustus into the well between her throat and her collarbone. Her body arched around it and then writhed away as he drove it in. Blood pooled around the wound on extraction.

Using Faustus wasn't an efficient way to dispatch the girl, but it was satisfying. Burrows focused on that spot of red until it appeared behind his eyes. His mind went numb as he retreated inside himself, alone, where no one could reach him for the first time in years. Here, now — this was the place he'd been seeking, the quiet that drugs and rituals and meditation and hiding out in the forest couldn't provide. He ran his hand down his thigh, over his ink. All this time, he'd been pointing the needle — *Omnis festinatio ex parte diaboli est* — in the wrong direction. The blood-streaked needle quivered in his hand, rising and falling with his breath. It wavered over her heart like a divining rod. Maybe he didn't need to kill her quickly at all. Then — crack — plastic splintered.

Geneva experienced déjà vu as she started to kick around in the trunk. Some faint memory clung to the whiff of wax polish. Maybe she'd dreamt of escaping from the trunk of a car before. How had it turned out? She searched for the taillight with her foot, planning to kick it out, thrash her foot around and hope someone would see.

Valerie lay still beside her: *Stop. Above us. The open space. He's there.*

Geneva registered the click of the trunk and the waft of cool air, external cues that had escaped her when she was inside herself feeling the rush. Then images flashed in front of her eyes. A pierced round hole filling with blood: *Pain.*

Val thrashed. Geneva's leg thrust through the taillight. But it didn't matter now. The lid was open. He was right there, hurting Val. She sat up and pulled her leg out. She stumbled over the lip, sprang from the trunk and hit the pavement in a fetal position with her knees and shoulder. In her mind, she leapt up and ran forward, pummeling Burrows with superhuman strength, attacking like an enraged bear. In reality, her hands were tied behind her and her eyes and mouth were bound. She couldn't see. She couldn't roar. And he was there. The outline of his hulking shoulders hovered on the edges of her senses as if in infrared. He smelled like car wax and doughnut grease.

A rush like wind, a high-pitched whine, surrounded Burrows. Geneva leapt from the trunk and landed on the pavement, trailing bandages, moving like an injured cat escaping. His quiet evaporated, the pressure began to build under his forehead. He turned to the girl, with the needle poised. And then—whump—she hit him square behind the eyes. He flew back. His ass struck pavement and gravel ground up his lower back. The impact rumbled down his spine like a Shadow Bus.

Then he was gone. Where? Spinning blindly Geneva pushed herself up to standing. She leaned back and reached behind her into the trunk. Val's hands clasped hers. Warm. Alive. She didn't want to let go. But Val's hands slipped out of hers pulling at the bandages on her wrists. When her hands were free, Geneva tore the blindfold from her eyes. They were on the side of the road surrounded by soy fields in the low light of afternoon. Burrows sat a ways off sheltering his head in the crook of his arm. He looked human there, unlike the monster she'd imagined him to be under the blindfold. She inhaled the rich soil smell, and turned her back on him, to see to Val.

The hole in Val's neck didn't look so bad, more like a bright pendant than a wound. But when she released Val's gag, she made a gurgling rasp as she drew breath and blood chugged from her throat.

Gravel crunched behind them. Geneva turned and kicked, aiming for Burrows' crotch again. He caught her shin and she tipped back, falling against the car. Her head scraped the lid of the trunk. The small of her back struck the edge. Burrows towered over her. She struck out, flailing her arms and he started to laugh. "The thing is, I have a size advantage."

Why would anyone hurt her? Hurt her and laugh? She cocked an elbow and clipped Burrows on the side of the jaw with a low smack of bone on bone. Pain shot up her elbow. But his eyes held fast on her, the space between his brows three long dark roads. "That's fine. Takes the edge off."

A glint caught Geneva's eye and she looked down to see the needle on the road. He'd dropped the weapon. Relief coursed through her. He'd release her to get it and then she'd have a chance.

"Nah, don't need it." He fumbled against her a moment, pressing her against the trunk. He pinned her there with a knee between her legs and then he grabbed her neck in his hands. "Be still, be quiet," he said squeezing each word into her neck.

Stricken, struggling, Geneva tunneled down into her own mind searching for a place inside herself running away from the approaching darkness. She reached a calming voice, a haven.

Val: *I'm right here. Come on. Stay with me. We're going to do this together. Think together. Let's take it to him. Think about the possibilities. Independence is overrated. Privacy's a thing of the past. Imagine what we could do... Intertwining fingers on your soul, invade your heart and make it whole...*

A purple coil of thought started to glow in the darkness and Geneva forgot about being choked and picked up on it... *harvest Sin and Chrome and Sea. Come and intertwine with me.*

Burrows grip loosened. She opened her eyes and saw him cringe. She lashed out: *Get back!*

He released her. His feet lifted off the ground. A lavender haze engulfed him and knocked him back. She turned raising her arms against the blast.

If you knew what we could do. You wouldn't be against it: Val continued.

Geneva lifted her head and peered between her forearms. She looked up into the empty gray sky, down the long silent road and over her shoulder at the still fields. A traditionalist, she was slow to catch on: *Wait, was that us?*

Burrows lay on his side, his legs splayed over the centerline of the highway. His head pounded, filled with chatter. A litany of pain and pressure swelled behind his optic nerves. It was exactly what he'd feared. He was trapped under the thoughts, immobilized. He realized he was lying in the road just as he caught a glint of silver streaking toward him over the horizon. He recognized the RV, Sync Chrome City was bearing down on him and he couldn't move. It'd roll right over him. He stared at death unblinking. He was not beyond caring, wracked with pain as he was, he always chose life. It was his. Why was his every choice stolen?

The RV stopped just in front of him, leaving his looking up under its tires.

Grugel got out, jumping: *Man, what are you doing here? You look like roadkill. Hit by a Shadow Bus. What the hell?*

Burrows made out the words. The pain faded back to average levels. Usual. Tolerable. He managed to get to his knees, stagger up. It was his life. His own. Sync Chrome City was here. New West was coming, his new friends, the boys in green. He had to get out. *Harvest Sin and Chrome and Sea*, the chorus resonated, lodged in his head, haunting. He rose to his feet and started running. No way, he'd be quashed by a song. Lame ass synth pop, and a couple of kids. No way. He slammed Geneva with his shoulder as he charged past her, sprinting into the soy fields.

"What the hell was that?" Grugel said. "What's with him?"

Geneva could barely hear him over the sound of Val's high-pitched excited laughter—that rollercoaster exultation again. In between fits, Val thought: *Whoa. Incredible. But I would like to see him run.*

"Right, yeah," Geneva said aloud. Clutching her shoulder, she lurched over to the trunk and untied Val's blindfold. The light sobered her. Val sat up: *We should go after him.*

Geneva looked out over the field. The sun, low in the sky, looked cold and distant. She wrapped her arms around herself: *It's too much.*

Val: *I know. It's weird. One minute you're eating Bismarks, the next someone's trying to hurt you.*

Geneva wished she had a coat to put over her T-shirt and Lydia's linen pants. Her jaw trembled: *We were hurting him. I mean, even if he... I still couldn't. That was a lot of...he was in a lot of—pain.*

Through the sound of her teeth clacking, Val's voice pressed through clearly: *Oh. OK, yeah. Wow. We can do that.*

"Um, guys?" Grugel wiggled his fingers back and forth between them. "Snap out of it. Am I, uh, interrupting something?"

"Yeah," Streker appeared beside them. Geneva flinched as he wrapped his trench coat around her shoulders, but she held on to the lapels. "They're talking."

Streker lifted Val out of the trunk in an easy motion. He was stronger than he looked. Looking down, Geneva spotted the needle lying by the road.

"Man, really? But Sync Chrome City." Grugel turned to the RV and back a couple of times. "No way. You mean without Sync Chrome City?"

"Yeah," Val said. Now that she was standing, a trail of blood oozed out of her throat and down her neck moistening the top of her T-shirt. But she was smiling so the gap between her front teeth showed. She looked cute and bloody.

Streker placed a couple of fingers to the side of Val's wound. "You're hurt." He massaged the torn pink edges of flesh and wiped the blood on his jeans. "It's not too bad, but let's get you in and fix you up."

"Shit," Grugel stomped one foot. "You mean we don't need Sync Chrome City? Isn't that gonna stall our easy ride?"

"No, we need it," Val said as Streker put his arm around her shoulders and began to lead her to the RV. "Not everyone can do what we can, yet. We still need a catalyst to wake the rest of them up."

Geneva got in their way. "No, this is crazy. We're not going with you."

"I wish you'd stop using that word," Val said.

Geneva pointed at Streker, "But he's an...an accessory. He gave me all that, crap, 'Come meet my mother, you'll really like her.' and then he...and he knew, knew we were best friends. Yeah, no, uh-uh."

They stopped. Val punched Streker on the shoulder. "You were an ass."

He hung his head. "I'm sorry. Really. I don't know why I trusted that guy. I think it was partly Da Lime. Blame it on Leo, guy loves everybody."

They started walking again, right towards her. She held up her hands. "That's not good enough. It's no excuse. You're still responsible for your actions."

"What are you going to do, stay by the side of the road?" Grugel's muffled voice came from the car. He was searching around in the trunk.

"No, we'll take that," she pointed ahead at the Mercedes.

Grugel looked up. "Steal my man's car?"

She held her arms out. "Your man tried to kill us. I guess we can borrow his car."

Val stepped around her. "We don't have time for this. It's a revolution." Grugel ran by her, too, carrying a round canister of car wax.

They entered the RV and left her standing alone in the road. She rolled her eyes and watched a few crows fly overhead across the flat gray sky. She bent and grabbed the needle. As soon as her fingers brushed it, it flashed blue: *Faustus.* The tips of her fingers went ice cold as she saw the needle plunging into a slim neck, Val's, and dipping into a thick thigh. She read pain, peace and agony off the needle like words on a page. She pulled her hand back, rubbed her fingers and rolled her eyes again. Well, what did she expect? The needle had a history. She thought about the bits and pieces of information that had passed her by, what Val and Streker had both said about Leo's Da Lime, how it drew people to her. The dangerous drug was a passed note with "Leo likes you" scrawled across it. She could exchange thoughts with Val and now with Faustus. It was too much to take in, a rush of, empathy, telepathy, psychometry. What was she going to do with it all? How would it change her? She wrapped the end of her T-shirt around her fingers and picked Faustus up. In the trunk of the car, she found a black encrusted piece of chamois cloth Grugel had missed. She wrapped the needle up and pocketed it.

When she turned around, the RV was still there. Val leaned out the door. She had a strip of white cloth tied around her neck, a spot of red soaking through the center, dashing, like a new punk look. "What're you doing? Come on."

Geneva stepped into the RV. It was no longer hazy, filled with the cloying cinnamon incense from New Year's Eve. It smelled like old carpet. Grugel was up front behind the driver's seat, smearing black car polish through his hair so it stood on end in three clumps. He stuck his tongue out, "Yaaah!" and leered as she got on board. In the dim light, Streker stood with his taut stomach exposed, the bottom of his T-shirt torn off. Val patted the chair next to her, sitting in front of the console. "Let 'em try to stop us now. We can do anything."

Darkness enveloped Geneva as she walked slowly to the back of the RV. On New Year's Eve, the glinting electronics on the black velvet had looked like stars. All around her they'd sparkled along with the electronic chords flowing over the chatter and laughter. She'd hidden in a corner, watching the Plug-Ins, unseen. That night, the RV had been warm with too many bodies and moist with breathy condensation. Now it was cold, dry, and silent. She stared at the console, a darker patch of black, until she could see the tiny squares of light reflected in Val's dark eyes. She felt like they were all floating in space on some leaderless mission. She wondered how they would get back. Val lowered a sleek pair of VR glasses over her eyes and handed Geneva another set. Streker dug a wire out of the console and unwound it to a black velvet chair big enough for two. He tapped a few buttons. "It'll be safe. We'll ease you in and out. Watch any one of those screens or all of 'em."

Streker took them in past the security sequences and in an instant they were connected to a thousand minds. Purple vines looped over them. Euphoria. Possibility. Power. She loved them all, these minds, these men and women. She'd do anything for them. *Now what? What do you want?*

The vines trembled and answers began to emerge: *Heal. Teach. Build. Help. Create. Love. Play. Sex. Relax.* Val: *Anything. Revolution. Change the world.* The students' minds pressed forward. Endorphins surged. The vines shook and the students dropped from them, disembodied, minds floating into space. The vines burst. Juicy droplets flew. The minds rose over the split and writhing vines up into emptiness. Streker: *Leaving Sync Chrome City. This is new.* The students clustered together picking up speed, propelled by hope. Val whooped: *Go. Go.*

Geneva grew warm, sweat trickled down between her eyes under the glasses. They were going to reach meteoric speeds, rushing forward like a launch party. Geneva's earthbound limbs twitched against the chair. Her temperature dropped. The sweat cooled on her brow. She sensed black holes ahead: seven of them. The danger seemed a vague, dream-like premonition, until she remembered the names of the lost guys: Chris, Michael, Don, Eli, Todd, Roger, and Doug were in comas at New West Mental because of this, Sync Chrome City. Only reality had such stark, crisp details. A launch like this, they weren't ready for it. She pressed the names out to the group: *Some of us are missing. Wait. Stop.*

But Val kept going: *Don't hold us back.*

Back? Geneva knew as soon as she thought about it, got it off Streker and the rest of them: *You couldn't be doing this without me.*

She saw Grugel in Sync Chrome City, his vines appearing as a stream of wires and data, just before she pressed out a last thought—*everybody out of the pool*—and yanked off her glasses.

He stood behind her as she sat shaking in the dark RV. "Yaaah, it's definitely more powered up."

She blinked at the purple cords flickering on the edges of her vision. Streker's head lolled on her knee beside the mottled velvet of the chair. She stood up and he moaned, falling back. "More dangerous, you mean. This could kill them. Look what happened to the guys." She turned to where Val was still under the glasses. "Get her out of there."

Grugel stepped around the chair and stood between her and Val. Muscles packed his small frame beneath his black wicked hair.

"These are people's minds," She faced off with him. "What the hell are you doing? You charge for this? Try to make a profit? Then, when they can't pay, what do you do, unplug them? Like a public execution? That's sick."

He grabbed her wrists, his forearms flexing from flesh to solid mass, and shoved her. "You are not going to stall our easy ride."

She went down fast, her wrists smeared with black wax, landing on her ass. Grugel swung his leg back like he was shooting for a target outside the RV, far across the road, "You understand, I'm not giving this up." His boot came at her, its black top scuffed, its thick sole caked with highway mud and gravel.

She gasped. Her lungs filled with stale carpet air. Pink flashes obscured her vision. He loomed over her, a leaning square torso and triangular face pointed down at her. On the edges of him, beyond her vision, back inside her mind, she felt the other students, racing forward. Then, falling into space. The RV screens went dark. Sync Chrome City shut down leaving their minds open, but alone, spiraling outward. Utopia really was nowhere and that where they were all going.

Grugel kicked Geneva in the hip where she lay. The blow landed, but barely registered as she felt the students fall. He pirouetted towards the screens. "What the...?"

Separated from Sync Chrome City, the students' minds seized. Grugel bent over one of the screens. Streker and Val slumped on either side of him. Streker's head fell forward. Val's dropped over the lip of the low chair. The screen glowed gray as Grugel resurrected it. "Damn, bitch. You told them. The Greenies come to shut us down."

Streker and Val's limp bodies began to twitch. Streker's shoulder hunched. Val's head bounced along the back of the chair. Below her glasses, her dimpled cheek flexed. The glasses slid to the side and the white slivers of Val's eyes showed; her eyes had rolled back into her head following her mind inside. Streker and Val were seconds from full-blown spasms as their minds trekked into territory their brains couldn't handle.

Geneva didn't want to lose them— any of them. Already, she wasn't quite sure where the students were; outside of their own heads for sure, cast out of powered down Sync Chrome City, but no longer housed in any space, tangible or virtual. She reached for them, pressing her thoughts out and felt their minds faraway, but she couldn't find them without letting go of her own tether, her body. Then how would she get back? She didn't know how to search that far outside of herself. She could not make the connection.

When she opened her eyes, Grugel stood over her, reached down and pulled her to her feet. Her hip burned as she put weight on it and her leg bent under her. He hoisted her dead weight, tucking an arm around her waist and pushing her around in front of him. Her head jerked back as he held her ponytails tight near her scalp, wrapping them in his hand. "We're getting out of here. No way I'm getting caught."

He pushed her forward past Streker and Val, their bodies slack, their minds floating.

As Grugel pushed her up toward the cab, the RV door opened. Leo's arms and legs splayed across the exit creating angles of light and shadow. "Hey ya."

Behind her, Grugel tensed. "Hey, man. You wouldn't be with the greens."

Leo ducked his head under the doorjamb. "Nah. Came for that one." He nodded at her.

Grugel pressed his body into hers and pulled her hair back at the same time, leaving no space between them. It felt more confining than the trunk. She could smell the wax polish in his hair mingling with the stale air. "Ah, you and Streker keep getting distracted. The game's about what's between your ears. Focus. This is our ticket." He said pulling her hair even harder. "Help me get Sync Chrome City out to the 'Way."

She jerked her head back hard —thwack—her skull connecting with Grugel's chin. His hands loosened in her hair. She pulled away and stood sideways between the two men, her hands out measuring the distance between them. "Nobody leaves."

She clenched her jaw remembering the way Burrows had flown away from her and landed in the middle of the highway. Blood streamed from Grugel's nose, the straight line of it bent. She could throw him away from her, crumple his body into the RV wall just by thinking about it. Her vision blurred and tears warmed the pinched corners of her eyes. "No. Sync Chrome City is over. We're going to stay here and let the cops gut this place, take them to the clinic, and you," she pointed at Grugel. "Wherever. This is a big contest of crazy. But I'll win if I have to. I'll scream the loudest. It's over."

Grugel glared. The tight edges of his eyes and mouth twitched. Leo stared at him. "Border's closed Grugel. Greenies all around. This is it for Sync Chrome City."

Leo tilted his head back and stretched his hand out simultaneously, so he looked like he was standing on parallel planes. "But don't let them lock you up in the clinic, Gen. They aren't the good guys, either. Come on, girl. Let's go before they bust in."

She shook her head, her hips dropped low. Grugel darted around her. He checked Leo as he went out the door. "Yaaah, plan B." Leo sidestepped, lunging, and grabbing Geneva's shoulder. She turned at a sharp sting, just in time to see the neon green liquid shooting into her arm. "Fuck! Get off me!" She swatted at the syringe and its emptied shell wobbled in her shoulder and then fell to the ground. Leo released her. "Trust me, girl."

The SLO-42 kicked in fast, sharing Leo's perception, and the flashing green lights in the distance beyond the door caught her attention. Dark shapes crawled toward her in the rose-colored dusk beyond the doorway. Field agents. One of them waved the blue current end of his taser at her. Leo had gotten the greens to let him into the RV to retrieve her telling them she was an employee of Friend-Me Co, but they only half believed him. They were ready to rush in and finish their mission to shut down Sync Chrome City and take the students to the clinic.

Leo wanted to get her out of there, bring her back to New West to his mother. But it felt like a challenging escapade, a diversion. The baseline of his persona belonged lazing under a tree somewhere, smiling up at the sun. Underneath the burst of Leo's chemicals, Geneva started to giggle. She knew it was wildly inappropriate, but the drug overrode her. "Lighten up," she said. "Why so serious?" Her high-pitched laughter shook her whole body as Leo grabbed her hand and led her out of the RV.

It was warmer than she remembered outside. Leo let go of her hand and crooked an elbow at Burrows' Mercedes. She watched three agents dressed in forest green creep toward the RV as she slid into the passenger seat. As they drove north, Geneva glanced in the rearview mirror and saw Grugel running in the opposite direction. He ran in a zigzag pattern, veering into the soy field. A flicker of blue appeared low in the field, and he faltered, lurching to the side as his leg went out from under him. Geneva looked down and loosened the drawstring on Lydia's linen pants. She pulled a side down to inspect her hip where Grugel had landed his boot. It was turning lavender in garish contrast with the scarlet strip of her underwear. She cocked her head at Leo and pouted. "It hurts."

"Mmm," Leo said looking at her hip out of the corner of his eye and treating her to a pleasant alchemy of prurient and concerned interest.

"People shouldn't think someone's only about what they've seen. Just because you're usually quiet, doesn't mean you won't yell. You know, just because I'm not about creating drama doesn't mean..." She crossed her arms over her chest and nodded her head once, floating high on the cloud of Da Lime. "Damn, dopamine addicts. Turn it into a test and I'll ace it every time."

The corner of Leo's mouth raised plumping his hollow cheek. "Yeah, I heard. You'll win a contest of crazy."

She sniggered. "Actually," she tapped her chest, creating the flutter of an external heartbeat on her breastbone as she stared ahead at the long-straight road. "I'm psychic. Really. Me."

From the edge of the soy field, Burrows watched Leo drive away, abusing Mistress M.D. by swerving unnecessarily on the straight highway. Paramedics followed the agents into the RV, they came out lowering two stretchers and hoisting them into the ambulances. The green lights flashed on the RV's silver surface and then sped away. The agents searched the side of the road and a couple of them ventured into the fields. Their electric tasers buzzed as Grugel fell. They finished their search. They got into the RV and three government Enviro-cars and headed down the highway toward New West. Burrows was alone again. It grew dark as he waited on the side of the road hoping to flag down a bus. Chill air crept underneath his brown jacket. His shoulders tensed. When the faint blue lights of a bus appeared from the south, Burrows stepped out onto the road and then back again. He wanted to be seen, not hit. The bus went by him and he thought he'd erred too far on the side of caution. But it stopped a few yards ahead of him. Its doors opened in a gassy exhalation. The bus driver was stranger looking than any of the Vary-altered people he'd met on the 'Way. She had huge blue eyes set deep into her round face. As he boarded, she winked. Her caked lashes left flecks of black beneath her eye. He moved quickly to the back of the bus. He was reaching for a privacy web, when the shroud beside him lifted. A frazzled Grugel appeared with a singed smell about him. "Yaaah, bitches, can't catch me."

~ 18 ~

INTERNSHIP

"The Mindscape material is also now regarded as an unnecessary psychometric tool and remains popular primarily as a children's toy. However, materials science made an essential contribution to the evolution of psychic potential. Mindscape helped early Awakening Minds, Geneva Weltraum in particular, conceptualize the Connected Ego, the Infinite Lattice and Psychic Space for the very first time." — *Becoming Psychic 101, A History and a Primer*

Leo clasped Geneva's hand as he led her up the walkway to the new pyramid-shaped building on the New West University campus. Its face was one huge triangular window made up of many smaller ones. The mounds of earth around the building were bare, yet to be landscaped. A landmark sign, however, had already been placed by the entryway. It read, "Friend-Me Corporation," in glistening silver.

"We're here to see my mom," Leo said, responding to the question Geneva had not vocalized. "What else would I do with a nice girl like you?"

Geneva's face warmed even as the chill winter breeze swept back her hair. The effects of the drug were wearing off. Beneath Leo's ethereal thoughts she recognized her own grounded undercurrents of perception. If she closed her eyes, feeling the wind through her lashes, she could see her thoughts: sunken orderly lines running beneath colored clouds. Under the influence of SLO-42, she knew what else Leo might plan for a nice girl like her and the thoughts were pleasant skin-to-skin, molten feelings. She also saw that as attracted as he was to Geneva, and the possibility she held for a new kind of romance, he'd still go back to the certainty of having Constance Monica Sherring as a girlfriend, if Coco so much as nodded his way. You couldn't fault someone for loyalty, but Leo's was frustrating.

Coco had made her choice. If she was letting her father's judgment keep her away from someone who loved her that was her problem. Maybe it was time to give Leo the choice instead of taking herself out of play just in case Coco changed her mind. All's fair in love and war. She tightened her grip on Leo's hand. She pulled him around to face her, pressed her body to his, tilted her head back and parted her lips. It was exactly what she'd imagined doing all last summer in the alley behind Ruby's. Now all he had to do was kiss her. Leo looked down at her, his eyes tinged with amber warmth. "Hey, hey now. I think I was supposed to bring you in directly."

Leo smiled. She took it as enigmatic, not outright, rejection. He was still holding her hand. She pouted. He'd abducted her. He'd drugged her. He owed her—a kiss at least. "You always do what your mother says?"

"Yep." he said nonplussed. "She's been good to me, an amazing woman. Come on, I'll introduce you."

There it was again, that loyalty. Hard to argue with, but still. Geneva returned her attention to the Friend-Me building before her. Its green-mirrored surface was completely out of sync with the rest of the red and beige brick buildings on the New West campus. Rumors about what went on in the basements of some of the buildings floated around campus. As a psychology student, however, she knew most of them weren't true. The administration had put a stop to animal experimentation after the revolution. It was wasteful, cruel, and unscientific. If animals were going to be tortured again for the sake of science though, this new building looked a likely place. The mounds of upturned earth, the unnatural green, and the ironic imperative of the name Friend-Me: It all said vivisection.

With her own good sense overrun by a residue of SLO goodwill, she followed Leo inside. It was reassuringly corporate, in maple and silver. A trim receptionist sat behind a computer at the front desk. Leo pointed to a small room with a green door to the right, “That's dispatch for the campus couriers." Then, he showed her to a large, windowed room filled with circular tables ringed by monitors. “This is where the Friend-Me mentors will be. Mom likes them to work together. That's why the circles."

Geneva nodded as he led her deeper in, to a bank of elevators. They rode up to the 14th floor where the elevator door opened into a huge triangular office, the tip of the pyramid, cast in greenish light. A woman knelt on an orange and brown patterned rug in front of a slim metal desk. She sorted through boxes, humming and occasionally clapping a hand to her thigh. When she looked up at them, her expression—half-smile and heavy-lidded eyes—felt familiar. It was the way Geneva herself looked after cramming all night for a test and awakening the next morning ready to ace it.

"Leo! Good!" the woman stood, stepped over the swirl of papers at her feet and held out her hand. "You've brought her."

Geneva felt the remnants of Leo's thoughts surge with love at the sight of the woman and the sound of her smooth low voice. Her own thoughts also spiked in recognition and not just because the woman's broad smile was clearly the origin of Leo's. She stepped forward past the woman's outstretched hand and wrapped her arms around the woman's waist, inhaling her nutmeg scent. The woman returned her embrace. For a moment, resting her head on the woman's soft shoulder, Geneva felt lighter, as if she'd just dropped her book bag after a long day. Relief swept through her. Seconds passed. Then she pulled away. The room went from blurry to sharp green, as she blinked back tears. She twisted her fingers through her ponytails. This woman was not her mother, was not a refuge. She'd just hugged Kendra LeMay, the head of New West's most innovative corporation.

Kendra peered into her eyes. She huffed, put her hands on her hips and faced Leo. "You drugged her. Are you out of your mind, child?"

"She was a little reluctant to come." Leo said. He gave his usual easy shrug. It was the same gesture anyway, but his plaintive expression, wide eyes, furrowed brow, made his face look ten years younger.

"Everyone's making bad decisions," Kendra said, looking pointedly at Leo who took shelter behind the desk. "But I'm glad you are here." She held Geneva's hands in hers and swung them side-to-side. "The world's first powerful psychic."

Geneva swayed. "Don't."

Kendra placed her hands on Geneva's shoulders steadying her. "Don't be afraid. There's nothing new, but so much to be discovered. 'Pure thought can grasp reality as the ancient shamans dreamed.' Sound familiar? It's Einstein."

Geneva pulled her hands away and shook her head. "No. You sound familiar, the way you talk. Those words. I know you."

Kendra put hands to hips and smiled. "So you have been paying attention."

Then Geneva made the connection to her childhood mentor on Friend-Me and understood why she'd been getting deliveries from the courier even when she was not on the Friend-Me network. "Nala?"

Kendra held out her hand again. "It's nice to meet you in person."

Geneva just stared at Kendra's red-orange nails. "My father was right. You've been spying on me, just like he said you would."

Kendra spread her arms wide. "He calls it spying. I call it synchronicity."

"An invasion of privacy," Geneva said.

"I didn't think your generation even cared about that anymore. Aren't you all neo-privates? A moot point regardless. What kind of privacy can someone who projects their thoughts expect?"

Geneva grasped her head in her hands as if to hold her thoughts in.

"Mom," Leo said.

"I'm sorry." Kendra said. "I noticed you when you first opened your Friend-Me account. We were just developing the process with the couriers. I monitored some of the journals and noticed you were unusual. It was easy to know what you wanted and needed. I became your Friend-Me mentor, Nala, to stay close to you. It's not so terrible child. Psychic powers are like everything in this world, more amazing than you could ever imagine, but also more mundane. It depends on what you are looking for. You project your feelings, but it's not a word for word translation. Not always. Mostly, we just get a general impression."

"Like with SLO-42," Leo said. "It gives you a taste of someone else, but it doesn't take you over."

Kendra frowned and waved a hand at the door. "Leave us."

No, don't, Geneva thought. Leo reacted as if he'd heard her, giving her an apologetic look, but he still rose obediently and disappeared behind the elevator doors. She was alone with Kendra LeMay. The woman's eyes, very much like Leo's but a darker shade of brown, stared through her. Feeling heavy and unsteady from the receding drugs, Geneva sank onto the least paper-strewn bit of rug she could find. "It's done. I'm here. Please, just tell me why."

Kendra LeMay knelt on the floor beside her and swept a hand over the rug. "Geneva, I want you to explore your potential, learn to control your abilities, see what you are capable of, what the future holds. I believe your abilities are our next stage of evolution. You will lead us to a new understanding of consciousness and what it means to be human."

Geneva shook her head. "No, I just want to graduate and get on with my life. I'm just a college student. I'm nobody's future. I haven't even got my own figured out."

Kendra made a clicking sound with her tongue. "Yes, and that's what college is for. A good leader is just someone with a driving passion who realizes they need other people to accomplish their goal."

Geneva pressed her palms against the rug and held her eyes wide so that the tears forming wouldn't spill out. Just one escaped. It splashed onto one of the papers, a document titled Conceptual Reality Project in CHEC with RFC-43 "Mindscape:" Subject 1 contract.

"You'll do it." Kendra said riffling through the papers around her. Then she reached forward and tugged a stack of them out from under Geneva's knees, the tear-stained sheet on top. "You'll do it to help Valerie, your friends, and Generation Utopia. These abilities are coming and if you don't know how to control them, your minds will betray you. All you have to do to prevent this is learn. Be willing. You might not be ready, but that's OK. No one ever is. You can be what you are and what you will be at the same time. That's life. That's synchrony. For the betterment of society, we have to learn how to use this ability that's coming whether we like it or not. I'd really like your help."

"This is the contract," Kendra said, flipping through the documents. "It gives you as many specifics as possible without wrecking the experiment." Her voice jumped an octave as she began talking faster. "Just sign there," she pointed to a line on a page. "And initial, there, there and there." She shuffled through the papers and handed them over. If she noticed the tear splotch on the first page, she didn't say anything.

Geneva took the thick slightly oily parchment in her hands. She skimmed the document: Conceptual Reality Project in CHEC with RFC-43 "Mindscape": Subject 1 Contract. It was filled with legalese. Her semester of Privacy Law aside, she'd need a lawyer to decipher it.

"What's RFC?" she asked.

"Really Fluid Composite," Kendra said. "It's a new material you'll be working with."

"And CHEC?"

"The Controlled Holistic Environmental Chambers, where the experiment takes place."

Geneva brought the last page to the top of the stack. The paragraph over the signature line read: As a result of participating in this experiment, I, the undersigned, absolve Friend-Me Corporation and the individual, Kendra LeMay, of any responsibility in the event of accidental death or dismemberment or instance of permanent disability including, but not limited to, coma, paralysis, seizures, mental trauma or loss of mental capacity or functionality. In addition, I, the undersigned, agree to commit to research and development of any findings from said experiment for a period of no less than two years and agree to uphold Friend-Me Corporation's full and proprietary interest in all such findings and the results thereof for a period of no less than 10 years."

Geneva's visions of vivisection returned. "I don't want to be a lab rat."

Kendra held out a pen. "Think of it as an internship."

The pen was standard Friend-Me courier issue, slim forest green with silver lettering. It looked like every pen she'd ever used to sign her name at the bottom of countless Friend-Me deliveries. She reached out, took it, rolled it between her fingers and stared at its nub of potent green ink. It signified a lifetime of acceptance.

She continued to look over the contract, lingering on each of the consequences.

Kendra twined the long russet yarns of the rug with her fingers. "You know, part of being alive, of being conscious, is being aware of your role in the world—history, future, culture, society—at this point in time. When I started Friend-Me Co., I wanted to create powerful connections between people. I thought of myself as a lone innovator in a time of stasis. But as it caught on, I discovered there were other people interested in the connections I was creating. I joined Psi-Aware and met Dr. Montgrave. She confirmed what I believed: that culture shapes who we are as people far more than the limitations of our bodies. Our bodies become what we imagine. She told me about the traumatized children coming to her clinic. Our children's brains were being changed by the connectivity of our culture, but faster than they could handle. Friend-Me contributed to the problem and now Friend-Me must help solve it. Even the government now agrees—the danger of being uninvolved outweighs the risks of plunging in—and it is funding this research. There's no going back, so we must go forward. This experiment will save tons of young people the grief you and Valerie have gone through."

Geneva considered. If she wanted to find out more about these powers, if she wanted to really help Valerie, here was an action she could take now. She silenced her thoughts, pushed aside her fears and scrawled her name at the bottom of the contract. Her usual steep slanted signature gained eccentric length and loops. She stared at it a moment and then put the page aside. In a flurry, she scoured the document and placed her initials GTW on each page. With each stroke, her anxiety lessened. This time she wasn't riding on the drug-induced high of Leo's buoyancy. She was feeling wave after wave of her own cool confidence. "I feel like I've just enrolled in Becoming Psychic 101."

"Well done." Kendra said. "You're about to embark on the most incredible adventure left to humankind—the exploration of the mind. It is time for us to venture in."

~ 19 ~

MINDSCAPE

"Friend-Me Corporation did play a role, as did founder Kendra LeMay, but I think the importance of that role has been exaggerated. We would have adopted the psychic curriculum, eventually. I don't like to use the term meddlesome, but I think it applies: the corporation and LeMay's involvement in the transformation was dangerously meddlesome." — *Save Giovanni: The Lost Men of the Psychic Wars,* S. Sherring

Tingling pain replaced the numbness in her legs as Geneva stood up from her cross-legged position on the rug in the middle of Kendra LeMay's executive suite at the top of the Friend-Me building on the university campus. She clutched the Mindscape Contract in both hands staring at her signature scrawled in permanent ink across the bottom of it. Probably, it occurred to her, too late, she should have at least asked her father's advice before signing her life over to Friend-Me. He'd been right about Friend-Me the first time. They were spying on little girls to gain a corporate advantage.

A door beside the elevator opened and Leo rushed out. "Mother, it's Sherring," he gasped, as the elevator opened. "I'm sorry."

A man with silver hair ducked as he stepped out accompanied by a blue uniformed officer. Geneva had seen photos of John Sherring, the President of New West University. In his smiling headshots, he looked handsome, but terribly ordinary, like an aging ball player. In person, all of his features were long, his arms and legs, nose and jaw. The stripes down his suit and across the broad tie knotted at his neck added even more length. In real life, he looked stretched thin.

Kendra LeMay pulled her tapered skirt down from where it bunched at her hips as she stood. Her patterned green and black blouse ballooned around her as she stepped forward. "President Sherring, you must be here to talk about the grand opening. We're just about moved in."

The top of her head reached just below his armpit. "It's over," the president said. Beside him, the guard's hands hovered over the holster wrapped around his waist.

Kendra tilted her chin up. "What's over?"

"This relationship," he said. "Between New West University and your corporation. You are no longer welcome on this campus."

Kendra knelt and lifted one of the boxes off the floor. Neither the president nor his guard made a move to help her. "The construction of the building is complete. Millions of dollars have been invested and we're about to begin. The last time we talked, we agreed. Friend-Me needs to be here. Sherring, you are not a mercurial man." She shifted the box on her hip. "So, what did I do to piss off New West?"

The president nodded at the guard who held up a handful of green vials. "I did not know part of your plan was to manufacture drugs on my campus. We found this in the basement. I believe this was made with your son's oxytocin. It's a complicated process. I can't imagine he's been doing this without your knowledge."

Kendra dropped the box on her desk. "Making SLO-42 isn't a crime. And Sherring, you are well aware—or could be—that we're using that drug to suppress students' psychic abilities at your internment lab. Thorazine isn't as effective as it used to be."

"Dealing SLO-42 is a crime. Especially, on my campus," he said. "I want you and Friend-Me gone by tomorrow morning."

Standing stock-still for once, by the stairway, Leo's eyes darted to his mother and then down. Kendra turned back to the president her hands planted on the edge of the desk. "You can't punish New West for my son's stupidity. When you entered the agreement with Friend-Me, you made a considered decision. You had good reason."

Geneva started toward Leo, bidden to comfort the hurt in his eyes. The president's voice rose. "I didn't know about your son's dealings. I didn't know you knew about Sync Chrome City. I didn't know you planned to speed this process up the entire time." Geneva jerked to a stop as the president caught her wrist. "Wait. What's this?" She looked from her signature scrawled in green ink, to him and back again. The wrinkles on his face appeared strategically placed to give him the authority of age without marring the smoothness of his cheeks.

"An employee," Kendra said.

The president dropped Geneva's wrist but pulled the contract out of her hand. As he scanned the page, steel gray flashed in his ice blue eyes. "No. This is not what we agreed to."

"It's exactly. Further research." Kendra replied.

"Test Subject?" The menace in the president's tone grew but his voice stayed low. He pointed at Geneva with his fist, the side of the contract balled up in it. "You cannot misuse my students. This ends. You lied to me, Ms. LeMay. I always had concerns that society was not ready for this. Our minds may be capable of more, but it doesn't matter if the majority of people are not ready for those changes and unwilling to invest in them. Becoming psychic would make us fundamentally different and we like the way we are. You are a visionary, but that doesn't mean you would lead us in the direction we want to go. Your vision could even be seen as a kind of genocide. You can't force this."

"I can't," Kendra said. "You can't force anyone to do anything. I'm well aware they have to make their own choices. But I can tell them what's stalking them, and I can come to their aid when I hear their cries of help. This is not some hypothetical. We're not debating some far-off future. This is not something Friend-Me can turn its back on. The genocide, as you call it, is underway. Our children are changing whether we like it or not. Young lives are at risk now."

"Because you put them there," the president said. "You said this was a completely natural occurrence and now I find that you've been speeding it up with SLO-42. You know what it's been doing to these children. They are not ready for this. We are not ready."

"But it's happening, and I think its been happening all along. Our children have been symptomatic for generations and our response has always been to drug them and now you are going back to the oldest solution of all—lock them away. Out of sight, out of mind. How will you rationalize this? Call it a lost generation?" she said.

"You will pursue this line of research no further," Sherring said. "I'm speaking both as the president of this university and as president of New West. You and your company are no longer welcome here."

At this, Leo took a protective stance at his mother's shoulder. His expression would have stopped Geneva cold. But the president had inches on him, and the guard had girth and the adults barely registered his presence. Kendra held out an arm protectively to hold him back as if they were coming to a sudden stop. Her eyes were locked on Sherring. The way they were focused on each other reminded her of the purple cords winding between her and Valerie. They looked like they were sharing an internal connection, having a silent conversation in a shared mental space. She saw confusion at the root of their anger. Neither Kendra LeMay nor the president had the ability to communicate the way she and Valerie had, sharing ideas and emotion directly. They had to talk to bridge the distance between them with words and be wary of a wrong one. It was easy to misspeak, misread, mishear, and misunderstand.

"The rebels were right. New West's a sham," Kendra said. "You didn't create utopia. You just took advantage of a situation and got rid of everyone you didn't like. Now I'm on the chopping block. Fine." She gestured to the boxes. "I haven't even unpacked. I'm a single woman who started out with a small business selling little girl's diaries. I know my place. You know you can afford to push me out precisely because I am not your enemy. I'm actually on your side. But how can you throw away our children?"

The president's extended arm began to shake. The contract in his fist rattled. He took the paper in both hands tearing it. The ripping sound seemed to carry on and on like a scream. "You are not bound by this young lady."

Geneva reached for a diagonal slice of the contract as it slipped from his hand and caught a jagged edge as it fell to the floor. "That's mine." *To help Valerie.*

The other half of the contract fluttered to the floor. The president stared at her. "What?"

"She didn't say a word. But you heard her. Valerie's one of the students you're interning at New West Mental. She wants to help," LeMay said.

Geneva nodded.

The president gestured to his guard and turned his back on them heading to the elevator. "You can do whatever you want, out there. We'll make our decision about this development when the legislative session ends in March."

Kendra threw the contract into the trash and turned to Geneva. "That's your new contract, then. That's how much time we have to help your friend. Less than three months."

A paper cut from the torn contract bled a thin red line across Geneva's hand.

Before leaving New West to become a guinea pig for Friend-Me out on the 'Way Geneva called home. Her father answered. Her mother was out.

"She's on assignment again. Something's brewing in Cascadia," her father said. "Is there something you need?"

"No, Dad, I just...love you." she said.

Geneva hadn't been outside of New West since she was five. Already the sight of the dingy 'Way and the transients living along it had her on edge, not to mention that she'd left behind the university, her family and everyone she knew to take part in an experiment. Pulling up to a high-fenced yard laced with concertina wire behind the low gray Friend-Me factory didn't make her feel any better. It was even worse when Kendra unlocked the chains and drove the Enviro-car through the gate up to the ramshackle house. Whereas Friend-Me corporate looked like the kind of place where animals went to tortured deaths this place looked like it hunted humans.

"This will be your home for the next three months," said Kendra as she followed her up the front steps. Kendra paused on the porch and fumbled in her purse. "After you enter the CHEC, Controlled Holistic Environmental Chambers, you will have no contact with the outside world until the experiment is complete. Do you have any questions?"

Geneva wished she knew what to ask. She shook her head no.

"Think of yourself as a plant about to be moved from a small pot to the yard. It will be traumatic to be uprooted. You bring just a little of your original self with you. The sudden rush of air feels noxious, but when you spread out, you'll grow."

She sounded like Professor Roundtree, but the metaphor was lost on Geneva when she entered CHEC house. The effect was immediately claustrophobic, and she wished she'd brought along a little more of her original soil. All that she had was her jacket and a fresh change of Face-in-the-Crowd clothes with an innocuous pair of white panties.

The CHEC house felt close, warm and stuffy like an unfinished attic. Everything was coated in a fluffy orange crème material that looked like insulation but felt like sponge.

"Lights," Kendra said, and a soft peach glow enveloped the room.

Geneva looked around. There was nothing in the house but the soft sherbet-colored fluff that coated the walls, floor and ceiling. There were no windows and only the entryway door. After looking around, she hurried up the staircase in front of her. Her sneakers sunk into the stuff. The upstairs of the house looked the same. There were a few unfurnished partitioned rooms coated in sherbet fluff.

Geneva went back down the stairs and pressed her hand into a wall. The scent of oranges rose. The goo oozed around her fingers. It was sticky damp and warm like dough. When she touched her fingertips to her lips, they tasted faintly sweet. The wall held the shape of her hand. "What is this?"

"That's the RFC - Really Fluid Composite. Marketing calls it Mindscape."

"Is there a bathroom?" she asked.

Immediately, a door opened in the side of what had looked to be a seamless orange wall.

Kendra smiled. "Through there. There's lots. You just have to explore. I'll leave you to it and send your teacher to you in the morning. Dr. Montgrave is a very special person. Very few scientists are prepared to stand up publicly for psi."

When Kendra left, the seam to the front door closed and Geneva was alone in the orange-crème Mindscape with no way out.

She managed to find a few comforts programmed into the house as a teaching tool by saying the right words in the right places. "Food," opened a little drawer filled with trail mix in the kitchen and "Water," extended a shiny orange working faucet near the bathroom. When she said, "sleep," in a small room upstairs, a nest of Mindscape, rose up out of the floor. It was not quite a bed, but when she lay down and wrapped it over her body it was soft and warm. Orange remained in her mind's eye long after she closed her eyes. It was difficult to gauge time in the windowless house, but she guessed it was nightfall. Her first night in the house, and she was already sick of seeing the color orange.

Geneva was sitting in the living room of the Mindscape CHEC house mushing the orange foam with her fingers when the front door reappeared. The wide-eyed woman who walked through it was familiar. She had a hooked nose and almond skin. The copper infinity symbol necklace swung over the high collar of her rust-colored sweater. She wore tights too and Geneva could not take her eyes off of the refreshing forest green color. "Dr. Montgrave?" she asked.

"I'm not with the clinic anymore. Just Friend-Me. You can call me Clara. How do you feel?"

Geneva pressed the orange-goo between her bare toes. "Weird. I'm a little bored. That's the last thing I expected."

"You are experiencing some sensory deprivation. That can be more stressful than too much drama. Sometimes it's more difficult to cope with mundane, daily life than to make a radical change. Did you find food? Water?"

Geneva nodded.

"Good." Clara plopped down cross-legged into the Mindscape in front of her. "Some of the basics have been supplied for you although we've worked them into the environment so there's still the exploratory feel. Mostly this house contains only what we are sitting on here. With the exception of its outward façade, part of the original 1905 building, the house is made of RFC."

She scooped up a mound of the floor and held it in her hands. "This is an ultra-light proton, high slippage, denatured transportable Really Fluid Composite, called Mindscape. I am one of a team of materials scientists and psychologists who created this substance for Friend-Me Co. We know it can do a lot. Since you have demonstrated ability with psychic projection, you will be the first to test its full potential."

She shaped the orange fluff into a ball and tossed it. Geneva caught the smooth, cool sphere and threw it back.

"I will teach you what I know," Clara said. She pulled and kneaded the ball a few times in a series of gestures that looked like Lydia Streker making cinnamon rolls. "This material is a combination of teleportable protons and viscous matter more easily susceptible to the vibrations of the mind. It's uniquely meldable."

As she watched, the stretched ropes of material grew shiny and bright like taffy. Clara reshaped it into a ball and began to spin and stroke it in her hands until it became translucent with a hint of yellow at its center. Clara tossed it. Geneva caught the warm sphere and clasped the smooth glass to her chest.

Geneva put it aside and tried to scoop up a glob of the floor. It didn't separate as easily as Clara made it appear. She tore a wad of the material up. As soon as it was in her hands, it felt less solid. It squished between her fingers and dripped back onto the floor when she tried to roll it into a ball.

Clara reached across her and picked up the glass sphere. "What you need to know is that the mind has the power to shape objects. We live in a conceptual reality. That knowledge is all you need to reach a de facto truth that you are capable of much more than you know and unlock your mind's potential. The Mindscape just gives us a way to process this new ability, to let us focus on what our hands are doing while our minds adapt. The brain learns and stores many things in networks which function outside of our awareness."

Geneva tried to shape the ball again, but the Mindscape still lay flat in her hands like soft dough.

Clara held up a transparent glass-like ball again now with a spiral strip of color through it like a bright orange peel. "You can do anything if you can harness the *vis viva*— the living force in all objects."

"How did you...?"

"With thought." Clara said. "I'm going to teach you to reify this substance. Mindscape is an abstract representation of infinite possibilities. I want you to imagine it as something simple, real, and attainable. Now cross your legs, close your eyes, and let's go to work. If anyone is capable of using this material, it will be you. While living in this house, you will learn to use it. You will need to, or the sensory deprivation will drive you crazy."

For the first time, Geneva understood why Val hated that word, because it implied that the changes happening to her were bad, that she was failing in a way eminently out of her control. She must have been—no, she must be—terrified and so alone. Geneva picked up another glob of Mindscape determined to prove that what she and Val could do was not crazy. When people saw what could be achieved, they would have to accept Generation Utopia.

~ 20 ~

ORANGE CRÉME

"Even those who have not had difficulty with their psychic studies to date, may struggle to attain the next level of development. An internship is strongly recommended. Students may also find it useful to participate in various meditation camps and workshops. Remember how even Geneva Weltraum struggled at first." — *Becoming Psychic 101, A History and a Primer*

Geneva was alone in the Mindscape house again. She'd had to admit, at first, that it felt good to be away from school. The atmosphere at NWU was so intense. Everyone was trying to follow their dreams or fall in love. Professor Roundtree said life was about, "being and becoming—constant transformation" which seemed true of New West students. It was so much work. They were all so busy becoming it seemed there was no time to think. Although wasn't that why they were at college?

Now she had time—too much—to contemplate and she was still failing. She hadn't managed to use the Mindscape. There were snow globe-sized tufts of it all around the house and scattered throughout the room she'd taken to sleeping in for longer and longer stretches. Her body had sunk into the orange sherbet-colored foam where she'd been curled up for days going on months. Sometimes the foam had a warm tone to it that meant it was daylight somewhere other times it was dim and grayish, meaning night. She felt hallow, but she was tired of the rations: the bread, the powdered juice, the reconstituted soups, and trail mix she'd been eating. She touched a few raisins and nuts beside her. She'd liked the food at first because it provided some relief from the homogeneous Mindscape. The nuts were firm, and the raisins were deep brown and wrinkled. But it wasn't working anymore. The peanuts were almost the same shade of orange as the Mindscape and the raisins had the same squish. Instead of changing the material, she felt like it was changing her and everything into a homogeneous blob.

Clara had been encouraging about Geneva's failures when she stopped by for training sessions twice a day wearing a relief of colors. "Don't worry," she said. "It takes time for the brain to create new connections. Even thinking of changing the Mindscape is progress. You are creating new patterns. I know that you hate the loneliness imposed on you by this work. But you are here because you want to find out what it means to be psychic. Once you find that out, you will never be lonely again. This isn't a magical wish in a fairy tale with terrible repercussions and a harsh moral. This is an ability that today will make you unique and tomorrow will transform us all. Your reasons for seeing this through can be as big or as small as you like. They can be as practical or as fanciful as you require, but if you stay and you do this, you will never regret it."

Inspired, Geneva had spent hours with Mindscape in her hands, hoping. But as the days passed, even Clara couldn't disguise her frustration at the lack of progress. Geneva emerged from one of their meditation sessions with a pancake of Mindscape smashed between her palms. "Stop trying so hard to control it," Clara scolded. "You have to free your intuition. Relax."

"Every time you say that I get tense. My intuition sucks," Geneva said.

"You have to concentrate on the outcome you want so your mind doesn't lock on the negative," Clara said. Her fuchsia top made her skin look a sallow orange. "Listen, I think we've gone as far as we can together. I've given you all the tools I have. It's time for you to use them: on your own."

Geneva had almost stormed out of the house then making for the now invisible doorway where Clara had entered, the spot she'd been staring at all afternoon, when she was supposed to be concentrating on shaping matter with her mind, "You're giving up?" But she'd stopped in the doorway staring out at the dingy 'Way and the bleak February sky. She could leave, but nothing had changed out there. She'd go back to the same uncertainty not knowing what to do, unable to help Val, unsure if Leo cared for her or was just waiting around for Coco to change her mind again. Leaving seemed pointless too. She closed the door behind Clara and didn't ask when she'd be coming back.

The worst part of being left alone in the Mindscape House was not knowing when she'd see anyone again. As soon as she was awake, Geneva wanted to be unconscious again, to bury her head in the orange-scented Mindscape and sink into sleep. She was so tired. Awake, her thoughts cycled. This was pointless. She could not help Val. She'd destroyed her future by coming here. She wouldn't graduate. She'd be kicked out of New West. She'd have to go live on the 'Way and work in the Friend-Me factory or live alone in the forest.

Geneva rolled over and scooped a ball of Mindscape out of the floor for the 365th time. She rolled it between her hands, closed her eyes and concentrated. *This time let it happen. Let it become glass.* She opened her eyes, and the Mindscape was—orange and viscous—exactly the same as the rest of the house. She pushed it back into the hole she'd taken it from. Maybe this was a trick and Clara was a magician. Maybe the "Mindscape" was just foam, and she'd been trying to do something impossible all along. Maybe she was the control in some experiment while someone else, somewhere—Valerie at the clinic?—had the real, malleable stuff. She wished she believed that, but she could still feel a connection to Val and knew her friend was still comatose, while she stayed here, in isolation, accomplishing nothing.

It wasn't fair. She couldn't do this. She didn't have the answers. She didn't know how to use this stuff, make it do or be anything else. Clara's logical explanations of quantum particles didn't mean anything, the world she described was nothing like her reality. Maybe it was something Valerie could have understood. She hadn't, maybe couldn't. Besides what good would it do, really, if she figured out how to manipulate the protons in the Mindscape and make glass spheres? They were good for nothing, and it was too late. The guys and Valerie were in comas imprisoned in New West Mental. Their minds were lost. The damage was irreparable. Geneva wasn't doing any good here. She was responsible, but powerless.

The wall behind her was scarred with long deep shadowed lines. She stood up and placed her fingers into the grooves. She couldn't remember raking her fingers into the stuff and wailing. But she knew she'd done this. There was no one else. It seemed so long ago that she could have felt that much emotion, had that much energy. She ran her hands down the lines.

She looked up to see Kendra LeMay staring at her. "Hi Geneva," she said in a soft voice as if speaking to a shy child. Geneva touched her matted hair, noticed the moistness under her arms and wondered if Kendra could smell her stink through the cloying orange Mindscape. It had been weeks since she'd bathed.

"Our time is almost up," Kendra said. She gazed at the shredded Mindscape floor and the scarred wall. "We're beginning to think we made a mistake. I know you are trying. Clara tells me you are. Maybe we fooled ourselves because we wanted to be right. We knew this would be hard, but we expected faster progress. It's not fair to keep you here if we're wrong. It's not healthy. I think we have to accept that either the Mindscape doesn't work, or you are not what we thought."

Geneva clasped her hands and thought about becoming clean, eating fresh food, seeing her mother. It was so tempting. But then, what? When she thought about leaving, she had to think about what came after that and nothing had changed, except that she was more miserable, than the day when she'd almost followed Clara out of the house. She still could not leave. Her problems were unchanged. Val would be in a coma. She would go back to the university. But she was not even a student there anymore. She'd dis connected herself even from that to be here. Now, it had become harder to go back than to go forward.

"No, I said I'd stay to see this through. I signed on," Geneva said, remembering even as she said it that Sherring had shredded the contract. But the paper itself had little value, whereas her act of signing it was irreversible. She remembered her scrawling signature and the relief she'd felt at the end of it. She hated LeMay for making her remake the choice.

Kendra shrugged. "OK, but soon it won't matter. They are casting a vote. Psychics will be one more undesirable element shut out of New West."

Geneva considered what the impact of a vote like that would mean: everything. They would never allow psychic studies. She and Valerie would be banished from the utopia her parents had created. But, if she could demonstrate the breadth of their abilities, nothing could stop them from claiming a completely new destiny. Alone again, Geneva kept envisioning LeMay's off-handed shrug. Like she didn't care one way or another. Even she had given up, even she no longer believed Geneva could make anything out of the revolutionary material.

So far, Geneva had failed to find either of the two things hidden in the Mindscape House she longed for most: a window and a phone. She intensified her search. She made another routine search around looking for them. This was her pattern: eat, drink, search methodically room by room—sleep.

One day she awoke from a dream. She couldn't remember any of it, except that it had contained the color blue. She immediately began her search. She walked throughout the entire house and said, "Window, window, window," until the syllables in the word separated and she wasn't quite sure how to pronounce it anymore or precisely what it meant. Still, no windows appeared anywhere.

She began to scream, "window" and sob, "window" pacing through the house, circling, until her limbs pulled her down on the floor of one of the small upstairs rooms. She muttered, "window, window" through dry lips with a swollen tongue. Her eyes burned as she stared unblinking at the ceiling. Finally, she closed them and just saw the window in her head, the four outlines, the great distance through it and the wispy clouds dissipating in the sky.

When she next opened her eyes, the light that struck them was colorless. It streamed through a clear panel revealing sky, in the ceiling of the orange-crème room was a window more beautiful than she had imagined. She sat up and dropped her head back to stare at it breathing deeply through each chakra from her sacrum to her forehead just as Clara had taught her. At the side of her window view, she could see wisps of green tree and a flitting sparrow. She sat cross-legged and stared into the sky as her mind uncoiled releasing the claustrophobic tension that had gnawed at her ever since she'd entered the house. She ate and slept and then returned to the window. It had grown wider. The tree held a nest in a misshapen branch.

Geneva sat up from where she'd been lying sunk into the spongy sherbet-colored floor of the Mindscape House. The ceiling looked different. There were waves on the surface of the orange goo overhead, variations of light and shade she hadn't noticed before. Depending on where she looked, patches were colored like buttercream or marmalade or blood orange. She got to her knees and wiggled her fingertips in the soft material at her sides. She leaned back and placed a hand behind her. She pressed down. It was warm where she had been sitting. It was cooler on the floor in front of her. Her body heat affected the Mindscape. It was not really such a leap from that change to what Clara insisted she could do: move the quantum particles and reshape them with her mind.

Geneva scooped a ball of the goo out of the floor. It was the same size and shape as each of her failed attempts. She began to knead it with the heels of her palms. Bits of it stuck to her skin. She stretched and pummeled it with her fists. She started to hum the Giovanni Hastings Musica melody in time with the kneading. The ball became smooth and satiny. It grew warm in her hands. She held it aloft. From underneath her eye, she brushed away a cool tear and lifted it on her pointer finger. She waved it back and forth and watched how it held its shape. The word for that: viscosity. She looked through it to the Mindscape dough. The dough adhered to certain principles. It was designed to move. She was meant to be able to move it or she wouldn't be here. It was the way to get unstuck.

She wanted to run, to shout, but she'd lose the moment. Instead, she sat very still and stared through the tear. She focused all her energy on it. Her mind ran to the ball, all around it and inside. Her mind pulsed with pleasure. So what she'd been doing before, trying to coax the ball to bend to her will was wrong. The opposite of what was wanted! Instead, she placed her mind inside the ball and let its curve shape her thought.

Then there were colors. It began with a yellow line of light bisecting the orange ball and trembling inside. Beneath the rind, yellow bubbled. Yellow burst out of orange seeds in the core and blossomed to deep red. The ball grew smoother and shinier until it became translucent. Geneva rolled it back and forth on her palm.

It was hard and solid and unlike anything else in the soft, sticky room, in the soft, sticky house. She closed her eyes tightly. Her lashes flicked her cheeks. Dr. Montgrave explained that once she put thought energy into an object it gained weight and a presence of its own that was reinforced when others saw it too. She wanted to share this reality not just with Clara and Kendra but with someone who cared, not just about the mindscape and its vast potential for profits, but about herself. There were things she was starting to realize and she wanted to share these ideas. Whenever she thought about that, she thought of Leo. She held the globe and sat by the door sending her mind outside of it to: *Leo.*

Hours later, when the door opened, he entered. "I heard you. I thought I'd stop by," he said.

His distant offhanded tone had unsettled her in the past, but now she had learned to see the possibilities in things that at first had no substance. He was earnest but cloaked his response in nonchalance to stave off rejection.

"You know what I want," she said.

She placed the glass globe shot through with yellow rays and red flowers in his hand then she grabbed his other hand and pulled him upstairs to the window room. She took off her clothes and pressed her lips to his. She sunk into the crevasses of his body. She hadn't felt comfort in a very long time.

~ 21 ~

BREAK IN

"At first you may feel overwhelmed by the Infinite Lattice. As you meet many minds, it may be difficult to keep track of your own. Rely on your unique way of visualizing the Lattice. The analogy to swimming is a good one. There's an innate element of danger in the environment, but it becomes less dangerous as you learn to navigate it. Remember there are many minds in Psychic Space to help you. It is less like swimming in an ocean and more like a crowded pool. Entering the Lattice is an essential part of mental development. When you feel restless, angry, or despondent, you most likely need to increase the pace of your psychic development. Spending more time in Psychic Space will be beneficial." — *Becoming Psychic 101, A History and a Primer*

Geneva and Leo made love upstairs in the Mindscape House. She opened her eyes and looked over Leo's bare shoulder into a profusion of Nootka-Rose-Ladyslipper blossoms. The wild rose honey scent dripped into her open pores. It filled her skin with expanding warmth until she felt ready to burst. Tendrils of steam rose off Leo's back like morning earth. She was up to her fingertips in his smooth shoulder blades kneading the muscles stretched across them. The red-striated lips of the flowers lapped at her sides. She took a deep breath settling underneath him. The air gliding petal smooth across her tongue left a trace of sweetness. It reminded her of sucking lilac stems. She exhaled letting his weight compress her. Her voice dropped into Hort-Audible tones talking to her lover as if he were a tender plant. "I can do it now. I can save them."

He lowered his torso onto her chest and his lips caressed the corner of her eye. Then he drew back, his lips glistening with her tears. "No one expects you to."

Her ponytails slid across the carpet, red-on-red. She laid her palms over his tawny nipples and pressed against his chest. Heat waves shimmered between them as she pushed him away. "No, I said, 'I can.' Look up. I can connect them."

She started to laugh until her body rocked with it. Leo turned over beside her on the bedroom floor and followed her gaze up. Delicate white roots dangled from the ceiling. Thorn-covered branches crossed the skylight and arched down into the room. Blossoms spread open wide above them, petal to petal.

"You did that?" His fingertips brushed her shoulder trailing a tingling sensation. When he held his hand up, the tips of his fingers were faintly green. "And this."

Geneva looked to see if she were turning colors, too. But she was still pink. It was the effect she was having on him. She couldn't stop laughing. Just this fall, she'd been afraid of killing the one rare hybrid entrusted to her by Dr. Roundtree. Now, in a moment of delight, she could Mindscape a hothouse filled with the flowers.

Leo stroked her back. "See, things don't have to be terrible to be true."

"I thought that," she said. "Gritty reality seems most real, but when things are beautiful and right, we always describe them as dreamlike and hazy."

"It's a problem," Leo said. "People don't picture the best possible outcome and they wind up living the awful reality they imagined instead."

"We can change that," Geneva said.

Leo shook his hand out and the pink returned to his fingertips. "I must have gotten some on me." He stood and the lean long line of him above her reminded her of seeing him for the first time at the Mansion Expansion dance. Then, she'd thought she'd be satisfied just to know his name. She rose and pressed her body to his one more time, her ribs aching from laughter. They stood naked and honey-coated surrounded by the heat of hundreds of exotic flowers. He held her head in his hands, petted her. "Come on. We should go."

At the dance, the guys had crowded her out of the way. Now, the thought of them sobered her. They would see her when she saved them. She pulled on her Face in the Crowd underwear, T-shirt, and khakis. Leo hummed behind her as she ran down the stairs. "How will we get back across the border?" she asked reaching for the door.

She froze as it opened, and Leo tensed beside her. Coco stood on the porch. The smoke-filtered Freeway sunset created a reddish nimbus around her head and shoulders as it shone through her blonde hair. Warmth rushed to Geneva's face. She grabbed Leo's hand and thought at Coco: *You had your chance.*

With the sun behind her, she couldn't see Coco's expression very well, but the nimbus around her dipped. "That's not why I'm here."

Coco gestured behind her. Eve's Cadillac was parked in the lot beside the house. The suspension was so low the chassis nearly touched the gravel. "They're voting tomorrow on whether our friends can be helped or not. We should be there. We should make them look us in the eye when they tell us we don't count."

Leo nodded. He went to the car and held the passenger door open. "Take us to the guys first. To Linden. It's Geneva. What she can do, its incredible."

Coco waved a hand. "Spare me details."

Geneva slid across the seat next to Leo. They waited while Coco made a call from the porch. "Just letting him know where we are," she said as she settled into the driver's seat.

Between Coco and Leo, Geneva twirled her fingers through her ponytails. She stared at the brown of her hair showing through her Gator-Tongue dye job and looked from Coco to Leo, one solid golden profile to the other. She had the not unfamiliar feeling of being small and foolish beside them. But things were different now. Her thoughts were audible outside of herself. She could shape matter with her mind. She looked at Leo. He loved her.

"You know," Coco said, watching Geneva in the rearview mirror as she backed out onto the street. "When I first met you, I was intimidated. You seemed so independent."

In Coco's controlled hands, the car sped unwavering toward Linden as the sky went dark. The president's daughter had no trouble getting them across the border.

Did she have to be beautiful, smart, and a great driver?

The corner of Coco's mouth turned up, but her eyes didn't leave the road.

"Sync Chrome City. It's like an addiction," Leo explained. "If the site goes down while you're on, it causes a mental rift. Or, if you use it too much, you get awakened. You know, gain access. I think that's what happened to our boys. But they couldn't quite handle it. So if the damage is caused by being unplugged, it makes sense that what might fix the problem is to..."

Coco veered off at the exit to Linden. "Plug them back in."

"But not in Sync Chrome City," Geneva said. "We want them outside that artificial environment."

Coco slowed the car as they hit the main strip into town and drove past the closed sandwich shop and the blue glow of the dimly lit high school. "We can't do that. Reconnect them to what?"

"To each other," Leo said. "Turn here and pull over."

Geneva looked at Leo. There was a chance it might not work out between them. Even though they'd made a connection, he still cared about Coco. What she had with him would either grow or it could be uprooted, wither and die when it would hurt most. It was a risk she was willing to take, to love him for a while, while it lasted.

Gravel crunched beneath the tires as Coco made the sharp right down the road to the clinic. "So how are we doing this?"

"I don't think we can just march through the front door. The lab coats at the clinic probably don't understand what's really wrong with the guys," Leo said.

"Worse, maybe they do," Coco said, pulling the car to the side. "I mean I can see why New West would have problems with a generation of psychics. It's destroying the last vestige of privacy." She killed the engine and turned to Geneva. "Not everyone always thinks the most complimentary things."

She sounded tense, and it was strange to think Coco might be jealous.

Coco reached over the seat into the black fullness of Eve's back-seat and returned with a flashlight for Geneva and a small pocket light for Leo. Geneva hefted the light. "We'll sneak around back."

"You're going to break into a government facility. You realize this could get you thrown out of New West. Permanently exiled. Or you might not come out," Coco said.

"You don't have to come in with us," Leo said. "In fact, it'd be better if you didn't. Stay here. If anything goes wrong, call the president and bail us out."

Coco, who'd been sitting with her long legs out the door, swung them back in. "You're right. Daddy wouldn't approve if I got caught inside. I'll sit tight."

Geneva caught an edge of bitterness in Coco's voice and tried to make out her expression in the dark. There wasn't time to decipher it.

Outside of the car, Geneva and Leo walked just under cover of the low hanging evergreens along the road to the clinic. She kept the flashlight pointed down at the brush. It ensured she wouldn't trip on a stray root but staring at the spot of light obscured everything else. She could barely make out the building when it came into sight ahead of them, a lumpish shadow in the night. The low, green building blended into its surroundings like an animal in hiding. There were no cars or lights around it visible from the forest.

They pressed close to the wall of the building to get through the dense bushes to the back. Brambles snagged her thin cotton T-shirt and thorns scratched her face and arms as she pushed through them. They walked the entire back of the building trying to spot any variation in its surface that might indicate an entrance. As they examined the paint, her flashlight dimmed and went dark. "I think we have to go around front after all."

Leo turned on the pocket light. Light flashed into the air for a moment before he snapped it down. "Wait, look at that."

Geneva turned toward the illumination of green and gray-green shapes trying to see behind the brightness. Then the pocket light flickered out too, leaving her in blackness.

"Useless." The bushes beside Leo rustled and she guessed he'd thrown the light aside. "The ground's different here. Careful." A rush of falling leaves accompanied the last syllable followed by thudding.

Kneeling, Geneva felt through the wet, slimy leaves in front of her. "Are you OK?" Brushing the leaves aside, her fingers ran over cold, rough concrete. As her eyes adjusted, the jagged outline of the bushes appeared framing the rectangle of black that had enveloped Leo.

He whispered from below. "There's steps, and a door."

She scooted down the stairway feet first. Rain-soaked moss lined the steep narrow stairs. It squished beneath her hands as she lowered herself down. The cold numbed her palms. There was movement below. As she reached the middle of the incline, Leo came into relief leaning against a gray door. He cradled his hand close to his body as if it were a slack-winged bird. "I cut my hand. I don't think it's bad."

Geneva touched his shoulder, nodded. She examined the door and plucked a New West Mental Health pass card from the pocket of her khakis.

"Where'd you get that?" Leo asked.

"Friend-Me," she said. "My last delivery. I thought you knew."

She ran it—click—over a sensor. Leo pushed the door open with his shoulder. "I thought we were breaking in—literally. This was easier than I..."

As they stepped into the bright clinic hallway, the door snicked to a close behind them. As she blinked, an elongated shadow, a tall man, bore down on them. "You don't think we have cameras?" A pocketful of green syringes — SLO-42—stuck out of his lab coat.

Geneva readied to bolt down the hall when Leo unclasped his hand and held it up. His nearly severed finger dangled. Leo's eyes went wide as he tumbled forward. His head cracked on the tiled floor at the man's feet.

"Shit," the lab coat said.

Geneva knelt and rolled Leo over. Scarlet red spilled down the front of him. A patch spread across his shirt where he'd cupped his hand to his chest. Blood streamed down his arm and began to pool on the tile.

The man turned, took a few quick steps and then turned back. "Stay, I'll get the first aid kit." He darted forward through one of the doors.

Leo looked up and winked at Geneva. He nodded at the empty hall. "It's just a finger. Go."

She nodded at him in surprise but didn't hesitate. She sprinted down the hallway trusting her instincts to take her the right way.

She ran right, left, right until she came to three doors in a row. Locked. Locked. Locked. From inside came, "Yaaah, do it now."

Grugel.

She pressed her hand against the steel door on the end and on tiptoe peered through the reinforced-plastic window. The doors connected to one long narrow bunkhouse. Inside, curtains separated several hospital beds. Unrestrained sheeted shapes lay in each of them. At one end, Grugel stood with several wires snaked through a barred window clutched in his hand. At the other end, Burrows hunched over one of the shapes. He lifted a limp figure off the bed.

Geneva's thoughts lunged for her friend: *Val.*

Returning sensation pricked Geneva's numb hand as she pounded on the door. "He doesn't care. He's trying to shut you down." Eve's narrow dark eyes appeared in the window. *Come on. This time let me in.*

The door swung open. Purple sparked out of the ends of the wires and danced across the beds. In front of her, Eve's eyes rolled back into her head. Her body dropped to the floor, convulsing. The bodies on the beds shook. Limbs thrust under the sheets. Purple coils unloosed around them. They were plugged into Sync Chrome City, but Sync Chrome City could not support them. So, they disconnected from everything, disembarked, disembodied. Their minds rushed past her falling into void as if she were standing on the precipice in front of the Big Top. They leapt past her off the ledge into the bay.

Electric violet lashed Geneva as she ran forward and grabbed the ends of the whips. Her arms elongated and her body burned with the sensation of stretched muscle. She gathered eleven ends into her hands, twined them together and fastened them around her wrist like a balloon bouquet. She tethered their minds. Instead of the nearby hospital tile, the floor sparkled purple far below. Discs of white flashed by as she descended. Dry heat rose around her. She was losing them. Their minds couldn't keep up with the evolution. They were detaching under the strain and falling free. *Maybe this is what's supposed to happen. Our entire generation sacrificed to unattainable perfection.*

As she fell, she heard Leo, "Call for help."

The lab coat responded, uncertain. "It's a secret facility."

"Fuck secret. My friends are dying. She can't hold them forever."

"Give them these. The SLO."

In a flash of green, Eve's mind separated and began to pull upward straining in Geneva's hands. She tightened her grip. *Is this what we want? To live out our days confined to New West Mental because we're unwanted?*

Eleven voices responded with opinions, but within them ran a thread of consensus: *We want to take our place.*

She grabbed at that thought. She showed them the Mindscape and the Nootka-Orchids. *We can learn to do this.*

She threw out a purple cord of thought, a long-tangled loop of an idea: *Utopia.* She unwound it in their direction speaking to Streker and Val who would understand and help her explain: *Sir Thomas More didn't believe his government could achieve it, but our parents tried. They taught us that it does exist. Maybe it's not New West. But if we've seen it, thought of it, envisioned it so many times...*

Minds grabbed on to the end of the cord continuing the thought. She felt Streker, Val, and others: *...then utopia is somewhere, and we are not lost.*

Yes. With a surge of effort, Geneva rooted her feet to the floor. She raised her arms, so her fingertips almost brushed the low ceiling. She made a trellis of her body and the purple cords wound over her. The tendrils lifted one by one off the sparkling desert floor. Uncurling purple tendrils, Geneva reached for those minds stretching to meet them. She repeated *utopia* over and over, like she did to the plants in the greenhouse on campus. The minds drew near and hooked onto the tendrils like buds. A garden grew across her. The room filled with soft, green light and the damp air dropped. Her skin sucked at the sudden moisture. She counted them. No one was missing. Eleven minds, detached from Sync Chrome City, had reconnected to each other creating an external neural net. They didn't need the Chrome tech. They didn't need New West. They connected to each other.

She opened her eyes and blinked to see that her arms were bare. The beds and the boys on them were unchanged although their limbs were still. Syringes littered the floor and green droplets trailed along the line of beds. At the far end of the room, Burrows rested on one knee, Val in his arms. His head hung. Sweat dripped down the top of his head and his lips formed a tight, dark arch beneath the shadow of his brow. At the other end of the room, Leo knelt plunging the last syringe of SLO-42, which was helping to anchor their minds to their bodies, into Grugel's arm where he sprawled on the floor.

Directly in front of her, the lab coat stared. He touched his lapel and spoke, "The president please. This is Dr. Klick. Yes, it's urgent."

With a grunt, Burrows lunged across the room. He lifted Val and kicked Klick in one swift motion. The doctor toppled to the floor. He moaned. "There's been a terrible tragedy."

Burrows kicked him again. "Shut-up." Teeth ground and cracked against bone as Klick's jaw caved-in. Leo rushed at them, head down. Geneva hit Burrows with*: We're coming. You've failed.*

Burrows checked her with his shoulder. Val's bare feet swiped her arm. "Stay the fuck away, freak. Leave me alone," he said. "They'll fear you too."

Geneva stayed rooted waiting for the last mind, Grugel's, to wrap around her. She couldn't leave the boys hanging. She looked at Burrows. *One day, you'll be one of them.*

He staggered past her carrying Val. Val's tether stretched thin. Finally, in a wave of green-relief Grugel's mind settled. Geneva curled the purple cords, back into their own heads, and tucked their minds—safe—inside their bodies. She left Streker, Eve, Grugel and the seven guys with visions of orange-cream frosted blossoms caked with loamy scent. Except for Val, who broke snap pea loose.

Geneva left Leo bent over the lab coat and ran after Val and Burrows. At the end of the hallway, past the reception desk, the front door to the clinic was shut, still. Outside, black forest surrounded the empty gravel parking lot. Alongside the building an engine hummed. Backed into the bushes by an open window was Eve's car. Burrows flung wires into the trunk and stepped into the passenger seat as the car rolled forward. It peeled out with Coco driving. Too late, Geneva placed that sarcastic tone that had sounded so strange in Coco's voice. She'd sounded like Burrows, or, she reluctantly admitted, like Val.

Leo came up beside her. "Come on."

They ran after the car. Gravel dust caught in her throat. The taillights shone ahead of them and then flickered out as the car cornered leaving them alone in the forest. Leo put a hand on her back as she doubled over clutching her knees.

"She helped him." Geneva said.

"Of all the times, to defy Daddy," Leo said. “Coco picks now.”

A familiar gassy exhalation sounded over her panting breaths. She started toward it blinking in the night until she could make out the huge shape. Swathed in black, with its lights out, parked in the brush, the shadow bus was nearly invisible. It wheezed as its doors opened and closed. Geneva boarded and saw the blond bus driver, blindfolded, bound and gagged lying on the floor beside her seat. One arm stretched over her head. Her hand gripped a round black knob as she operated the doors. Her cheeks were stained with black streaks. Leo took off her blindfold. The underside was smeared with mascara. Her red eyes narrowed. She sucked in air as he removed the lipstick-stained gag. Her washed out pout stretched into a grimace. "That creepy jerk."

~ 22 ~

POLITICS OF PSYCHICS

"It was a lesson we could have learned from our own revolution. When the time for change arrives, it cannot be forsworn. Things on the fringe, laughable ideas that ignite the passion of a minority, are the ones to watch. Change evolves. The shifting begins far in advance, but then roils suddenly to the surface unstoppable. It's very like tectonics. I don't want to sound too much like a psychic geologist, but it is an interesting idea, that these shifts are part of our essential framework, built into our very earth." — *Save Giovanni: The Lost Men of the Psychic Wars*, S. Sherring

Burrows hesitated at the edge of the crowd of Psi-Aware protesters in front of Old Main on the New West University campus. He watched the wind whipping their hair across their contorted faces. He told himself it'd be fine. He could enter the crowd of people and not one of them would notice him. They were too caught up in their fervor. He'd just make his way to the steps of the administration building. Even while he told himself this, he stood still. Just because the minds weren't pointed at him didn't make them less sharp. It'd be like stepping into a field of knives and trusting that they would stay sheathed.

A line of television crews, cameras and neatly dressed newscasters there to report on the historic vote were the first gauntlet.

As Burrows squeezed by a young TV reporter in a tight pink suit, he heard a familiar voice rising behind him, "Well, I do have a Ph.D. in physics and on the basis of what we know, we have to take our intuitions seriously. It's time to stop snickering. We can be telepathic." He turned and saw Lydia Streker shaking her frizzy-haired head at a young reporter. She wore a yellow T-shirt that said "Deming Fest: Dem Right Fun!" across her chest. Her son stood beside her.

Burrows had done this very effectively, created this crowd in hopes of throwing New West into civil war, but now it was inconvenient. He'd meant to foment unrest to meddle with New West's perfection, reveal a few cracks and maybe begin to tear it apart. He'd never thought there would be this many people though who wanted to be psychic. There were more of them than there had been counterrevolutionaries and there was usually a lot more energy in opposition. He'd never imagined that you could get this many people to stand around holding signs and chanting, "Yes, Psi!" Yet here they were. They looked damn foolish. They'd do their cause more harm than good. But their numbers were annoying, and Lydia Streker was on TV.

As he pushed past the media, the crowd grew tighter. Burrows shoved them aside with his shoulders to get closer to Dr. Montgrave. He could see the expression on her face and could tell she thought that protest was distasteful too. It served her right. She was one of them. The only difference between her, Friend-Me Co., and these fanatics was that she had been willing to wait. These people wanted things to happen faster. He supposed having her clinic fill with comatose patients had changed that. Did she really think the world needed a bunch of psychics? Burrows would make sure the president knew Clara Montgrave was no different than the Psi-Aware crazies.

As they closed in on the steps, the people were packed shoulder to shoulder. Beside him Coco yelled, "Excuse me!" as she shoved

Valerie's chair into each shift in the bodies to create an opening. Burrows followed her, braced for pain. They were nearly at the steps, immersed in the crowd. He was taller than most of the people, which afforded him some relief from the claustrophobia, but the people standing on the steps blocked his view. The pressure on his chest and back from the crowd was bearable. As long as they didn't turn their thoughts to him, he could make it. But people were unpredictable. They could crush you without warning.

When the forward movement stopped, Burrows was jammed among the crowd. Coco could no longer coax the people ahead of them to move. There was no place to go. We're trapped, he thought, and struggled for breath. Looking down, he saw the wheels of the chair at the base of the steps. He unstrapped Valerie and lifted her into his arms.

"Hey. Hey man. I'm with you. With Psi-Aware. And so is this girl. She's sick because of what the government's done. Tell them." He pointed at the camera in front of the crowd. "Tell them, I've got something to say. Follow me."

He thrust her over the crowd hoisting her higher and moving her forward. "We'll take her to the president."

The crowd moved up the steps into the rotunda. He climbed up with her and reached the president as he began to speak. "I've just received some information that, while disturbing, might make our decision here today easier. Some students were seriously injured at New West Mental Health. Secrecy is no longer an issue. I can tell you everything."

The crowd hushed as the earth moved beneath their feet.

Geneva leapt out of the shadow bus driven by Alice as soon as they reached the New West campus. The wind pushed against her as she ran to the administration building. A throng of people, protesters, and reporters, stood on the lawn. She could see the Psi-Aware fanatics and the Neo-Privates yelling at each other. Their faces were red and contorted. Their mouths were wide open with lower teeth bared but the syllables they spoke were carried away by the wind. It made sounds a meaningless jumble. As Geneva pushed into the midst of the protest, she was buffered from the wind. Ahead of her, on top of Old Main the New West flag rippled, evergreens segmenting its golden circle. Holding her hands out in front of her and mentally shoving people aside, she jogged through the crowd. *Move. Move. Move.* She pulsed the thought forward and watched the people jolt out of her way. The people ahead turned to look at her with wide eyes.

Go on and look, Geneva thought, *just get out of the way*. She searched ahead for Burrows and Valerie. She continued to press her thoughts in front of her creating static charged shocks. She pointed at the steps up the administration building. By the time she reached them, people had stepped aside and cleared a path for her, a white part. She raced up the stairs and paused at the top to get her bearings looking back over the crowd with the Friend-Me pyramid distant behind them. The guys circled behind her; Leo, left, Streker, right. Ahead, silent people filled the rotunda. They listened to a deep clear voice.

"President Sherring," Leo said.

The narrow doors were propped open. Geneva pushed into the building and through to the center of the crowd. She looked up to see the president standing on the third-floor landing talking to a man with his back to the crowd. "No, don't. She has done nothing. She is powerless in all this."

Burrows turned. He cradled Valerie in his arms in the white clinic robes. He dumped her body over the third story railing but held her wrists, so she dangled above the crowd like a porcelain doll. They gasped and took a step back leaving Val suspended over the marble floor. If Burrows dropped her, Val would fall on top of the New West crest in the center of the golden circle. Burrows shrugged off the president's hands. Valerie's chin lolled on her chest. Her feet pointed toes down.

A dull roar shook the building. Geneva lurched from side to side. Leo and Streker grabbed her shoulders. People dropped to their knees around her. Burrows let go of one of Valerie's wrists. Her body tilted toward the floor. Her arm hung. Her wrist red where Burrows had grasped it. He clung to the railing with his other hand and Valerie swung in pendulum arcs.

Geneva stretched her arms up. She blinked as a skiff of plaster dusted her face. A crack etched through the dome of Old Main. A white blur passed in front of her, and a woman dropped to the ground. Blood gushed around the chunk of ceiling embedded in the back of her head. A wave of people moved toward the doors of Old Main and toward the arched doorways ahead of the hallways.

Everything Geneva had learned was useless. She could manipulate matter with her mind. If she meditated, focused her thoughts, she could effect a slow change, fix the roof maybe. But the building was collapsing over the people now and Valerie was falling. Bodies surged around her and thoughts*: Get out! Earthquake! Mother.*

She stood firm keeping her arms raised. She wouldn't leave Valerie. At least she could do that. Then she saw a flash of familiar purple light. Valerie's eyes blinked open above. The room strobed purple. Geneva saw flashing lines of thought whipping around the dome, leaping from person to person. In the middle of the chaos, the light pulsed toward an interwoven voice, a shared synapse. The individuals were united in one thought: *Door!*

Val*: Just get the dome.*

Just the dome. Just. The ground swayed. The floor buckled and Geneva reached out for the synapse, the one unified thought, and made a connection.

Everybody here. She directed. *Everybody now.* People's attention turned. It was as if she were standing naked, dipped in clay, and they began to approach her with paintbrushes. Leo squeezed her shoulder. She looked up at the dome splintering above them. She pictured it solid, the pieces fused. *We can do this. Now!*

The people's minds turned to the ceiling. The room became still and silent, except for the low rumble and the intermittent thump of falling bricks. The people were rooted in place, looking up. Bricks and chunks of marble and bits of plaster began to float through the air and land on the floor. The cracks in the dome above filled with purple light. Its surface flowed. It became smooth and transparent showing blue sky, cumulus clouds and the waving New West flag.

A rush of spring air sank to the bottom of Geneva's lungs. Valerie had pulled her other hand up to grab Burrows arm. She clung to his thick forearm as he shook her. Valerie: *Powerful.*

"Get away, get off me!" Burrows screamed.

Then, Valerie was falling.

Geneva waited for the impact, bone against bone. It never came. The crowd raised their arms, too. For a moment she couldn't see anything but the backs of people's upturned hands. When they moved away, across the room she could see Valerie crowd-surfing, but lost sight of her as she was lowered to the floor in a huddle of people.

A multitude of strangers hugged Geneva. She turned and saw Lydia Streker's frizzy wind-swept hair, tear streaked cheeks and enormous smile. "That's what I'm talking about. I heard you honey. I heard you. You did it."

Geneva looked at the translucent dome. "Not just me."

"I know," Lydia Streker, said her ample chest puffing. "Damn right, we all did."

“Up there,” Leo said.

Geneva and Lydia darted through the crowd and up the staircase. The president stared over the railing. Moaning came from his office. They found Burrows huddled in a ball next to the president's desk clutching his head in agony.

Lydia Streker rushed by, knelt by Burrows and raised her arms. She looked like she was going strike him some swift blows with her elbows. Then she took a deep breath and rocked on her heels. She stuck out her tongue and waggled her fingers. "Psychic, ha. There's nothing to do but wish you the blessing of instant karma. If you're lucky you'll get the consequences right away and won't have to atone for them in the next life. If you're lucky. Namaste."

~ 23 ~

LONG DISTANCE LOVE

"Again, to understand the trauma of the Psychic Rift, you have to look at historical and cultural context. Simpatico was an unknown concept, and certainly not a shared value as it is today. Our idea of shared mind—Connected Ego, Psychic Space, the Infinite Lattice—would have horrified them. Even those few who welcomed psychic abilities could not have fathomed our achieved extent of psychic connection. There was little evidence of what would be accomplished. Even trained psychics, of whom there were few in secret government programs, had achieved, at best, merely 50 percent success." — *Becoming Psychic 101, A History and a Primer*

Geneva held tight to Leo's waist as the scooter purred along the lane toward the Senator's Mansion. Her ponytails, freshly dyed a dangerous Gator Tongue red, whipped around her face as she turned to look at the lawn. "Horses?"

"It's a luxe pad," Leo said.

She pressed her face to his hair. It smelled of peach. "I can't believe Coco invited me."

"She kind of had to. You're the thing," he said. "Besides, I don't think there are any hard feelings."

Geneva didn't think so either, not between her and Coco. As far as she was concerned, Leo had made his choice. He was with her now, no matter how gorgeous Coco looked when she opened that door. Leo parked his scooter next to the Friend-Me Co. trucks alongside the mansion. "We've always been friends."

She caught the trace of bitterness in Leo's voice and realized it was true. Leo and Coco were good friends no matter how many times she dumped him.

"I don't think I can forgive her," she said.

Leo cupped her face in his hands. She could tell he knew she wasn't talking about Coco anymore. She was asking about Valerie, again—still—of course. She waited for recriminations. He had to be tired of her worrying about Val. She was tired of it too, but she couldn't stop, "What if I can't?"

"That's probably OK," he said.

He kissed her. He tasted peachy, too. She rang the bell. Coco opened the door in a rush of sunlit orange. She wore a breath-catching smooth tangerine dress that fell to her knees, the most flattering length. Eve stood beside her busty in strapless periwinkle. The girls embraced Leo. Geneva hung back out of habit, but Coco hugged her too, her arms sugar-polish soft. Eve shrugged her shoulders and gave her a half-smile. "Welcome," Coco said. She pointed through the French doors toward a ballroom filled with Mindscape. It smelled like an orange ocean. "The party starts now. You can set up."

Leo pulled his Sound-Wield wand from his backpack. "I'm going to get started. You OK?"

Geneva looked at the guests, in gowns and tuxes, standing knee deep and uncertain in the Mindscape. In the August heat, the orange waves across the floor and layered on the walls and ceiling took on a sweaty sheen. "This is too weird. But," she pointed to the buffet table. "My parents are over there. I'll be fine."

"Introduce me later?" he asked.

She hugged him. "Of course." As she navigated the crowd, one bewildered guest, a woman holding up the ends of her paisley gown, stood stiffly amid the foam. She turned to her tuxedoed partner, "I don't know what's happened darling. Last year, there was elegant dancing and excellent hors d'oeuvres."

Wedges of orange and yellow fruits filled the buffet. All the foods had been imported from C-town under the new trade agreement Geneva's mother had negotiated. Geneva recognized flavors from the Ruby's tropical sundae and tried to remember the names: mango, passion fruit. The nuts were crisp, light and summery: macadamias. Leo started his Sound-Wield set with timpani and mandolin and a cascade of golden light.

When she reached her parents, her mother drew her in. "Honey, I'm so glad to see you."

Geneva pressed her face to her shoulder. She hadn't felt so close to her in such a long time. They didn't let go until President Sherring approached. "Ambassador, you've done a remarkable job with the C-town assignment," he said.

Her mother released her and shook the president's hand. "Thank you. I think we'll all benefit. AeroFlux agreeing to manufacture Enviro-Cars to our specifications is the real coup and they are happy to retool now. There's not as much business in the airline industry." She gestured to the buffet table. "The other things though, I'm not sure how much we'll want foods like these or really be able to get them. Frankly, I don't understand how C-town did and I couldn't find out easily."

President Sherring nodded. "Not much demand anyway, I suppose. New West is too independent. I think we were right on that score. It makes sense to be self-reliant when it comes to the essentials. It increases our security, our sense of well-being. Good things, however, are meant to be shared, enjoyed all around. Going into this next phase, that's got to be clear. Well," he gestured to the guests. There were few genuine smiles around the room as the guests attempted to mingle through the Mindscape in pretense that this was just another cocktail party. "I suppose we'd better get on with our demonstration. They look restless."

The partygoers silenced as soon as Sherring clapped his hands. They'd been waiting for some signal to be let in on the surprise.

"Attention everyone, please let me introduce Dr. Clara Montgrave. She will explain our unusual décor this evening."

There was light applause as Clara held her hand high in the middle of the room and the crowd parted around her. Leo bathed her in a circle of light that made her copper gown shimmer.

"This lovely orange fluff at your feet is a new material called Mindscape," Clara began. "It's the latest Friend-Me Co. innovation. There's a very complicated explanation involving slippery protons and quantum particles but, since this is a party, let's keep it light."

The guests murmured agreement.

"The magic of this material is that it is specially designed to be shaped by thoughts: our thoughts. You can move this material with your mind and with enough practice make it into whatever you can imagine. Please join me in a demonstration." The infinity symbol around Clara's neck swung as she scooped a sphere of Mindscape out of the floor. "Everyone please take a handful, like so."

The begowned and bejeweled guests struggled to emulate Clara's easy gesture. They tore up wads of Mindscape like cotton candy. Strands stuck to their fingers. Geneva's parents managed spheres after a few tries. But the New West University students dipped down and came up easily with balls. The guys juggled theirs waiting for the rest of the guests.

Lydia Streker approached Geneva, pouting, with a drooping lump of Mindscape in her hand. "None of the young people are having any trouble."

Geneva rounded out Lydia's Mindscape with a few pats. "Don't worry. Clara makes it look too easy. It took me months to learn. It makes me jealous to see how easily my friends can pick it up now."

"Well, I'm not giving up," Lydia said, tossing her ball in one hand. "Some things are easier to learn when you are young, but we all have the capacity. The brain gets better with use. We can think revolutionary thoughts until we die. You paved the way, now we all have to catch up."

"Does everyone have a ball?" Clara asked, as her orange blob turned to glass. "First, will it crystal clear. Then, concentrate on adding color." Stripes of red flowed through her sphere.

Overhead Leo swung on silver chains and switched the music to a string suite as he wove streamers of orange and yellow light like sunshine through the crowd. The guests stared at their globes.

Her mother, holding a murky sphere, whispered. "Is that your Leo?"

Geneva nodded—her Leo—her cheeks warmed.

As the string music trailed off, Clara held up her carmine-laced orb. "How did you do?"

The guests held spheres with varying degrees of translucence palms up. Most of the students raised colorful balls. They were nothing more than paperweights and baubles, but they were made of Mindscape and mind.

"Good. It takes practice. Focus. Now, let's work together. I think we're all tired of walking through Mindscape in our ball gowns. Let's do something similar to this orange goo on the floor," Clara said. "Look down. Close your eyes. Join hands if you like. It's time to use our collective consciousness for a change."

Lydia clasped Geneva's hand. "This part I'll like," she whispered.

Leo changed the music to steel drums and the lights pulsed pastel. The orange faded. The waves flattened. The floor smoothed into clear glass. Lydia clicked her heels, "Ohhh." Eddies of pink and yellow and turquoise began to swirl under the surface of the translucent ballroom floor. As Kendra LeMay walked over to them, colors pooled under her steps.

"Mr. and Mrs. Weltraum," she said, shaking Geneva's parent's hands. "You really have remarkable daughters. Everyone saw what Geneva here did and Valerie's blossomed now that she's learning control."

Geneva followed Kendra's gaze across the room, where the New West students had raised a ring of knee-high glass bulbs around a sparkling crystal floor and begun to dance. Valerie and Streker circled each other tossing garnet-colored globes between them. Geneva sighed. She'd meant to look for Val first thing and had forgotten. Maybe it was time to accept that it was OK. She wasn't Val's keeper. Her sister could take care of herself.

Her mother saw where she was looking. "You two getting along better?"

"A little. We're speaking, anyway," Geneva said.

"You two living together, both starting to awaken was difficult," Kendra said. "It was very hard for her to be around you while her powers were developing. It was hard on you too. That's why you've felt intertwined and yet distanced. You had to get away from her to discover your talent and she needed to be away from you to be able to cope with hers."

Geneva sighed. "I kept trying to help her, but I was aggravating the problem."

"I told you not to be roommates," her father said.

"Don't blame yourself," Kendra said. "Sync Chrome City sped everything up before your minds were ready. That's what caused the seizures."

"*Omnis festinatio ex parte diaboli est*," Geneva said. "All haste is the work of the devil."

Her mother winked at her father. "Slow down, you move too fast."

"On the other hand, it's not good to stand in the way of progress. Having a lot of hope and nothing to pin it on, no action, almost lead us into civil war. President Sherring has assured me that New West will restore funding to Friend-Me so we can research and develop psychic powers on campus and New West Mental Health will be shut down permanently," Kendra said. "I'm excited that Valerie is going to come work with me. We need to develop the curriculum so we can start teaching the skills, slowly, to the next generation. There's a lot to be done. People are warming to the idea of telepathic, empathic and telekinetic abilities, but there's concern about what it will mean. Some people will be afraid to let their children learn something that's difficult or even beyond their own abilities. Our work begins." Kendra turned to Geneva. "Are you sure you won't join us? We could really use your help."

Geneva shook her head. "I'm sorry. I have other plans."

Leo swung down beside them putting an arm around his mother. "Am I interrupting something?"

"I was just trying to get Geneva to come work for me after graduation and I think she was turning me down," Kendra said.

Leo gave her a questioning look and in return she gave him: *We have to talk.* "Mom, dad, this is Leo."

"Fantastic light show," her father said.

"I was just the opener," Leo said. He pointed toward the doors. "You won't believe who Coco got for the main event."

The band had more deviant Varies than Geneva had ever seen in New West. The five people standing by the French doors were practically animals. There were two bearish guys, a squirrel woman, and a couple with black tattooed masks across their eyes.

"That's Giovanni Hastings Musica from down the 'Way," Leo said.

"That's really them?" Geneva asked. "They're a real band then, not synth?"

"Yeah." Leo said. "Coco tracked them down in Portland and they agreed to make the trek up."

Geneva smiled. "I knew it! I knew they were real."

"Go on," her mother said.

Leo pulled her toward the front of the room. As Giovanni began its dark chords the students danced and changed the Mindscape. The rounded bubbles grew long and spiked, coming up from the floor and down through the ceiling. The ballroom became a cave of amethyst, garnet, emerald and onyx stalagmites and stalactites. The guests wove through them drinks in hand. Geneva and Leo stood at the edge of the ring watching the band play and their friends dance. Geneva pressed her back against Leo as Intertwining Fingers began. They sang the chorus along with the raccoon-ish-looking vocalists.

As the song ended, Geneva gave Leo*: I wish people were made of Mindscape.*

He hugged her. *No, you don't. You'd be some kind of super villain.*

She watched their friend dancing with fluid arching bodies, no longer emulating the shaking jolts of seizures, instead looking like the electric violet lashes of their minds. *This all would have been easier, if we could have just thought: change.*

Leo stroked her hand. *Now we can start to educate people.*

Geneva turned to him. *I'm going away.*

"Come on," he said, he held her hand and led her out through the French doors. "I like it when you are in my mind, but let's talk."

He walked her out to the pool behind the house. The setting sun made silhouettes of the horses grazing in the president's pastures. Geneva and Leo sat on the edge of the pool and dipped their feet in the water. "I talked to Dr. Roundtree," Geneva said. "I joined one of his research projects for post-grad work, but it's in the Cascadian wilderness, outside of New West. Roundtree thinks there is a teleological aspect to the psychic powers that needs to be explored.

We know that technology, Sync Chrome City, caused the psychic abilities to manifest sooner than they otherwise would have. But not for me. I didn't need that electronic connection, mine manifested organically. It was a natural evolutionary step that happened faster than we thought was biologically possible. We don't know why. Why now? Why me? I'm going to do graduate research study. I guess my thesis will be myself, I'll beat other people to it and be my own best lab rat."

"In the wilderness?" Leo said. "Sounds dangerous. You're brave."

Geneva shrugged. "I guess. I'm excited about the research, but I'm sad. It's bad timing, for us."

"Not so much," Leo said. "I still have to finish school and I'm working on my music. Besides, we're too new for promises. I mean, right now, I feel like I want to be with you forever, like I could say that, but what if things change? It's too early to say we're a sure thing."

"I know. I want to be with you. I just want to know what else is out there first." She circled her feet through the water. There was no way to be sure. She might just be projecting her feelings onto Leo. Maybe he didn't feel exactly the way she did. Maybe it wasn't organic. Maybe it wasn't real.

He touched his feet to hers below the water. "We'll see how things are when you get back. We'll hope and see what happens."

~ 24 ~

THE FUTURE FOREST

"We return always to Geneva Teresa Weltraum. She more than any other figure, even Valerie Freeman, embodies the spirit of the generation and her story most accurately explains the Psychic Rift and Saga. Even the most historically precise interpretations cannot avoid the compelling story of her tragic romance with Leo LeMay. In hindsight, we see so much unnecessary pain." — *Becoming Psychic 101, A History and a Primer*

"Even so, there's no question that Geneva Weltraum is the hero of our time and C.G. Burrows no less than a villain: a shark among seals." — *Save Giovanni: The Lost Men of the Psychic Wars*, S. Sherring

Geneva stood at the back of the Big Top as President Sherring began his fall quarter kickoff speech standing behind the NWU podium with Kendra LeMay. She already felt different from the other students, older, immune to the opening day energy. Kendra had arranged for Geneva's time in the Mindscape House to count as an internship for college credit. She just had to take the test she'd missed and then she'd be a graduate student, leaving all this behind.

"You could say we'll begin teaching Becoming Psychic 101," President Sherring said. As the Big Top filled with applause,

Geneva checked her watch and left for her Privacy Law final. The test was a snap. She'd never gotten around to studying, but with her new powers of concentration, she didn't have to. She scanned her textbook before the test and when she sat down to take it, the information flowed line by line in waves behind her eyes like an open book.

Afterwards, she headed to the on-campus headquarters of Friend-Me Co. The Nootka Rose-Ladyslippers planted around the base of the green pyramid looked healthy. Their dark leaves lifted, and their petals fluttered in the cool breeze off the bay. The new hybrid had passed its test, too. It had become heartier and withstood the cooler weather. Geneva inhaled the marine-rose scent. The corrosive Rust Red Sea with its encroaching iron tang seemed far away. She felt light. No more tests. She still carried some nervous energy inside of her, but she understood the source of it and knew what to do now. Her new certainty felt like seeing a color other than orange in the Mindscape House, a relief.

Inside Friend-Me, Geneva nodded at the receptionist and took the elevator down. The world held many possibilities, as it always had, but now she had chosen a direction. She would follow her destiny and Burrows knew the way.

Burrows injected the last syringe of SLO-42 into the corner of his eye and contentment washed over him. They had him on a mellowing blend of Kendra and Leo LeMay, four syringes a day. Between that and his twice a day meditation routine, he'd conquered the pain of his telepathy for the first time in 30 years. Other people's presence registered as light pressure, tolerable. He no longer knew what they were thinking about him and could therefore stand to give them the benefit of the doubt. Animosity sloughed off him and left him at peace. Compared with the energy and certainty of the person he had been, he felt lethargic. He missed his drive, though he knew bitterness and anger had fueled it. Being superior had been fun, but it wasn't worth the agony. So, he took the drugs and buried his telepathy.

At the moment, he didn't have a choice. By sweet irony, New West's philosophy didn't make provisions for wrongdoers. There were no prisons or penalties. They had already done their worst to him—exile. The people he'd wronged most, Valerie and the president, had argued on his behalf. They valued knowledge over revenge. They'd turned him over to Friend-Me for research. He lived in the basement of the drug and psychic lab. Across the hall, New West's researchers were also making hybrid animals who could withstand the rising Rust Sea fish-rats and dog-turtles. Although the briny smells and squeals were not ideal, at the moment living in the lab among the other test subjects was a fair trade. He was learning. He wasn't becoming a neurosurgeon, scooping into people's brains like he'd wanted, but he was finding out a lot about the chemicals within them and the way minds worked. They were examining slices of his mind to see where it was different and what had caused his telepathy. They thought they were getting closer to the key to unlock the mystery of consciousness.

So, he wasn't surprised, after the Friend-Me lab tech called, "Visitor," to see Geneva standing in the lab wrapping her bright red ponytails around her fingers. Because she knew he'd murdered Valerie's parents—a point of fact damning even in New West—and had kept it to herself, he had expected she would show up at some point to extract a price. In return for protecting his privacy, what would she ask?

Geneva held the huge brass padlock in her hands until it warmed and expanded with a pop. She pushed open the thick steel door. The basement lab had been outfitted with a futon and a rug, but it was still mostly beakers and vials strewn across black counter tops. Burrows sat with his back against a cement wall staring into an open Friend-Me journal. He was expecting her. She got:

They couldn't keep you out. Go ahead. He expected her to hurt him, again. It was weird to think she could.

"Come on in. I've had my shot," he said getting up, straightening the bedding on the futon and raising it into a folded couch.

She looked at the row of green vials of SLO-42 lining the nearest countertop, the juice Burrows needed to take every day. She walked over to the countertop and picked up one of the vials. She held it up to the dim fluorescent light where it turned from black to murky green. It was a sludgier looking stuff than she was used to, highly concentrated. She fingered the syringe.

"I can," she said. "I thought about it. I really thought about it, whether it was actually possible to forgive someone for murder. But it is. It just is. They couldn't do it. Valerie wouldn't. Right now. But once they see, once they open up to it and they can feel each other so intensely like right inside at the heart where it matters. Then, they will. They would."

From Burrows she got: *But I killed.*

"It wasn't you. You were in pain. No, stop, it's not just an excuse. Just stop thinking that for a moment."

Burrows tried. He knew what it was like to have thoughts stinging in his head, carrying the burdens of others. It made her feel that what she was about to do would be OK. Would work out OK, anyway.

"Thank you," she said. "You would never have done that. You would never under any circumstance have done that. You would never do that. You aren't meant to hurt *anyone.*"

She said it like a mantra, and he winced when she pushed that last word in to him, through the sludge of drug dose suppressing that part of his mind, protecting him from the pain. She pushed it in and watched him take it. He gave her: *I deserve it.* She felt his regret, his repentance. Not that he had killed Valerie's parents so much, in truth he hadn't known them, but sadness about losing his dealer, a peppy guy named Mason, Mace.

"I liked him," Burrows said. He hadn't had many friends.

Geneva felt bad for having that power, a niggling bit of guilt she was always going to have if she stayed around here, knowing that for no good reason she had power over all these people, because she knew both their secrets and how they felt about them. Her power over others gave her an inherent moral ambiguity. It would be impossible not to abuse it. She couldn't be psychic and be a good person, she figured. In Burrows' case, she would not even try. She needed him to take her to her destiny. "Burrows, I forgive you."

She felt Burrows both wanting this relief and trying to resist it. He didn't want to be so easily satisfied, to have the emotions tugged out of him as if he were watching a mass-market movie or saying, "I love you, too." The emotions came anyway. Relief and thankfulness washed over him, and his mind leaned into hers and sighed. Geneva felt guilt now because she'd used his guilt to get what she wanted, compliance.

"Tell me," she said. "Tell me what you know. What frightened you?"

He rubbed the side of his jaw, running his nubby fingers through the scars, visible through his shorn beard. He didn't want to talk about this, but he would, because she had paid the price, she had power over him. "I'll go there, but I want to actually tell you," he said.

He knew he didn't deserve the concession, but he didn't want her in his mind. She agreed. She also didn't enjoy the feeling of forcing it, of tearing thoughts out of another's head. It was better if he was willing.

"OK," she said. "But I'm going to follow along. I want to know how you feel about it.

He frowned but nodded resigned. There was no way to keep her out of his head. She could go where she wanted. He stroked his beard some more, a habitually nervous tic. It was another thing they had in common. She was still winding her ponytails around her fingers.

"It was just a little girl sitting under a tree."

"Me."

"You."

"What scared you?"

"She did. You did." he said. "She was sitting and glowing and it was like she, everything, was going to pop open."

Like a wound.

Like a seed. She corrected, pressing him. He saw the girls again in the back of his trunk bound together. He felt the old fear and the new guilt.

Burrows balled his hands into fists and rose off the couch. "I wish you wouldn't do that."

He stepped towards her, towering over her. She was glad he couldn't feel that she was afraid. She didn't back up, not an inch. She held still even when he grabbed the syringe.

"An extra dose if you don't mind," he said. "This is really hard for me, you know."

"No, I don't care. So, it's hard," she said. Then she whispered. "But you're forgiven."

He plunged the syringe into his arm and then looked up at her. He threw it onto the futon. He gave her a cold look. "I have to forgive myself."

She looked down. That was harder. "What kind of tree was it?"

His mind went blank.

"What kind? Madrona? Fir? Maple?" she pressed.

His mind clicked emptily over various responses, but it pulsed as she spoke the words. There was something hidden there. It was what she wanted. *Come on.*

"It had long droopy branches with tiny shoots and leaves."

"Blossoms?"

"No. Yes. Pink."

"A weeping cherry."

He shrugged.

Geneva yanked her backpack from around the shoulder. She unzipped the side pocket and brought out the dried cluster of leaves, the Friend-Me delivery from early last year, when it had all started. "They looked like these."

He nodded.

"When I was in school on the last day of elementary school before the revolution, I was all alone on the playground. It was before Valerie came to live with us. I touched that tree and I felt." She paused and the feeling washed over her again, the golden glowing expansiveness—she could do anything. She looked at Burrows. "Do you miss it?"

His hands immediately went to his jaw. "No," he said.

But he did a little.

"No," he said. "This is better, understand. The peace. The quiet. That's all I need."

She did get it. She understood that the dull murky layer of SLO-42 haze was better than the sharp stabs of pain. Without the distraction, he could access the better parts of himself here: his wits and his humanity. But he was still scarred inside. He might never want to be around people, know more compassion. He would never feel joy again. She placed the vial, the one she'd picked up and was still holding into her backpack. "You were born in the wrong time. One evolutionary step too early."

"No, not that. Don't do that. Don't take that," he said.

He was so afraid to live without the drug, for now. It made her smile. It made it easier.

"I need you to come with me. We're not done. Becoming Psychic 101, what they are going to do. Teaching it is just a start. I haven't been able to figure it out. I haven't been paying attention. I couldn't get my head around it. I kept wondering, 'Why me? Why now?' Like you're thinking. You just want the peace and quiet. I thought that's what I was supposed to do, be, and then I was hit with this destiny thing and I'm a big superhero/super villain. I'm Giovanni Hastings. I have the power. I could go either way. But I was asking the right question all along, 'Why me?' I don't think it's just me. I have to know, but I don't want to stay here and have them try to pull the answers out of me like a lab rat-fish thing. I want to find out for myself."

He couldn't keep his eyes off her fingers, going down the row of vials and moving each one into her backpack. If she dropped one, she knew he would catch it. She watched how much effort it took him to ignore the vials, to sit down and clasp his hands together. Letting go, letting her take the drug he needed. He didn't understand yet that he was going with her.

"My father said once that learning the mysteries of the world doesn't spoil it. It doesn't have to make things less interesting. It doesn't have to destroy our faith. We have to believe things can only get more miraculous," Burrows said. "I haven't believed that—ever."

"You think your Dad never gave you anything better than Mistress M.D."

He nodded.

"But he said that," she placed the last vial into her backpack. "Here's the deal. I'm going North into the Cascadian wilderness. I'm doing a research project for Dr. Roundtree to start my graduate work. I never did figure out what I wanted to do with my life. If I stay around here, I think I'll be treated like some kind of psychic messiah, some hero. I can't."

She got: *You don't want to be the hero. I don't want to be the villain.*

"Exactly, or vice versa if it comes down to that. So, you're coming with me. You're the only one that's felt it before. I haven't felt it. You are going to help me find the *unus mundus*, the world mind. It's not just me and us awakening. It's everything. It's why you and Valerie and Senator Sherring and Constance are so sad. They've lost that connection with nature. This lab," she pointed back toward the room of animal experiments. "There's the problem."

"They'll come after us," Burrows said.

They would. New West, Friend-Me, the people on the Freeway; when they realized she'd taken Burrows with her. But that's not what Burrows meant: *The trees.*

The idea filled Geneva with an expansive rush. She couldn't resist the impulse to press back at Burrows, all the thoughts that came to her: *The source is in the trees. It's teleological, natural. It's the wayrrul. It's the quantum flirt. It's the aboriginal power. It's the trees.*

He cringed, resisted her thoughts: *I wish you wouldn't.*

She felt his: *Fear.*

"We feel fear before we know what we're afraid of," she said.

She didn't tell him what else she'd picked off his subconscious. That The Freemans, and his friend, Mace, were alive. He hadn't killed them after all. It seemed safer to travel alone with him if he still carried his guilt for the murders—was trying to reform. It would keep him committed to taking the SLO-42 to keep himself in check. She didn't feel bad about the omission. He had kidnapped her, taken a stab at Valerie and threatened Coco. If he thought she had forgiven him, he would owe her. What gnawed at her was that she hadn't told Valerie. She'd didn't want Valerie following her into the wilderness, as she surely would have if she'd known her parents could be there. But there were no guarantees.

Geneva knew she was different, but she did not know how in the world it had happened. She pushed Burrows again: *We're going forward. We're going to find it, our way, our new way together.*

On their way out, Geneva uncaged one of the hybrid rats with webbed toes and lacy flying fish wings. The friendly creature clung to her and its freedom. It burrowed into her neck and she felt it exhale and relax. As she stroked its soft and scaly back, she watched Burrows unlatch another cage and free another of the rat-fin beings, which quickly crawled up to his neck, and curled around it.

The four of them left the lab and headed North into the dry Cascadian wilderness and toward the drowning islands of Pacifica.

EPILOGUE: THE GIOVANNI HASTINGS STORY

There once was a boy with such unusual talents that his parents thought there must be something wrong with him. They took him to a doctor. The doctor, who had been trained to diagnose trouble, thought there was indeed something amiss.

"What should we do?" the parents of the boy, Giovanni Hastings, asked. "Medication?"

The doctor held his head in his hands and pondered. Finally, he referred them to a specialist. The neurosurgeon claimed to be able to see into Giovanni's head from the outside. He put Giovanni into large machines and shot rays through his head and took pictures of his young brain. Then he held the pictures up to the light and hemmed and hawed and pointed at spots.

"I propose surgery," he said, at last. "Of a most unique sort. We must remove Giovanni's brain and feed it to the world. Then everyone will gain these unusual talents."

Giovanni's mother, Mrs. Hastings, nearly fainted on the spot at this dramatic proclamation although, in truth, she'd imagined just such drastic measures.

"If we do this, what will happen to Giovanni?" Mr. Hastings asked.

"He will be without brain," the surgeon solemnly responded.

Giovanni's parents took the boy home directly. This was not the kind of decision one made on the spot in a doctor's office. The neurosurgeon apologized that in this most unusual case, he did not have any pamphlets he could send home with them to help them make an informed decision. An operation of this sort had simply never been performed. It was the first of its kind. Mr. Hastings noted the excited gleam in the neurosurgeon's eyes and the way he said "performed." It made him hesitant.

However, that afternoon, Mrs. Hastings spied on her unusually talented Giovanni as he played in the abandoned yard with the neighborhood boys. Giovanni had always been the leader of games. He had, after all, most unusual talents. Shortly thereafter, the telephone rang. It was the excited surgeon. "Have you made your decision?"

"I think it must be done," Mrs. Hastings said. "For the good of everyone."

The media got hold of the story. Probably the surgeon's office assistant had made the first call to the attractive television reporter. Certainly, the gleaming-eyed neurosurgeon was pleased that the story was out, all the better to make him well-known. Giovanni was, in fact, a very media-friendly boy, pleasant to look at even on large screens. Soon his rosy cheeks were ubiquitous. Mrs. Hastings gave interviews explaining why she was willing to sacrifice Giovanni's brain.

"For everyone's good," she repeated.

It was a popular phrase with the public. The tabloids, however, vilified her. She was a terrible mother, an attention-monger. They rolled out their largest type for her: MOTHER ASKS SURGEON TO REMOVE CHILD'S BRAIN!

Mr. Hastings, on the other hand, was a terrible interview. He didn't have much to say, so the reporters, eventually, left him alone. They pressed the neurosurgeon for details instead. He described the procedure incision by incision, his eyes gleaming all the while.

"What about Giovanni?" a reporter asked. "What will happen to him?"

The neurosurgeon said that not all of Giovanni's brain would be extracted. He would leave the primitive reptilian portion of brain to control Giovanni's emotions. This would give him a small chance at survival.

"The amygdala is shaped like an almond," the surgeon said, as the reporters scribbled furiously.

The next day almonds were ubiquitous shown in insets above Giovanni's rosy cheeks. The tabloids used more large type: BOY WILL BE LEFT WITH ALMOND FOR BRAIN! Sales of almonds skyrocketed. The public relations executive whose responsibility it was to make sure people ate more almonds worked overtime to take advantage of the windfall publicity. Finally, all her carefully prepared facts about the health benefits of almonds, and the history of almonds, and clever witticisms about almonds saw the light of day. Due to her efforts, almonds gained positive associations in the minds of all people for years to come. All her hard work paid off, but of course there was also a certain amount of luck involved and the results were difficult to quantify. Lots of dollar signs were added at any rate.

Politicians got involved rapidly in the Giovanni Hastings' situation so that they could also take advantage of the windfall publicity and set them themselves up handily for re-election. Also, they wanted to be seen as doing something and respond to the concerns of their constituencies.

"It's wrong for a mother to remove her child's brain," they declared.

Politicians proposed laws prohibiting the removal of a child's brain and prohibiting the eating of brain. When that infuriated a small but vocal ethnic minority that considered the eating of crab brain to be a great delicacy, they amended that law to prohibit the eating of human brain, specifically, which would, in all probability, scientists declared, lead to outbreaks of disease and madness.

Because some politicians and scientists were so adamantly against the removal and eating of Giovanni's brain, other politicians and scientists took the opposite side and became vehemently in favor of it. Later, everyone heralded these early adopters. Sensible people merely asked questions: What were Giovanni's amazing talents? Would eating his brain bestow the powers upon everyone who ate of them or would it cause disease and madness? They could not make up their minds about eating Giovanni's brain without understanding all of the facts. Other people took great offense to this. The audacity of asking! Who did these sensible people think they were? No one owed them any explanation.

As a benefit of all this discussion, every person learned a lot about the workings of his or her brain. The field of neuroscience, previously considered a bit of crockery and certainly beyond the ken of the average layperson, expanded considerably. Soon even the smallest child could name all the hemispheres of their brain and neurotransmitters and, of course, everyone knew about the center of emotions, the almond-shaped amygdala. And nobody perpetuated that right brain, left-brain misinformation any longer, because everybody knew the brain worked holistically through complex, interconnected electro-chemical mechanisms.

Meanwhile, other things went on in the world. And they were not going well. They were going to hell. People stopped laughing at wild-haired prophets who talked about the "end of the world" and the "end times." They weren't so funny anymore, except for their continually and radically unkempt hair. They could be right. It was time for drastic measures.

The tide of opinion shifted.

“The early adopters were right,” people said, including on the front page of The Herald daily newspaper. “We might as well eat Giovanni's brain.”

Giovanni was now 10 years old. The gleaming-eyed surgeon was still around and anxious to perform. The laws were restored. Childrens' brains could be removed, and anyone could eat whatever they liked (almonds were still very popular). A date was set for the procedure to remove Giovanni's brain and the maker of the leading brand of almond milk developed a formula for a tasty brain milkshake. The milkshakes were very popular even without the Giovanni Hastings' brain supplement.

As the date for the long-awaited event approached, the removal and consumption of Giovanni's brain, an investigative reporter asked a sensible question, "Would there be enough brain to go around?"

Oh, the audacity! In fact, there would not.

This sparked another firestorm of controversy that threatened to flare into endless debate. But for the first time, Mr. Hastings himself offered an opinion. He gave a, for once, engaging interview proposing that the younger generation alone eat Giovanni's brain and gain the unusual talents. It was a culturally acceptable plan, because they all said they wanted what was best for their children, even though some parents secretly, selfishly, if truth be told, did not want their kids to be able to do anything unusual. Particularly, they did not want their children to do what they could not do. But no one would say this culturally inappropriate truth out loud. Some of the older population also thought the brain might kill you and wanted none of it. So, this solution worked for them, too.

Eventually, even the surgeon and Mrs. Hastings agreed to forgo their portions of Giovanni's brain for the sake of the children. To be sure, they put it to a vote. Some people voted yes because they believed eating Giovanni's brain would save the world. Other people voted yes because they thought the procedure was doomed to fail and they were tired of the endless debate and they were too old to eat the brain anyway, tasty almond milkshake or no. Overwhelmingly, people voted to kill Giovanni Hastings and feed his brain to children.

On the night before the operation, as Mrs. Hastings sat around absently stroking the top of Giovanni's head, a masked man with enormous shoulders broke into her living room and kidnapped the boy. Soon after, the masked man appeared on TV threatening to kill the boy the good old-fashioned way by gunshot. He said he would cut off Giovanni's head and hide it away until the amazing brain inside rotted, lost to hungry consumers of tasty almond milkshakes young or old forever. Soon everyone asked in a unified voice: Who was this masked man who had stolen Giovanni, kidnapped their futures, and deprived their children of brain and potentially world-saving unusual talents?

The investigative reporter worked overtime trying to find out who was the angry man behind the mask. Using the clue of his enormous shoulders, she uncovered some interesting facts:

1.) The man was an escaped convict.

2.) He had had amazing abilities as a young boy and had been operated on.

3.) The gleaming-eyed neurosurgeon had removed all but the almond-shaped amygdala of his brain and subsequently made the man angry. Always angry.

"Is it true?" The reporters questioned the neurosurgeon. "Why didn't this important fact ever come up during all of our endless debates?"

The surgeon gleamed. "Not relevant," he said. "That was then, and this is now."

The angry man allowed an investigative news team to shave his head on TV so that everyone could see the latticework of scars left on his skull from the operation. He submitted to a brain scan, which revealed only the almond-shaped portion of his brain. The rest of his head was filled with a medical foam replacement patented by the gleaming-eyed neurosurgeon.

Meanwhile, the search for Giovanni was underway. No one knew where he was except the angry man who wouldn't say. He said they would never find Giovanni, but the police continued to look. Many private citizens took up the search too, but the most tireless searchers were Giovanni's four best friends from the neighborhood who missed their playmate very much. He had always been the leader of their games with the best imagination and most unusual talents. They looked for Giovanni day and night and long after they were supposed to come inside for supper. But the angry man was right, Giovanni was well hidden, and no one could find him.

So, Giovanni, tied up in an abandoned warehouse, had to save himself using his unusual talents. After his escape, he went directly to the clubhouse in the abandoned yard near his home where his four playmates hugged him and listened joyously to the recount of his escape. Giovanni embellished a bit adding Cerberus and Cyclops. His friends were glad to see him. Afterwards, Giovanni announced a press conference.

All the reporters, including the investigative one, came to hear Giovanni's announcement.

"I am 12-years old now and I have spent most of my life listening to people talk about whether or not to eat my brain," Giovanni said. "But it is my brain and here is what I have decided: I would like Dr. Skillings to remove all of it."

At this, the neurosurgeon's eyes reached the limits of their capacity to gleam.

"Even," Giovanni continued, "the almond-shaped amygdala. And I don't care for any foam filling."

"But how can you live without any brain?" the surgeon protested. "An empty head? That will surely kill you!"

"I'll have my eyes," Giovanni said. "The optic nerve is part of the brain."

The crowd of reporters murmured. By now, everyone knew this to be true, but no one had thought of it.

"What will happen to your brain?" a reporter asked.

"Will you feed it to the children, Giovanni?" another shouted.

At this, Giovanni gestured to his four friends standing on the stage beside him. "My friends will try it first. If they gain my unusual talents, then all the other children may share the tasty almond milkshakes, too."

The angry man, who was allowed to attend the press conference in the custody of an armed guard because it made good media, raised his hand. The reporters looked up expectantly and Giovanni called on him, "Do you have a question?"

The man stroked his hideously scarred head stuck between his enormous shoulders and fidgeted nervously in his orange jumpsuit. Between clenched teeth he said, "You'll regret this, kid."

"That is not really a question," Giovanni said. "But the world is coming to an end, and we have to try."

"That's what I thought too," the man snarled, shaking his enormous shoulders. "Didn't work out so good."

"That was then, and this is now," said Giovanni.

Despite the warning of the angry man, that afternoon a team of surgical technicians led by Dr. Skillings, of the gleaming eyes and bearer of the patent for medical foam, removed Giovanni's brain, every portion of it including the almond-shaped amygdala which was fed raw to Giovanni's four close friends. The texture was terrible, but it didn't taste bad, a little cinnamon-y.

Afterwards, everyone waited anxiously to see if the four friends would gain amazing abilities. Giovanni's parents waited anxiously to see if their son had miraculously survived brain extraction. The neurosurgeon waited anxiously to see the result of his great experiment. The angry man waited anxiously as he had every day of his life since his own operation for his anger to fade and his head to stop hurting. The investigative reporter didn't wait for anything. She was investigating a possibility no one had thought of and was already digging up some interesting leads.

As it turned out, the four friends gained unusual talents even more amazing than Giovanni's. They could lift large objects just by thinking about them. They could communicate with each other telepathically. They could read minds. They could heal injuries and stop pain. They could levitate through the air. The Giovanni Hastings Milkshakes were rapidly distributed around the world and hastily consumed by most of the world's children. After drinking the GHMs, the world's children gained an immediate understanding of each other and managed to solve most pressing global problems on the spot. They established an entirely new educational system and sent their parents back to school. As it turned out, eating Giovanni's evolved brain was just a catalyst that unlocked latent abilities undeveloped in the populace.

Giovanni Hastings awoke, and he was the same old Giovanni, but with a strange gleam in his eyes. His head was not empty. It was filled with compassion and empathy for all the world's children. He could see their perspectives with his remaining brain—his gleaming eyes—and communicate with them effortlessly all at once. Giovanni's parents were happy. His mother was first to enroll in the new school system. His father didn't want to, he said he was too old to learn new things, and that was OK, too. The world's children declared Giovanni their heroic leader and created the worldwide holiday Giovanni Hastings Day during which everyone ate sugared-almonds and drank milkshakes and wore crowns of almond leaves and decorated their houses with almonds, too. The woman who had run the almond marketing campaign had become very, very rich and then retired. Now almost everyone planted almond trees in front of their homes and down city streets and ate as many almonds as they wanted for free.

Although there was no longer any need for prisons and there were no guards, locks or keys, the angry man still lived in his cell holding his hurting head in his hands. The neurosurgeon offered to remove the rest of his brain and the medical foam, but the angry man didn't want anything to do with him. No one really did. Now that they could see how Giovanni's eyes gleamed with enlightenment and compassion, the gleam in the neurosurgeon's eyes just looked creepy by comparison and made everyone extremely nervous.

While his friends went on making improvements in the world and enjoying their new super heroic powers and setting up schools, Giovanni paid a visit to the angry man.

"I'm sorry about the way things turned out for you," he said. "I was lucky my friends suggested sharing my emotions."

"My friends only teased me," the man said. “My parents weren't interested, either."

"I think you should at least take medicine to dull your pain," Giovanni said. He handed the man a couple of pills. "Then you won't be so angry."

"But somebody has to be angry. Where there's a hero, there's a villain. That's the way it goes," the man said. "Besides, it's all I have left. It's my identity: the angry man.”

But Giovanni insisted that the world was different, so the man took the pills and sighed. "So, that's it then."

"No, there's more," Giovanni said. "I've been in touch with an investigative reporter. She's been asking, ‘Why you? Why me? How come our brains evolved before everyone else's?’"

The man had not thought much that. His head hurt too much. “Those are good questions,” he admitted.

Giovanni handed the man a bottle of pills. "Keep taking these so you won't be so angry. You and I are going to find out together the true source of our unusual talents."

And the man did as Giovanni Hastings said because Giovanni Hastings, the hero, had saved the world.

Shel Graves is a reader, writer, and utopian thinker who lives by the Salish Sea. She is a solarpunk author published in the anthologies *Glass and Gardens: Solarpunk Summers* and *Glass and Gardens: Solarpunk Winters* from World Weaver Press edited by Sarena Ulibarri. Shel earned her MFA at Goddard College, Port Townsend, a utopia which no longer exists. Shel is an ordained animal chaplain with the Compassion Consortium and as Shel Graves Animal Consulting, www.shelgravesanimal.com, aims to create a culture of compassion and pay attention to animals.

May we all be confident, at ease, playful, and safe.

www.ingramcontent.com/pod-product-compliance
Lightning Source LLC
Chambersburg PA
CBHW060809310726
48980CB00002B/282

* 9 7 9 8 9 9 8 5 4 8 6 0 4 *